D0606967

Dear Mr. M

Also by Herman Koch

The Dinner
Summer House with Swimming Pool

Dear Mr. M

A NOVEL

Herman Koch

TRANSLATED FROM THE DUTCH BY SAM GARRETT

HOGARTH
London / New York

Translation copyright © 2016 Sam Garrett

Published in the United States by Hogarth, an imprint of the Crown Publishing Group, a division of Penguin Random House LLC, New York.
hogarthbooks.com
crownpublishing.com

HOGARTH is a trademark of the Random House Group Limited, and the H colophon is a trademark of Penguin Random House LLC.

Originally published in Dutch in the Netherlands as *Geachte heer M.* by Ambo Anthos, Amsterdam, in 2014. Copyright © 2014 by Herman Koch. This translation originally published in the UK by Picador, an imprint of Pan Macmillan, London.

Grateful acknowledgment is made to Charlie MacPherson for permission to reprint an excerpt from *The Black Box* by Malcolm MacPherson, copyright © 1998 by Malcolm MacPherson. Used by permission.

Library of Congress Cataloging-in-Publication Data
Names: Koch, Herman, 1953– author. | Garrett, Sam, translator.
Title: Dear Mr. M : a novel / Herman Koch ; translated from the Dutch by Sam
    Garrett Hogarth.
Other titles: Geachte heer M. English
Description: First American edition. | London ; New York : Hogarth, [2016] |
    "Originally published in the Netherlands as Geachte heer M. by Ambo Anthos,
    Amsterdam, in 2014."
Identifiers: LCCN 2016010024 (print) | LCCN 2016020843 (ebook) | ISBN
    9781101903339
Subjects: LCSH: Authors—Fiction. | Teenagers—Fiction. | Teachers—Fiction. |
    Missing persons—Fiction. | GSAFD: Mystery fiction.
Classification: LCC PT5881.21.O25 G4313 2016 (print) | LCC PT5881.21.O25
    (ebook) | DDC 839.313/64—dc23

ISBN 978-1-101-90332-2
eBook ISBN 978-1-101-90333-9

Printed in the United States of America

Jacket design by Christopher Brand
Jacket photography by Angelo Morelli/Millennium Images, UK

10 9 8 7 6 5 4 3 2 1

First American Edition

For
Cootje Koch-Lap
(1914–1971)

Herman Koch
(1903–1978)

Anyone who thinks he recognizes himself or others in one or more characters in this book is probably right. Amsterdam is a real city in the Netherlands.

Haynes: [*To crew*] Pull the power back. That's right. Pull the left one [throttle] back.

Copilot: Pull the left one back.

Approach: At the end of the runway it's just wide-open field.

Cockpit unidentified voice: Left throttle, left, left, left, left . . .

Cockpit unidentified voice: God!

Cabin: [*Sound of impact*]

—Malcolm MacPherson, *The Black Box*

Teacher Mortality

1

Dear Mr. M,

I'd like to start by telling you that I'm doing better now. I do so because you probably have no idea that I was ever doing worse. Much worse, in fact, but I'll get to that later on.

In your books you often describe faces, but I'd like to challenge you to describe mine. Down here, beside the front door we share, or in the elevator, you nod to me politely, but on the street and at the supermarket, and even just a few days ago, when you and your wife were having dinner at La B., you showed no sign of recognition.

I can imagine that a writer's gaze is mostly directed in- ward, but then you shouldn't try to describe faces in your books. Descriptions of faces are quite obsolete, actually, as are descriptions of landscapes, so it all makes sense as far as that goes. Because you too are quite obsolete, and I mean that not only in terms of age—a person can be old but not nearly obsolete—but you are both: old *and* obsolete.

You and your wife had a window table. As usual. I was at the bar—also as usual. I had just taken a sip of my beer when your gaze passed over my face, but you didn't recognize me. Then your wife looked in my direction and smiled, and then you leaned over and asked her something, after which you nodded to me at last, in hindsight.

Women are better at faces. Especially men's faces. Women don't have to describe faces, only remember them. They can tell at a glance whether it's a strong face or a weak one; whether they, by any stretch of the imagination, would want to carry that face's child inside their body. Women watch over the fitness of the species. Your wife, too, once looked at your face that way and decided that it was strong enough—that it posed no risk for the human race.

Your wife's willingness to allow a daughter to grow inside her who had, by all laws of probability, a fifty-percent chance of inheriting your face, is something you should view as a compliment. Perhaps the greatest compliment a woman can give a man.

Yes, I'm doing better now. In fact, when I watched you this morning as you helped her into the taxi, I couldn't help smiling. You have a lovely wife. Lovely and young. I attach no value judgment to the difference in your ages. A writer has to have a young and lovely wife. Or perhaps it's more like a writer has a *right* to a lovely, young wife.

A writer doesn't *have* to do anything, of course. All a writer has to do is write books. But a lovely, young wife can help him do that. Especially when that wife is completely self-effacing; the kind who spreads her wings over his talent like a mother hen and chases away anyone who comes too close to the nest; who tiptoes around the house when he's working in his study and only slides a cup of tea or a plate of chocolates through a crack in the doorway at fixed times; who puts up with half-mumbled replies to her questions at the dinner table; who knows that it might be better not to talk to him at all, not even when they go out to eat at the restaurant around the corner from their house, because his mind, after all, is brimming over with things that she, with her limited body of thought—her limited *feminine* body of thought—could never fathom anyway.

This morning I looked down from my balcony at you and your wife, and I couldn't help but think about these things. I examined your movements, how you held open the door of the taxi for her: gallant as always, but also overly deliberate as always, so stiff and wooden, sometimes it's as though your own body is struggling against your presence. Anyone can learn the steps, but not everyone can really dance. This morning, the difference in age between you and your wife could have been expressed only in light-years. When she's around, you sometimes remind me of a reproduction of a dark and crackly seventeenth-century painting hung beside a sunny new postcard.

In fact, though, I was looking mostly at your wife. And again I noticed how pretty she is. In her white sneakers, her white T-shirt, and her blue jeans she danced before me the dance that you, at moments like that, barely seem to fathom. I looked at the sunglasses slid up on her hair—the hair she had pinned up behind her ears—and everything, every movement she made, spoke of her excitement at her coming departure, making her even prettier than usual.

It was as though, in the clothing she'd chosen, in everything down to the slightest gesture, she was looking forward to going where she was going. And while I watched her from my balcony I also saw, for a fleeting moment, reflected in your wife's appearance, the glistening sand and the seawater in slow retreat across the shells. The next moment, she disappeared from my field of vision—from our field of vision—in the back of the taxi as it pulled away.

How long will she be gone? A week? Two weeks? It doesn't matter all that much. You are alone, that's what counts. A week ought to be enough.

Yes, I have certain plans for you, Mr. M. You may think you're alone, but as of today I'm here too. In a certain sense, of course, I've always been here, but now I'm really here. I'm here, and I won't be going away, not for a while yet.

I wish you a good night—your first night alone. I'm turning off the lights now, but I remain with you.

2

I WENT to the bookstore this morning. Copies are still piled up beside the register, but then you probably know that already. You seem to me like the kind of writer who goes into a bookstore and the first thing he does is look to see how many inches his own work takes up on the shelves. I imagine you might also be the kind who's bold enough to ask the clerk how sales are going. Or have you become more reticent about that in recent years?

In any case, there's still a big pile of them at the front desk. There was even a potential customer who took one and turned it over and over in his hands, as though trying to measure its importance by weight. I had a hard time not saying anything. *Put it back, it's not worth your time.* Or: *I highly recommend that one, it's a masterpiece.*

But I couldn't decide so quickly between such extremes, and so I said nothing at all. It probably had to do with that big pile, which already spoke volumes. Anything piled up high beside the register is, after all, either a masterpiece or anything but—there is no middle ground.

While the customer was standing there with your book in his hands, I caught another glimpse of your photo on the back cover. I've always felt that there is something obscene about that expression you wear as you look out into the world. It's the expression of someone pulling on his swim trunks with unbearable slowness on a busy beach, with no hint of shame, because he doesn't care whether people see him. You're not looking at the reader, no, you're challenging him to look at you—to *keep* looking at you. It's like one of those contests to see who'll avert their eyes first; a contest the reader always loses.

By the way, I still haven't asked how you slept last night. And what you did with that suddenly empty space beside you in bed? Did you stay on your own side, or did you slide over a little more toward the middle?

Last night you listened to music: that CD you never put on when your wife is home. I heard your footsteps all over the house, as though you were trying to make sure you were really alone—how you opened windows everywhere, then the door to the balcony too. Were you trying to drive something out, to exorcise it? The smell of her, perhaps? People in love, when the object of their affection is not around, will bury their nose in a piece of their sweetheart's clothing. People whose love has run its course throw open the windows, the way you hang an old suit out in the wind if it's been in mothballs too long, even if you know full well that you'll never wear it again.

You were out on the balcony, and I could hear you singing along. It's not the kind of music I'm fond of myself, but I understand how someone who likes such music might write such books. You had it turned up pretty loud, by the way, just a little short of public nuisance. But I'm not fussy about things like that. I didn't want to be the killjoy on your first evening alone.

Why, by the way, didn't you dare to come downstairs yourself that time, to complain about my music being too loud? Why did you send your wife?

"My husband's a writer," she said. "He can't stand noise."

I invited her in, but she took only a few steps into the hallway, she didn't want to come any further. I noticed her craning her neck at one point, trying to catch a glimpse of my apartment. I looked at her face, and at the same time I smelled something—something I didn't want to go away quite yet.

A few hours later, on my way to bed, I passed through the hallway and that scent was still there. I stood there in the dark for a long time, as long as it took for me not to smell it anymore. In any case, I didn't throw open any doors or windows to drive out her scent. I waited patiently until the scent felt that it was time to go.

As I saw that evening close-up, she is indeed no longer the young girl who came to interview you for the school paper back then. How did you put it? "One day she showed up toting a notebook and a whole list of questions, and to be honest she still isn't finished asking them."

What was the first thing she asked you, after she stepped over the threshold? "Why do you write?" A question schoolgirls are prone to ask. And what did you tell her? What answer would you give these days?

At the dinner table you tend to be silent. Not that I would be able to make out the words themselves if you did talk, but the sound of voices comes through the ceiling quite readily. I hear the tick of silverware on the plates and, in summer, when the windows are open, I can even hear the glasses being filled.

While your mouth is busy grinding your food, your head is still in your study. You can't tell her what's occupying you. She wouldn't understand anyway, after all: she's a woman.

So the meals go by in a silence broken only sparingly by questions. I can't hear what she's asking, I only hear that she's asking a question. Questions to which you must reply with only a nod or a shake of the head.

If I don't hear you respond, that means you're moving your head, the head itself is in your study: it can't speak, only move.

Later, after you get up, she clears the table and puts the glasses and plates in the dishwasher. Then she withdraws to the room on the side facing the street, where she stays until it is time to go to bed.

I still haven't figured out exactly how your wife passes those hours alone in that room. Does she read a book? Does she watch TV with the volume down low or off?

I often imagine to myself that she just sits there—a woman in a chair, a life that goes by like the hands of a clock, with no one ever looking to see what time it is.

You will have noticed by now that I've put on some music of my own. I'm sure it's not your kind of music. I've cranked up the volume on my stereo a little louder, to more or less the same level as on that evening when your wife came down to ask if I could lower it a little.

I know that you, as a matter of principle, will not come down. You have to be able to send someone else, you're not the kind to come down yourself. Which is why I turn up the volume a little more. The sound of it could now, I believe, rightfully be described as a public nuisance.

I have no fixed plan. In any case, I regret the fact that a pretty young woman like that is condemned to your company, that she withers away by your side.

Now I really do hear the doorbell, you're quicker than I expected.

"Could you perhaps turn the music down a bit?"

I won't try to describe your face, describing faces is something I leave completely to you.

"Of course," I say.

After closing the door in your face—your undescribed face—I turn the music down. Then I gradually turn it back up. My guess is that you won't come down again.

I guess right.

Tomorrow you have a signing session at the bookstore, I saw the poster in the window. Will the line of people waiting for your signature be long or short? Or will there be no line at all? Sometimes those big piles beside the register don't mean a thing. Sometimes it rains, sometimes the sun is shining.

"It must be the weather," the bookstore owner will say when no one shows up.

But someone will show, in any case. I'll be there.

I'll see you tomorrow.

3

I SOMETIMES wonder what that must feel like, mediocrity. By which I mean what it feels like from the inside, for the mediocre man himself. To what extent is he aware of his mediocrity? Is he locked up inside his own mediocre mind and does he run around tugging at doors and windows, trying to get someone to let him out? Without anyone ever hearing a thing?

That's how I often imagine it, as a bad dream, a desperate scream for help. The mediocre intelligence knows that the outside world exists. He can smell the grass, hear the wind rustling through the trees, see the sunlight coming through the windows—but he also knows that he is doomed to stay inside for the rest of his life.

How does the mediocre intelligence deal with that knowledge? Does he try to buck himself up? Does he realize that there are certain boundaries he will never break through? Or does he tell himself that it's not really all that bad, that this very morning, after all, he finished the crossword puzzle in the newspaper without any noticeable sign of exertion?

If you ask me, there's only one real rule of thumb, and that rule says that you'll never hear people of above-average intelligence mention how smart they are. It's like millionaires. You have millionaires in jeans and scruffy sweaters, and you have millionaires in sports cars with the top down. Anyone can get a catalogue and look up the price of the sports car, but I'll give you ten-to-one odds that the scruffy sweater guy could leave the same car behind in a restaurant for a tip.

You're more the kind with the convertible. Even when it's raining you drive with the top down, past the outdoor cafés down by the beach. "As early as kindergarten, teachers noticed that I was exceptionally intelligent." It's a subject that often (too often, to the point of nausea in fact) comes up in your work and in interviews. "My IQ is just a fraction higher than that of Albert Einstein." I could go on—"When, like me, one possesses an intelligence found among barely two percent of the population"—but why should I? There are women who say out loud that every man turns and looks when they walk past, and there are women who don't have to say that.

In fact, you should see your face when you're extolling your own intelligence. Your face, and the look in your eyes. It's the look in the eyes of a rabbit that has misjudged the distance to the other side of the expressway—and realizes too late that the headlights bearing down on it are already too close to dodge. A look, in other words, that doesn't believe itself for a moment, that's paralyzed by the fear that the first tricky question will expose it as a fraud, once and for all.

A mediocre writer serves a life sentence. He has to go on. It's too late to change professions. He has to go on till the bitter end. Until death comes to get him. Only death can save him from his mediocrity.

His writing is "not without merit," that's what we say about the mediocre writer. For him, that's the pinnacle of achievement, to produce books that are not without merit. You really do have to be mediocre to go on living once you've realized that. To go on caring about a life like that, that's what I should really say—to not prefer death.

The line at the bookstore wasn't so bad after all. It had rained a little earlier in the morning, then the sun came out. The people were lined up to the door, but they were all inside. Not a bestselling author's kind of line. Not a line out to the street, or all the way around the corner, no, just the normal kind of line you'd expect for a writer in whom interest has been waning for the last decade or so. Lots of middle-aged women. Far past middle age, I'm sorry to say—women no one turns to watch as they go past.

I took a copy of *Liberation Year* off the pile and went to the back of the line. There was a man in front of me. The only man there, except for me. Everything about him told you that he wasn't there of his own free will, as they say, but that he'd come along with his wife, the way husbands go with their wives to IKEA or some furniture outlet. At first the man feigns patient interest in an adjustable bed frame or a chest of drawers, but before long his breathing grows labored and he begins tossing increasingly desperate glances toward the checkout counters and the exit, like a dog smelling the woods after a long trip in the car.

And it was his wife who was holding your book, not him. Women have more time than men. Once the vacuuming is done they open a book—your book—and start to read. And that evening in bed they're still reading. When their husband rolls onto his side and places a hand on their stomach, close to the navel or just below the breasts, they push that hand away. "Leave me alone, okay, I just want to finish this chapter," they say, then read on. Sometimes women have a headache, sometimes they're having their period, sometimes they're reading a book.

Again, I'm not going to attempt to describe your face. The expression you wore when I put my copy of *Liberation Year* on the table for you to sign. Suffice it to say that you looked at me the way you look at someone you've never seen anywhere but on the other side of a counter. Across the counter at the drugstore, for example, the cashier you suddenly run into on the street: you recognize the face, but have no idea where from. Without the context of the counter, the razor blades, and the painkillers, you can't place the face.

"Is it for someone special?" you asked, the same way you'd asked the people in front of me. Meanwhile, you looked at my face. The face that seemed familiar to you, but that you still couldn't pin down.

"No, it's for myself."

You sign with a fountain pen. A fountain pen you screw the cap back onto after each signature or personal inscription. You're afraid that otherwise it will dry up. You're afraid that you yourself are going to dry up; that's what a dime-store psychologist might conclude, before going on to ask you more about your parents and your childhood.

"And the name is—?" The cap was already off, the fountain pen already poised above the title page, when suddenly I thought about something. I looked at your hand holding the pen, your old hand with the clearly visible veins. As long as you continue to breathe, the blood will keep on transporting oxygen to your hand—that's also how long you'll be able to sit at a table in a bookstore and sign books that are not without merit.

What I thought about was this: I thought about your face poised above your wife's face, your face in the semidarkness of the bedroom, your face as it slowly approaches hers. I thought about it from her perspective, how she sees that face approaching: the bleary old eyes, the whites of them not completely white anymore, the chapped and wrinkled lips, the old teeth, not yellow but mostly gray, the smell that passes between those teeth and reaches her nostrils. It's the same odor you smell when the sea pulls back, leaving behind it on the beach only algae and empty mussel shells.

The odor is so strong that it overrides the normal, old-man smells: the smell of diapers, of flaking skin, of dying tissue. Yet, a little more than three years ago, there must have been a night when she saw a future in all of that. A night when she decided that having a child by that uncongenial-smelling face could be regarded as an investment.

That your wife was able to see a future, I can almost believe that. But what kind of future did *you* see? She saw a child that would grow first inside, then outside, her body. But what about you? Did you see yourself waiting at the gate of the elementary school, later, amid all the young mothers? As an admittedly old but famous father? Did your fame, in other words, make you free to bring a child into the world at a ridiculously advanced age?

Because what future awaits her, your daughter? All you have to do is look at the calendar. That future, namely, doesn't exist. Even if it all goes unexpectedly well, from a point somewhere halfway through high school she'll have to make do with nothing but the memory of her father. In the middle of those "difficult years." Those same difficult years during which her mother once knocked on your door in her capacity as reporter for the school paper.

You spoke my name, and once again looked at me with that gaze in which—somewhere far away—something like recognition had begun to dawn. As though you heard a song that sounded vaguely familiar, but you couldn't come up with the name of the singer.

Your fountain pen scratched across the page. Then you blew softly on the letters before closing the book—and I smelled the odor. You're almost done for. One signature, one inscription on a title page separates you from the grave and oblivion. That's another thing we need to talk about: the future, after you're gone. I could be mistaken, of course, but my impression is that it will go quickly. In southern countries, the dead are buried the very same day. For reasons of hygiene. The pharaohs were wrapped in bandages and buried along with their most prized possessions: their favorite pets, their favorite wives . . . I think it will look something like that. The Big Forgetting will begin the very same day. You will be buried along with your work. Of course there will be speeches, and the list of speakers will be impressive enough. Full or half pages in the papers will be dedicated to the importance of your oeuvre. That oeuvre will be collected in a leather-bound, seven-volume edition, subscriptions to which are open even as we speak. And that will be that. In no time, separate volumes of the luxury edition will start popping up at secondhand book sales. The people who have subscribed won't show up to collect the series—or they'll be dead—on the day it appears.

And your wife? Oh sure, she will go on playing the widow for a while. Maybe she will even play hardball and forbid some biographer to cite from your personal correspondence. But that doesn't seem like a very realistic scenario to me. Guarding access to correspondence is more the kind of thing the older widows do. The widows with no future. Your wife is young. It won't be long before she starts thinking about a life without you. She probably already thinks about that with some regularity.

And by the time your daughter turns eighteen and has to apply for an official document (a passport, a driver's license), the person behind the counter will already be asking her to spell her surname. Perhaps she'll still say: *I'm the daughter of . . .*

Who's that?

Yes, that's how it will end. You won't live on in your work, but in the child you brought into the world in the nick of time—just like everyone else.

Maybe you've noticed that, so far, I have been extremely discreet in dealing with your daughter as a private individual. I have not, for example, made any attempt to describe her. In situations where she was physically present, I have left her out of my descriptions. In the tabloids, faces of the children of celebrities are sometimes rendered unrecognizable, in order to protect their privacy. Your daughter's presence yesterday, for instance, when your wife left in the cab, is something I have not mentioned. I remember how she waved to you through the rear window of the taxi. From my balcony, I could see her little hand waving. I saw her face, too, but I won't describe it.

And I've left her out of your shared dinners, because you yourself always do too. Your wife brings your daughter to bed before you start in. The silent dinner. You are, of course, completely within your rights to feed your daughter beforehand and then put her to bed. There are couples who think that in that way they can keep something alive, something of the old, romantic days when it was just the two of them. With no children. But how is that supposed to work when your daughter grows older? Will she put up with that silence the way her mother does? Or will she, like all children, fire off questions at you? Questions that can only help you out. That could make you a more rounded person—even now, even though she's not quite four.

There are wars in which only military targets are fired upon, and there are wars in which everyone is a target. You, more than anyone, know exactly which war I'm referring to. You write about it. Too often, to my taste. Your new book, too, harks back once again to that war. As a matter of fact, the war is the only subject you have.

Which brings me straight to today's sixty-four-thousand-dollar question: What does a war do to a person of mediocre intelligence? Or perhaps: What would that same mediocre intelligence have done without that war?

I could help you out with some new material. The women and children have meanwhile been herded to the air-raid shelters. Nothing prevents me now from handing you the new material on a silver platter. That in doing so I consider you a military target is something you should take as a compliment.

The material, by the way, is perhaps not entirely new. It might be better to speak of old material seen from a fresh perspective.

I am going home now.

The first thing I'll do is read your book.

4

You're up unusually early this morning. Especially for a Saturday. The clock beside my bed said nine when I heard you in the bathroom. Judging from the sound of it, you have a stainless steel shower stall and an adjustable showerhead—you have a predilection for the powerful jet, from the sound of it; the noise it makes when you open the tap is, in any event, like an April downpour pounding on an oil drum.

I close my eyes and see you holding out one careful hand to test the water. By then you have probably already undressed, a pair of striped pajamas hangs neatly over the back of a chair. Then you step into the shower. The thrumming of water on the steel floor becomes less loud. All I hear now is the normal splash of water on a naked human body.

Generally speaking, though, you're more the kind for the tub. For endless soaking, I mean. With scents and bath oils, and afterward a lotion or a cream. Your wife who comes to bring you a glass of wine or port. Your wife who sits on the edge of the tub, lowers her hand into the water, and makes little waves with her fingers. You probably cover yourself with a thick layer of bubble bath—to keep her from thinking the wrong kind of thoughts. Thoughts about mortality, for instance. Or about copyrights passing automatically to the next of kin.

Do you own a toy boat? Or a duck? No, I don't suppose so. You wouldn't permit yourself such frivolity, even in the bath your mind keeps thinking about things that leave other people stumped. That's too bad. A missed opportunity. With mountains of bubble bath and a boat you could reenact the sinking of the *Titanic*: on that fatal night, the captain turns a deaf ear to all warnings about icebergs and the ship disappears, its stern sticking up at an almost ninety-degree angle, into the icy waters of the North Atlantic.

What I do judge you capable of is farting. A loud fart, with a rush of bubbles that roils up like thunder to burst through an iceberg of bubble bath. But I doubt that makes you laugh. I see an earnest expression. The earnest expression of a writer who takes everything about himself seriously, including his farts.

In any case, this morning you opted for the shower, a rare exception. I'm sure you have your reasons. Perhaps you're in a hurry, to be on time for an appointment. Maybe it has to do with your being home alone and unable to warn anyone should you become unwell. You wouldn't be the first writer to be found dead in the tub.

I think about you as the water pours over your body. Not for very long; it's not a particularly pretty thought. My impression is that older people tend to choose the shower in order not to have to look at their body. Please do correct me if I'm wrong. For you that's not a problem, apparently. Apparently you can stand that, the sight of a body whose folds and crinkles seem above all to be a foreshadowing, indicators of a near future when that body will no longer be around.

As far as I can tell from here, your wife never takes a bath. Even though she's the one who has nothing to be ashamed of. Before the mirror, under water, only half covered with a hastily wrapped towel, it doesn't matter, she can take pleasure in who she is. But she never stays in the shower for more than a couple of minutes.

Personally, I regret that. I'm not made of stone. I am a man. During those two minutes I've often thought about her, just as I'm thinking about you now. Hanging over that chair at such moments is no pair of pajamas, but a white towel or bathrobe. She herself is in the shower by now. She closes her eyes and raises her face to feel the jets of water. She welcomes the touch of water on her eyelids like a sunrise, the start of a new day. She shakes her head, briefly but vigorously. Drops of water fly from her wet hair. Somewhere in a corner of the shower stall or close to the bathroom window you can see a little rainbow.

The water pours down her neck. Don't worry, I won't go into any greater detail about the thoughts that come next. I won't defile her beauty; not out of respect for your feelings, but out of respect for her.

So the actual showering lasts barely two minutes. But after that she stays in the bathroom for a long time. To do things, I suspect. Sometimes I fantasize about just what those things might be. Sometimes I wonder whether you still fantasize about things like that on occasion, or whether they are just more annoying details to you.

This morning I'm having some doubts about that new material. The new material I could give you. Last night I read your book, hence the doubts. Yes, that's right, I read *Liberation Year* in one sitting. I am purposely avoiding terms such as "in one fell swoop" or "at a single stroke"—I simply started around seven in the evening and by midnight I was finished. It wasn't as though I couldn't put your book down, or, even worse, that I needed to know how it ended. No, it was something else. That same thing you sometimes have in restaurants: you've ordered the wrong dish, but because you're ashamed to leave too much behind on your plate, you go ahead and eat more than is good for you.

It's hard to pinpoint exactly. In fact, I've had the same sensation with all your books. You take a bite and start chewing, but it doesn't taste like much. It's hard to swallow. Odds and ends become stuck between your teeth. On the other hand, though, it's not really bad enough to summon the waiter and demand in a huff that the dish be brought back to the kitchen.

I think it's far more simple than that: even wolfing down a miserable meal adds to our stockpile of experiences. We've eaten absolutely everything on our plate. We feel our stomach bracing itself for a serious bout of indigestion. Perhaps we order a cup of coffee and something on the side to help our stomach out a bit.

And so, around midnight, after having put away *Liberation Year,* I turned on the TV for a few minutes. Bouncing from channel to channel, I finally arrived at National Geographic. I was in luck, the program that was starting was one I always enjoy. *Seconds from Disaster,* about aviation catastrophes. You see how the passengers—the unsuspecting passengers—place their luggage in the overhead compartments and fasten their seat belts.

Sometimes it starts earlier than that. During check-in. The passengers put their suitcases on the scales and are handed their boarding passes. They are looking forward to a well-deserved vacation or a reunion with distant relatives. But we, the viewers, know that they can forget all about that vacation and that family reunion. None of that is going to happen.

At the same moment, in another part of the airport, at Gate D14, a Sunny Air Boeing 737 is fueling up and receiving its last-minute inspection. The technicians discover "nothing unusual," as they will later tell the members of the investigative committee. Most of the parts, broken into tens of thousands of little pieces and spread at great depths over an area of dozens of square miles, have now been recovered with the help of the most modern equipment. In a vacant hangar, investigative committee specialists set about putting the plane back together, using those tens of thousands of pieces of the puzzle. It takes months. When they are finished, the final product still looks more like a jigsaw puzzle than a plane. It will, in any case, never fly again. The only reason for the reassembly is to determine the cause of the disaster. Was it a technical defect, or was it human error? What does the black box tell us? Can we learn anything from the final conversations between the pilot and the air-traffic controllers?

"Left motor has failed . . . right motor has failed . . . we are going down to thirty thousand feet . . ."

Suddenly, the little dot on the radar screen in the control tower ceases to be a dot.

"Hello, Sunny Air 1622 . . . ? Do you read me, Flight 1622 . . . ??? Hello, Flight 1622?"

This all comes much later. The important thing is the beginning. In the beginning, everything is still in one piece. I usually think even further back in time. I think about the passengers. How they put on their socks and shoes that morning. How they brushed their teeth and then took the taxi or the train to the airport.

"Have we got everything? Do you have the tickets? What about the passports?"

Personally, I'm in favor of a black box that starts registering information much earlier. Not just the last half hour of conversation in the cockpit, but *everything.* The true extent of a disaster has a tendency to be tucked away in the details.

In the note to the neighbor lady who has promised to feed the cat: *kitty chow only in the morning, in the evening half a can of cat food or fish, raw heart 1x weekly.* Barely twelve hours later, the hand that wrote those words has disintegrated at an altitude of thirty thousand feet. Or become lost amid the wreckage. That morning, that same hand tore a sheet from the roll of toilet paper, folded it three times and carefully wiped his or her backside. It's partly about the senselessness of it all, in hindsight. Looking back on it, he or she might as well have skipped that wiping, or at least not done it so carefully.

But let's stick with the hand. During the final hours of its existence, the hand—at an altitude of thirty thousand feet and moving at a speed of almost six hundred miles an hour—flipped through a magazine. The hand reached out and accepted a can of beer offered it by the stewardess, the fingertips registering that the can was, if not icy cold, at least cool enough. In a moment of inattention the hand stuck one finger in a nostril, but found nothing large or solid enough to worm out. The hand was run through a head of hair. The hand was placed on a denim-covered thigh—at that very moment, in the cockpit, the pilot looks over at his copilot. "Do you smell that?" he asks. Any number of little red lights blip on above their heads.

The aircraft banks sharply and quickly loses altitude. The cabin fills with smoke. At home the cat stretches out on its rug by the fire and pricks up its ears: that must be the neighbor lady with the kitty chow! Sometimes the plane explodes at high altitude, at other times the pilots succeed in putting it down, with two stalled engines, on a military airstrip on some coral atoll. A landing strip that is actually far too short for aircraft that size. That evening the cat lies in the neighbor lady's lap and purrs. If it's a nice neighbor lady, she will adopt it. It doesn't matter all that much to the cat, as long as some-one keeps buying kitty chow and fish and heart.

Last night I read *Liberation Year* and this morning I think about you as you take a shower. I have hesitations, as I've already mentioned, about the new material. They say that with most writers everything is already fixed in place, that after a certain age no new experiences are added. You've said that yourself, in more than one interview. I can hear and see you saying it, most recently on that Sunday-afternoon cul-ture program.

"After that age, there really aren't any new experiences to have," you said—and the interviewer was feeling kindly disposed, he pretended it was the first time he'd heard it.

I don't hear the shower above my head now. You're dry-ing yourself off, you'll shave, then you'll get dressed. With every air disaster, there's always that one passenger who ar-rives too late and misses his flight. That passenger, too, put on his socks and shoes that morning. *I could have been on that plane,* he thinks. His life goes on—that evening, he's able to simply put his socks in the wash.

What if you had felt drawn to another apartment back then, and not this one? I don't know, maybe you let your wife decide. It *is* a lovely street, after all: old trees, lots of shade, barely any traffic, almost no children playing outside. That last point is a bit of a shame for your daughter, you probably should have thought about that a bit more. But it's certainly the ideal street for a writer who believes that no new experiences are going to come along.

When you moved in, you didn't bother to introduce yourself personally to your new neighbors. No need to do that. That's what your wife is for.

"We're the new neighbors," she said, and put out her hand.

A small, warm hand.

"Welcome," I said.

On that occasion, your profession remained unstated. That came later, the time I had my music on too loud.

On *Seconds from Disaster,* there was an older couple who had never flown before. The plane tickets were a present from their children. Like all the other passengers, the older couple was played by actors. In the reconstruction of the final minutes of Flight 1622, they turned to each other for support. The children, too, were interviewed. The children were not played by actors. The children were real.

I'm not sure, in other words, whether the new material would be of any use to you. So I'll just give it to you in its most unpolished form. You're completely free to do whatever you like with it. If you have any questions, just come downstairs.

There are books in which the writer appears as well. As a character. Or there's a character in the book who enters into a discussion with the writer. I'm sure you know the books I'm talking about. You wrote some of them yourself.

That's what makes this different. I'm not a character. I'm real.

In high school, something happened that changed the rest of my life. In high school, children spread their wings. They no longer test their boundaries to the point where they've been drawn, they go beyond them. They no longer see their parents and teachers as adults who lead them by the hand, but as obstacles on the road to self-fulfillment. They crush an insect, just to see if they can do it, and then feel regret—or not.

The new material starts here. I doubt whether you can do anything with it. But whatever the case: here's where it starts.

5

It was the year when teachers were dropping like flies. Suddenly, there they went. Not a month passed without the entire Spinoza Lyceum being summoned to the auditorium, where Principal Goudeket would make yet another "sad announcement." Of course you had to keep your mouth shut and look serious, but what we mostly felt was a sense of justice having been done. The announcements never made us sad. There was something comforting about this massive falling by the wayside. If only by reason of their age, teachers were turning out to be vulnerable. They were not, in any case, immortal, not like we were.

A teacher who that very afternoon had been carping at you about the homework you hadn't done or about your general lack of enthusiasm might not show up at school at all the next morning. That none of these deaths were preceded by a long sickbed served to amplify the comforting effect. No endless hospitalizations, failed radiotherapy, or other delays—nothing that could have made the dying any more human.

Mr. Van Ruth was our math teacher. Whenever someone's attention lagged, he would point threateningly out the window at the Rietveld School of Art & Design, a few hundred yards from our school but hidden by the trees, and say:

"If you'd rather play with clay and crayons, they've got a place for you."

Suddenly, one morning, he didn't show up. It was the day after an early autumn storm, the trees had already lost some of their leaves and so, for the first time that year, the tip of a roof at the Rietveld School was visible through the branches. I remember clearest of all the empty space in front of the chalkboard, never again to be filled by his lanky frame.

I thought about the morning of the day before, when Mr. Van Ruth had put on his socks and shoes before cycling as usual to the Spinoza Lyceum.

Mr. Karstens used to sit on an especially high stool behind his desk in the physics lab, which was supposed to make him look less short. "There are some people present in this room who will never understand a thing about physics," he said on Monday morning, breathing a deep sigh. On Tuesday he was dead.

During the memorial service in the auditorium, Principal Goudeket found it fitting to refer to Mr. Karstens's family situation. We found out, for example, that the physics teacher did not have a wife, but two "growing boys" he cared for on his own. The principal left out the important details. Was Mr. Karstens's wife still alive? Or were the two growing boys now completely on their own?

Whatever the case, the detail about the sons added a human twist to the man's death. Besides being a physics teacher who was ashamed of his own dwarfish stature, and who therefore never dared to come down off his high stool even once during the whole period, he was suddenly also a father with two growing boys who waited for him to come home.

But the sons had never been in the picture before, no one

had ever seen them in real life, which served in turn to almost completely undermine the human element. There was even a remote possibility that they were just as relieved as we were. That's right, maybe the growing boys were above all relieved, because at last they could do whatever they wanted—go to the snack bar for takeout every night and stay up watching TV until far past midnight—and no longer had to walk down the street beside a father who was too short.

But such possibilities invariably went unspoken during the memorial services in the auditorium at the Spinoza Lyceum, so that we were left only with the image of two growing boys sitting in a darkened kitchen, their empty plates in front of them, waiting, because there was no one left to take care of them.

Miss Posthuma lived by herself on the ninth floor of an apartment building close to the road going out of town to Utrecht. I had been to her home once to discuss my reading list for that year's English lit class. From her living room window you could see the rowers skimming across the mirrored water of the River Amstel. And later, as darkness fell, you saw the lights of cars on the highway crossing the Utrecht Bridge. Somewhere a clock was ticking. Miss Posthuma asked if I wanted another cup of tea. She had hair that she kept short and wore in tight little curls and she had a high voice, without any real bass to it, the kind one often hears in women who have never had an orgasm in all their born days. It was a voice that fluttered around the room like a little bird, without landing anywhere, as though anchored to nothing and not really connected to the earth; just like Miss Posthuma, in fact, in her ninth-floor apartment high above the world and the people in it.

Then, suddenly, I clearly heard that voice ask if perhaps I preferred something other than tea, that she probably had a bottle of beer somewhere in the fridge. I saw too that something broke in her expectant expression when I stood up and said it was time for me to be getting home. Something in her face shifted color almost unnoticeably. Out on the street I looked up one last time at the ninth floor of the building, but there was nothing about the lights along the outside gallery to show which apartment was hers.

It didn't cause much consternation when Miss Posthuma didn't show up at the Spinoza Lyceum one morning. Only later did I hear that they'd had to break down the door to her apartment. But Goudeket's memorial speech never once mentioned the word "crowbars." It was clear as a bell that the principal had been unable to find anything worthy of note as theme for his little speech. This time there were no growing boys or other pathetic or heartwarming details to make Miss Posthuma, who had been found dead in her own home, a little more human. Goudeket came up with nothing better than "her enormous dedication to our school and her pupils"; under the hard fluorescent lighting of the half-empty auditorium, that sounded like less than nothing, as though the big oblivion might as well get started right then and there.

And then there was that one spectacular finish, a finish that went out with a resounding bang, flying glass, and blood. Harm Koolhaas ("Harm" to the juniors and seniors who had social studies with him) made his mistake less than half an hour after a midnight landing in Miami, when he took a wrong exit in his rental car, a white Chevrolet Malibu, and ended up in "the wrong neighborhood" (thus spake Goudeket).

The two men he asked for directions at the badly lit gas station were never found. It appears that Harm Koolhaas had tried to roll up the window on the driver's side and back away fast, but that this maneuver ended with a loud smack against a parked car. According to the gas station owner's testimony, one of the men had just enough time to poke the barrel of his pistol through the crack in the window. Meanwhile, the second man opened fire on the windshield.

Harm Koolhaas wore fairly fashionable corduroy trousers and carried a beaded bag over one shoulder, from which he would invariably produce his pack of Javaanse Jongens rolling tobacco at the end of class. When he walked down the hallway, it was always with a bit of a bounce in his step.

Somehow we couldn't reconcile the two images—the trousers and the beaded bag on the one hand, the corpse hanging out of the car with its neck twisted at a strange angle on the other. As though the halls, the classrooms and auditorium of the Spinoza Lyceum were the worst possible preparation for a violent demise in an American B-movie.

During the traditional moment of silence, I thought about that gas station on the far side of the Atlantic. I saw the bright red TEXACO letters, and the red-and-blue flashing lights of police cars. The policemen were chewing gum and they wore sunglasses, even though it was far past midnight.

I tried to place Harm Koolhaas's death in some kind of perspective. I went back in my mind to his arrival at Miami Airport, to the moment when he was handed the keys to the white Chevrolet Malibu, to his walk across the parking lot beneath a dazzling canopy of stars . . . Did he have that beaded bag slung over his shoulder in America too? Had he brought along a few extra packs of Javaanse Jongens, just to be sure?

And while I was thinking about that bag and the packs of rolling tobacco, I realized that I would have to go back much further than that, to the baggage check-in at Schiphol, the flipping through a travel book about Florida at thirty-five thousand feet above the Atlantic, the happy, excited prospect of touching down on American soil. Or maybe it all started much earlier than that, as he put on his shoes and socks the morning he left. Harm Koolhaas standing in front of the mirror in his corduroy trousers, running his fingers through his hair.

In this case too, there was no wife or growing boys to miss him. The social studies teacher was still young and unattached, "in the prime of life," as Goudeket read aloud from his notes. He could go to the airport on his own and didn't have to turn and wave to anyone after going through customs. In all probability, he sauntered first past the shops with duty-free goods. After that, the number of people who saw him in real life decreased drastically, until finally he disappeared from sight altogether.

Because the body of our history teacher, Landzaat, was never found, no memorial service was ever held in the auditorium in his honor. In the case of a missing person, after all, there is always the hope that they may pop up somewhere. That someday they may resurface and announce themselves, at a police station, or at some remote farm miles and miles from the spot where they went missing, badly confused and suffering from memory loss, clothes torn and smeared with mud, but—thank God!—unharmed.

As the days and weeks went by, that hope grew scanter. A photograph of him remained hanging in the classroom all year long. Purely out of laziness, because no one ever thought of taking it down (who knows, perhaps it's hanging there still). Back then it had already begun to curl at the edges and the colors had started going drab. It was a small photo—a Polaroid—showing Mr. Landzaat grinning and baring his characteristically long teeth all the way up to the gums. Where his pupils were, in the whites of his eyes, you could see two red dots from the flash. His hair was wet, probably with sweat from dancing at the school party where the Polaroid picture was taken.

Yes, when it came to dancing at school parties Mr. Landzaat was a real go-getter. Without so much as a how-do-you-do he would grab a girl by the hand and drag her out onto the dance floor. And the girls rarely put up a fight. Jan Landzaat was a popular teacher at the Spinoza Lyceum, perhaps *the* most popular. The horsey teeth were nothing but a minor shortcoming in his eternally tanned and youthful face. Another minor defect was his own awareness of how popular he was, and of how he made the girls giggle and blush.

When our class took a field trip to Paris, he remained at the hotel bar later than the other teachers. He drank his Pernod without water or ice, and told funny stories about back when he had taught at the Montessori Lyceum. Stories that made all of us laugh, including Laura Domènech, a junior like me.

"At the Montessori, they're completely nuts," Landzaat said. "Like some holy sect. The smile of beatific certainty. Of *faith* in that certainty. I'll tell you, I was so glad to get out of there!"

Then, for the second time, he laid his hand on Laura's forearm, the only difference being that this time he didn't remove it again right away. We all saw. We saw that Laura didn't pull her arm away. We saw how Laura took the elastic band out of her ponytail and shook loose her long, black hair—how she then put a cigarette between her lips and asked Mr. Landzaat for a light.

Jan Landzaat, too, had almost certainly put on his socks and shoes before leaving his temporary rental in Amsterdam's River District that Boxing Day morning, to spend a few days with "friends in Paris." And because it was "on my way anyway," as he told us later that same day, he had swung by Terhofstede, a cluster of houses belonging to the municipality of Sluis, some three miles from the coast of Zeeland Flanders.

His tempestuous affair with Laura Domènech had ended a little less than two months earlier. He tried to be light-hearted about it, but with each passing day his face bore more and more traces of collapse. The color of his skin faded from brown to yellow, he began forgetting to shave, and there were mornings when the smell of alcohol made it to the desks all the way at the back of the classroom. Often he would remain standing at the board for minutes, lost in thought. You'd have to repeat your question a couple of times before he would reply.

But not that one time, not when I raised my hand and asked if there was any truth to the rumor that Napoleon had ordered his sixteen-year-old mistress drowned in the Seine. Mr. Landzaat turned slowly and looked at me. His red-rimmed eyes had dark, heavy bags under them, as though he'd been up weeping all night.

"And why should *you* suddenly be interested in that?" he asked.

The house in Terhofstede belonged to Laura's parents, who were spending their own Christmas vacation in New York, giving Laura and me the run of the place. At first, when Laura told him she was dumping him, Jan Landzaat couldn't believe his ears. And when he heard why and for whom, Laura said he'd looked disgusted.

"With *him*?" he said.

The little white house was at the edge of the village. When I woke up in the morning I would lie there and look at Laura's long, black hair fanning out over her pillow. Sometimes I let her sleep, usually I woke her. The frost made

flowers on the windowpanes and there was no heating upstairs, so after that first night we moved the mattress down to
the living room and slept in front of the antique coal stove.

In fact, we didn't get up often. Every once in a while, just
to do some shopping in nearby Retranchement, which had
one shop. It was too cold to cycle so we walked, holding each
other tight the whole time. When we went back to the house
we had bottles of cheap wine, beer, eggs, and bread.

The difference between night and day faded to a timeless
vacuum in which we had eyes only for each other—for our
attempts to get closer and closer together. In the warmth of
our zipped-together sleeping bags, on the mattress in front of
the coal stove, the world began all over again each day, each
hour, each minute.

So in that timeless vacuum it didn't surprise us much to
find, after we had got dressed and walked to Retranchement
to replenish our supplies, that it was Boxing Day and everything was closed. We lingered there for a while, before the
plate glass window of the closed shop, struggling with the
idea that the world actually stuck to something like opening
times. It was the coldest day of that whole week, a fine haze
of snow was blowing across the paving stones. Night seemed
to be falling again already, or else it was already getting light
again—on that score, too, there was no longer anything like
absolute certainty.

And so, empty-handed, we started in on the trip back to
our warm bed in front of the stove. Just outside Retranchement the road makes a slight bend, halfway through which
one catches sight of the first houses of Terhofstede, including
the white one that belonged to Laura's parents.

She was the first to see the car parked outside the garden
gate. Someone was leaning against the fender, only a vague
form at this distance, but still, unmistakably, a person. It was

Laura too who immediately recognized the cream-colored Volkswagen Beetle as belonging to our history teacher.

"Oh, no!" she said. She grabbed my arm and tried to pull me back down the road. At this point in the bend there were no houses or trees to hide behind. Our only hope was to backtrack as quickly as we could.

At that moment, though, the figure hoisted itself off the fender and walked up onto the road. He waved.

"Oh, no!" Laura said again. "This is just too horrible!"

I pulled her up close, threw my arms around her. I didn't ask how Mr. Landzaat knew where we were. His behavior in the last few weeks had become increasingly desperate. First he had accosted Laura in the bicycle shed at school, panting and pleading for a chance to talk. Later there were the phone calls when all Laura could hear was the sound of his breathing.

One night she had woken up with a strange feeling, and when she slid aside the curtain of her bedroom window she saw him there. He was standing under a lamppost, looking up at her. She couldn't see his features clearly, but she could feel his look of reproach.

For obvious enough reasons, at school she hadn't dared to complain about our history teacher's behavior. That would have resulted, at the very least, in the two of them being kicked out of the Spinoza Lyceum. And telling her parents about it was completely out of the question. They were modern, to a certain extent (or at least that's what they called themselves), and you might even say they were understanding. But between being understanding and actually understanding something yawns an unbridgeable chasm—a chasm so deep that you often can't see the bottom at all.

And so I had taken Laura in my arms and held her tight. She started sobbing quietly.

"Take it easy, love," I said. "Take it easy. Everything's going to turn out fine. I'll make sure it all turns out fine."

Then I let go of her and stepped out into the middle of the road. I raised my hand and waved to Mr. Landzaat. I waved as though I was happy to see him.

6

THIS IS the point at which I leave you up in the air about how things went from there, a technique you apply regularly yourself—a digression at a moment of suspense, a story within the story.

In *Liberation Year,* that story within the story begins when the four children start on their long journey on foot to the part of Holland already freed by the Allies. The trip takes ages and is rarely suspenseful. We, the readers, would rather get back as quickly as possible to the interrogation of the Wehrmacht defector. But for pages on end you make us hop over frozen ditches along with those children. That they dye their hair along the way is, in fact, extremely implausible in that last year of the war, when even the direst necessities were rationed. Implausible and boring. The children are such pains-in-the-ass, the reader doesn't really give a damn whether they survive the trip or not. You end up hoping they'll be arrested and spirited away, and the sooner the better. *Off! Off with them! Off with this book!*

Another reason why I pause here is because I'm curious to hear whether my tale of teacher mortality sounds at all familiar to you. Especially the part about the two high-school students and the teacher who just won't go away. What I'm wondering is whether you have any idea how it goes after that, but to be honest I have no doubts about that anymore.

At the risk of getting ahead of myself: Isn't it an ironic twist of fate that your most commercially successful book should be entitled *Payback*? I've always liked that title. You were never particularly in form after that when it came to titles—nor when it came to writing books either, come to think of it—but that's another story. The story within the story of your life, you might say, of your dwindling writer's career.

And then, isn't it a much more ironic twist of fate that *Payback* should be your only book based on real events (not counting *The Hour of the Dog,* which was about your first wife—a different genre, if you ask me)?

Suddenly I can't help thinking about my visit to the book-shop a few days ago. Not the day that you were there signing, but the day before that. The moment when the customer finally put *Liberation Year* back on the pile beside the register.

After the initial relief, I also felt a certain disappointment. Because, as a matter of fact, I still wish you the best possible sales figures. What could be better than for as many readers as possible to see for themselves that, after a dozen books, two plays, and almost half a lifetime, the writer of *Payback* no longer cuts the mustard?

That afternoon, by the way, I also noticed that there weren't a lot of your books on the shelf. *Payback* is pretty much obligatory, of course, but your other work was thinly sown. I asked the salesperson about *The Hour of the Dog* (talk about glaring titles), but he informed me that that particular title was "no longer in print."

No longer in print . . . There are words, sentences, and phrases that, in all their simplicity, say much more than they seem to at first: *two months to live, never heard of it, dead on arrival . . .* For a writer, *no longer in print* must fall somewhere in that same category.

I saw that *Payback* is now entering its twenty-seventh print run. I sort of like the new cover, vaguely American with all that red and blue. And that new picture on the back cover—at least you're not one of those writers who hopes to cheat time's advance with a single vague and grainy photo.

You try to keep up with the times, even on the backs of your books. That too, though, is a form of mortality. Every five years the cover is rejuvenated, while the writer and his work go on aging for all to see.

I took care to stop and read once again the text on the back cover. There was no significant difference from the text on the back of the first edition I have here at home. I own several editions—three, to be precise. When it comes to covers, I think the movie edition is the ugliest. Those red, dripping letters! What could the publisher have been thinking? A bloodbath? It's a pity, because a title like *Payback* already speaks so clearly for itself. Why would you want to add anything to that?

And then, beneath those dripping letters, in a sort of *Gone with the Wind* setting, the photos of the three stars. That's the second crucial mistake. An intentional mistake to boot, made only to pump up sales. And indeed, after the movie came out, *Payback* began its second life, as they say, and made the bestseller list for the second time in five years.

Movie or no, you should never put pictures of the book's characters on the cover. That only cramps the reader's fantasy. You force him to keep seeing the faces of the actors in the movie. For someone who has seen the movie first and then, out of curiosity, goes on to read the whole book, that might not be so bad. But anyone who reads the book first is faced with a dilemma. During the reading he sees the faces of all the characters in his mind's eye. Faces he wants to assemble with his own fantasy. No matter how those faces may be described. Despite your superfluous descriptions of noses, eyes, ears, and hair color, each reader constructs his own faces in his own imagination.

Three hundred thousand readers; that's three hundred thousand different faces for each character. Three hundred thousand faces that are destroyed at one fell swoop by that one face in the movie. As a reader, it's pretty tough to remember that imaginary face after seeing the actor on the screen.

Two high school students mastermind their teacher's perfect murder. That's the first line of the text on the back cover.

Two factual inaccuracies, in the very first sentence. Because we never masterminded anything—and it was anything but perfect.

There's no need for me to cite the rest of the text here, you know well enough how it goes. That first sentence wasn't there on the first eighteen editions, it was added only for the film version. But it's been on every edition ever since. The book has been molded to fit the movie. A movie that differs from the book on a few essential points. Just as your book differs from reality on a few essential points. From the real events on which it's based.

Those latter differences are understandable enough. You ran into a few blank spots that your imagination had to fill in. And I must say: Hats off! You got awfully close.

But not close enough.

How would you like to have the chance to fill in those blanks all over again? A revised edition of *Payback* in which the unsettled questions are settled at last? If I were a writer, I wouldn't be able to resist the temptation.

It was a little less than a year ago that you moved in

upstairs. That would never be possible in a novel. Writer moves into apartment above . . . well, above what? A character? No, I'm not one of your characters. I'm a flesh-and-blood human being on whom a writer has loosely based a character. In a novel, it would be completely implausible. Too much of a coincidence. Coincidence undermines a story's credibility.

There's only one area in which we accept coincidence, and that is in reality. "Such a coincidence!" we say, and then we dish up a juicy anecdote in which coincidence plays a major role.

Conversely, you could say that the coincidence that has made us neighbors is only plausible because it takes place in the real world.

You could never come up with that yourself, people say. At least, a writer never would.

I remember so clearly the afternoon when I went to see the movie version of *Payback*. There weren't very many people in the theater, it was a matinee. I remember the moment when the high-school students appeared on screen for the first time. The boy takes the girl by the arm.

"I want you to know that I care about you more than anyone else in the world," he says, and I couldn't help laughing at such a totally unnatural and implausible line, spoken by an even more implausible actor—the kind of actor you see only in Dutch feature films. I laughed so loudly that I was hissed at from all corners of the darkened theater.

People read a book and imagine the faces themselves. Then they go to the movie version and the imaginary face is destroyed by the face of the actor on the silver screen.

With me, that was totally different. In both the book and the movie, I kept seeing the same face.

My own.

7

THE POSTCARD came this morning. A postcard . . . there's something touching about that, something from days gone by. The same days gone by to which you belong, where your roots lie, you might say.

You yourself are all too pleased to make a show of those days gone by. In interviews you never fail to emphasize your lack of confidence in modern inventions. Computers, the Internet, e-mail, cell phones—all things you keep at bay.

"My wife does all my e-mails, I'm too old to start in on that."

"Sometimes I hear the cell-phone conversations people carry on in the train and I ask myself whether we've made any real progress since the days of the Neanderthal."

"I write the first version in longhand, then I type it over. On an old-fashioned typewriter, yes. I tried it once, writing on a computer, but had the feeling right away that I was checking in passengers at an airport. Or working at the local branch office of a bank."

Every once in a while you go too far with it, and the coyness shines through. Like when you cast doubt on the sense of electronically amplified guitars.

"Why for God's sake does a guitar need to be amplified?

When I hear it, I always have the sneaking suspicion that the guitarist isn't really technically competent, that he's trying to mask that by making as much noise as possible."

Who are you trying to impress with comments like that? Probably those readers who, like you, grew up during World War II. Those readers who (like you) believe that after a certain age there are no new experiences to be had.

Otherwise, of course, you have every right to do what you do. Writing on a typewriter, why not? It's not about whether people are right or wrong to live in the past, it's about whether or who they're trying to impress.

If you ask me, that's what you're out to give your readers: a potbelly stove rather than central heating, a bike with coaster brakes, a teacher you address as "Mr." and "sir," rather than a teacher who tries to be just as young as his pupils. Just as young and sexy, I should really say—the latter above all.

As a matter of fact, you're sort of right to be so naive. Those cell-phone conversations really are completely vacuous, of course, but then so are all conversations. Including those held around the old-time cracker barrel. There's no reason to wax nostalgic about how those cracker-barrel conversations were more edifying than the ones carried on today in a train that is—per usual—running late ("Hi, it's me, no, we're standing still again, where are you?").

People prefer to talk about nothing at all, it's been that way for thousands of years and everyone's fine with that. To say nothing, quite intentionally, of e-mails and text messages. E-mails and text messages facilitate social contact the way a laxative facilitates defecation. But when one takes an overdose of laxative, as we all know, the result is only diarrhea.

You, in fact, are doing the right thing when you write

longhand and then type your sentences letter by letter on a blank sheet of paper: that forces one to think slowly. For the sake of convenience, I won't go into whether a mediocre mind is served at all by thinking slowly. It's the idea that counts.

The reason your wife sent a postcard is because an e-mail or text message would be a no-no. Her handwriting is cute, it's—I say this without duplicity—girlish. Handwriting with lots of round shapes in the letters, and with round, open dots over the *i*'s. Psychologists say that open dots over the *i*'s are an indication of egocentrism, but when it comes to that, if you ask me, you have to draw a sharp distinction between men and women.

Sometimes I run into the postman while he's filling the boxes down by the front door. At other times, like this morning, he's still busy sorting the mail out by his cart.

"Give it here, I'll do it," I say.

"Are you sure?"

"Sure. People have to help each other, right?"

That's the way it goes, all the time. Completely natural. A nice, normal man lends the postman a helping hand. Only in the course of a subsequent reconstruction, in black and white and with an ominous voice-over, might one see something abnormal in it. Only with the advantage of hindsight concerning what happened next, and with the aid of tendentious music, does being handed mail that is not addressed to you take on something sinister.

I always wait until the postman has walked on with his cart before starting to fill the boxes. I look at each package or envelope before slipping it into the appropriate mail slot. For me, it has never been anything but plain old curiosity. Or healthy interest, if you will. On the basis of bank statements, subscriptions, and warning notices, I get to know my neighbors better. I never go too far. I study the blue envelope from the tax service for no longer than a second, then put it in the mailbox of the one to whom it is addressed.

Sometimes I imagine that I am being filmed by someone in a van parked across the street. A nondescript van with the name of a construction or plumbing firm on the side. An undercover operation, with a hole drilled in one of the *o*'s of "construction," the glass of the camera's lens visible perhaps only from up close. A telephoto lens, the images are blurry, grainy—but nothing strange is going on. I don't take any mail upstairs with me in order to steam open the envelopes at my leisure. I don't look at the envelopes any longer than is needed to read the name of the recipient. Personal letters are becoming less common, unmistakably so, and postcards only show up during vacations.

That is how I looked this morning at the postcard from your wife. I moved it up closer to my eyes, as though I were having trouble reading the address. Fortunately, girlish handwriting is very easy to read. For the space of a single second, I thought about the van across the street. That's why I shook my head briefly, as though realizing my mistake a bit too late—as though it had taken me a second to see that the postcard was not intended for me, but for my upstairs neighbor. Then I smiled. I flipped the card over, glanced at the picture on the front, and put it in your mailbox.

They can do all kinds of things these days. They can zoom in on a grainy picture and blow it up a million times. Imagine that there really had been a van parked across the street this morning: by zooming in and blowing up enough they could have seen which postcard I had read in a second and to whom that postcard was addressed.

There was nothing visibly suspicious about it, but still, they could have reconstructed my knowledge of her whereabouts based on the combination of text and picture.

That was the real reason why I shook my head. Why I smiled. I smiled because now I knew where she was. And I shook my head because, of course, I should have figured that out for myself a long time ago.

8

AFTER COMING out of the shower last Saturday, you went to the café across from here. When I heard your door shut I walked out onto my balcony, where I can see the street. You don't know how to make coffee. You don't know that butter should be kept outside the fridge. You would only burn yourself if you tried to heat some milk.

You took a seat outside and opened the newspaper. After a few minutes you looked around to see if anyone was coming to take your order, but none of the waitstaff had come out yet. You were the only customer. You put down your paper and turned in your chair, the better to peer into the restaurant itself.

It was a lovely day. One of the first sidewalk-café days of the year. Sunlight bounced brightly off the big windows. You shielded your eyes with one hand and peered inside, but you probably couldn't see a thing. If you had looked up, you would have seen me standing there. If it hadn't been so far away, you probably could have seen the smile on my face. I felt for you. Really, I did.

The café is a fairly new one. Even before it opened, everyone was saying what an asset it would be for the neighborhood. For this quiet neighborhood. In fact, La B., the restaurant, is the only place around. A normal café where you can drink a cup of coffee in the morning and a beer at the end of the afternoon, we don't have anything like that.

After about ten minutes, you were clearly fed up. You put your paper down on the table and went inside. You were in there for a long time. I pictured the undoubtedly deserted interior of the café. From somewhere behind a door that was open a crack you heard vague noises, as of someone loading cups and glasses into a dishwasher.

"Hello?"

No response.

"Hello?"

Then, finally, a girl came shuffling out of the kitchen. It was only Saturday morning, but she was already exhausted. You only wanted to order a cup of coffee, but in a café like this that's never a simple matter.

"I'll be with you in a minute," the girl said reproachfully, as though you had tried to barge ahead in line.

Meanwhile, outside, your newspaper was lifted momentarily by the wind, but remained on the table. It would have been too much, you having to chase a runaway newspaper—a needless addition to a scene that was convincing enough as it was.

You came outside again and sat down. You'd obviously had enough of the newspaper for the moment. First that coffee. A good four minutes later, the girl finally appeared at your table in person. She asked what you would like. You looked up and squinted. She was standing with her back to the sun, you couldn't see her face very clearly. How old might she be? Nineteen? Twenty, tops. The generation that has no idea anymore who you are. You could tell that from her body language. *A pain in the neck,* that body said. *A troublesome old man who shows up at eleven o'clock on a Saturday morning, for*

God's sake, to order a cup of coffee. We've only been open for an hour, what's wrong with this guy?

She didn't quite pull out a memo pad to jot down your order, but almost. Then she disappeared inside, only to come out again three minutes later. Empty-handed, of course: three minutes is not nearly enough time to pour something into a cup. She gestured, she pointed, she shrugged—and you looked up at her, your hand shielding your eyes from the sun. From my balcony I couldn't make out a word, but I had the feeling I could tell what was going on. I'd experienced it myself once, when I went there for a cup of coffee shortly after the opening. The milk. It was eleven o'clock in the morning, but there was no milk left. I saw the girl point in the direction of the local shops. She would be pleased to go get some milk, but she was alone. She couldn't leave the café unmanned: this old fussbudget could understand that, surely?

Is it at such moments that you miss your wife? I don't know whether you thought about her that Saturday morning. I did, in any case. I lowered my eyelids and tried to imagine her on the sun-drenched gravel beach. She was sitting, her arms wrapped around her knees, on a towel she'd spread out on the gravel. Your daughter was just coming out of the water with a bucket and a little shovel. I thought these things because I was still assuming that she had gone somewhere far away, to one of the Canary Islands, or at the very least to some resort on the Mediterranean.

I still have a copy of the women's magazine from a few months ago with the portrait of her in the section called "Partner Of," where the wives of famous men are interviewed. About how wonderful and intelligent those men are. About that first meeting at the public reading or film festival, when lightning struck.

You have women who wait in the soccer stadium, beside the underground passage that links the stadium to the training field. They shout things at the players. They ask for an autograph, for the hundredth time. They want to have their picture taken with the player. They have a dream. They have their sights set on a soccer player, and it doesn't really matter which one. Any player who can make that dream come true is eligible.

The women who cruise the literary evenings, film festivals, and theater cafés are different. Yet their dream is essentially the same as that of the soccer women. A husband with a famous face. To the outside world, they maintain that they're primarily interested in the substance. In his talent. Still, a writer with a flashier car always has a prettier—younger—wife than the writer with only a public transport pass. The playwright dependent on public grants has to make do with factory seconds from the outlet store. The sculptor sloshed by eleven each morning has to make do with a woman with red-rimmed eyes who, just like him, reeks of wet ashtrays and soured wine.

How did your wife put it again in "Partner Of"?

"I had done a book report on *Payback* [. . .] It was my senior year at high school. A girlfriend and I mustered up all our courage and called the writer for an interview in the school paper. I still remember how long I spent in front of the mirror that day. I couldn't decide between my miniskirt with high heels or just a plain old pair of jeans. At the last moment, the other girl couldn't make it, and I showed up in the skirt [. . .] at first sight, that spark [. . .] never went away again [. . .] older than my father [. . .] hurt my mother the most [. . .] never wanted to see me again."

What interested me, though, wasn't so much the interview as the photo that went with it. Your wife, leaning against an ivy-covered wall. In jeans, wearing Adidas sneakers. It's a white brick wall, the outside wall of a house, in the upper left-hand corner you can see a little bit of a drainpipe, painted green, and a small window—belonging to a bathroom or a shower?

It doesn't say so in so many words, but it was immediately clear to me where that picture was taken. Probably at the same spot where your wife was interviewed. You yourself have made only sporadic mention of your "place in the country," as you call it in some interviews. Your "second home," or more frequently your "second work space," because of course the work must go on: so that readers won't think you're goofing off at that second home, just lolling on the couch beside the fireplace.

In the nearby town of H., they're oh-so proud to have a famous writer living close by. A real, still-living writer who shows up now and then at a sidewalk café along the market square; who orders fried fish or a dish of mussels at the local seafood restaurant. It doesn't literally say that either in "Partner Of." But if you read carefully, it's in there. The name of the town—H.—is even mentioned outright, as an example of the kind of respectful deference one still finds in the provinces.

"At the supermarket, people let me cut ahead in line, because they know that I'm his wife [. . .] rather embarrassing, really, but on the other hand I still enjoy it. That never happens in Amsterdam, anyway."

The way she puts it, I think, is rather sweet. I see her face. How it glows with pride. But it's also glowing a bit with embarrassment. That's your wife, to a tee. Or perhaps I should say: that's all the women whose portraits appear in "Partner Of."

When I flipped over the postcard this morning and looked

at the picture on the front, it took about three seconds for the penny to drop. It was a photograph of an old city gate. A gate in the wall of a fortified town. *Greetings from H.* was printed in red letters at the bottom.

Then I went upstairs to find that women's magazine. After rereading the whole "Partner Of" interview, I turned my attention to the photo. How many little white houses could there be close to the town of H.? How many little white houses with ivy on the wall? With a drainpipe painted green?

I took an even better look at the photo. Your wife looked good. Rested. Healthy. Her hair pinned up, a few blond locks had come loose and hung down around her ears. Little earrings. Now I saw something else too. To the right of her face, a tile was affixed to the wall. A tile with a number on it. A house number.

The little tile with the number on it was partly hidden from view by her pinned-up hair. It could have been just that one number, or the final cipher of a larger one.

The number was a 1.

9

Once again, I hesitate. We now have two narratives running side by side. Or three, actually. The stories within the story. You yourself love that technique; as we've seen already, you make full use of it in both *Payback* and *Liberation Year.*

So I'm hesitating. For a moment, I ask myself what you would do if you were in my shoes. Go ahead here with the next day—the day after the postcard arrived—with me driving down our street, after setting the navigation system for the route to H. ("A navigation system?" I hear you say. "What kind of gizmo is that?" I see you shaking your head after I explain. "What's wrong with a road map?" you ask— and, once again, you're not completely wrong about that.)

I could, of course, also toss you some new material. The way Laura Domènech, Mr. Landzaat, and I greet each other at the garden gate of the house in Terhofstede—up to the moment when the three of us go inside and the history teacher gradually begins to disappear from sight.

Or I could go on with last Saturday: the third parallel narrative. You got up from the table outside the café. You still hadn't had your coffee. I raced to take the elevator down and followed you on your walk through town. That's already a lot less suspenseful—at least for you. After all, you were there too. At most, it might be interesting to your readers.

What does a writer do during the weekend? What does he do on a normal Saturday (and Sunday)—a day when his wife is not at home?

But like I said: you know that better than I do.

Landzaat threw all his body language into the fray to make clear that something had really changed in his attitude toward Laura. That he was not here to accost her again.

"Laura," he said quickly when we came close enough for him to see the expression on her face. "Laura, please! Let me . . . let me explain first. Let me say what I have to say."

He spread his arms, his palms facing forward. *Look, I've come unarmed,* that expression says in some cultures. Here, with us, it was meant above all to express innocence and helplessness: he would make no attempt to touch her, let alone embrace her.

Laura snorted, it sounded like a sob. I glanced over at her, but saw that she was not crying. The look in her eyes was cold, perhaps even colder than the polar wind that blew fine-powder snow across the paving stones in front of the house.

"What are you doing here?" she asked.

First she pointed at the house, then made a broader sweep with her arms, a gesture meant to take in the entire whitened landscape that surrounded us. Our landscape. The history teacher hadn't looked at me even once.

"I'm here . . . I'm here to say goodbye, Laura," Mr. Land-zaat said. "I'm here to say that it's over for me too, now. That's what I wanted to come and say to you. I won't bother you anymore."

I looked at his face. He hadn't been waiting for us in his car all this time, it seemed, he had been outside, standing by the gate. His cheeks, shaven for a change, were grayish.

Under his eyes, or perhaps I should say under the dark-blue bags under his eyes, I could see a few burst blood vessels, purple and red. He tried to smile, but the cold probably clanged against his teeth—those long teeth that appeared for a moment between his lips, which were already a dark blue as well—because he closed his mouth right away.

"I . . ." He pointed to the cream-colored Volkswagen Beetle—"I'm leaving again right away. I'm on my way to Paris. To see friends."

"Oh, really?" Laura said. The history teacher was hugging his upper body now with both arms, and rubbing those arms with his black-mittened hands. "I'll only stay for a minute," he said, and as he said that he glanced at the front door of the house. "I thought . . . maybe I could come inside to warm up. I just want to explain. So that we can part as normal . . . as grown-up individuals. If that's okay with you, Laura."

Now, for the first time, he looked at me. I couldn't see my own eyes, but I knew the look that was in them. *You came here of your own free will,* I looked. *Now you'd better blow out of here right away, of your own free will.*

For your own good. I looked then, for good measure—but the history teacher had already taken his eyes off me.

"Laura?" he said quietly. "Laura?"

Laura stamped her boots in the snow.

"For just a minute, then," she said at last.

And so we went inside. Landzaat took off his coat and mittens and warmed himself by the stove. In front of the stove was our bed—our unmade bed. His shoes were almost touching the mattress. *I won't bother you anymore,* he'd told Laura—but here he was anyway. Our history teacher was inside. Inside of something that had at first been only for us.

"There's almost nothing left in the house," Laura called

from the kitchen. "We just went to do some shopping, but the only store in the village was closed too. And if I make coffee now, we won't have any tomorrow morning."

"Don't worry about it," Mr. Landzaat called back. "A glass of water is all right." He rubbed his hands together, cupped them and blew into them. "Wow, it's so cold," he said.

Now, from the kitchen, I heard the rattling of bottles.

"We've still got . . . ," I heard Laura say. "Wait a minute, what's this? Eau-de-vie. There's still a little left. You want that? A glass of eau-de-vie?"

No, I said in my thoughts. *Not eau-de-vie.* But Laura couldn't hear that.

"Well, I wouldn't say no to that!" Mr. Landzaat shouted. "I still have to drive, but one little glass couldn't hurt."

Then he turned to look at me—and winked. He winked, and at the same time he bared those long teeth, all the way up to the purplish gums.

I didn't look at his face, only at his mouth and his teeth. If I had teeth like that I would keep my smiling to a minimum. In my imagination I saw Mr. Landzaat nibbling at a carrot. Then I imagined him holding an acorn between his fingers. Would he sink those teeth into the acorn right on the spot, or would he save it for the long winter?

You have two kinds of teachers. The first kind behave like adults. They want to be addressed as "sir" or "ma'am," they don't put up with backtalk or stupid jokes in their class-room, if you can't behave then you can stand out in the hall for an hour, or they'll give you a note to take to the prin-cipal's office. In everything, they emphasize the inequality between themselves and the pupil. The only thing they ask for is respect. And usually, they get it.

The second kind of teacher is mostly scared. He lowers

himself out of fear. He pulls a boy's hair, just as a joke, he plays soccer with the kids at recess, he wears trousers and shoes that bear a distant resemblance to our own trousers and shoes; he wants, above all, to be liked. Sometimes we, the pupils, play along for a while. Mostly out of pity. We act as though we really do like the frightened teacher, we let him believe that he's popular. Meanwhile, however, the frightened teacher has awakened our animal instincts. Animals can smell fear a mile away. Within the herd, the nice teacher is the straggler. We wait patiently for the right moment. An unguarded moment when the nice teacher stumbles or turns his back on us. Then we pounce on him collectively and tear him limb from limb.

Both the authoritarian and the frightened teacher belong to the most mediocre category of human being. The term "*high* school," in fact, is completely misleading: there's nothing high or mighty about it, it's the deep rut in the middle of the road. They only make it seem like you're being taught different things: what it really comes down to is spending six years under the yoke of the most stifling kind of mediocrity. Nowhere is the odor of mediocrity more pervasive than at a high school. It's a smell that works its way into everything, like the stench of a pan of soup that has been bubbling on the burner too long. Someone turned down the gas and then forgot all about it.

"So, are you two surviving out here in the cold?" Mr. Landzaat asked. He was trying to sound jovial. He did his best to please, to act as though it was indeed all a thing of the past, the desperate overtures in the bicycle shed, the panting phone calls, the shadowing of Laura all the way to beneath her bedroom window. *Dead and buried,* he was trying to say. *You two have nothing to fear from me.*

But he was still standing there, warming his hands at the

stove. Above all, he was standing too close to our bed. He shouldn't have come.

Before I could answer him, Laura came in carrying the bottle of eau-de-vie and three glasses. They weren't shot glasses, they were tumblers. She slid aside the two dirty plates off of which we'd eaten our fried eggs and bacon that morning, and put the glasses on the table.

"How much of this stuff are you supposed to pour?" she asked, twisting the top off the bottle.

"Not very much," I said.

"All right, looking good," Mr. Landzaat said. Still rubbing his hands, he stepped away from the coal stove and sat down at the table. Laura lit two candles and put them on the windowsill. It seemed to be just a smidgen darker outside than it had been a few minutes ago—it had started snowing again.

"Well, here's to you!" Mr. Landzaat said, holding up his glass. But when neither Laura nor I made a move to imitate his toast, he raised the glass to his lips and took a big gulp. "Ah," he said, "just what the doctor ordered." He glanced at the dirty plates. "Must be nice, a house like this without your parents around? Able to do whatever you like?"

Laura's forehead was creased in a frown. She rolled her glass between her long, pretty fingers, but she still hadn't taken a sip.

"Why are you here?" she asked quietly, without looking at the history teacher.

Mr. Landzaat raised the glass to his lips again, but put it back on the table without drinking. He leaned forward a bit and placed his hand on the table, not far from Laura's. I shifted my weight and the wooden chair creaked loudly.

.   .   .

"Laura," he said, "I've come to say that I'm sorry. Not about what we . . . us, the two of us, I'm not sorry about that, but about . . . afterward. I shouldn't have . . . I acted like a schoolboy. I shouldn't have kept calling you. But I simply couldn't accept that it was over. Now I can."

He smiled and bared his long teeth again. The combination of heat from the coal stove and the first slug of eau-de-vie had caused two rosy blushes to appear on his gray cheeks. *Like a schoolboy,* he'd said. *I acted like a schoolboy.* I didn't take it too personally. After all, I wasn't a schoolboy. A boy, yes, but not a *schoolboy.* It wasn't so much insulting as pitiful, this frightened man comparing himself to a schoolboy.

Laura looked at him silently. Mr. Landzaat knocked the rest of his drink back in one go. Then he wiped his mouth with the back of his hand. His lips were no longer a dark blue either, they were redder.

"I wanted to ask you to forgive me, Laura," he said. "That's why I came. To ask your forgiveness."

"That's good," Laura said.

Mr. Landzaat sighed deeply. His eyes were glistening, I saw. I took my first slug of eau-de-vie, then set the glass down on the table a bit too loudly. The history teacher looked over—not at me, only at the glass.

"I hope, when the vacation's over, that we can go back to how things were in class," he went on. "That we can act normally toward each other. As friends. That we can stay friends."

"No," Laura said.

Mr. Landzaat stared at her.

"Act normal in class, okay," Laura said. "That's mostly up to you. But I don't want to be your friend. You're not my friend. And you never have been."

I felt a deep warmth rising up inside me. The heat began

somewhere in the pit of my stomach and made its way up. It was not the kind of heat the coal stove gave off. This heat came from inside. A proud warmth that wanted to get out.

"Laura, I realize that I . . . carried on," Mr. Landzaat said. "That's why I'm here to apologize. I lost my way for a while there. My senses. I . . . I couldn't think about anything else. But now that you've forgiven me, can't we just be friends? I would really like that. Maybe we should let it go for a while, but after that . . . I mean, after Christmas we'll be seeing each other in the classroom a couple of times a week. At school. We'll see each other in the hallway, on the stairs. It's not like *nothing* happened, Laura. You can't just wipe it out. I'm very fond of you, and that's something *I* can't just wipe out. It would be weird for us to act as though nothing had happened."

There was a sentence bouncing around in my head. A line from a movie. *Maybe you didn't hear correctly, buddy. Maybe you didn't hear what the lady said.* Then the script would have me stand up as a sign that the conversation was over. It was high time he started the car and drove on to Paris.

But I didn't say anything. I was sure now that it was better not to say a thing. As we'd come down that last stretch of road into Retranchement, I'd whispered to her a few times that there was nothing to worry about. That I would protect her. But Laura didn't need protecting. She did it all by herself. Landzaat was flat on his back. He was flat on his back the way a dog lies on its back to expose its soft spot, as a sign of surrender to a stronger opponent.

I have to admit that then, for the first time, I entertained the idea that a person like Mr. Landzaat might not deserve to live. That he was not, so to speak, worthy of living. Back in the olden days, when the gladiators fought and the loser had behaved in a cowardly fashion, the crowd would give the thumbs-down. I gave the thumbs-down to him right then.

Finish him off, Laura, I thought. *Once and for all. That's what he came for.*

"I think it would be better if you left," Laura said quietly. "I really don't feel like this at all."

Mr. Landzaat picked up his empty glass, raised it to his mouth, and put it back down. He glanced at the bottle, then looked at Laura.

"You're right," he said. "I'll leave. Maybe I shouldn't have come."

But he didn't get up.

"I . . . ," he started. Now he picked up the bottle and screwed the top off. "Anyone else?" he asked. Laura shrugged, I didn't do anything. After he had topped up our drinks, he filled his own glass—almost halfway to the top.

I looked out the window. It was now almost completely dark. In the light of the only streetlight along this stretch of road you could see the snow swirling down in flurries that grew heavier all the time. I thought about the advice parents and other grown-ups would give. Better not to drive in weather like this, especially not when you've knocked back a few glasses of eau-de-vie. But we weren't grown-ups. Mr. Landzaat was the only one here who had passed the age of consent, long ago. He didn't need anyone else to tell him what was good for him.

For us—for Laura, and certainly for me—the best thing would definitely be if, at a considerable distance from this house, he were to slip off the road and smash into a tree or an embankment.

"If you plan to get to Paris, Mr. Landzaat . . . ," I said.

"Jan," he said, "please, call me Jan." When he looked at

me I saw that the eau-de-vie had reached his eyes now—something about the whites of them, something watery that reflected the light from the little candles.

"It's getting dark," I said. "If you want to get to Paris tonight, it's about time you left."

Mr. Landzaat sighed deeply and took his eyes off me. "Are you happy, Laura?" he asked. "Tell me that you're happy with . . . with *him*. If you don't dare to say it with him around, I'll take you along with me to Paris. But if you tell me that you're really, truly happy, then I'll be out of here in ten seconds. But I need you to look at me, Laura. Please. That's the only . . . the last thing I'll ask of you."

"Go away," Laura said. "Get out of here, you idiot."

I looked at the bottle of eau-de-vie, it was more like a clay flask than a bottle. I thought about whether it might be heavy enough to crush someone's skull.

"Look at me, Laura," Mr. Landzaat said. "Look at me and say it."

I picked up the bottle and weighed it in my hands. I pretended that I wanted to pour myself some more eau-de-vie, but I was mostly assessing the bottle's heft.

"I'm happy," Laura said. "I've never been happier than I am with him. Never in my whole life. You look me in the eye, you jerk! Look! You look me in the eye and tell me what you see."

We stood outside by the gate while Mr. Landzaat tried to start the Volkswagen. It felt like hours passed, but then there was a loud pop and a white cloud of exhaust. I had both arms around Laura and was holding her tight.

"Sweetheart," she whispered in my ear. "My love."

The car moved a few inches, almost imperceptibly to the

naked eye. It took a moment for us to realize that the rear tires were spinning desperately in the fresh snow. Mr. Landzaat turned off the engine and opened the door.

"No traction," he said after he'd climbed out. He kicked the rear tire, then took a few careful steps up onto the road. Almost right away, he slipped and fell—or pretended to slip and fall.

"It's like a skating rink out here," he said.

I felt Laura's hand under my coat, her fingers under my sweater and T-shirt, her nails against my skin.

"I'm really sorry about this," Mr. Landzaat said. "I wanted to leave. You saw me try to leave. But I'm pretty much powerless. Is there a hotel somewhere in the village, maybe?"

10

AFTER THE tunnel, the landscape changes. I won't try to describe that landscape, I think you can picture it just as clearly as I do. First you have the cranes along the waterfront, the pipes and tubes of the refineries, the little lights blipping on and off at the tops of the power pylons, but after the tunnel everything becomes flatter and emptier.

White vapor is coming from the cooling towers at the nuclear plant. Stacked up high along the dike are blue sea containers bearing names like HANJIN and CHINA SHIPPING. The road's surface consists of sloppily laid concrete slabs, as though the road itself were only temporary, as though it could just as easily be somewhere else tomorrow.

A few curves later and the cooling towers and containers are behind me, in my rearview mirror. In front of me the new landscape opens up—little dikes lined with poplars, pastureland with a few sheep or horses, a brick steeple in the distance.

As I've already noted, one should do one's best to banish coincidence from a novel—from a made-up story. Coincidence fits better in the real world. The real world is its ideal habitat. Only reality is glued together with coincidence.

In both *Liberation Year* and *Payback,* nothing is left to coincidence. Coincidence ruins the credibility of a writer and his story, you're quite aware of that. In your books, therefore, everything has to do almost fastidiously with everything else. The children are able to find their way into the liberated zone of the Netherlands *because* the eldest of the two boys once went there on vacation with his parents. The Wehrmacht officer understands Dutch (something his interrogators don't know) *because,* in prewar Berlin, he was infatuated with a Dutch girl. Might that Dutch girl, the reader wonders even at that point, be the same one who is now in hiding close to Amsterdam's Old West Church? And indeed, when they meet later on in the story (under less felicitous circumstances), can you really call that a coincidence?

Something similar happens in *Payback*. The history teacher, Mr. Landzaat (in your book you call him Ter Brecht—a name that's a bit too contrived to my tastes) listens to the weather report on the car radio on his way to Terhofstede (Dammerdorp in *Payback*). What you're suggesting is that he knows it will start snowing later that day. He takes into account the possibility that he may become stranded; you force the reader to suspect this along with you. Still, he drives on. Here the book parts from the truth. The truth, as is so often the case, is much simpler. Mr. Landzaat was probably hoping that Laura would react differently, but I don't think he ever consciously considered the weather.

He was standing outside, in the freshly fallen snow. At that point, he really wanted to leave. Today, still, so many years later, I firmly believe that.

So imagine that it hadn't started snowing, or that it had been snowing only lightly. Then he actually would have left. He would have spent the rest of that Christmas vacation with his friends in Paris. You would have had no premise for your book. Instead, out of desperation, you might have written yet another book about the war.

. . .

It's market day in H. I drive once around the city center and finally park the car outside those same city walls that I saw only yesterday on the postcard.

Here is my plan: I go to a café for a drink. I strike up a conversation with the bartender or the waiter. After a while, I casually mention your name. *The writer, yes. He has a country home somewhere around here, doesn't he?* Then I change the subject right away. To the best place in H to buy mussels, for example. With a little luck, I'll already have an idea of the general direction I need to go in to find the white house with the address that ends with a 1.

But that's not the way it goes. Coincidence, apparently, has alighted in H long before I arrived. The sidewalk cafés around the market square are chock-full of customers. And while I'm walking around trying to find a seat, I spot her. She has her sunglasses pushed up over her hair like a barrette. On the table in front of her is a half-empty glass of white wine. Beside her glass is another one. A glass of pink lemonade, with a straw. The end of the straw is hidden from sight in a little girl's mouth.

How could I be anything but thankful for such a fluke? I am grateful to coincidence. I can skip the whole search mission, the way I would probably skip over it in a book. Just like the descriptions of landscapes and faces. If this were a book, with a made-up story, some readers would now definitely be crying out that it's all awfully coincidental. Maybe they would even stop reading.

But not you, I think. *You won't stop.* I act as though I'm scanning the tables at the sidewalk café, like I'm looking for a place to sit. Across from the chairs occupied by your wife and daughter, there is precisely one vacant seat. There are plastic shopping bags lying on the chair, but if you took those away, someone could sit there.

"Excuse me," I say, "but is this seat taken?"

I look at her. I look at her face as though suddenly something is dawning on me. As though I'm seeing a vaguely familiar face that I can't quite place yet.

"I . . . ," I say. "Is . . . are you . . . ?"

She squints in the sunlight and looks up at me. I move a little to one side, so that my shadow falls across her face. Now it's her turn to look up at me as though at someone whose face she can't immediately place.

"But . . . ," she says.

"Well, I'll be," I say. "It is. You're . . . I live downstairs from you. I'm the downstairs neighbor."

"Right," she says. "The neighbor. You're the neighbor."

"Yeah. I'm . . ." I point over my shoulder, at the market square—"I was going to do some shopping. I'm not too far from here."

Then comes the part I learned by heart; the important thing is to make it come out sounding as natural as possible. "I'm staying in K.," I say. "Close to here. At a bed-and-breakfast. I came here for the nature reserve, the wetlands at S. I'm a photographer. I photograph birds. This is such a coincidence," I add. "I didn't know . . . I mean, are you here on vacation?"

I had thought about this on the drive down. Would it be possible for me to know that you have a country cottage close to H.? Possible, yes, but not absolutely necessary.

"Birds," your wife says.

"Uh-huh," I say. "Well, you know, it's only a hobby. I do other animals too—I *photograph* other animals too," I correct myself quickly. "Nature. Everything in nature."

This is the point at which I look around. Is there another

free table somewhere? No. There are other vacant chairs, but that would only mean that I would have to sit down with other people. My hands are already resting on the back of the chair with the shopping bags on it.

It's a heads-or-tails moment. You've tossed the coin, it spins as it falls, it rolls off under a chair or table. You bend down and pick it up.

Heads it's me: *But I won't bother you any longer. I should be moving on.*

Tails it's her: *Oh, how thoughtless of me . . . Please, sit down.*

It's tails. She leans over, takes one of the shopping bags off the chair, then the other, and places them on the ground beside her own chair.

"Can I take your order?"

Suddenly there's a girl standing beside me, a girl carrying a wooden tray. I glance at the table, at the glass of lemonade and the glass of white wine.

"I'll have a beer, thanks," I say.

I slide the chair back and sink down onto it. Only then do I look straight at her. I smile. She smiles back. There's no need to describe her face—you see her face in your mind's eye.

"Who's that man, Mommy?"

There's no real need for me to describe your daughter's face now either, but I can't leave her out of the story any longer. If I were to leave her out, what follows would be impossible to understand.

"That's our neighbor," your wife says. "That's what he just said. Our downstairs neighbor."

Then your daughter looks at me for the first time. I look back. I look at her face. In that face, your genes have won the battle. That's a pity. It's not an unattractive face, it's just not a girl's face. More the face of a man. Not a boy. A man's face with girlish hair. She has your eyes, your nose, your mouth. Her eyes aren't watery like yours, the skin on her nose is still white, unmarred by blemishes or hair, when she laughs one sees no brown or grayish teeth, but otherwise she's simply a copy—a three-year-old, female version of you.

I state my name. Then I ask hers.

She tells me, and I say that I think it's a pretty name. *A little far-fetched, a little affected, maybe a little too special*—but of course I say none of that. Who picked this name? You or your wife? I'm betting on you. A daughter of yours, you must have felt, couldn't have just any old name.

"Well, isn't that a coincidence!" your wife says to your daughter. "He has the same first name as Papa."

So now you know my name too. You already knew, of course. Or rather, you should have known—only a few days ago, you wrote my name at the front of your new book. At the front of *Liberation Year*.

For [. . .], you wrote. *Hope you have fun reading this.*

Fun reading—yes, that's what writers sometimes write at the front of their books, you're not alone in that. *Have fun reading this.* I don't know how that works with you, but I rarely have fun while I'm reading. *Fun reading* makes me think of someone who slaps his knees in mirth as he turns the pages.

A reader reads a book. If it's a good book, he forgets himself. That's all a book has to do. When the reader can't forget himself and keeps having to think about the writer the whole time, the book is a failure. That has nothing to do with fun. If it's fun you're after, buy a ticket for a roller coaster.

That we share first names is yet another indication that we find ourselves in the real world. In novels, characters never have the same first name. Never. Only in reality, the real-life reality that takes place in the here and now, do people have the same name. When people have the same first name, you have to state the surname in order to distinguish between them. Or come up with a nickname. *Big-mouth Bill,* we say, to keep loquacious Bill and quiet Bill separated in our minds.

I have to keep the conversation going, I think, but right then the girl comes back with my beer. I raise my glass in a brief toast, then take a sip. A smaller sip than I'd like.

"We have a house," your wife says, before I have time to think of anything to say. "About five miles from here. A cottage. It's at the bottom of a dike; in the distance you can see the ships sailing into the estuary of the W. Heading for A. harbor."

I look at her. I look her straight in the eye. Don't hold her gaze too long, I warn myself. *How did the two of you get here? I mean, you left in a taxi. But you didn't take it all the way to H., did you? The taxi must have brought you to the station in Amsterdam. But I noticed yesterday that there's not even a station here in town. Yesterday, when I was wondering whether to come by car or by train. The closest station is in A.*

"We usually take the train to A.," she says now, answering one of the questions I didn't ask. "At least, when it's just the two of us"—she nods at your daughter—"that way, [. . .] still has the car back home. Then we take a taxi from A. We have a car here too. A little secondhand Subaru."

When she speaks your name, she smiles briefly, and I smile back briefly, as though we're both realizing at the same moment that she has spoken my name too. Indeed, it's something you'd never see in a book. At least *I've* never seen it in a book. I find it particularly endearing, in fact, the way she mentions the make of the car. A Subaru . . . Most people would be ashamed to drive around in a Subaru, but the way she mentions it is off the cuff. A secondhand Subaru. A little car, and it doesn't matter if it's a Subaru because it's only used as a local shopping cart anyway.

That's it, it occurs to me then. It's all in that word "little." House—*little* house. Car—*little* car. The apology is already bound up along with that. You may be a famous writer with money in the bank who can afford a second car and a second house, but by calling that second house and that second car a *little* house and a *little* car—a *little secondhand* Subaru—it's all smoothed over. With her qualification of "little," your wife is telling me: *It hasn't all gone to our heads.*

"Today we rode our bikes here," she says. "The weather's so nice. It was fun, wasn't it?"

"It was really windy," your daughter says.

"But on the way home we'll have the wind at our backs," your wife says. "It will blow us all the way home."

She puts her arm around your daughter and gives her a little squeeze. Then she smiles at me again.

"I want to go home now," your daughter says.

"We'll go in a minute," she says. "You haven't finished your lemonade yet."

"I'm not thirsty anymore."

Your wife picks up her wineglass—it's still half full. I see her glance, before taking a sip, at my almost-empty beer glass.

"Yes, we should be going now," she says without looking at me.

"I'll be off too," I say. I toss back the rest of my beer and look around. I act as though I'm looking for the girl to bring the bill.

By then I already know what I'm going to do. I mustn't sit around here, I mustn't foist my company on her any longer, that would only make her nervous. I'm going to walk around the market. I announce that too. *I'm going to take a little look around the market.* From behind the stalls I can keep an eye on the sidewalk café, without being noticed. *About five miles from here,* that's what your wife said. I can follow them in the car, not right behind them the whole time, no, that would be too obvious. Just pass them a couple of times, then wait further along to see which turn they take. A cottage. It's at the bottom of a dike; in the distance you can see the ships sailing into the estuary of the W. A house number ending with a 1—it shouldn't be too hard.

But coincidence, apparently, isn't finished with us yet. A shadow suddenly falls over the sidewalk café. When we look up we see the clouds slide across the sun. Gray clouds. Dark gray. Rainclouds.

"Oh, goodness," your wife says. "We'd better hurry, we don't want to get wet on the way home."

Then it's her turn to look around, but the girl with the serving tray is nowhere to be seen. Now, in the distance, we hear a rumbling. I look at my empty beer glass. Silently, I count to three.

"Looks like a real thunderstorm coming up," I say. "If you want, I can give you a ride home. No problem at all."

"You don't have to do that," she says.

"Really, it's no bother."

"I don't want to get wet, Mommy," your daughter says. "I want to go home."

Your wife bites her lower lip. She looks around again, then up at the sky. Thunder rumbles again. Closer now.

"But what about the bikes?" she says. "No, we better wait here for it to blow over."

"But I want to go home *now,* Mommy."

"You can pick up the bikes later on," I say. "My hotel's not too far from here. In K. Later this afternoon. Or tomorrow.

I'll pick you up at your house and bring you back here. No problem."

A flash, a brief silence, and then a clap, followed by a rolling rumble.

Just like back then, I think now. And the next moment it occurs to me that you would always be sure to say that. *Just as it was before.* Yes, you'd make it easy for the reader, or rather: you would do everything in your power to keep the reader from missing the correspondence between one event and the other.

What do they call that again, when a narrative motif is repeated in a different form? Long ago, a snowstorm gave a story a different twist—gave someone's life a different twist. And now, years later, a thunderstorm tosses something my way. An opportunity. Opportunities. A surprising twist.

"My car's parked just outside the wall," I say. "I can swing by here and pick you up."

I point to the curb in front of the café, where at that same moment the first raindrops begin spattering against the pavement. The sky shifts from gray to nearly black, the red-and-white-striped canopy above our heads begins to flap—people slide their chairs back and hurry inside.

"That's very kind of you," your wife says. "But I wouldn't—"

The flash and the boom arrive almost simultaneously. Someone shrieks. From around the corner, somewhere a few streets down, comes a roar—the sound of tiles sliding off a roof, or perhaps more like a truckload of gravel being dumped on the street.

"That was a direct hit," says a man holding a newspaper over his head. Through a split in the canopy, a fat rivulet of water is now clattering onto one of the tables. Your daughter has stood up. She has both hands pressed against her ears, but she hasn't started screaming or shrieking. I see the look in her eyes. It's more like amazement. Maybe even fascination.

I push my way past the tables and out onto the street. Supposedly to see where the lightning has hit, but in fact to get a better look at the sky. To my regret I see, just past the church steeple, the first patch of blue peeking out from behind the clouds.

"I'll get the car," I say, once I've walked back to where your wife and daughter are standing. "Wait here."

Before your wife can object, I've turned up the collar of my coat and am striding down the street, past the market square where the merchants are still doing their best to pull their wares in and out of the rain.

I look up at the sky again. There's already more blue up there than a minute ago; white, sunlit clouds are piling up beyond the steeple. I've already reached the street that passes through the city walls when I turn around again and take another look up at that steeple.

It's like I've seen it somewhere before—not like a déjà vu, no; really seen it. The steeple is flat on top. You can't really even call it a spire, somewhere three-quarters of the way up the old part stops and something new begins, something that once, at least, more than sixty years ago I reckon, must have been new. The steeple has been rebuilt. Not restored. Reconstructed. In an architectural style that has aged faster in sixty years than that of the church itself.

Then I suddenly remember it; not literally, not word for word, but I resolve to look it up when I get home—which I did a few days later.

The Spitfire dove and strafed the rooftops. Thin ribbons of fire spouted from its cannons. Then the plane dropped something, something that from this distance looked like

a milk can. The children watched the can spin around
and around . . . and the next moment it hit the church
steeple. A ball of fire. Stones came raining down. The
children ran for shelter in the doorway.

When they came out a few minutes later, the spire
was gone. Just a scorched framework at the spot where
only recently it had poked so proudly at the sky. Wisps of
smoke roiled up, like the smoke from a cigarette laid in
an ashtray and then forgotten.

We won't go into your literary style here. I see how you
went about doing it. I look up at the steeple, and I sense how
at that moment I am literally standing in your shoes. You
have stood here before too. Like me, you looked up at the
steeple, blown to pieces and then rebuilt after the war. You
let your imagination run wild. Then you decided to use the
steeple.

Who knows, maybe the church tower at H. will, in the
near or distant future, serve as a stopping-off place in a "literary walk." *In the footsteps of the writer M . . .* The participants
in the walk are wearing gray and green jackets. Hiking jackets. They are no spring chickens. They're not much use to
society anymore. Only those with too much time on their
hands go on literary walks.

The guide will point at the steeple. "This is the church
tower that was bombed in *Liberation Year,*" he'll say. "No,
ma'am, I see you shaking your head, you're quite right. In the
book, the steeple is located in the eastern Netherlands, the
part that was already liberated in 1944. But the author truly
did let himself be inspired by this steeple for that evocative
scene in *Liberation Year.* He simply moved the steeple somewhere else. That is the artistic liberty of the writer. He picks
up a church—a steeple, a church spire—and sets it down

somewhere else, at a spot in his book where it serves him best."

A little less than fifteen minutes later I park my car in front of the sidewalk café. Meanwhile, the sky has cleared up completely. My heart is pounding. I climb out and, for the second time that day, my gaze sweeps over the tables, but your wife and daughter are no longer there. Most of the bikes are parked at the french-fry stand on the market square. Entire families are seated on the benches around it, eating french-fried potatoes from paper cones. On one of those benches your wife has just handed your daughter a napkin, to wipe the mayonnaise from her lips.

Hands in my pockets, I saunter over to them. "It's pretty much cleared up now," I say.

"My daughter is really tired," your wife says. "If it's not too much trouble, we'd like to take you up on your offer anyway."

11

IN THE movie version of *Payback* there's a scene where Laura and I are walking down the beach hand in hand. We're barefoot. Laura is wearing a dress, I have my jeans rolled up to my knees.

"So what now?" Laura asks.

"What do you mean, what now?" I ask.

A wave washes around our feet. The beach is deserted, yet everything tells you that the director wants this to be a summer scene. Why on earth did you agree to let them move the action from winter to summer? Now something essential is gone: the weather. It was the heavy snowfall, and nothing else, that forced Landzaat to spend the night in Terhofstede. There was no hotel, he had to sleep upstairs, in the attic. We lay downstairs on our mattress in front of the coal stove. That night we barely slept a wink. We lay close together, we kept our clothes on for once. We needed to be prepared for anything, we told ourselves.

This is a point on which the movie departs from the book. Having things happen in summer makes us, however you look at it, more culpable. The man remains the same obtrusive history teacher, but he is at liberty to drive on to his friends in Paris. In the movie, Mr. Landzaat too is more culpable than in reality. The viewer in the theater has prior knowledge. The real story, after all, has already been all over the media. The history teacher disappears without a trace. *Why doesn't he go away?* the viewer asks himself. *Why doesn't he leave the boy and girl alone?*

Every once in a while we heard the bed creak above our heads. We held our breath. Landzaat must not have slept much that night either. One time he got up, we heard his footsteps on the wooden floor, then he came down the stairs. Laura crept up closer to me. We heard the toilet door and, after a bit, the hissing rush of piss. It sounded very close by—it was like he was pissing all over us, Laura would say later. It was, in any event, something you would rather not hear.

The next morning we awoke to sounds from the kitchen. We stayed in bed and pulled the blankets up even further, so that only our heads were poking out when Mr. Landzaat put his own around the door.

"Coffee's ready," he said. "How do you like your eggs?"

At the breakfast table, barely a word was spoken. The coal stove was still warming up, so both Laura and I had blankets draped over our shoulders. I noticed that Laura, too, was doing her best not to watch the history teacher's long teeth make short work of his fried eggs.

"So, here we go again," he said, getting up to put on his coat.

But during the night a lot more snow had fallen. Our first glance at the VW, almost buried now beneath a thick, white blanket of it, destroyed any hope of Landzaat's speedy departure. But we tried anyway. We put on our gloves and did our best to wipe the snow from the windows and hood. We used a shovel I found in the shed to dig out the wheels, but now the car wouldn't even start. At the very first attempt, the starter seized up and fell silent.

Through the snow-smeared windshield of the Beetle, Laura and I couldn't get a clear look at the history teacher's face. We looked at each other. Little white clouds of breath were coming from Laura's mouth. Then she squeezed her eyes shut tight. It had stopped snowing—the unbroken cloud cover was the color of wet paper and seemed to hang right above our heads, like a suspended ceiling. It felt like ten minutes or more went by before the car door finally opened and Mr. Landzaat climbed out.

"There's no garage in this village, I guess," he said. "But do you know if maybe there's a town or village close by where they've got one?"

I remember clearly the way he stood there. His lanky frame in the snow. He had come uninvited. He had finished all our eau-de-vie and eaten the last of our eggs. In the middle of the night he had released a loud, clattering stream of urine into the toilet. But we were young. If he were to leave now, we would have forgotten about him within the hour. In summer he could have left. But not in winter.

"There's nothing in Retranchement," I said. "I'm afraid we'll have to go to Sluis."

Without thinking about it much, I'd said "we." I glanced over at Laura, but she had taken off her gloves and was blowing on her fingers to warm them up.

"How far is that?" Mr. Landzaat asked. "Sluis?"

"Three or four miles, I guess. About an hour's walk, when the weather's normal. A little more than that now, probably."

Sooner than I'd imagined, a tacit agreement had been made that I would accompany him—that I would at least show him the way.

Laura had already turned away, her arms clutched around her middle. Lifting her feet up high above the snow at every step, she went back into the house without a word.

"Or do you two know someone here in the village who might let us call a garage?" Mr. Landzaat asked.

"We have to do some shopping anyway," I told the teacher. "Our supplies are nearly gone. We might as well walk."

Move the action from winter to summer and you get a different story. It's not like moving a church steeple—it's more drastic than that.

Your wife is in the passenger seat beside me, giving directions ("At that little road up there, turn left"), your daughter is slouching in the backseat with her head against the door; in the mirror I can see her eyes fall shut now and then—a few more minutes and she'll be asleep.

For the sake of saying something, I comment on the landscape, on how vast it is, how big and empty—it's almost as though I'm *describing* the landscape. Your wife says that's what attracted you to this place most, it's a place where you can literally clear your mind.

Then we're there. I park on the dike in front of the white house. And there the Subaru is too. A blue one. The door to the house is at the back. I help with the shopping bags. She wakes your daughter. I carry the bags down a paved pathway. I see the green drainpipe, the ivy, the little window to the toilet or shower, the house number ending in a 1.

Now we're inside. A living room with an open kitchen. Your daughter runs to the TV and turns it on. Your wife takes a few things out of one of the shopping bags and puts them in the refrigerator. Then she stops what she's doing and looks at me.

She could offer me something to drink, but I can tell from her expression that she doesn't feel like it. Maybe she's done enough already today, maybe she's tired. What she wants most now is to be left alone.

But I remain standing. Cartoon figures move across the TV screen, soundlessly for the moment. I take a step toward her, and almost immediately I see something shift in the look in her eyes. *This is the downstairs neighbor,* I read in her eyes, *but how well do I know him, anyway?* The house is isolated, from the road one can see or hear nothing of what's happening inside. It's sort of like accepting rides from strangers. The realization, too late, of how stupid you've been.

I raise my hands slightly—something meant to resemble a reassuring gesture—but I'm aware that reassuring gestures, above all, can be interpreted in any number of ways. No doubt about it, the serial killer you've invited inside in good faith would start with a reassuring gesture.

She has closed the door of the fridge and lowered the shopping bags to the floor. She is looking at me wide-eyed.

I need to say something, or else I need to say goodbye and leave. But I stand there. I still don't say a word.

Then your daughter calls to your wife.

"Mommy?" she calls out. "Mommy, are you coming to watch TV too?"

Why Do You Write?

12

THAT'S THE way it goes, a writer's life. He gets up, he show-
ers, he dries himself off—just like the rest of us. But soon
afterward, the first problem presents itself: breakfast. He's on
his own today, wife and daughter have gone to their country house, he doesn't know how to use the coffee machine.
Under duress—on the heels of a shipwreck, a nuclear catas-
trophe, an earthquake—he might be able to wrest it from his
memory. A filter. Ground coffee. Boiling water. But today,
the end of the world has not arrived. It's Saturday and the sun
is shining. Across the street from his home is a newly opened
café with a patio. He closes the door behind him and takes
the elevator down.

The girl who finally comes outside ten minutes later (no,
that's not the way it went, he had to go in and get her!)
clearly has no idea who she's talking to. She mumbles something about milk that they don't have. She can't leave the
café behind untended, that's her excuse. "But I'm here, aren't
I?" he says. "I'll hold down the fort for a few minutes." But
the girl shakes her head. "I can't do that," she says. She hasn't
been working here long. Only on Saturdays. She's only a college student. *So what are you studying?* he could ask. Instead he
stares irritatedly into space. He lays his hand on the flapping
pages of the newspaper.

It's been happening more often lately, people who fail to recognize him. Young people especially. Entire generations who no longer read his books. He could grouse about how it's all the school system's fault. The high schools, after all, don't even teach literature these days! But deep in his heart he knows that it has nothing to do with the educational system. It's oblivion that beckons—a finger beckoning to him from a freshly dug grave. Nothing to get hysterical about. The promising talent, the breakthrough at middle age, and finally the forgetting. The forgetting that comes before the ultimate silence. He's at peace with that. All experience is worthwhile, he tells himself.

Turning the corner of his own street—he has abandoned the prospect of coffee, black coffee is one thing he can't handle on an empty stomach—he sees a couple coming toward him. Not a young couple, somewhere in their late fifties he guesses. Their children have probably already flown the coop, they're out for a walk together, the shared void of a Saturday morning—of an entire weekend! He sees it in their eyes right away: looking, looking away, looking again. As they pass him, they nudge each other. They laugh guiltily and greet him with a nod. He takes a little bow, *yes, it's me, it's really me,* then goes on his way.

He passes the bookshop window. The poster with his face on it is still stuck to the glass. *From 3 p.m. to 4:30 p.m., your book signed by . . .* He looks at his face on the poster and then at his face reflected in the display window. Find the differences. The face on the poster is younger than the one in the window, true enough, but not blatantly younger. When he gives a reading at a library, he sees it in the expressions of the female librarians who welcome him. All along, they've been expecting him to be a pompous ass. A pompous ass who allows only flattering portraits of himself on the backs of his books. Digitally manipulated photos that remove all pimples and moles. *It's amazing,* he sees the librarians thinking, *in real life he looks almost exactly like the photo. Age becomes him.*

Not like N, he thinks. N who always has them change the lighting on his wrinkled face to make it look like a portrait by a Dutch master. A viceroy. A Roman emperor. A Greek idol. The writer portrayed here, those photos seem to shout, lives in the certainty that most women would still give an arm and a leg to have his almost-octogenarian body perform a low-flying mission over their own. *And he's probably right,* M thinks. He glances one last time at both his faces in the display window, then walks on.

There are writers his age who do things differently. They get caught up in their own rejuvenation. They prance about in cream-colored sneakers. All Stars! They wear flashy red jackets and buy sports cars. They drive the cars from library to library. They see to it that the sports car becomes part of their look, just like the jacket and the All Stars. *I may be seventy-eight, but inside my head I'm younger than all of you put together,* that's what they try to communicate with their getup. "The important thing is to stay curious," they tell the one hundred and twenty middle-aged women gathered around them beneath the harsh fluorescent lighting of the library. "That's what keeps you young." When the reading is over, the middle-aged women throng to the table where the author is signing his books. As they help the writer spell their names correctly ("It's for me: *Marianne* with two *n*'s and an *e* at the end"), they are thinking about only one thing. Not about the stale odor that would probably waft up from the cream-colored All Stars, were this fantasy to pan out. All of them would gladly put up with that, as they would with the endless moaning and groaning and the way the eternally young writer's tongue tastes of too much red wine. Red wine the morning after a party, a puddle left in a glass with a cigarette butt in it too. He uses that same tongue to lick them all up and down, but it takes a god-awfully long time, it seems like it will never end. The next day they call all their girlfriends. "You'll never guess who stayed over at my place last night . . ."

Today M is fairly lucky. The library where he's expected to turn up is within walking distance, in a neighborhood at the edge of his own town. The worst thing about giving a reading in Amsterdam is the audiences. The audiences here radiate a certain self-importance, to put it mildly. What they radiate above all is the fact that they could be attending so many other, perhaps even much more interesting performances, matinees, or concerts. Still, on this sunny Saturday, they are here, with you, in the library. They're raring to go, but make no mistake about it: they're not about to settle for the same old song and dance, not like those provincial bumpkins who, for lack of a richer cultural agenda, go gladly to see an older, visibly dwindling writer.

At the door to the library he is welcomed by a woman who introduces herself as Anke or Anneke, or something like that. He didn't really catch the name, or rather: his hearing picked up the vowels and consonants in a certain sequence and sent them on to his brain, but upon arrival they all fell apart, like some appliance or machine you've stripped down despite your better judgment—a toaster, the engine block of a moped—but then can't put back together for the life of you.

Anna (Agnes? Anneke? Anke?) extends a hand—it's a dry hand; he glances down at his fingers to see whether there are flakes of eczema sticking to them.

What is it with these lady librarians? he asks himself, not for the first time, as he follows her past endless rows of borrowed-to-tatters, dog-eared, and therefore totally unappetizing

books. *Why do they all wear their hair the same way?* He has
nothing against women with short hair. On the contrary.
Short hair, even a crew cut, can look splendid on a woman.
But this isn't like that. This is *easy* hair, easy to keep up, like
a front yard full of paving stones rather than a lawn.

The library itself is one of those responsibly renovated
buildings, everything dressed in a motley (low-threshold!)
newness meant to seduce readers into doing their book-
borrowing here; the same way the churches tried, not so very
long ago, to draw in unbelievers with pop music during the
services. In the olden days libraries were merely dusty, he
thinks, introverted. Today they all do their best to look like
airport departure halls.

"Do you have any objection to signing during the intermission, and after the reading?" the librarian asks; they've
stopped in a corridor hung with posters and bulletin board
notices.

How could he have any objections to that? That's what
he's here for, isn't it? Why do they always ask that?

"And would you like to stand or sit?" she goes on. "We
have a table and a rostrum, so you can choose. Do you use
a microphone? What would you like to drink during the
reading?"

He looks again at the librarian's easy hair. When you stop
to think about it, it's simply a slap in the face, walking around
like that. There's no need to have one's hair cut in the ugliest
possible fashion. But "have one's hair cut" seems the wrong
way to put it too. Far more likely that she wields the shears
herself. That's cheaper. *What do I care how I look,* they say to
themselves and the outside world. Then they attack their hair
with the scissors.

Suddenly he feels exhausted. The rest of the afternoon
stretches out before him like an empty plot of land without

trees or buildings, a vacant lot beyond the reach of any zoning ordinance. The female librarian has asked him a number of questions, one after the other. He's already forgotten the first and second ones. They usually ask these questions much earlier on. They call you three to five months in advance. He used to answer the questions himself. Microphone. Sit/stand. Drink. Sign. For the last few years, though, his wife has done that for him. They usually call in the evening. At an inconvenient moment. During the eight o'clock news. They have a keen nose for moments when you really shouldn't be bothering people.

These days he just stays on the couch in front of the TV and lets his wife answer the phone. He looks at the images of a bombed-out city, of a suburb retaken from rebel hands, he has the volume turned down low.

"He'd rather stand," he hears Ana say, "but a table is okay too."

"Of course, he'd be happy to sign."

"If the room's not too big, there's no need for a microphone."

"Just plain water. And during the intermission he likes to have a beer."

This last comment is perhaps the most important of all. The core of the reading, the pivot, or perhaps more like the tipping point. You can put up with anything as long as you're allowed to slowly sink back into yourself after fifty minutes. The questions that come after the intermission he answers rather offhandedly. But the beer calls for a separate mention. Experience has made him wiser. They used to ask him during the pause whether he would prefer coffee or tea. Whenever he mentioned beer, they would raise their eyebrows. Then one of the lower-ranking librarians would be sent out on a scavenger hunt. Sometimes she would come back just before the intermission was over with one bottle that had, unfortunately, not been refrigerated. By the time they found a bottle opener, the reading was over.

"No, it's not that far, is it?" he hears Ana say. "He'll walk from the station."

That's right, they always ask that too. Whether he wants to be picked up at the station. No, he doesn't want that. Nothing is worse than to have the blathering start long before the reading itself has even begun. No, that's not true, there is one thing that is much worse than being picked up, and that's when they insist on bringing you to the station *after* the reading. In a cramped car, the blanket covered in dog hair has to be tossed onto the backseat to make room for you. Normally, the passenger seat slides back further than that, but the handle broke off yesterday. There he sits, the bunch of flowers or bottle of wine in his lap, his knees jammed up against the dashboard. The engine turns over. "There's one question still on my mind, something I didn't dare to ask in there . . ." All the way home on the train, the odor of dog clings to his clothes.

"Would you like some coffee? Shall I take your coat?"

He doesn't want any coffee, he prefers to hold on to his own coat.

"How many people are you expecting, more or less?" he asks, for the sake of having something to ask. In order not to have to look at the librarian's haircut, he pretends to examine a poster announcing a comedian who will come here soon to talk about "his profession." The picture shows the comedian wearing a funny derby, a nutty pair of plastic spectacles, and a fake mustache glued to his upper lip. *Anyone who lets themselves be portrayed like that on a poster should be taken out and shot,* he thinks. Right here, the moment he gets to the library, or else at home, in his sleep—with a silencer, of course; it would be a pity to wake anyone up with the blast.

"We have about twenty reservations," the lady librarian says. "And there are usually about twenty more who show up. But, well, you never know. It's such nice weather . . ."

And what if it had rained? he thinks, trying to imagine how she must have looked as a young girl, long ago. Where did it go wrong? At which age did that face slam shut like a book no one felt like finishing? What would she have said if it had been raining—*You never know, it's raining out?*

"I need to use the restroom," he says.

She leads him to a space with a photocopier and a book-case filled with loose-leaf binders. A coffee machine is sputtering in the corner. This is where the toilet is.

He tries to fend off the thought that the librarians use this toilet too. Standing at the little sink he takes a few deep breaths and looks in the mirror. The final moments alone—the trick is to make these moments last as long as possible. Sometimes he fantasizes about not coming back at all, about how the librarians would glance at their watches with concern. "He's been in there for fifteen minutes. I hope nothing's happened to him? Could you go and sort of knock quietly, Anneke?"

It would be a nice addition to his obituary: *found dead in the restroom of a library where he was about to read from his own work.* And then? What else would the obituary say? He looks in the mirror, and suddenly he can't help thinking about his mother. What if she could see him like this, he thinks. Would she be proud of him? He suspects she would. Mothers are not hard to please. They're always proud, even of a writing career that's nearing its expiration date. Thoughts arise in his mind about her troubled deathbed, her mouth trying to smile at him, trying to reassure him, *go on back outside, go have fun with your friends, Mommy's just a little tired.* And with no clear transition, he thinks then about his young wife. About Ana. Instead of a youth full of discos and a new boyfriend every two weeks, she chose him. Sometimes he thinks he stole those boyfriends and discos from her, but that's not true. She decided of her own free will to share her life with a writer, a writer who was aging rapidly, even then.

He flushes the toilet for form's sake, then steps outside.

13

THE READING begins. He sees about thirty people in the audience, most of them women, not one of them younger than fifty-seven, he guesses. Four or five men, tops. One man is sitting in the front row, he recognizes the type: they often have beards, they come to the reading wearing sandals or hiking boots. This one, for a change, has on a sleeveless khaki vest with a wealth of pockets, zippers and rivets, the kind photographers and cameramen wear; there are marking pens and ballpoints sticking out of a few of the pockets. His broad, hairy, and tanned arms are crossed at his chest, the chairs on both sides of him are unoccupied, and he has a pair of (reading?) glasses pushed up over his peaky, mussed-up hair. The hair of a troublemaker, M knows, a man in bad boy's clothing who, like the bewhiskered ones in sandals, saves the impertinent questions for after the break. *What do you actually think of your own work? What do you get paid, anyway, to come here and read a few bits from your book? Can you give us one good reason why we should read your books?*

Further back, toward the middle of the room, he sees two other men. Colorless men. Men in sport jackets and striped shirts who apparently could think of nothing more pleasant to do on this Saturday afternoon than accompany their wives to a reading. Deep in his heart, he feels an almost nauseating contempt for men like these. He's a man too. Would he ever attend a reading at a library—a reading by a writer like him? No, never. Not even if all other options had been exhausted.

Startled, he sees a familiar face in the audience: his publisher. He vaguely recalls a phone call from him about a week ago. "There are a couple of things I need to talk to you about," his publisher had said. "Maybe I'll pop by the library." Were they planning to dump him? he'd wondered during the phone call. No, that wasn't likely. His sales might be dwindling, but his name is still one everyone would be pleased to have in their stable. He could find another publisher at the drop of a hat. It seems more likely that they just want to discuss that interview Marie Claude Bruinzeel asked about, the one he's succeeded in putting off till now. "Please!" M had said. "Don't do that to me!"

All the way at the rear, in the backmost, almost empty row of chairs, is another man. A young man. Well, youngish . . . about thirty years younger than he is, that's for sure. The man's face looks familiar to him somehow, but he can't quite place it. Might be a journalist, you always have to watch out for those. It wouldn't be the first time that his own remarks, made in the familiar hominess of a library reading room, would end up twisted around completely in the pages of some free local paper, torn out of context and then drawn to his attention by his publisher's publicity department. *I never knew you felt this way about racism/the environmental movement/ home birthing,* someone—the publicity assistant on duty that day, or else his editor—would scribble at the bottom of the clipping. No, neither did he. More or less that way, but not exactly that way.

When he opens *Liberation Year* to the first page, he is struck by a mild dizziness. It's a dilemma each time: the longer he reads, the less blather he has to listen to, both from the audience and from himself. *Where did you come up with the idea for the book? Do you write in the morning, or in the afternoon? Do you use a computer, or do you write longhand? What do you think about the rise of right-wing radicalism in Europe? Does your wife read your books before they go to the publisher?*

The answers, too, he knows almost by heart. He always remains polite. He smiles. He lets his gaze roam over the faces of his audience. Lately he has started fantasizing about a flatbed truck showing up about halfway through the reading and rounding them all up. *Calm down everyone, stay calm, there's nothing to worry about. It's only a drill, you're being evacuated for your own safety.* Then the tailgate closes and the truck drives out of town. At a clearing in the woods, the audience has to climb down. *Take it easy, people, don't look back, just walk on quietly until you're out of the woods.* Only when they catch sight of the freshly dug pit do they realize what is about to happen.

"I write longhand," he says. "I need to feel the words flow down my arm." He hears himself talking, as though someone else were giving these answers. A spokesman or press officer. He starts reading. From the first sentence, he has the feeling that the text is not his own, that it was written by someone else. He has that feeling more often lately, but it usually overcomes him in his own study: he rereads the things he wrote months ago, and suddenly each word is new. In fact, he can't remember ever writing this text. That's one of the advantages of old age. The forgetting. Something old will sometimes look new the very next morning. But this is different. He reads the words about the resistance group, pinned down behind the railway embankment by an ambush, the description of the landscape, the sunrise, a duck quacking in the distance, and not only does it seem like the work of another writer, but like text from a writer he wishes he had nothing to do with. *What a load of tripe,* he thinks, *there we go with that war again. The Dutch resistance, what a bunch of schmaltz.*

At first he doesn't notice that he has stopped reading. He looks at his hands, his fingers on the page of his own book. *These fingers will probably never freeze off, not in the years still allotted to him,* he thinks, *but they* will *disappear.* He looks at the faces in the audience. A few of them may already be walking around with some disease, but will only get the diagnosis next week. *Only a couple of months left, ma'am . . . six months at most.* He shakes his head.

"Could I ask how many of you have already read my book?" he asks, trying to win time. A few fingers are raised.

"I had hoped to read your book before coming here this afternoon," a woman in the second row says. "But the library has it lent out all the time. I'm on the waiting list."

He looks at her, no, not really, he looks at her face, at everything except her eyes. He has never understood why people would want to *borrow* a book. All right, maybe because they don't have a lot of money, but there are so many things you might choose to deny yourself for lack of money. He himself finds it filthy, a borrowed book. Not as filthy as sleeping in a hotel where the sheets haven't been changed and you're forced to lie among the last guest's hair and flakes of skin. A book with wine spots and a crushed insect between the pages, with the grains of sand from the last reader's holiday falling out as you read.

"So why don't you *buy* my book?" he asks; he tries to smile, but only succeeds halfway. He can't see his own face—if it's a smile, then it's a fairly contemptuous one, he suspects.

"Excuse me?"

The woman is staring at him, startled. He hears someone chuckle, but otherwise the room is mostly silent.

"Are you that poor? Can't you afford a book that costs less than twenty euros?"

He is still looking at her face, then at her hair—it has a wave to it and is obviously dyed: a color like that is biologically impossible at her age.

"I—" the woman starts in, but he beats her to it.

"How much did you have to pay the beautician who did your hair this morning?" he asks. "Four times the price of my book, I estimate. But still, you'd never cut corners on that beauty parlor. You would never want to be seen with a head full of gray ends just to save enough money to buy my book."

Now the room is truly, completely still, no one is chuckling anymore.

He sees the librarian glance at her watch. *What's this?* Then he realizes: it's time for the intermission. During a reading, time fades away. Or no, it becomes something else, time does: outside, people are walking around in the sunshine, a van misses a motor scooter by a hair, a waitress's hand takes a glass of wine from a tray and places it on the table of the sidewalk café. But here in the library, time has followed a different logic, like that of water seeking the shortest route to the sea—or to the drain, rather. It is, literally, lost time: time you'll never get back again. An intermission has been imposed. A commercial break. "We'll be right back with more stories and anecdotes from M, the writer. Don't go away. Feel free to remain seated." Most of those present don't even need to be encouraged. Now they are being entertained; when this is over there gapes the chasm of a Saturday afternoon, the panicky fear of boredom.

"Would you like coffee or tea?" the librarian asks.

14

"LONGHAND, FIRST. Then I type it all out on the machine."

"Do you write in the morning or in the evening?"

"I start early in the morning. Nine o'clock. Not at ten to nine, and not at ten past nine. Nine o'clock on the dot. I don't wait for inspiration. I made a pact once with my subconscious mind: If you prompt me with ideas, I'll keep up my end of the bargain. I'll make sure I'm at my desk every morning at nine. You can count on me."

There is some muted snickering from the audience. They think it's a good joke, but he's serious. It may be the only thing about his writing practice that isn't a joke, it occurs to him.

"Do people ever recognize themselves in one of your characters?"

"That happens, yes. The opposite happens more often, though. That people whose face and body I've described most accurately don't recognize themselves at all. There are simple tricks for that. Changing the person's profession, for example. Or turning a man into a woman. The more precise you are in describing faces and personalities and objectionable traits, the less people realize that it's about them. No one sees themselves the way others do. And then there's something else: they simply don't believe it's possible. They can't believe that you, the writer, would be ruthless enough to portray them in such a terrible way. Even if it's a perfectly accurate portrayal. But there is no other choice. As a writer you have to approach the truth as closely as possible, even if there's collateral damage. 'Never marry a writer,' my first wife's mother once said. 'Before you know it, you'll find your whole life in some book.' "

Suddenly he falls silent. How did he arrive at this, for God's sake? His first wife? Her mother turned out to be right. In *The Hour of the Dog,* he had painted a merciless portrait of her. After the divorce. A reprisal, pure and simple. And as recognizably as he could. She had left him. For someone else. For more than a year she'd had something going with Willem R, the eternally drunken painter. Willem R had visited their home, eaten dinner at their table, and he—the cuckold—had suspected nothing. He had labored under the mistaken impression that his first wife was not at all charmed by the painter's drunken gibberish. He'd had no qualms about them going off on jaunts into town together, meeting up for lunches or dinners. R poured red wine down his gullet without really tasting it. He stank a little, there were spots on his shirts and holes in his black turtlenecks. At the table he used his napkin to dab at his forehead, his sweat smelled of wine too, it was simply unimaginable to him that his wife would even allow the painter to touch her with his fingertips, which were undoubtedly covered with an invisible layer of stale sweat too. That she—and here the imagination reeled and all M could do was groan quietly, his eyes clamped shut—would tolerate Willem R's chapped, perennially purple lips on hers . . .

He wrote *The Hour of the Dog* in six weeks. In a fury, growling and writhing in his desk chair. When it was finished, his publisher tried to warn him. Only for form's sake, he realized later—so much later that it was far too late already. No publisher could pass up a book like that one. The readers couldn't either. *The Hour of the Dog* became his second bestseller, after *Payback*. Most critics thought it went too far, all that dirty laundry and overly intimate detail. An embarrassing display. And they were right. It started when he read aloud a passage from it on the Sunday afternoon culture program, and the interviewer let a brief silence fall when he was finished. He had almost snorted with pleasure as he'd read that excerpt, laughter had risen now and then from the studio audience, but now the silence was total.

"It's almost as though you'd beat her to death if you ran into her tomorrow on the street," the interviewer said. "Or am I mistaken?"

"Beat her to death?" he'd replied. "Beat her, no, of course not . . ."

Back at the house, he had started reading. Starting at page one. It hurt right away. Each sentence, each word caused him pain—in a deep, dark, and previously vacant spot between his heart and midriff. How could he ever have let it come to this? What had he been thinking, for Christ's sake? What business did readers have knowing that his first wife had cheated on him with that smelly, shoddy painter, R? The details were the worst of it. Her physical imperfections, her bizarre habits, how she scratched at the mole above her lip when she lied to him about where she had been and with whom. The same mole he had called one of her "seven beauties" and which he had always made her vow never to have removed. Now he had shared that scratching at the mole with tens of thousands of readers. Just like her habit of wanting to show up everywhere—dinner dates, birthdays, train stations and airports—far too early, because she was afraid they would otherwise come too late or miss their train (or plane).

Having arrived at the dinner address or birthday party, they were always forced to walk around the block a few times, at airports they spent hours nosing through the duty-free shops. He had always found that endearing too, but now he used it against her. In *The Hour of the Dog* he had blamed it on "her bourgeois fear of being caught red-handed," and called her "a whore who feels guilty about her profession."

He had tried to call her that same afternoon, after the broadcast, but the phone was answered by the painter, who announced that he must have a pretty good idea why she didn't want to talk to him anymore. A few minutes after they hung up, the phone rang. He picked it up on the second ring, but it was a girl—a girl's voice, asking whether he might consider doing an interview for her school paper.

Less than a year later, the drunken painter died. M felt no glee when he heard about it. Regret was what he felt, mostly. He never looked at *The Hour of the Dog* again, and when his publisher started talking about an inexpensive paperback edition he said he needed time to think about it. In the last few years he had seen his first wife a few times in the café of the artists' club. She tended to sit on the glassed-in porch, and she always had a glass of white wine in her hand. One time he watched as she let her head sink down into the lap of an old poet. By then Ana was no youngster anymore, yet at such moments M still felt ashamed. Another time he had been very close, he had already slid back his chair and was about to walk up to her and apologize. But just at that moment his first wife, who was sitting at the bar beside an octogenarian concert pianist, tossed back her head and laughed loudly. The laugh was much too loud, dry, and without resonance—the laugh of someone who wants everyone to know that she's doing fine. He sat back down again. For the first time he felt sincere compassion for her, and the next moment he was disgusted by that feeling all over again. Compassion. It was almost worse than the things he'd written about in *The Hour of the Dog.*

He looks up at the audience, but in fact he's not looking at all; he lets his gaze wander over the faces in the group, afraid as he is to establish eye contact with any one person in particular.

A woman raises her finger.

Do you ever see your first wife anymore? Have you ever had the chance to explain to her why you did what you did?

"Do you have any advice for Dutch teachers who use your books in their classes?" is what the woman really asks.

He breathes a sigh of relief. When he smiles, he feels the skin on his lips stretch painfully.

"I remember quite well how that used to go at school," he says. "We had a teacher of Dutch literature who would just start reading aloud from something. Outside the sun was shining, from the windows of our classroom you could see the ducks floating in the canal. The teacher read, and after that he talked about what was so special about that particular book. Why it was that the writer had created nothing less than a masterpiece. My Dutch teacher was what they call an 'inspired teacher,' he sincerely loved literature. He tried to communicate his enthusiasm to us. But the whole misunderstanding lay precisely in that enthusiasm, for how can you love literature and then decide to read it aloud in front of a classroom? That's the last thing books are for, isn't it? Or, to put it differently, those who love literature keep those books at home. They don't take them along to a high school. And they certainly don't read aloud from them. That misunderstanding continues, right up to this very day."

"But then how *are* we supposed to do it?" the woman asks—she's not so very old, in any case a few years younger than the average person present here today, he thinks. "How are we supposed to get young people to read?"

He sighs deeply.

"You yourself work in education, I suppose?"

"I teach Dutch at a secondary school."

"I was afraid of that. In your question I detect that other major misunderstanding. Namely, that young people—or invalids, or vegetarians—should 'have to read.' That's completely unnecessary. We shouldn't want to force anyone to read, just as little as we should want to force people to go to the movies, listen to music, have sex, or consume alcoholic beverages. Literature doesn't belong in a secondary school. No, it belongs more on the list of things I just mentioned. The list that includes sex and drugs, all the things that give us pleasure without any external coercion. A *required* reading list? How dare we!"

Then, in the front row, the man in the sleeveless vest raises his hand.

"In *Liberation Year,* you wrote about a sympathetic Nazi and an evil Jew," the man says. "Did you have a particular reason for that?"

"No," he answers. "Except that sometimes I feel the need to show that stereotypes should be seen through. Not every Nazi is just a Nazi, and not everyone in hiding is automatically a good person."

"You talk about stereotypes," the man says. "But wasn't it precisely the stereotypes about Jews that led to the Holocaust?"

"That's true, I'm very aware of that. But in my book, the Jewish man in hiding is not a stereotype. He is a man of flesh and blood, with good and bad traits."

"But as a writer you must know how careful you have to be about that. There are plenty of readers who will be all too pleased to read about an unsympathetic Jew. And that group of readers will only see their own prejudices confirmed in your portrayal of the Jew in hiding."

"First of all, I never think in terms of groups of readers. And even if I wanted to, I could never help the prejudiced to rid themselves of their prejudices, to the extent that those people read my books at all."

"But you did once write an extremely enthusiastic pamphlet about Fidel Castro. About Castro and Che Guevara and the Cuban Revolution. And you have never distanced yourself from that. You even refused to sign a petition calling for the release of political prisoners in Cuba."

He suddenly feels flushed. *Here we go again!* It's become a bothersome habit, the way they remind him at every opportunity about his pamphlet on Cuba and Fidel Castro. He's already addressed that sufficiently on more than one occasion, hasn't he?

"I *was* enthusiastic about the revolution in Cuba," he says. "In fact, I couldn't understand those who *weren't* enthusiastic about it. I visited the island, and I was struck by the aura of excitement there. It was almost electric. People had dislodged a cruel dictator with their own hands. The Cubans were visibly proud of that. Everywhere you went, you saw only happy, smiling faces and thumbs raised in victory."

"While a little further away the executions were taking place and the corpses were being bulldozed into mass graves," the man said. "But I suppose you didn't take a look over there?"

"Those were mostly traitors and collaborators. Every revolution has its victims. But it was definitely not the pitiful or the *good* who were shot there."

"And who decides that, whether they were good or bad? Is it you? Or is it all those so-called revolutionaries?"

If they only knew what he really thought, he thinks. Then he would have to pack his bags and run for it. That would be the end. He doubts whether the reading clubs full of bored housewives would still come to see him at the library after that. Sometimes he fantasizes about an ending like that, a final twist to his writing career: at the last moment, with one foot already in the grave, he would say what he really thought. Then he would jump into the coffin as quickly as possible and pull the lid shut behind him. In his books he let those thoughts shine through dimly at best, for those with ears to hear, for those who could read between the lines. That was what a writer's freedom was all about, it was in fact perhaps the *only* freedom: to think things through to their logical conclusion, and then to ease up on the gas. What the reader finally encountered was never more than an echo of those logical conclusions.

If he were to write down what he really thought, in its rawest and most unabridged form, it would all be over, just like that. The readers would turn their backs on him in disgust. Bookshops would refuse to sell his work. The rare critic would dedicate a final, concluding article to his oeuvre, the main gist of which would be that now everything "must be seen in a different light," including his earlier, never-renounced love of Communist dictatorships. He would have to turn his Order of Merit back in. A statue, or even a plaque bolted to the wall beside the front door to his house (*In this house, from . . . to . . . , lived and worked the writer M*), would be out of the question. A future biographer would (if Ana gave him permission—but she would, they've already talked about that a few times in a roundabout way) delve into his correspondence and have little trouble finding "the first signs of his later derailment." In certain circles, though, his popularity would only increase. Circles in which no one, not even he, would want to be popular. Those circles would do all they could to co-opt the writer and his work, but that wouldn't be too easy, the books were too unruly for that, and their author too elusive. The Netherlands would ask itself out loud whether it is allowable to be proud of an author like him, whether the author and his work should be seen separately. A "national discussion" would ensue, the kind of public brouhaha the Dutch all know and love. As always, the double-standard straightedge would be taken out of the drawer. The same double-standard straightedge a socialist mayor of Amsterdam applied years ago to bar from the city a writer who had visited apartheid South Africa, while the public advocates of leftist dictatorships and left-wing concentration camps, including himself, could simply go on living there.

No, he thinks then, that's not how it will go, not at all. He can say whatever he feels like. At most, people will laugh at him. No, not even at most, they will do *nothing but* laugh at him. Another war would have to come along before he could be relegated to a "right" or "wrong" camp. And it would also depend on who won that war as to whether he would be arrested, liquidated, or simply have his head shaved and be dragged around town atop a manure wagon. Or, in the event of a different winner: the statue, the Order of Merit, and the street named in his honor—the victors are the ones who get to choose between the manure wagon and the statue.

His gaze sweeps the faces in the audience. At last, he looks at the man in the sleeveless vest. He could do it, he thinks, it's possible. An experiment. A corner of the veil. He could acquaint them with a glimpse of his real opinions. Maybe it would make Monday's papers, maybe not. Maybe Marie

Claude Bruinzeel would cancel their interview. Or maybe she would be even more eager to talk to him. He clears his throat, coughs into his fist. An experiment.

"Let me tell you something about good and evil," he says. "Or better yet, about right and wrong."

15

BARELY FIFTEEN minutes later—the librarian has glanced at
her watch a few times by then—it is suddenly over. That's
how it goes, there is a time to come and a time to go. What
really gets the librarians' goats are the writers who don't
know when to stop. The writers who would like to hear
themselves talk all day. Colleague S is notorious on the cir-
cuit. He has no qualms about going on for an hour longer
than agreed ("I see another question there at the back . . .")
and when it's over they almost have to drag him to his little
red sports car in the parking lot.

Around noon, librarians are eager to escape. Especially
on a Saturday or Sunday. They still need to swing by the
supermarket, or they have a sick nephew coming over for
the weekend—which means they like to stick to the sched-
ule. Organizations that hire you in for a Friday or Saturday
evening are a different story, though. There they start off by
asking whether you'd like to join them for a bite to eat beforehand, and, if so, if you could arrive no later than two and
a half hours before the reading. And afterward they assume
you'll join them in one for the road at the most authentic pub
in the village. They tell you stories about your colleagues.
Colleagues who helped close down the pub. "Colleague N
hung around here till three in the morning." "It took four of

us to drag colleague C up to his hotel room." "Colleague D fell asleep in the backseat of my car, we just let him lie there." You know you will only disappoint these people if you head home before midnight. "Colleague P is a real party animal, he got up on this same table and started dancing." You feel obligated to do something. Something, it doesn't matter what. Something that will allow the organizers to describe their evening with you as *unforgettable* too, or at least link it to some juicy anecdote. "He passed out right here, facedown in a bunch of flowers, then he went out on the village square in the pouring rain, stripped, and sang 'The Internationale.'"

"I need to catch the last train," he always tells them. "I have to get up early tomorrow, I need to get on with my book." He sees the disappointment on their faces right away.

But all he ever wants to do is go home. He's boring—that's how they'll remember him later too. In the car on the way to the station he remains silent, not out of unwillingness, no, the words have simply dried up, he's said enough for one day.

The lady librarian has come up and is standing beside him, not too close—she probably finds men scary and dirty. She thanks the writer, she thanks the audience, then she hands him the bouquet of flowers. Applause. He steps down from the podium, sits down at the table with books, and screws the cap off his fountain pen. A little line forms. He can't make out the first name, the librarian asks if he'd like something to drink, music is suddenly coming from a loudspeaker somewhere. Lame music, with neither head nor tail. When he asks for a beer, the librarian looks worried. A woman places her book on the table in front of him, open to the title page, and hands him a slip of paper with text on it, written in blue ballpoint.

"Would you write that in it, and then under that your

name and 'have fun reading' and 'Amsterdam' with the date above that?"

For Els, because you were there for me when the others had already given up, a big kiss from your Thea.

"Why, of course," he says.

The line grows shorter. One last dedication—*for Maarten, for your 60th birthday*—and it's over. Beside the door, through which sunlight is streaming, stands his publisher, talking to the lady librarian. M recognizes the pose—the publisher has his elbow cupped in one hand, with the other hand he supports his chin, the index finger pressing against his cheek. Interested. A listener.

M is just about to get up when a shadow falls across the table. Standing there is the "young man" from the back row. Once again his face seems familiar to M. His first instinct is to glance at the man's hands. They usually wait till the very end, till everyone's gone, the aspiring writers who try to leave him with a copy of their unpublished manuscript. Hundreds of typed pages, often without paragraph breaks, printed in a font that is too small and frequently with even smaller spaces between the lines—all in a wrinkled, dog-eared envelope or bound together with a big rubber band.

Long ago, he sometimes took those packages home with him and read the first few sentences. Then came the staring at pages packed too full with letters, as though the sentences and characters were fighting for space on the page, as though they were about to be crushed, like people in a heaving crowd on a city square.

But the man's hands are empty. M braces himself for a question, a question the man didn't dare to ask with everyone else around. How one goes about writing a book. How to get started.

M takes a copy of *Liberation Year* from the slightly diminished pile (eight copies sold today, he estimates, and then you had the man with a bulging plastic bag from which he produced M's entire oeuvre, and not only the books he'd written in their entirety in the course of a long writer's life, but also all the collections, anthologies, and yellowed literary journals to which he'd ever contributed, "if you'd just jot your name down here, and here . . . ," the man said). He opened it to the title page.

But this man has still said nothing, asked nothing. He leans across the table of unsold books and looks around a few times, as though making sure no one can hear him.

"Yes?" M says—looking him straight in the eye. He adopts an interested expression. "What can I do for you?"

16

FIFTEEN MINUTES later he is sitting with his publisher in a dark and empty old-fashioned pub around the corner from the library. His publisher raises his glass to his lips and nibbles at the foam. M himself has almost finished his first beer.

"About that interview," his publisher says. "With Marie Claude Bruinzeel."

M sighs. He knows Marie Claude Bruinzeel's reputation. First she'll try to lull him to sleep during an ample meal with beer and wine. She will praise his work, as well as his attractive appearance—his pronouncedly masculine features that have become only more irresistible with the passing of time. Then, without warning, she will zoom in on his mother. On "the lack," on the absence of a mother during his formative years, the years that formed him as a writer. "Do you still think about her often?" Marie Claude Bruinzeel will ask as she orders another bottle of Pouilly-Fumé. *Every day,* he replies—he should reply, but he doesn't. He shrugs. "Oh, well, you know . . . ," he says. Then she moves right on to the childhood photos. From her bag she produces a photograph of him as a boy, sitting on his mother's lap. "She was a beautiful woman," Marie Claude says. "You take after her. Did her physical beauty influence you later on, when it came time to choose your own women?" She mentions the names of a few vague relatives whose addresses and phone numbers she had wheedled out of him on a previous occasion. "Your cousin, V, told me that you've never been the same after your mother's death. That you steeled yourself. That your aloofness these days can be traced back to that dramatic event."

He tries not to think about the final days, but he can't help it. The closed curtains, the doctor's footsteps in the hall, the consoling hand on his cheek. *Your mother, it's over, boy.* That sentence. That word. "Over." A sentence he would carry with him for the rest of his life, he knew that even back then. And then the leave-taking in the bedroom. He had never known that the dead could lie so still. Truly still, not the way a person or an animal sleeps, no, as still as a vase on a table—an empty vase, without flowers. His mother, that which had been his mother until a few hours ago, was already somewhere else, in any case not here. He had heard somewhere that the human body becomes twenty-one grams lighter at death. The faithful attributed the difference to the departure of the soul. But he was not religious, or at least he did not believe in souls that could be weighed on a set of scales.

He was alone with her for a few minutes, with what was left of her, while in the hallway his father spoke to the doctor in a muted voice. He promised her something, he promised it in a whisper.

I'll always carry you with me, he whispered. *From now on, you're here.* And he raised his finger to his head and tapped it softly—it is a promise he has always kept.

Now he thinks about his cousin V. What's he been doing, shooting his mouth off about aloofness to some journalist he doesn't know from a bar of soap? Cousin V, with whom he used to play in the sandbox at his parents' home. After his mother died, his father sold the house and they moved to an apartment in Amsterdam. In one of his books—he doesn't remember which one—he spoke of the house with the sandbox as "the last house in which I was ever happy."

"I'm afraid that an interview with Marie Claude Bruinzeel is not on," he tells his publisher. "I've started on something new, I'm in the middle of it, more chattering about the last one will only disturb my rhythm."

His publisher sighs, it's probably the same sigh he breathes with all his authors when they're "being impossible." He's referred to it before as "the spoiled artist routine," but then he was talking about a colleague who refused to let his wife appear in "Partner Of."

"Working on something new? Already? What's the hurry?"

M reads his publisher's expression: the raised eyebrows, the almost shocked, in any case not happy look in his eyes, the mouth forming a botched smile, the jaws clamped together just a little too tightly.

"Is that so strange?" he asks. "I just happen to feel better when I'm working on something. Especially in a period when a new book comes out and everyone suddenly has something to say about it."

"Sure, sure, whatever works for you. It's just that I think it would be a pity if *Liberation Year* were to disappear from the public eye too quickly. Anyway, Marie Claude Bruinzeel is thinking more in terms of a portrait of your entire career. A seven-page spread in the magazine. Lots of pictures."

At the mention of pictures, he groans inside. He knows them all too well, the photographers who insist on coming up with "something special" at the expense of his old face and dwindling old body. Photographers with truly original ideas about how that special something should be given form can be counted on the fingers of one hand, that's his experience. "I was thinking about taking you to a slaughter-house," they tell him on the phone. "Or else photographing you in a sauna, with only a towel around your waist." There are photographers with lamps and umbrellas, photographers who take fifteen Polaroid pictures before getting down to the real stuff, photographers who claim that "two and a half, maybe three hours should be plenty." When he invites them to his home they poke around in all the rooms, then stand there shaking their head for a long time, and finally, like every photographer he has ever invited to his home, take a picture of him in front of his bookcase. The occasional joker asks him to lie down on his bed. Another requests that he take off his striped shirt and replace it with a white one, only to start biting his lower lip half an hour later and breathe a big sigh. "If you don't mind, I'd like to try it one more time with the striped shirt." After that the photographers go out onto the balcony and stay there, sunk in thought, for a long time, or slide a table over to the window. "I don't know what's with me today," they sigh, shaking their head again.

"I'll think about it," he tells his publisher.

"Okay, but not too long. They have a deadline. We have to jump on it by Monday at the latest, otherwise they'll ask someone else."

17

M OPENS the front door of his apartment house and takes the elevator up. As he passes the third floor, he can't suppress a smile.

"Who was that you were talking to, there at the end," his publisher had asked in the café.

"Oh, just some fellow," M replied. "Just someone who wanted to know how you get to be a writer. You know the type."

When he gets out on the fourth floor, he is still smiling. He thinks about what he needs to do. He could call Ana, no, he *must* call Ana, but he can do that later too, he thinks, tonight or tomorrow morning.

Once he's inside he walks straight through to the kitchen, takes a beer from the fridge, opens it, and raises it to his lips. In the living room he puts on some music—the CD he often listens to when he's home alone. He thinks back on the final part of the reading, the moment when the man in the multifunctional vest stood up and stomped out of the room.

"I'm not going to listen to any more of this!" the man had shouted.

M tries to recall exactly what it was that prompted that—he seems to have pretty much forgotten it already. It started with Cuba. M felt no desire to admit being wrong about Cuba. He still found it all a bit too smug, all these people who suddenly turn out, after the fall of the Berlin Wall and collapse of the Soviet Union, to have predicted long ago that there could never be any future in Communism.

"Do you know the great thing about revolutions?" he'd asked the man in the vest. "The essence? The essence is that first everything has to be torn down in order to actually start all over again. Right down to the ground. Barricades, burning cars and buildings, a statue roped and pulled from its pedestal. It is, to start with, a celebration. The laughing faces, the bearded revolutionaries atop a captured personnel carrier, the thumbs raised, the fingers making the victory sign. 'If it can happen without bloodshed, why not?' you might say. There are examples of revolutions in which no one was killed. Nonviolent resistance, peaceful revolutions, soldiers with a rose stuck in the barrel of their rifle, cheering women with carnations in their hair. But there is also something unjust about nonviolence. The soldiers who put down their guns, who refuse to shoot at the crowd, are we really supposed to accept them all with open arms? Can there really be forgiveness for the secret-police informers, the collaborators, the dictator's sweethearts who fed human flesh to his crocodiles? Or should they all be finished off as quickly as possible, without trial? Their guilt, after all, has already been established. No lengthy legal proceedings are needed, are they? A revolution is a blackboard wiped clean with a wet sponge. Cleaned completely. But the teacher is still standing at the blackboard. Are we supposed to give him a second chance? Should he be allowed to once again cover the blackboard with his explanation of how things work? Or is it our blackboard now?"

Then the discussion had grown heated. The housewives

had begun shifting uneasily in their seats, their eyes flitting back and forth between the sleeveless man and M. "Good and evil," he had said at a certain point, staring straight at the man, "is far too simplistic, it leads only to generalizations."

He should have stopped right there, M realizes now. He should have let it go. But he knows himself better than that. Winning by points was too easy, it had to be a knockout.

He has opened the doors to the balcony and is standing outside now, the can of beer still in his hand. It's coming back again, word for word.

"When you look at the history of the twentieth century," he'd said, "you can only conclude that those who were committed to the good account for just as many or more victims as those who knew deep in their hearts that they represented evil. Lenin, Stalin, Mao, Pol Pot: all of them, based on their belief in what was good, had millions of people slaughtered. The fascists, the Nazis, though, always did as much as they could on the q.t. They went to great pains to keep the locations of the death camps a secret. When the war was winding down, they did all they could to cover their tracks. Even today, they still deny what they did. But what does denying the Holocaust amount to, except the voice of a conscience? Anyone who denies the Holocaust is in fact saying that it didn't happen because it's too horrible for words. They weren't that evil, the deniers shout. We're not that evil either, they go on in the same breath. It's so horrible, we can't believe people are capable of that."

Before this point—somewhere halfway through M's monologue—the sleeveless man had stood up and made for the exit. Even though M hadn't even started saying what he really thought. He had barely taken the corner of the veil between his fingers. *Enough is probably enough,* he'd thought. If the troublemakers start leaving the room at the very first jab, perhaps it *was* better to keep one's real thoughts to one's self. A few minutes later, the lady librarian glanced at her watch.

From his balcony he looks at the sidewalk café where he had failed to drink coffee with milk this morning.

He leans forward, not too far; when he stands on a balcony he always has the same fantasy—that you lean over too far and lose your balance. The center of gravity. The upper body is suddenly heavier than the lower part, the feet leave the ground, you try to catch yourself, but it's too late.

M can see a bit of the balcony that belongs to his downstairs neighbor, a little corner of a white wooden armrest, a flowerpot with only soil in it.

He knocks back the rest of his beer, steps inside, and closes the balcony doors.

18

MARIE CLAUDE Bruinzeel is sitting at a window table in the café across from his house, all the way at the back of the dining room that is otherwise deserted on this Monday morning. She doesn't get up when M sticks out his hand, but then he realizes why. She's interviewed him once before, a public interview in a room at some book fair. It had gone uneasily at first, but afterward they had kissed each other three times on the cheeks, like old acquaintances.

He takes her hand and leans across the table. Once she catches his drift, she raises her cheek to him—but remains seated.

"It was sweet of you to call me yesterday," she said. "It gives me a little more leeway with my deadline."

Sweet. He lets the word sink in for a moment, he doesn't remember them being so familiar before. This ice must have been broken as well during the last interview, he suspects.

Today there actually is milk for the coffee. And it's not the girl from last Saturday who brings it to the table, but a thin man with a shaved head and a fuzzy little beard.

"The cappuccino was for . . . ?" he asks before putting the cup and saucer down in front of M with a slightly too-elegant gesture, causing a bit of foam to spill over the edge. It's a superfluous question, because Marie Claude Bruinzeel's nearly full café-au-lait is already in front of her. When the thin man leans across their table, M sees something in his earlobe, an earring, a piercing, or something in between the two, something black in the shape of a snail or a shrimp. Through the wispy beard he now sees a few spots on the man's face. Not pimples. Spots. It's not something that can simply be turned on and off, this constant observing of superabundant detail; he is a writer, he tells himself, but the vacuuming up of details is purely obsessive. Often, after a day in the city, or a meal in a crowded restaurant, he comes home exhausted by all those faces and their irregularities.

He watches as a glop of foamy milk runs down the side of the cup, onto the saucer. But he's not going to say anything about it. In a café like this, run by amateurs, things are what they are. Either there is no milk at all, or else it runs over the edges, there is no middle ground.

Now he looks at Marie Claude Bruinzeel's face. He had forgotten how pretty she is. A bit too much makeup, perhaps, but not the kind of makeup that's intended to hide anything, rather to accentuate everything that's already there. She's wearing her hair up; he follows a few loose strands all the way down to her neck, then lets his gaze travel back up via her chin and glossy red lips until he is looking her straight in the eye.

One of the rare advantages of an interview: you can keep looking into the interviewer's eyes for a shamelessly long time, and when that interviewer is a woman, as is now the case, a woman as pretty as Marie Claude Bruinzeel, you can even keep looking for longer than might be good for you.

He's good at it, at looking. He is never the first to avert his eyes.

"Well, I didn't have too much going on," he says. "My wife is out of town. I'm home alone."

He said it without ulterior motives, but it could easily be interpreted as a pass, he realizes immediately. Oh, but then so what! She's part of the target group. His target group. He may be old but, after all, she's here because of his talent. If she had no interest in old men with talent, in babbling on about that talent, she would have picked a different profession.

"I'm all yours, Marie Claude," he says. That may have been a bit too much, too smarmy, but he says it with a smile. He knows that women like it when you say their first name out loud. Not too often, then it becomes too possessive, but in exactly the right dosage. Casually. Besides, it's a name he enjoys pronouncing, as though he were ordering something in a French restaurant, a *spécialité de la maison* that isn't on the regular menu.

She returns his smile. It's an agreement that meets with their mutual approval, he knows. During the ninety minutes that the interview takes, he is allowed to keep looking into her brown eyes. By way of quid pro quo, he is expected not to be too stingy with his answers. Besides an inside look at the wellsprings, at the workings of his talent, he must also give her something that has never been made public before. An illegitimate child. A life-threatening illness. A manuscript tossed in the fire. He wonders when she will start in about his mother.

"So," she kicks off, "have you fallen into the proverbial black hole after finishing *Liberation Year*? Or not yet? Actually, you don't seem to me at all like the type for black holes."

For the first fifteen minutes his answers run on automatic pilot. Not too brief, not too long. He only shifts his eyes away now and then to look outside, to pretend he's thinking about a question. But there's not a lot happening outside. He sees his own quiet street, the big old trees and, catty-corner from where they are seated, the entrance to his own building. He can see no further than the corner. Around that corner, the postman has just appeared with his cart.

He hears himself talking. He's given all these answers before. In fact, he would really like to give very different answers, new answers to old questions, but he knows from experience that that would not be wise. The new answers are seldom better than the old. He used to read over the interviews he'd given, both before and after publication, but he's stopped that. He can't stand to be confronted with his own waffling anymore; in print it's often even worse than in real life.

"The black hole doesn't exist," he hears himself say. "Nor does writer's block. Those are the cowardly excuses of writers without talent. Ever heard of a carpenter with hammer's block? A carpenter who installs a parquet floor and then doesn't know what kind of floor to put in next?"

He tries to smile as he says this. He tries to seem lively by making gestures to go along with the example of the parquet floor. He raises an imaginary hammer and pounds an imaginary nail into the tabletop beside his cappuccino. *I have to make this look as though I'm doing it for the first time,* he tells himself, but the look on his face, he suspects, will betray his boredom. So instead he concentrates on Marie Claude Bruinzeel's eyes and imagines how he would look into those eyes if this wasn't an interview at all, if he were simply sitting across from a pretty woman whom he would later invite to come to his place for a drink or "something other than coffee."

What he's actually waiting for is the moment when she will start to plumb the depths, or rather, the moment when she will step across the border between his public and private lives. He could of course dig in his heels, he could adopt his

coldest, most impassive expression and shake his head. *Sorry,*
that's my own business. But he knows that's not how it works
with Marie Claude Bruinzeel. He only wonders what it's
going to be. His mother? The loss? The other women, both
before, during, and after his two official marriages? Or perhaps, after all, the approach of death? His own death. What's
left afterward.

One more time he pulls his gaze away from Marie Claude
Bruinzeel's brown eyes, purportedly to think about yet another question (*Are you finished with the war now? Or is there*
still a book about that subject somewhere inside you?), but in fact
to take a little break, to catch his breath, to see something
normal. The postman is still one door down from his building, he takes the bundle of mail out of his cart and distributes
it in the letterboxes.

Maybe a postman would have been a better example than
a carpenter, he thinks. What about the black hole of a postman after he has handed out all his letters? Could he, tomorrow or the day after, when starting another day's round,
suddenly find himself faced with a mail block?

"The question is not whether I'm finished with the war,
but when the war will be finished with me," he replies, not
for the first time. "The same applies to the book. Whether
there's another book about the war inside me is not something I decide for myself. The book does that. The book
always gets there before I do."

Then, suddenly, she is at his mother. He does his absolute
best not to look out the window again. No visible body language that Marie Claude Bruinzeel might use to jump to a
conclusion. The thin man with the wispy beard was at their
table only a minute ago, to ask whether everything was satis-
factory and if there was anything else he could do for them.

She had ordered an espresso, he another cappuccino, but in a café like this one, he knows, an eternity will pass before they arrive.

The "loss"—the word is there already, in her very first question. Whether he thinks there is a connection between the loss of his mother and the war. Or whether the fact that he returns to that war so often in his books has less to do with the war itself than with the fact that his mother fell ill in the middle of it. And whether there is perhaps also a connection between the age he has mentioned so often, the age after which he's said no new experiences come along, and the fact that his mother died shortly after he reached that same age.

He grimaces. He shouldn't do that, he thinks. He grimaces in spite of himself. *This is all much too private,* he should reply. *I'd rather not talk about this.* He has to hand it to Marie Claude, she's done her homework. No, it's more than just homework, she's taken a few things and added them up, made new connections. Unexpected connections that no one else has made before, as far as he can recall. At least not in this way and all at the same time.

He has written about the war and about sick mothers. About dying mothers and the sense of loss. And about the age at which everything coagulates, the age after which the new experiences are no longer really new and can, at best, only be compared with the old ones—only he's never done that all in the same book.

"To start with the loss," he says to gain time, but then he doesn't know how to go on anymore. He wants to stir his coffee, but his cup is empty. "I miss her," he says. "I miss my mother, perhaps now more than ever."

Marie Claude Bruinzeel looks at him expectantly with her big brown eyes. She's waiting for his next sentence. A next sentence in which he'll explain himself further.

He clears his throat. *I can always take it out of the interview later on,* he thinks. *Take out the worst of it.* But then he mustn't forget to ask to see it before publication, for just this once, by way of exception.

"At first, it's mostly the shock," he says. "Or no, not really a shock, because you've seen it coming for months already. The illness. The treatment. The hope of recovery. The relapse. You're prepared for it. But it's still strange when it really happens. I kept hoping for a miracle, right up to the very last day. And then it happens anyway. From that moment on, you cross a line, all that's left is before and after. With each day that you move further away from that line, the things that happened before become more important. Become clearer, take on more portent. You don't want to forget your mother, but above all you don't want to forget what it was like before. And then there are emotions you don't often hear about in connection with death. The first is the novelty. *This is real,* you think. *This is happening to me.* No one else can say that. It was in the middle of the war, that fact is not unimportant. Death was hardly an uncommon event. There's a platitude people still use these days: 'There are worse things, aren't there?' Back then, that was really true. There were worse things happening in the world than the death of someone's mother. Around the corner from us, a week before my mother died, a collaborator was shot as he cycled down the street, and then finished off with a bullet to the back of the head. Two weeks after my mother died, a British bomber was hit by German antiaircraft fire right above our house. I remember the burning tailpiece, the smoke and flames, the impotent screeching of the propellers as they tried and failed to keep the bomber in the air, the explosions of the ammunition going off in the hold; you hoped, no, you expected to see men jumping out of it, the pilot, the crew, that they would use their parachutes and float to safety. But that didn't happen. The bomber listed over, cut a huge arc, and crashed in a field a couple of miles away. The first thought that came to me was that I had to tell my mother about it. I had even started formulating a description, in my mind I was describing the bomber's last few moments in the air. And less than a minute later I realized that I had been living like that for a long time, everything that happened to me in my life, on my way to school, at school, on the way home, I had always shaped it right away into the story I would tell when I got home. To my mother, sometimes to my father, but mostly my mother. The downed bomber was the first story that I experienced all on my own, that I didn't have to tell to anyone, that didn't even have to become a story."

He pauses for a moment—he knows what's coming, he had set himself up for it, consciously or not.

"Because your father wasn't there when your mother died?" she says now, indeed. "He wasn't even in Holland. Was he?"

"Wait, there's something else I need to say. When someone has been ill for a long time, there's always a sense of relief when it's over. Relief on behalf of the sick person who no longer has to suffer, but above all on your own behalf. It's difficult to admit, especially at the age I was then, but I felt an enormous relief because everything could finally be cleared out of the house. The curtains could be opened again to let in the light. *This is where my life begins,* I thought to myself. *My new life. My life free of sickbeds.* But there was also another thought. *I want to see even more bombers go down,* I thought. In those days, the war was already getting closer, it was the summer of the Normandy invasion, only a matter of time before it would reach us. I hoped it would come to our town as well. I felt guilty about finding the crash of a bomber more exciting than my mother's death, but at the same time I could keep that feeling of guilt all to myself. It was *my* guilt, and I no longer had to make a story out of that for anyone either."

There he stops. There's more he could say about liberation and loss, but he decides to keep that to himself. For a book, he has been thinking for the last twenty years, but now he doesn't even think that anymore.

The sense of loss started about thirty years after his mother's death, and it has gone on right up to this day. The first years there was only the relief and the liberation, and the feeling of guilt about that—what people called "coping" or, even worse, the "process of grieving." Sometimes he missed his mother, but more often he didn't. In some way he couldn't explain, she had become a part of him. Literally. That's how it had felt to him on the evening she breathed her last breath. A quiet, whistling breath it had been; after that came complete silence.

There was no such thing as a soul, but out of that thin and at the same time swollen body, something had indeed risen up. He had looked around, perhaps it was already on its way to a heaven that didn't exist when it saw the son standing at the foot-end of the bed.

I'll always carry you with me, he had whispered to the dead body later that evening, but the promise had in fact been superfluous. She had already done it herself. With a final effort she had freed herself of her body and slipped into the body of her son. There, somewhere deep and distant, at a spot no one but him even knew was there, she would remain for the rest of his life.

That was why he had never hung up photos of her in his house. The photos were in a box, sometimes he took them out. Six months ago with his daughter, for the first time.

This is your other grandma, he'd said, *the grandma who isn't here anymore.*

But he didn't have to look at the pictures every day. He remembered her better without them.

"Your father wasn't there," Marie Claude says. "Your father wasn't at home when your mother died."

No. He shakes his head. He feels tired. He's already talked too much, remembered too much. *Do we really have to go on now about my father?* He feels himself closing down, it is time to wrap things up.

What he won't go on to tell Marie Claude Bruinzeel, in any case, is about how he feels the loss these days. After thirty years. *I miss her,* he thinks. *I carry her with me, inside myself, I have no pictures of her on the wall. In the meantime, the distance between her death and myself has grown and grown. But it's all lasted an awfully long time.* That's what he has started thinking in recent years: it's lasted long enough.

The thirty years after she died he dreamed about her often. In those dreams she was always already ill, sometimes she was lying in bed, in other dreams she shuffled slowly around the house.

But after those first thirty years the dreams disappeared too. Thirty years without his mother, that was still doable. But fifty years? Sixty? He misses the dreams.

"Your father had enlisted in the German army. That summer he was fighting on the Eastern Front," Marie Claude Bruinzeel says.

"They couldn't reach him right away," he says—but this no longer interests him. He wants to go home. What he'd like to do most is go right back to bed. Close the curtains, shut his eyes. "My father did come home as soon as he could, when he heard about it. And he never left me alone again after that."

Except for while he was in custody for collaborating with the Germans, he halfway expects her to say then. Or else she'll ask him whether his father's leaving for the East was perhaps an escape, away from the sickbed of his wife, the relationship with whom—to put it mildly—had cooled in those years.

But she doesn't. She stirs her espresso, which arrived along with his cappuccino—even though he didn't notice it, the moment when the thin man brought their orders has come and gone.

"The Netherlands Institute for War, Holocaust and Genocide Studies recently started a new investigation of the unit your father served in," she says. "Have you heard about that?"

He grimaces, but he would be better off not grimacing, he warns himself. He has heard about that investigation. He was above all surprised to hear that there were people work-ing at the institute who apparently thought that an investiga-tion like that made any difference. Pretty much everything had already been nosed through, hadn't it? Maybe they had nothing better to do. Maybe they needed an investigation that no one was interested in anyway, simply to justify the salary they were paid out of taxpayers' money.

He says that he has heard about it. He sips too hard at his overheated cappuccino—tormentingly slow, a white-hot riv-ulet slides down his gullet; he feels the tears come to his eyes.

Why is she starting in about this? He's already tossed her far more material than he was planning to, hasn't he? He can't remember ever having revealed so much about his mother's death.

"The results of the investigation won't be published for a few months," she says. "But I have my connections at the institute. The tentative conclusion is that it was no standard army unit your father was in."

He says nothing, he wipes the tears from his eyes with the back of his hand.

"His unit operated behind the lines," Marie Claude Bruinzeel continues, keeping her warm brown eyes fixed on his. "Not behind *enemy* lines, but in the area already taken by the regular army. They carried out special missions there. I don't think I need to tell you what those special missions involved back then."

To keep from having to look into her eyes, he shifts his gaze to look outside. The postman's cart has now stopped in front of the door to his own building, through which a man has just come out. The man pauses and, from the looks of it, is saying something to the postman.

The neighbor, M recognizes him right away. The downstairs neighbor. Whenever he comes across him "in the wild," he sees a face that seems vaguely familiar, like that last time at the restaurant, at La B. Ana had to tell him that it was the downstairs neighbor sitting at the bar, drinking a beer. Now he recognizes him immediately.

The neighbor and the postman are talking. M sees him shrug, the postman laughs, he leans over his cart and hands the neighbor a pile of letters.

"Well?" he hears Marie Claude Bruinzeel's voice. "Did you know about that special unit?"

"Do you know what it is, Marie Claude?" he says. "Here in Holland there were millions of people who mostly did nothing at all. The vast majority sat at home on the couch and brooded. Less than one percent joined the resistance, maybe a little more than one percent went looking for adventure in some other way. By joining the army that was moving on to the Russian steppes, for example. I can't help it, but I've always felt more admiration for the people who at least did *something*. Even if some were on the good side and others perhaps on the wrong side."

Meanwhile, the postman has walked on with his cart, the downstairs neighbor has started distributing the pile of mail throughout the various letterboxes—he pauses for a moment, he looks at something, something in the mail, and flips it over. From so far away, he can't make out what it is. An envelope? A postcard? Now the neighbor looks around, flips the letter or card over again, stands there with it in his hand for no longer than three or four seconds, then tosses it in the letterbox at the top, to the left of the door, the boxes for the fourth floor, M's letterbox.

"But you don't really mean that, do you?" Marie Claude says. "In fact, what you're saying is horrible. As though someone who volunteered for a death squad was only looking for a little adventure."

He breathes a deep sigh. His father never tried to hide anything from him. The uncomfortable details were something he had never withheld. Bit by bit, he had told M everything. The retaliatory measures. The executions. The mass graves. *No one is innocent,* his father had said. *Least of all me. If you don't want to get your hands dirty, you should stay at home beside the fire.*

"I'm tired," M says. "Actually, I'm drained."

Only then does he notice the unshaven man standing beside their table. The man's hair is disheveled in an intentional way; hanging over his shoulder is a bag, a bag that can only contain a camera, M realizes, and he feels his heart sink a few inches, a feeling like hitting an air pocket, an elevator going down too fast. The man has even more bags with him, round bags, cylindrical bags, bags with a number of zippers, and a tripod with an umbrella attached to it. It takes him a few minutes to spread it all out over the four empty chairs at the table beside theirs.

"Are you two more or less finished?" he asks. He looks around, taking in the café interior, peers squintingly at the tables outside. He sighs. "I can't decide between in here or outside," he says. "In half an hour, forty-five minutes I'll have everything set up, then an hour, ninety minutes for the pictures themselves, so if I could get started it would be real nice."

Then he looks at M for the first time.

"You're a writer, aren't you?" he says. "I guess you must have a bookcase at home then. Maybe we could finish up there. A couple of pictures, just so we have those."

Life Before Death

19

SHE WASN'T attracted to him right away.

"There's a boy coming, he's a junior," David Bierman had told her. "He might be somebody for you."

Laura had done her best to look as uninterested as possible.

"Not that he's quite your type," David went on. "He's no one's type really. But he *is* one of those people you have a strong opinion of right away. You either think he's something special, or you think he's a complete asshole."

At the party a few days later, David pointed him out across the room. The boy was sitting slouched down in a leather armchair, his green rubber boots crossed casually at the ankles; he was holding a tumbler filled almost to the rim with some clear liquid—it wouldn't be water, Laura thought.

He was, above all, very thin, thinner in any case than she liked them. She wanted a boy to have some substance to him. Flesh. Warm flesh that gave a little, pliable flesh under soft skin, not bones sticking out everywhere. This one had gone to no trouble to disguise his thinness, she had to give him that. Atop his tight-fitting jeans he wore an even tighter T-shirt that crept up a little to reveal a white section of stomach and a navel surrounded by blond hair.

But the rubber boots were what drew your attention

most; they were half-Wellingtons—the boy had turned down the tops to reveal the light-green insides. *Who wears rubber boots to a party?* was the first thing she thought. But later she would often think back on those green boots.

Laura herself was in the habit of getting up each morning half an hour before her parents and her brother, who was two years younger than she was. Half an hour was what she needed to shower, wash and blow-dry her hair, and put on her makeup. But there were days when she didn't do the makeup. She would just spend half an hour in the shower, gradually turning down the tap from hot to ice-cold. Then she went to school with her own face—the water treatment kept her cheeks a soft pink all day long—and she saw how people looked at that face of hers.

That's right, I can get away with it. She looked back. *I don't need it, the mascara, the eye shadow and lip gloss. Even after a shipwreck, after months of bobbing around on a wooden raft in the burning sun, I'll still be irresistible.*

The thin boy with the rubber boots broadcast a similar message. Not exactly the same message, because even with the best will in the world you couldn't call him irresistible, but like Laura he knew that the other people's eyes were on him.

She couldn't deny that she was curious—if only for the space of a few seconds—about how the boy in the green rubber boots kissed. Then she forgot about him.

The party was almost over when Laura suddenly found herself standing beside him, at the table where earlier in the evening there had been wooden planks with cheeses, baskets of French bread, and dishes of peanuts and raisins, and where at this hour of the night, except for a single flattened and melting triangle of brie or Camembert, there were only some bread crumbs and peanut shells left.

The boy looked at her. No, it wasn't just looking: he was sizing her up. Not from head to toe, it's true, but from a point on her forehead, somewhere above her eyebrows, down to her neck. She saw his eyes, which were an almost translucent blue.

On his thin, well-nigh emaciated face—his jaw and cheekbones seemed ready to poke through the skin—was the same blond down she had seen before around his navel. Soft hair, not bristles. He hasn't started shaving yet, she could tell.

"So you're Laura," he said.

He grinned, peeled the triangle of cheese off of his paper plate, and held it up for her. She shook her head vigorously, not so much because she wasn't hungry, but because of his self-satisfied tone.

So you're Laura. As she watched him stick the cheese, rind and all, into his mouth in one bite, she suddenly realized what that sentence meant, and she felt her cheeks start to glow.

So you're Laura could only mean that David had talked to him about her beforehand too. In her mind she heard David's voice: *This girl I know . . . she could be right for you. You'll either like her immediately, or think she's a huge bitch.*

That next Monday she saw David in German class, first thing in the morning.

"Well, what did you think of him?" he asked.

"You were right," she said. "He really is a complete asshole."

.   .   .

Now, on this day after the day after Christmas, as she waited in her parents' house in Terhofstede for him to come back, she thought about that first meeting.

After tossing some more coal on the fire, she lay down on the mattress. Every once in a while she got up and went to the window. Hours seemed to have gone by since he and Landzaat had left for Sluis; there was no clock in the house, and at his insistence they had left their watches at home too. "We're going for total timelessness," he'd said. "When the sun comes up, then it's light. And when it's dark, it's dark."

At some point she must have fallen asleep: outside now, except for the glow of the streetlight, there was total darkness. She got up and opened the front door. The snow had stopped, there was no wind, it felt like the air was frozen too, as though you could break it into tiny pieces and then crumble it between your fingers.

She pulled on her boots and walked out to the road, through snow that came up almost to her knees, past the history teacher's car and on to the crossing in the middle of the village where the streetlight stood. Here, in the hard white light, the sight of the snow hurt her sleepy eyes. She halted. A few houses further up on the left lived a farmer from whom her parents sometimes bought potatoes and onions. The farmer also kept an eye on the house when they were gone; one time he had replaced a pane of glass that broke during a storm. She thought she remembered the farmer having a telephone—but who would she call? Her parents in New York? Somewhere in one of the pockets of her traveling bag was a slip of paper with the numbers her parents had handed her on the day they left. The number of the hotel, but also the numbers of her aunt and uncle in Amsterdam, and the neighbor lady. She tried to figure out what time it was in

New York, but she wasn't sure. *A six-hour time difference,* she
remembered her father saying, but here in this stock-still,
frozen landscape, beneath the light of the streetlamp, the
concept of time seemed to have lost all meaning.

And what would she say, anyway? *Don't be startled, nothing
really terrible has happened, but . . .* She vaguely remembered
the farmer's living room, where she had been maybe two or
three times. Dark, heavy furniture, she recalled, a table with
a plastic floral tablecloth. The farmer himself was so big and
broad that he barely seemed to fit in the living room and had
to duck under every doorway. His face was red, probably
from working outside so much, she thought.

She imagined him standing there as she called her parents
in New York: he would only be able to hear her side of the
conversation (*I don't know exactly how long ago . . . A couple of
hours, for sure . . . It's dark here now*) and he would draw his
own conclusions. He would take his coat down off the rack,
put on his cap, and help her look—or he would immediately
call the police. She turned around and walked back to her
house.

She had already passed the teacher's car and was just about
to lay her hand on the garden gate when she heard someone
shout her name. And even before she turned around she felt
something warm, something warm inside, so warm that the
cold air no longer had a grip on her.

She slipped a few times as she started running toward
him, as fast as the snow allowed. She had already seen it,
and later she would often remember it that way too: that
they would meet right under the light of the streetlamp, that
they would embrace, cover each other's cold cheeks, eyes,
lips with kisses—*like in a movie,* that was what she was thinking when, only a few yards from him now, she realized that

he was alone. For a moment she focused on a spot some-where behind him, the point where the snow-covered wil-low stumps on both sides of the road dissolved into darkness.

He himself wasn't running; he stumbled toward her, it looked as though he was limping. The next moment they had hold of each other. The kisses, the tears—there was snow, or ice, in his lashes she saw after they had stopped kissing for a moment to look into each other's eyes.

"Sweetness," she said. "My sweetheart."

He was crying too, or at least something wet and shiny was running from the corners of his eyes down to his upper lip.

"Where's . . . ?" She looked again at the road behind him, disappearing into the darkness.

"Isn't he . . . ?" He nodded toward the house. "Isn't he here?"

She looked straight into his eyes, then shook her head slowly.

"I lost him," he said.

20

LATER—AND FOR years—Laura would think back on this moment, their movie moment beneath the streetlamp, think back on it and ask herself again and again whether she had noticed anything strange in his behavior at that point. Anything unnatural in his voice when he said, *Isn't he . . . ? Isn't he here?*

What does someone's voice sound like when they're acting as though they really don't know where someone is? Someone who's pretending that he truly doesn't have the slightest idea what has happened to that other person? The voice of someone you know well—whom you *thought* you knew well, she corrects herself again and again during the days, weeks, months, and years following Jan Landzaat's disappearance.

I lost him. As though he were talking about a little child who'd disappeared from sight in a busy department store or on a crowded beach. Herman had pulled up a chair and sat down beside the fire, his head in his hands. So that he wouldn't have to look at her? With the passing of time, with the passing of more and more time, this last detail too would take on greater significance. In her memory he remained sitting there, for longer and longer, so long that he finally didn't look at her at all.

"Did he act guilty? Or let me put it differently, did he seem conscience-stricken to you?"

The darker of the two detectives turned a page in his notebook and gave her a friendly look—serious, but still, above all, friendly.

She was sitting between her parents on the living room couch. Her mother had made tea, then poured it into Duralex tumblers. It was easy to see that the detectives, if they drank tea at all, were used to having it served in cups on saucers, or at the very least in sturdy mugs; every time they picked up the glasses they would burn their fingers and then set them down quickly again.

"If you'd like another sugar waffle, help yourself," her mother said.

Laura looked at the face of the friendly, darker detective. A handsome face, boyish. The other detective was big and solid, a square head with blond, stubbly hair.

"I don't know," she said. "I really don't know."

She felt her eyes stinging, and a few seconds later her mother's hand on her shoulder, her fingers softly kneading her shoulder through the material of her sweater.

What exactly was a guilty or conscience-stricken impression? That he didn't seem confused? Not truly upset? All right, he had avoided looking at her as much as possible as he told his story, but did that mean anything?

"You know that clump of woods, a mile or two before Sluis?" he'd said. "They're not really woods, just a clump of trees at that bend in the canal. I had to take a piss. I went into those trees, further than I normally would, I wanted him to be as far away from me as possible. It was freezing, of course, it all took a little longer than normal. When I was finished and I turned around, he was gone."

She tried to imagine what he was describing, but she'd always had a bad sense of direction, she didn't even know which clump of trees at what bend in the canal he was talking about. Still, she was sorry later that she hadn't asked any questions, that she had let him tell the story from start to finish without interrupting him even once.

"For a moment, I thought he was monkeying around," he continued. "I mean, that's the kind of teacher he is, Landzaat, right? One of those guys who slaps you on the shoulder and tries to act cool."

And yes, at that moment he had looked up at her, she suddenly remembered that. After he had said that thing about acting cool, he had paused—for no more than a couple of seconds—and looked her straight in the eye. *That's the kind of teacher he is, right?* he'd said with his eyes (and with that little pause). *The kind of teacher who seduces a girl from his class during the field trip?*

Laura had only shrugged.

"Anyway, he was gone. Because I thought he was horsing around at first, I didn't try to call for him right away. Maybe he's off behind a tree or crouched down in a ditch, watching me the whole time, I thought. I didn't feel like having him make a fool of me."

Was it snowing then? she could have asked, but didn't. If it had been snowing, that would make it more believable that he had lost sight of their teacher. But it hadn't snowed, she was almost sure of that. All right, she had fallen asleep a couple of times while he was gone, but during the little walk from the front door to the streetlamp she hadn't crossed fresh snow—she would swear to that if she had to, if the dark, handsome detective asked her to.

"The first thing I did was climb up to the highest spot I

could find. But when I couldn't see him from up there either, I walked back a ways, along the canal, the way we came. Then I started calling his name."

But what about his footprints? she had felt like asking—and once again, she didn't. *His footprints in the snow would have told you which way he went, right?*

"It was weird. Suddenly I wasn't sure how to yell for him. 'Mr. Landzaat' or 'Sir' sounded way too formal. And I didn't want to shout 'Jan' either, that would almost make it sound like he was my friend. So the first few times I just shouted 'Hey!' and 'Hello?' After that I shouted 'Landzaat?' and that sounded good. 'Hey, Landzaat! Stop messing around! Come out where I can see you, man!' I must have shouted that ten times in a row, and the more I shouted, the more I realized what a ridiculous name that is, Landzaat."

Laura looked at his face, where the aversion was clear to see, as though he were talking about something filthy that he'd stepped in by accident. And then he raised his eyes to meet hers again and repeated the teacher's name.

"*Land*zaat," he said, placing added stress on the first syllable—and it was true: if you repeated the name often enough, it became just plain ridiculous.

But now she heard something else in that name too. By putting the stress on *land,* he was implying—perhaps unintentionally, but perhaps not—that there was another *zaat,* another seed you could think of besides *Land*zaat.

And not hayseed or birdseed either.

Seed that she, Laura, had let into her body (she was on the Pill, condoms in her view were an annoying interruption and otherwise a lot of messy business), seed that she may on more than one occasion have wiped from between her legs with a T-shirt, a towel, or the corner of a sheet. Yes, that's the way he was looking at her now. His aversion was no longer limited to the history teacher. While in full possession of her senses, she had allowed the teacher with the long teeth to slip his dick inside her and squirt her full of seed.

"Oh, blech!" he shouted, then turned his gaze away from her.

The detective with the square head leaned forward for another sugar waffle, took a big bite of it and, as he chewed, let his gaze travel over the bookshelves covering the walls. Laura's parents rarely watched TV, in the evening they would sit at their respective ends of the couch with a glass of wine and a book. The detective looked at the bookcases the way a child in a deathly still museum might look at an abstract painting, a twelve-by-twenty-foot painting consisting only of smudges and stripes.

"A new witness has turned up," the darker detective said. "Someone who says they're sure they saw Mr. Landzaat and your friend close to the Zwin."

Laura looked at him, doing her best to seem inquisitive.

"You're familiar with the Zwin?" the detective asked.

Her mind raced. She couldn't just act dumb. Her parents had bought the house in Terhofstede when she was still a baby. During the summer vacations they had gone to the beach at Cadzand, or driven to Knokke where you could rent pedal cars and ride along the boulevard. In the fall and winter they took long walks, the first few years with her little brother in a carrier on her father's back, atop the old earthen fortifications around Retranchement, along the canal to Sluis, and to the Zwin, a nature reserve, a bird sanctuary: there, when the tide was out, you could hike across the sandy flats where marram grass and thistles grew, but you had to watch out for the water's return. On two occasions they had been caught unawares. Her father had handed over the carrier with her little brother in it to her mother and lifted Laura onto his shoulders. Wading up to their waists, they had safely reached the dunes.

"Sure, the Zwin," she said.

"What I meant was, whether you know where the Zwin is," the detective said. "With regard to Sluis. And to Terhofstede, of course."

She remained silent. She wasn't quite sure what to do; any answer she might give could be the wrong one. She thought of all the American cop shows where suspects only let themselves be interrogated in the presence of an attorney. *I want to call my lawyer,* said the veterinarian who was suspected of murdering his wife, and then you already knew that he must have done it.

When you walked from Terhofstede to Sluis, you didn't go by way of the Zwin. It wasn't even a roundabout way to get there. The Zwin lay in the complete opposite direction.

The square-headed detective had stopped chewing on his waffle. The dark detective tried smiling as he drummed his fingers on his notebook, then he breathed a sigh and shrugged.

"Maybe you would—" he began. "Maybe you'd like to just—"

"It's been a very tiring afternoon for Laura," her mother interrupted him. "Maybe she's answered enough questions for one day."

21

IN THE last week of summer vacation, she and her friends were going to the house in Zeeland for the first time—the first time, that is, with no parents around. Besides David Bierman, she invited Stella van Huet, Michael Balvers, Ron Vermaas, and Lodewijk Kalf. Stella was the one who had the most trouble getting her parents' permission, she'd had to listen to a long sermon full of warnings and possible doomsday scenarios in which the word "condom" had actually come up a few times. In the end, however, a reassuring phone call from Laura's parents had cinched it.

A few days before they were to leave, Laura got a call from David.

"Remember that guy at my party?" he asked.

For a moment, during the brief silence that fell, Laura thought about asking *Which guy?* but decided against it almost immediately. Somehow she sensed that David would know right away that she was only playing dumb—and this intentional playing dumb would make him think that Laura had developed a particular interest in the boy. That was certainly not the case, she told herself, but she couldn't deny that even now she could see the green, folded-down boots in her mind's eye.

"Yeah?" she said. "What about him?"

"He flunked this year," David said. "When school starts again, he's going to be in our class."

Laura could have answered with *Yeah?* again. *Yeah, what about it, what's it to me?* But she knew she could never make that sound believable.

"I've been thinking," David went on—to her relief—after another brief silence. "He's got some problems at home. His father has had a girlfriend for years. His mother just found out about it. But they're not getting a divorce. They're going to stay together, at least until he's graduated, that's what they told him. He's an only child. He sits at home in the evening, between two parents who have nothing to say to each other. I go hang out with him at his house sometimes. To the outside world, the parents act real cheerful, like nothing's going on. They think his friends don't know about it. That he wouldn't have told anyone. But even if he hadn't said a thing, it's so obvious. The mother with her red-rimmed eyes. The father who wolfs down his supper without tasting it and then gets up from the table as fast as he can. By that time, Mom has almost finished the bottle of wine. 'I wish they'd get a divorce,' he says so himself, 'it's just so incredibly awkward.' Whenever one of them is alone with him, they try to get him to take sides. It drives him nuts. Looking at it objectively, of course, it's all his father's fault. His mother's in pain, she sits around crying all the time, she tries to make him feel sorry for her, but he doesn't want to deal with it. Most of all, he doesn't want to be disloyal to his father. 'You're not really supposed to say this,' he told me, 'you're not even allowed to think it, but somehow I understand my dad. I understand that after almost twenty years of being married he started getting claustrophobic. You know my mom, David,' he says, 'you know what I mean.'"

Laura could tell where David was going with this. A sob

story. A story meant to soften her heart toward this boy. After which he would ask whether Herman could come along to Zeeland. It would be good for him to get away from it all. The situation at home was unbearable.

While David was starting in on a character sketch of the boy's mother, in which the phrases "borderline hysterical" and "always moping" came up more than once, Laura thought about it. She wasn't completely opposed to the idea, she admitted to herself. Maybe the boy was simply arrogant and annoying, and there was nothing more to it, but on the other hand there was something about that skinny body and those odd boots that had kept her fascinated over these last few months. And now, suddenly, new information had come up. *He's an only child,* David had said. More than the story about the stifling parents, it was this news that placed the thin boy's attitude and behavior in a different light. There were certain adjectives that were always mentioned in the same breath with being siblingless: "spoiled" and "egocentric" were the most common. Hard on the heels of those came "pitiful" and "lonely." When you really thought about it, it was hard to come up with any positive adjectives for an only child. "Only" already sounded rather lonely and pitiful—as though, except for that single, only person, nothing else existed and never would. *So you're Laura.* She replayed the sentence in her mind. Already it sounded different. She saw again how he held up the runny wedge of cheese for her to take, then stuffed it into his own mouth, rind and all. Only children were asocial, that's what people said, they got everything their heart desired, they never picked up after themselves, and when you were doing the dishes you had to flap the dish towel at them, or literally force it on them, otherwise they'd just stand there watching while other people stacked the dripping plates and pans on the counter. She thought about the skinny, egocentric, spoiled, pitiful, lonely child in his green rubber boots, in between his silent parents, his father thinking not about his son but about his girlfriend, his mother opening another bottle of wine because there was no future. It was at that moment that Laura made up her mind, and that was precisely how she would remember it later too. But she wasn't going to make it easy for David, if only to keep him from jumping to the wrong conclusion.

"So what do you think?" David asked. "It's your parents' house. I figured I'd better ask you first. I haven't talked to him about it yet, so you can always say no. But I bet he'd love to come along."

"I don't know . . . ," Laura said. "I mean, we're such a tight group. Shouldn't we ask the others about it first? They don't even know him."

She was glad that David couldn't see her face.

22

THREE DAYS later, on Friday morning, they met up at Central Station. The first leg of the trip would take them to Flushing, then they'd go by ferry to Breskens, and after that take the bus—which ran only once every two hours—to Terhofstede.

As was to be expected, the thin boy showed up wearing his rubber boots. David introduced him to the others. The boy shook hands all around, starting with Stella.

"Hi, I'm Stella," she said. From her cheery tone and the way the others were acting, it was clear that they had all been filled in on the boy's painful situation at home.

"Herman," he said.

When he got to Laura, he smiled. "Hello," he said. "We've met before, haven't we?" She thought he was only pretending not to remember her. He reached out to shake her hand, and his left hand joined the right. He laid it atop hers and gave it a little squeeze. "I just want to say that I'm so happy you invited me to join you," he said. "I mean, the only person I really know here is David. Thank you, Laura."

She looked into his eyes, which were more gray than blue, but with something glistening behind that gray, something much lighter, a winter sun appearing for a moment from behind gray cloud cover—it wasn't easy to hold his gaze for long.

"Of course," she said, releasing her breath for the first time since he'd taken her hand. *So he's not a complete asshole,* she thought. *A complete asshole doesn't say things like that.*

They found an empty compartment and, with a little shifting and squeezing, they all fit in. None of them had much in the way of luggage; no suitcases at least, suitcases were for old people. Michael was the only one who hadn't yet tossed his duffle bag up onto the rack. He unzipped it and pulled out a squarish bottle of Dutch gin.

"Anyone up for a shot?" he asked.

The bottle went around. David was the first to raise it to his lips, then Ron and Michael. Lodewijk, Laura, and Stella shook their heads. "It's only ten o'clock!" Lodewijk said. "Please!"

As last, the bottle arrived at the thin boy—at Herman. He took a slug; Michael was already holding out his hand for the bottle when Herman tilted his head all the way back, without removing the bottle from his lips. They watched breathlessly as little bubbles rose through the liquid, bubbles roiling to the surface like in an aquarium. His Adam's apple bobbed up and down a few times, the train rattled and lurched as it crossed a switch, and the mouth of the bottle came loose from Herman's lips, spilling gin down his chin and neck. He rested the bottle on his thigh and screwed the cap back on.

"So, now my parents are dead and gone," he said.

For a few seconds it was very quiet in the compartment— only the sound of the iron wheels on the tracks. Herman wiped his mouth and handed the bottle back to Michael.

"Sorry, I didn't mean to startle you guys," he said, looking at them one by one. "My parents are still alive. Unfortunately. All I did was erase them, I needed to do that."

He laughed loudly, David was the only one who laughed

along with him, but not from the bottom of his heart, Laura noticed.

"Do you . . . want to talk about it?" Stella asked.

Stella's father was a psychologist, but more than that: her father too had traded in his wife six months ago for one of his female patients, twenty years his junior.

"If I started talking about my parents, I'd bore all of you all the way to Flushing," Herman said. "That's part of it. The other thing is that they don't deserve it. They're basically a couple of losers who should never have had children."

Another silence.

"But don't worry," Herman laughed. "I'm not a total downer. I'm really happy to be here. Really." He waggled his head a few times, then closed his eyes. "Well, almost," he said.

"If you ask me, you're just really pissed off at your parents," Stella said.

Herman opened his eyes again and looked at her. "Not pissed off, no. Just disappointed."

On the boat from Flushing to Breskens they bought gravy-roll sandwiches. David, Ron, Michael, and Herman had a can of beer along with theirs, Lodewijk had coffee, Stella a glass of mineral water. Laura drank tea.

As they lounged along the railing on the rear deck, David and Herman held up their half-eaten rolls to the diving gulls. Laura squinted at the water foaming around the hull, and then at the coastline fading into the distance. She thought about her own parents, with whom no one could find fault. On the contrary, all her friends, both boys and girls, agreed that she had the greatest parents in the world. "I wish my father was like yours," Stella had said to her once. "What do you mean?" Laura asked. "I don't know," Stella said. "Your father just has a way of looking at people that's so . . . so *normal*. Yeah, that's it! Your father looks at me the way he would look at an adult. And he talks to me that way too. My own father always has this pitying look in his eyes, and he always talks in that kind of undertone. 'Maybe you'll understand it someday, Stella.' That's what he said to me recently. I don't know what it was about, just something stupid, about what time I had to be home or something. 'I'm not one of your patients, Daddy!' I shouted at him. But he didn't even get mad. He just stood there with that pitying smile on his face."

The boys were especially charmed by Laura's mother. She translated British and American literature into Dutch; the last few years she had also started writing poems that were published from time to time in literary journals. Her first collection was going to appear that fall. But when Laura brought friends home, her mother always stopped working and made the loveliest sandwiches for them. Poppyseed and sesame-seed buns with pickled meat roll, ham, minced beef, herring, and mackerel.

"You have really nice friends," she had told her daughter once they'd all gone home. "Well, then?" she went on, after a pause, in a quieter tone. "Any of the boys you like more than the others?"

"No," Laura said.

"That David—his name *is* David, isn't it?—he's very handsome."

Upon which Laura said she was going to her room, she had homework to do.

Laura's father used to work as an editor for a national newspaper, but for the last eighteen months he had been presenting a popular current-events program on TV. The best part about him, as Stella said, was that he stayed so normal. He had every reason to get a swelled head. People on the street nudged each other when Laura's father walked by, sometimes they asked him for an autograph, which he always gave without complaint. Even during vacations on faraway foreign beaches, people would come up to him. "We don't want to bother you," they would say, "but we saw you in the distance and my wife said to me: 'Is that who I think it is?' Look, she's sitting up there in front of that café, could you just wave to her? Are these your children?" Laura's father never lost his patience with these kind of encounters, he waved to the woman in front of the café, he squatted down between the children for a photo, he handed out autographs on the backs of beer coasters, napkins, and placemats, sometimes with a big Magic Marker on a T-shirt, and one time even on the inside of someone's thigh, at a beach resort in southern Spain—the Dutchman in question was covered in tattoos and wore only a pair of swimming trunks, so he had rolled up one of the legs of those trunks, right up to his crotch. "Here, if you would," he'd said. "I'll tattoo it on myself, later." Laughing, Laura's father complied.

Not long ago she had gone out to lunch with him at a restaurant that had just opened. When they came through the revolving doors, all the customers looked up. Dozens of pairs of eyes followed as the waitress led them to their table—the best spot in the house, Laura saw, with a view of the canal. During lunch, too, people kept looking at them. Laura saw them lean over to each other and whisper, smile, then look again. But her father bore these gazes too with calm and patience.

"You know what's funny?" he said. "You're seventeen now."

She stared at him blankly.

"You know these people are looking at us and asking each other: 'Is he there with his daughter, or with some girlfriend thirty years younger than him?' Two years ago, they wouldn't have wondered at all. That's something new. Fantastic!"

Laura couldn't help but blush, but her father had risen halfway out of his chair and kissed her on the cheek. "So," he said. "Now they have even more to whisper about."

Ever since her father's face became a regular feature on TV, her parents' marriage had been accompanied by a never-ending flow of rumors about extramarital affairs. Photographs sometimes appeared in the gossip magazines, showing him leaving a nightclub or disco with a girl barely older than his own daughter. And there was that time, in one of those magazines, that a fashion model had claimed she'd been having a secret affair with him for almost a year. But her father dismissed it all with a laugh; he even brought the gossip rags home and tossed them on the kitchen table. "Look what they're writing about me now," he said. "It's obviously a slow season for news."

And Laura's mother laughed along with him. In the evening her parents still lay across from each other on the couch with their books, the way they always had, and filled each other's wineglasses. At school, though, it sometimes made things tough for Laura. Her friends tended not to read those magazines, but some of the teachers did. It was hard to put a finger on it: something pitying about the way Mr. Karstens, their physics teacher, looked when he asked about homework she hadn't finished; Miss Posthuma, in English, who never looked at her directly and always started shuffling papers around on her desk when Laura came up to ask about some British or American novel on their required list. You couldn't really know for certain, there might have been other reasons too. Mr. Karstens was short, and short men often don't like pretty girls. Miss Posthuma, as David once put it, was "clearly a reject, as a specimen of the female sex." They had all laughed at that. "A specimen that should never have made it out of the factory." Her homeroom teacher had called her aside one morning and asked if there was anything she wanted to talk about. "Your grades are generally quite good," he said, "but sometimes you seem a little absent-minded in class. Are you doing okay, or is there something you'd like to talk to me about?"

Her homeroom teacher was also their history teacher. His name was Jan Landzaat, and he had a friendly, not-unhandsome face, but his teeth were a bit too long. He was one of the more easygoing teachers, he would talk to you off the record, as though the two of you were on an equal footing. He was also one of the few teachers who came to class in jeans and a sweater; most of the others preferred sport jackets and ugly gray or light-brown slacks made of some barely definable synthetic material, with a sharp crease down the front of them. Those teachers probably thought this colorless outfit lent them a kind of natural authority in the classroom, but for the students it only undermined their credibility. How could someone who dressed like that, someone obviously so oblivious to the devastatingly ugly, actually have anything interesting to say about distant countries, exotic species, or writers at home or abroad? In class you always tried to look at a spot beside them or above their head, and generally maintained the greatest possible physical distance between yourself and the teacher in question. Whenever that distance was reduced, for example, when you had to come up to the front of the class, you couldn't help but notice that they emitted a peculiar odor, like wet clothing kept in a bag too long. Some of them had horrible breath too, that smelled like dead flowers in a vase, or, as in the case of Mr. Van Ruth, the math teacher, as though he had mashed a whole cheeseboard between his teeth the night before.

Laura looked at the fresh, boyish face of her homeroom and history teacher, tanned above the collar of his burgundy fisherman's sweater, and wondered whether it could really be, whether there was a real possibility that she could trust this man; that she could tell him that her absentmindedness had to do partly with the sport coats, the slacks, and the stench of rotten water in a vase.

"Is everything all right at home, for instance?" he asked.

"What do you mean, Mr. Landzaat?" she asked, to win time; she knew exactly what he meant, of course, she was only disappointed to find that her easygoing homeroom teacher apparently read the same magazines as his ugly, stinking colleagues.

"Listen, why don't you call me Jan?" he said.

Was everything all right at home? It was a question she'd asked herself too in recent weeks and months. Yes, her parents were nice. Nice people, that's what everyone said, from her friends and classmates to the parents of those same friends and classmates—and even some of her teachers. The teachers fell into two categories: those who thought it was rather interesting to have the daughter of a famous TV host in their class, and those who openly broadcast the message that she shouldn't expect to get better grades just because her father was a celebrity. The former category sometimes had her stay after class, supposedly to talk about her homework or some paper she had to write, but in fact to have her give them a glimpse of the world of television. The second category, understandably enough, hated everything that fell outside the bounds of the middling. Laura sometimes suspected them of giving her bad grades on purpose, but she could never prove it. The magazines talked about what her father earned each year. An annual salary that a teacher would probably have to work for half their life to earn . . . or their whole life, come to think of it. At the start of the new school year, the geography teacher asked all his students where they had spent their summer vacations. Laura had started in enthusiastically about the trip she and her parents and younger brother had made across America in a camper. From the East Coast to the West Coast. Halfway through her description of the big waves and the surfers off the beach in Malibu, the geography teacher had interrupted her. "Perhaps we should give your classmates a chance to tell us about their vacations, Laura. We haven't all taken a big, long trip, not like you." Then he took his eyes off her and looked around the class. "Is there anyone who simply spent the summer in our own, beautiful Holland?"

Mr. Landzaat smiled with his lips closed. "Only two weeks of school left. You looking forward to the vacation?"

"Yeah," she said.

"And what's your family going to do? Where are you going?"

Earlier in the year her parents had bought a house in France, in addition to the one they already had in Terhofstede. The new house was in the Dordogne. They would spend most of July and August there, but before that they were going to Cuba for two weeks. In the last week of the vacation she would go for the first time with her friends and without her parents to Terhofstede.

"We're not really sure yet," she said. "Maybe we'll stay in Holland and go camping. Or go to France," she added quickly, because "stay in Holland and go camping" sounded a little too far-fetched for a family with her father's income.

"Oh, yes, France! Now that you mention it: Do you already know which field trip you want to take?"

In late September, all the junior classes were going on a field trip. You could choose from a week of kayaking in the Ardennes, a week in West Berlin, or a week in Paris. So many students had signed up for Paris that they were going to have to draw lots.

"Paris," Laura said. "But I don't know whether that'll happen. You know about the lottery, I guess, Mr. Landzaat?"

"Sure," he said. "And call me Jan. I have good news for you, actually. I'm one of the three chaperones going along to Paris. The lottery has to be impartial, of course, but there are always a couple of candidates who, in view of their academic performance, might be better off spending a week in the Ardennes, just to whip them into shape."

Had he winked? It happened so fast—a barely perceptible fluttering of the eyelid—that Laura thought for a moment she had imagined it, until he winked again.

"You have to keep this to yourself, Laura," he went on. "But we select certain students in advance. The lottery comes after that. Are you particularly fond of kayaking?"

She shook her head. "Not particularly."

"Fine, then I'll make note of that." He rummaged a bit through a pile of papers on his desk. "The other teachers who are going along are . . . that woman who teaches English, what's her name again?"

"Miss Posthuma."

"Right, Posthuma . . . and the third one is Harm. Harm Koolhaas, social studies. He's okay. He had no problem whatsoever with giving the lottery a little helping hand."

Laura was seventeen now, as her father had rightly noted. Grown men turned their heads and whistled as she walked down the street. It could be. It was possible. Jan Landzaat, history teacher at the Spinoza Lyceum, was openly flirting with her. She barely had to do a thing. It wasn't like being an actress who tries to get a role in a movie by going to bed with the director. It might've seemed that way a little, but only vaguely. It was actually something very different, she told herself. Jan Landzaat was not unattractive, he probably thought so too. There were rumors. He was new here, he'd only started at the Spinoza this year, before that he had taught at the Montessori Lyceum. There was a lot of contact between the students at both schools: friendships, relationships, they went to each other's school parties. The rumors spread quickly, the way rumors usually do, with a kind of snowball effect. The Montessori had almost six hundred students, the Spinoza more than eight hundred. At the top of the hill the snowball was still very small and fit perfectly in the two hands that formed it and then let it roll; halfway down the slope it had already gathered so much snow that nothing and no one could slow it down. It started with the story that the Montessori Lyceum had suspended Jan Landzaat because he had been involved with one of the senior girls, then the story went on to say that the two of them had had plans to get married: the history teacher, people said, had been about to leave his wife and two little children. Then it was only a small step to Jan Landzaat's wife coming home and finding the two of them on the couch, to Jan Landzaat's wife barging into the classroom in tears to confront the teacher with his adultery—in the scene at the teacher's home, in Laura's imagination, his pants had been down around his ankles and the girl was the first to see the wife standing in the doorway, while he himself hadn't noticed a thing. She had tapped him on the shoulder to warn him, but he'd gone on licking her throat for at least another thirty seconds. In the classroom scene the wife was toting a rolling pin, like in a comic strip or a B-movie, Mr. Landzaat had to climb out the window to avoid a beating. The rumors reached their zenith with stories about more than one girl filing complaints against the history teacher for pawing them. That was about a month after he started work at the Spinoza Lyceum. After that, someone—no one could remember exactly who—noted that it would be awfully strange for the Spinoza to simply hire a teacher who had committed such serious offenses at his former school. And just as they had gone from bad to worse, the rumors now turned and went the opposite way. If the worst was unthinkable, then the less worse must be based on falsehood too.

The snowball did not melt, nor did it explode against a tree trunk; no, from then on it grew only smaller and smaller. Like in a film run back frame by frame, it rolled to the top of the hill again, where it finally ended up in the same hands that had originally formed it.

In the meantime, did the history teacher's reputation suffer under all this? Not really. At least not among the students. True or untrue, Jan Landzaat was indeed a more than averagely handsome fellow, or in any case no dirty old man; no one knew exactly how old he was, but he couldn't have been much more than thirty. Laura had seen him one time with his wife, she had come in the car to pick him up on a Friday afternoon. She remembered how Mr. Landzaat had leaned down to kiss her on the lips. Then his wife had opened the back door of the car and two little children had climbed out, two little girls, whom he picked up and hugged in turn. A nice young teacher with an equally nice young family. What could be more natural than for a teacher like that to feel closer to his students than to his gray-mouse colleagues in their dull slacks and sport coats? The juniors and seniors were allowed to call him by his first name, the way they also did with Harm Koolhaas, the social studies teacher who was Jan Landzaat's friend. Harm Koolhaas also acted more like an eternally young adult. But still, it was different with him. Rumors went around about him too, albeit of a very different nature than those concerning Jan Landzaat. Harm Koolhaas, they said, had no wife or girlfriend, and wasn't looking for a wife or girlfriend either. He was careful not to blatantly favor the boys in his class, but *you can smell something like that miles away,* David said once. It wasn't that the social studies teacher was compromised by his predilections: times had changed. But it remained a soft spot—in an emergency situation it was something one could push against or pull on, and keep doing so until something in him broke or tore.

Jan Landzaat had asked her how she was doing, whether everything was all right at home. For a moment, she had considered confiding in him. Considered telling him something about her father; the history teacher, after all, was an expert in the field of real or fabricated rumors. About the incident at the restaurant, for example, the moment when her father had leaned across the table to kiss her on the cheek. How he had gloated over people's glances and the whispering—people who were not famous like him, people who had to go through life with an unfamous face. At the moment it happened she had been too bewildered to react, but later, in her room, she had played back the whole scene in her mind, over and over. Her father had enjoyed the fact (he found it fantastic) that those people might think something other than that he was there having a grilled-cheese sandwich with his nearly full-grown daughter. Without asking himself for a moment what Laura thought about it. And she saw the problem with her own attitude right away too. After all, wasn't it childish of her to make such a big deal out of it? She imagined how her father would respond. *Oh, sweetheart,*

*did that bother you? I never meant it that way. But if it bothers you,
I promise that from now on I will never make a public display of how
much I love my daughter.* Then he would laugh it off, the same
way he laughed off the stories and pictures in the gossip rags.
I'm not allowed to kiss my daughter anymore, he would tell her
mother at the table. And then her mother would laugh out
loud too.

For very different reasons, she couldn't express her doubts
about her father's behavior to her best friend either. To Stella.
Stella would have thought she was crazy. *Your father looks at
me in such a normal way,* Stella had told her. *The way you look
at a grown-up.*

"I'd really love to go to Paris," she said. "West Berlin
doesn't appeal to me that much, and the Ardennes would kill
me. Do you think it's possible, you think I have a chance,
Jan?"

And as she was calling her homeroom teacher by his first
name for the first time, she placed her left hand on the tabletop, not far from the sheet of paper with the various field-
trip destinations on it; not far either from the teacher's right
hand, the fingertips of which rested on the bottom of that
sheet of paper. Well-tended fingers, Laura saw, no flaky skin,
neatly manicured nails.

"That shouldn't be a problem," Jan Landzaat said. "Like I
said, some people deserve it more than others."

She gave him only a few moments to let his gaze rest
on her hand, then pulled it back from the table. With both
hands she now tucked her hair behind her ears, then pulled it
all the way back in a ponytail and shook it loose again.

With most boys, blushing started at the cheeks, but with
Mr. Landzaat it was his neck that turned red first. Then it
rose quickly from the collar of his burgundy sweater across
his chin, around his mouth, and up to his forehead—like a

glass being filled with pink lemonade. Maybe the blushing had started even lower, Laura thought, and therefore earlier, somewhere right above or right below his navel.

Today he would not get to see her hands again. She leaned forward a little and placed them on her thighs, close to her knees, so they were hidden from sight beneath the table. For the time being, Jan Landzaat would have to make do with the memory of the girl's hand on the tabletop, maybe it would come to mind again when he went to talk to Harm Koolhaas and Miss Posthuma about which students should be exempted from the lottery—which students deserved more than others to go on the field trip to Paris.

23

As a matter of fact, Herman really didn't help with the dishes. And when the table was being cleared he had to be egged on before he finally stood up with a sigh, piled up two or three plates, and took them, along with one single fork, one knife, and one glass, to the kitchen—then sank back down in his chair and lit an unfiltered Gitane.

There was nothing to be done about it, but the two girls were always the ones who started in on the dishes. Lodewijk usually dried, David was an old hand at cleaning the table; with a wet cloth he wiped and polished until the wooden tabletop gleamed as though it had never held a plate. Meanwhile, Ron and Michael saw to the floor, one of them wielding the dustpan, the other the brush, but that was pretty much it.

"Your turn, Herman," Stella said on the third or fourth evening, when Lodewijk, for a change, had lowered himself with a sigh into the easy chair by the fire.

She was standing in the doorway, holding out a checkered dish towel. Herman glanced left and right, as though checking whether she was talking to someone sitting beside him. "I thought that's why we brought two women along," he said. "Why else? Can anyone explain that to me?"

But when he saw the look on Stella's face, he slid his chair back anyway. "Only kidding. Ouch, my back!"

The first couple of days were sunny, but on the third the weather turned. Rain and wind. That evening they even lit the coal stove. Lodewijk had put on a white, knitted sweater and rubbed his hands together to warm them.

"So what's wrong with you, anyway?" Herman said to him as he took the dish towel from Stella's hand. "Are you sick or something?"

A thick book lay in Lodewijk's lap, a book with a marker sewed into the binding. Lodewijk had a penchant for Dutch authors from before the war.

"Are you sick, or just too lazy to dry the dishes?" Herman said when Lodewijk didn't reply. "I mean, I'm happy to take over for you, but the dishes will never be as dry as when you do it."

Laura was still standing at the table with the last few dirty glasses in her hand; she saw Herman wink at her, but looked away quickly.

"I'll come and inspect them later on," Lodewijk said without raising his eyes. "And if I find even one drop on them, I'll make you start all over again."

Michael and Ron, busy applying dustpan and brush to the floor around the coal stove, both laughed. Lodewijk lifted his feet a fraction of an inch, so they could get under them.

There was a smile on Herman's face, Laura saw, but his eyes were not smiling along.

"That sweater of yours, Lodewijk, is that made from sheep?"

"Baah," Lodewijk said.

Laura took a step toward the kitchen, but couldn't get by, not with Stella and Herman standing in the doorway.

"Did your mom knit it for you?" Herman asked. "Did she catch that sheep and knit it into a sweater?"

Laura came a step closer; as though by accident she knocked one of the glasses against Herman's forearm. When he looked at her she raised her eyebrows and shook her head. "Okay," she said cheerfully. "Shall we get going?"

"What's up?" Herman said as he took the first cup from the rack and slowly wrapped it in the dish towel. "Did I accidentally touch on a taboo here? Sheep? Knitting?"

Laura had closed the kitchen door behind them and held her finger to her lips. "It's his mother," she whispered. "She's ill. Very ill."

In a voice close to a whisper, she told Herman the gist of the story. Lodewijk's mother had an operation six months ago. For a while the prospects had been decent, but now it seemed she had only a few months to live. Lodewijk's father had died when he was eleven. He had no brothers or sisters. *Which means he's an only child too,* Laura almost said, but caught herself just in time. Her main feeling was one of amazement—at herself, for realizing only now that she was here in the same house with two only children.

"Okay," he said when she was finished; meanwhile, the plates, glasses, knives, and forks had piled up in the dish rack. Herman was still working on the first cup. "But that's not good, of course."

"No," Laura said, but then she looked at him. "What do you mean?" she asked. "What's not good?"

"That you guys protect him by not talking about his mother. I mean, I didn't know about it. But if I had, I would have said the same thing just now."

Despite herself, Laura felt her face grow hot. "It's not like that, we don't avoid talking about his mother," she said. "We talk about her all the time. We ask him how she's doing. Before the vacation started we all went to see her in the hospital. We brought her presents. Flowers. Bonbons and things. It turned out that she wasn't allowed to have most of it, but it was the thought. The whole thing was pretty intense. His mother was all yellow in the face, I mean, I knew her when she was still healthy. All swollen up. Horrible. But we acted as normal as possible. We joked around and Lodewijk's mother actually laughed with us, even though you could see that it was hard for her. Michael had made this thing for her, from two clothes hangers and a piece of wood, a thing she could put on the bed so she could read a book without having to hold it up."

"It turned out she never read books," Stella said. "Only gossip magazines. But anyway, like Laura said, it's the thought that counts."

"Oh, fuck," Herman said; he folded open the dish towel. The cup was in it, its handle broken off. "Maybe I made it a little too dry," Herman said. It was one of her mother's favorite coffee cups, because it had belonged to *her* mother before that, but Laura couldn't help laughing.

"What is it?" Stella looked over her shoulder. "Herman!" she said when she saw the cup and the broken handle in the dish towel. "What are you doing? Haven't you ever dried dishes before? Look at this pile. Come on, get a move on."

"Yes, ma'am," Herman said; he looked at Laura and made a face. A childish face—like a little boy whose angry neighbor lady has just seized his soccer ball.

Laura half expected him to toss the broken cup into the garbage pail under the counter, but he didn't. He placed the handle carefully in the cup and put it on a shelf above the stove, along with the round canisters of coffee, tea, and sugar. Then he took a plate from the rack and started drying it.

"What I meant to say was really something else," he said. "The whole thing about Lodewijk's mother is terrible, sure. But you shouldn't make a taboo out of it. You all go to visit her in the hospital. Fine. But if you're not allowed to joke about things anymore, then in fact you've already signed her death certificate. Generally speaking, parents are ridiculous creatures. If all you do is ask Lodewijk politely and worriedly about his mother's health, then you're not taking him seriously anymore, as the son of that same mother. What you're really saying then is that you've already given up on her."

"Yeah, they say that sometimes," Stella said. "That it's better for the survivors to look death in the eye. Not repress it."

Laura couldn't help sighing. Stella had a way of sprinkling conversations with secondhand psychological theories she got from her father. Usually misquoted, and always at the wrong moment.

"But, Herman," she said, "you didn't know that Lodewijk's mother was seriously ill, but would you still have started in about his knitted sweater even if you *had* known? Do you mean that, really?"

Herman looked her straight in the eye; his look was no longer cold or tough, more like amused—naughty.

"Maybe I would have adapted the text a little," he said. "I probably would have asked: 'Lodewijk, who's going to knit those disgusting sweaters for you when your mom's not around anymore?'"

Laura held Herman's eye and didn't blink. *How can you say something like that?* That's what she thought she should say right then, but what she was thinking was quite different. It had to do with what Herman had said earlier. *Generally speaking, parents are ridiculous creatures.* And also with something else he'd said, a few days ago on the train, when he used the gin to raise a toast to the death of his own parents. "Ridiculous," that was the key word. Laura had always felt that her parents were nice and friendly. That's what they were, wasn't it, nice and friendly? Everyone said so, even her friends. You almost couldn't ask for nicer parents. But sometimes those nice parents were a pain too. No, not a pain: they were ballast. A weight around your neck that made you walk around a little bent over all the time. Her famous father with his corny jokes at his daughter's expense. Her mother sticking her head in the sand, so that she could have a glass of red wine with her husband on the couch at night. She couldn't help it, but suddenly she felt jealous of Herman—jealous of his parents. Normal, tiresome, selfish, failing parents you could be angry at. Parents you could wish dead and forget about with a few slugs of gin. She was even a little jealous of Lodewijk. Lodewijk, who was already a half-orphan, and who would soon be rid of it all, of the never-ending nagging of parents.

Herman must have seen something in the way she looked. Something, a change in her expression, because he smiled at her, with his lips and with his eyes.

"They are disgusting, aren't they, Laura?" he said. "Lodewijk's sweaters?"

And she smiled back, it was no effort for her to smile back at Herman with her eyes, she knew that.

"Yeah," she said. "Disgusting."

24

ON THE last day of the trip, Herman surprised them with a meal he had prepared all by himself. Under the guise of a lone bike ride, he had gone to Sluis and secretly done all the shopping. When he came back no one was allowed into the kitchen. Herman said he didn't need any help.

"It smells great!" Lodewijk called out from his chair beside the fire, while the girls set the table with glasses and plates Herman handed them through a crack in the kitchen door. "Can you give us any more information? Like what time we're going to eat? We're famished!"

But no answer came from the kitchen. It was almost dark when the door flew open with a bang and Herman came into the room, clutching the handles of a huge pan in his mittened hands. "Hurry up, fast, a trivet!" he said to Stella, the only one who had already pulled up a chair at the table.

"Come on!" he said. "What are you people waiting for? If it gets cold, it's ruined."

He disappeared back into the kitchen and returned carrying a platter with three smoked sausages, still in their plastic packaging with the brand name UNOX on them. "Scissors?" he asked Laura. "Are there scissors in the house?"

"Hotchpotch," said Ron, who had already lifted the lid off the pan.

"Maybe more of a dish for a winter's day," Herman said. "But I figured, the weather being what it is . . . And the days will be getting shorter again soon anyway," he added, disappearing back into the kitchen.

Stella dished it up, Laura cut open the plastic packages, and Herman returned with a frying pan half-filled with a sputtering-hot liquid.

"Look out, this is hot as hell," he said. "Has everybody dug their little foxhole? The mustard's in the kitchen. Michael?"

"Beautiful!" said Lodewijk, who had already started in. "Really, Herman. Fantastic."

The day after Herman had teased Lodewijk about his sweater, they'd all gone for a long walk, first to Retranchement, then along the canal to the Zwin. At one point Herman and Lodewijk fell behind the others, and when Laura turned around she saw Herman put an arm around Lodewijk's shoulder. Those two had become closer since that walk in a way that was clear to everyone. Herman asked about the books Lodewijk read and, on occasion, Lodewijk sneered at their classmates, "that bunch of illiterates" who barely read at all, or if they did, only the "wrong books," which would end up on their required reading lists anyway.

"Be careful not to get any on you," Herman said now to Lodewijk. "Under the circumstances, we wouldn't want your mother to have to start knitting again."

"You know, I think I *will* spill something on myself," Lodewijk said. "Then at least I won't have to wear this sweater anymore."

At first, Laura had been amused by the way Herman and Lodewijk tried to outdo each other with ever-blunter jokes about Lodewijk's deathly ill mother, but in the end it seemed to take on a strained quality—especially for Lodewijk. It was as though the brusque jokes fit Herman to a tee, like a sweater made to size, not a bit too small or too big, while with Lodewijk it was more like a pair of jeans that were really too tight for him, but that he wore anyway because he thought they made him look slimmer. Lodewijk had always been funny, but his humor was more of the wide-eyed sort, as though he was amazed by everything that happened. Now it was as though Herman had awakened this blunt side of his character.

"It really is delicious, Herman," Laura said. "It has something . . . something . . . special. Onions?"

Herman was just in the process of dishing up a second helping, but he was the only one. He jabbed his fork into a big piece of smoked sausage and swung it onto his plate. "Garlic," he said.

Laura watched as he cut the chunk of sausage in two, wiped it through the glob of mustard on his plate, and stuck it in his mouth. She had always thought hotchpotch with raw endive was kind of childish. A typical boy's dish. The kind of thing boys could squeak by with when it came to cooking. Fried eggs, spaghetti and tomato sauce, chili con carne— hotchpotch belonged in that same category. It was the kind of thing that was almost impossible to ruin, but the boys would stand around in the kitchen for hours anyway, acting important, as though they were fixing a three-star meal.

"It's one of my mother's recipes," Herman said. "With garlic. That's the way she always made it."

"Made?" Ron said.

"When she was still happy," Herman said.

"There's one of those traditional butchers on our street who makes smoked sausage from pigs that have always lived outside," Stella said. "You can really taste the difference."

"And what is it you taste, exactly?" Herman asked. "Mud? Shit?"

"No," Stella said. "Just meat. Real meat. Not this chemical garbage."

"I've seen those traditional butchers too," Herman said. "And I've bought smoked sausage from them. Once, but never again. The 'traditional butcher' is perhaps the greatest misnomer of our age. And his smoked sausages along with it. That meat has all kinds of things in it: tendons, nerves, bits of crushed bone that get stuck between your teeth. And the whole thing packaged in a thick, tough skin that you end up chewing on for hours. They probably use the hog's foreskin for that. No, I swear by Unox. Chemical garbage, my ass. It slides right down the gullet, the way smoked sausage should."

Laura was half expecting Stella to come back at him with arguments about poison or environmental damage, about toxins that piled up inside the body when one ate factory-made food, but she did something different. She cut off a piece of the Unox sausage, jabbed her fork into it, and stuck it in her mouth.

"Now close your eyes," Herman said, "and tell me what you taste."

Laura shifted in her chair, she didn't know exactly what was happening, but something was. Apparently she'd missed out on the fact that Stella had not yet tasted the smoked sausage, not until Herman had started talking about its chemical benefits. Now she watched as Stella chewed slowly, her eyes closed, and saw how Herman looked at Stella. He had never looked at Stella that way before. Laura felt her cheeks tingle, and she reprimanded herself silently. *Not now!* All week, Herman had treated Stella as though she was a bit naive, a naive and rather unworldly girl who never got further, during their walks and dinner-table conversations, than the deposition of dime-store profundities that she'd picked up from her father. That was all true enough. But Stella was also something else, something that Laura knew she herself was not. Stella was *sweet*. Perhaps even innocent. Stella could look at you in a certain way . . . Laura always had to lower her eyes or turn them away when her closest girlfriend looked at her like that. She had tried it in front of the mirror once: she had opened her eyes so wide that the tears came, she had thought about lovely, innocent things—but not in a million years did she come close to looking the way Stella did. No, Laura was not sweet. She was lots of other things—pretty, irresistibly so perhaps, although all too aware of her own irresistibility— but she would never be sweet, or innocent, or "vulnerable" (the fashionable word these days). More like the very opposite. Stella had actually said that to her after Laura told her girlfriend about the blushing history teacher, about how she had wrapped Jan Landzaat around her finger in order to secure a place on the field trip to Paris.

"When it comes to things like that, you're a lot cagier than I am," Stella had said. At first, Laura had objected to that qualification, because most of its connotations seemed negative to her. But later, at home, in front of the bathroom mirror again, she had to admit that Stella was right. She had smiled seductively at her mirror image, and now she saw it herself. "You definitely are a cagey one," she said to herself out loud—then burst out laughing.

"You're right, Herman," Stella said now. She looked at him with her lovely, innocent eyes, Laura saw, and now she saw something else too. Stella *beamed*—there was no other word for it, it was like she was illuminated from inside by some invisible source of light or heat. "It tastes a lot better than I thought. How can that be?"

"I was just thinking," Laura said. "When we get home, shall we all go to the hospital and visit Lodewijk's mother again? Like, the day after tomorrow? Or else early next week?"

She might have been imagining it, but it looked as though Lodewijk froze for a moment inside his knitted sweater. She didn't have much time to think about that, though. Herman and Stella seemed not to have heard, they were still looking only at each other.

"But school starts again next week," Ron said.

"Well, so what?" Laura said. "We can go after school, right? When are the visiting hours? We'll buy some nice things to eat and a book—a whole bunch of magazines," she corrected herself quickly. "What do you think, Lodewijk? It's a good idea, isn't it?"

"She's not in the hospital anymore," Lodewijk said.

Now everyone, including Herman and Stella, looked at him.

"She's at home," Lodewijk said. "They can't do anything more for her at the hospital. She told them she wanted to go home."

"But . . . ," Laura began.

"The neighbor lady's taking care of her now," Lodewijk said. "At first I felt bad about coming along with you guys, obviously, but when I said I'd stay home my mother wouldn't have it. She said I should just go and enjoy myself."

"Jesus," Michael said. "That was big of her."

"You know what's funny?" Lodewijk said. "Or no, not funny, more like ironic. That neighbor lady has lived in the apartment next door ever since we moved in, but we always thought she was a horrible old witch. Lived there all that time alone. No husband. No children. About sixty, I guess. And way too tall, maybe that was why, that's what I always figured. A woman who's two heads taller than you, no man would go for that. But whatever, right at the start, as soon as my mother fell ill, the neighbor lady offered to help. And she didn't just offer to help, she was really there whenever you needed her. Since my mom came home, she's even started cooking for us."

"You see that sometimes," Stella said, "that people who you don't expect it from suddenly turn out to have a really warm heart."

"And you know what else I think?" Lodewijk said. "It's so weird. A kind of premonition. When I left last week, the way my mother looked at me. I was already at the door with my backpack on when she asked me to come and give her another kiss. Even though I'd just done that. She's already so weak, but she threw that skinny, swollen arm of hers around my neck. She squeezed as hard as she could. 'My sweet boy,' she said. 'My sweet, sweet boy.' It was only when I got to the bus stop on my way to the station that I realized it. She was saying goodbye to me. She won't be there when I get back. She wanted me to go away so she could die in peace. Like an old cat that crawls under the kitchen counter. So I wouldn't have to be there when it happened. And at the bus stop I thought: *I can still turn around and go back. I can stay with her.* But I got on that bus anyway. I'm here with you guys, instead of with her. And so do I feel guilty all the time now? In some ways, yes. In other ways, though, I hope I was right. That she really will be dead when I get home."

No one said a word. Stella, who was sitting closest to Lodewijk, laid her hand on his, but Lodewijk looked at Michael.

"Have you still got that bottle of gin around somewhere?" he asked. "I think I feel like something stronger than tea tonight."

25

WHAT THE kitchen counter resembled most was the stadium field after a rock concert. Here there were no empty cans, though, no shards of glass and shredded sheets of black plastic, but filthy pans, plates, cutlery with the caked-on remains of mashed potatoes, scattered butt-ends of endive and globs of dried-up mustard—Herman hadn't even thrown away the potato peels. But the garbage pail was still pretty much brimming over, Laura saw when she lifted the lid.

"That's what you get when boys try to cook . . . ," she said, fishing a wooden spoon out of the garbage.

Stella had already pulled on the rubber gloves. "Oh well, it was a sweet thought," she said. "What'll we do, just start anywhere?"

After the boys had polished off the rest of the gin, Ron got his guitar and Michael came down with his saxophone. Herman had been sitting in the easy chair by the stove the whole time, his legs wide, smoking one Gitane after the other.

"I did the cooking," he said. "Tonight I'm exempt from kitchen duty."

At the first notes from Michael's saxophone, Laura caught Stella's eye and gestured to her to come into the kitchen.

"Did you really like that Unox sausage, or were you just pretending to?" Laura asked. She was standing behind Stella, a little to the left, so that she didn't have to look her friend straight in the eye; she did her best to make her voice sound normal, but didn't quite succeed.

"What do you mean, 'just pretending to'?" Stella had moved all the plates and cutlery from the sink onto the counter and sprayed a stream of green detergent into the tub of hot water.

"You should have seen yourself," Laura said. "And heard yourself. 'Oh, that's *delicious!*' I mean, I know how you always look at every can and jar to see how much artificial flavoring has been added. Everyone knows that. No one believed you. Only Herman, maybe."

"I was just trying to be nice." Stella started in on the first plate—according to the same method as always, Laura knew: first she scrubbed off the caked-on remains with the scouring pad, then ran the dishwashing brush over the plate, and finally she rinsed off the suds under the cold tap that she left running beside the dishpan the whole time; glasses she held up to the light before putting them in the rack. "He doesn't help out much, okay. He's lazy, but he's also not used to it, you can tell that. If you just ask him to help out, he does it, really. And cooking tonight, that was all his own idea. So then why sit around and whine about a Unox sausage."

Laura took the first plate from the rack. She raised it to right in front of her eyes, examining it for a spot of endive or mashed potato that Stella might have missed—but found nothing.

"But there's a big difference between not whining and acting as though you're being served haute cuisine, I guess. And the look on your face when you said it . . . It was really too bad you couldn't see yourself."

Stella was running the brush slowly round and round the next plate, but now she stopped. She turned halfway and looked at Laura.

"Can I ask you something, Laura?"

It was one of those moments when you cross a certain line unawares, Laura realized only too late. Suddenly you're on the other side and can't go back. Laura would think back on this moment often, later, the moment when she, without knowing exactly how it had happened, found herself somewhere she didn't want to be.

She could feel her face growing hot, and cursed herself. It had all gone too quickly. She knew the question that was coming next, and she knew that she could never lie as long as she was looking straight at Stella.

"Do you *like* Herman, Laura?"

Straight through the dish towel, Laura pressed her fingers hard against the edge of the plate she was still drying, but when nothing broke off, she dropped it instead.

"Oh, shit!" she said.

The plate didn't break into dozens of shards on the tile floor, not the way she'd hoped. Instead, it broke neatly into three fairly even pieces, which remained lying at her feet.

"He's too skinny for me," she said, bending down to pick up the pieces. "And those rubber boots. I don't know, but somehow I always find myself hoping that I won't be there if he ever takes them off."

She stood up, and now she did look Stella in the eye.

"He's just not a boy for girls," she said. "Not obviously, I mean. Not the first one you think of when you think about boys." She didn't blush when she said this—because it was the truth. "He's not my type," she added. "Maybe he's yours. As far as I'm concerned, you can have him. Enjoy yourself."

And then she really did have to turn away. She turned her back completely, then tried to take as long as she could to stuff the broken pieces of plate into the packed garbage pail.

26

As soon as they had gathered at the bus stop the next afternoon with their bags and duffels, it started raining softly. Only a drizzle at first, but a few minutes later they saw the rain rolling in curtains across the fields from the direction of Retranchement. There was no shelter for them to huddle beneath, they did their best to keep dry under the trees on the deserted village square. Laura closed her eyes and listened to the rain rustle through the leaves. She had gone upstairs early the night before, but barely slept a wink all night. Downstairs in the living room she'd heard Michael on his saxophone and Ron playing his guitar, punctuated occasionally by laughter, and also the sound of someone throwing up into a bucket in the little hallway between the kitchen and living room. At breakfast that morning Lodewijk had been quieter than usual, and after pushing away the plate of bacon and eggs David had made for them, he stood up with a groan and said, almost in a whisper, that he was going out for a breath of fresh air.

"Do you want me to go with you?" Stella asked.

Lodewijk closed his eyes and shook his head—a shake barely perceptible to the naked eye, followed by more groaning, as though the slightest movement caused him pain. "No, just leave me," he whispered.

The attic was divided into three bedrooms, separated only by thin wooden walls. In other words, you could hear everything: snores, sighs, farts—and the friends always left the doors open till way past midnight in order to go on talking. The girls had a room to themselves; David, Michael, Ron, and Herman slept in the big room in two beds and on two mattresses on the floor. Lodewijk had the smallest room all to himself. It was only big enough for a single bed. Sometimes he would complain loudly that the others were making too much noise.

"Maybe there are people here who would kind of like to sleep!" he shouted—but he didn't actually close his door.

It was almost light out when the others finally came upstairs. Laura turned to face the wall and heard Stella—or at least she assumed it was Stella—come into the bedroom, then the sound of a zipper: a drawn-out sound, the sound of someone doing their utmost to open a bag as quietly as possible.

Somewhere in the hallway or outside the door there was whispering, but she couldn't make out what was being said— let alone by whom.

"She's asleep," Stella whispered back.

The zipper was closed again, the planks in the wooden floor creaked softly when Stella took the few steps that brought her to the doorway. Now Laura heard a soft squeaking, a sound she hadn't heard that whole week, but she knew immediately what it was.

They're closing the door! Except for the soft squeaking, she heard only the pounding of her own heart beneath the blankets. *They're closing the door so I can't hear what they're going to do . . .*

With a short, dry click, the door closed.

Laura counted to ten, her heart pounding faster and

louder, then rolled over slowly—the bed, too, creaked at the slightest movement.

Gray daylight was coming through the red-and-white checkered curtains of the attic window, touching the floor—and Stella's bed, where her travel bag lay atop the blankets. Without making a sound, Laura lowered her feet to the floor. A few seconds later she was at the door and pressing her ear against the wood.

At first she could make out no distinct noises, then came a shuffling and the sound of one of the other doors opening and closing again.

"You want to take your bag with you, Lodewijk?" The voice was Herman's, he didn't seem to be trying to speak softly at all. "Maybe you still want to brush your teeth or something?"

"Shh!" That was Stella. Laura pressed her ear to the wood so hard it hurt; for a long time there was nothing, until suddenly she heard David's voice.

"The bed all the way at the back, Lodewijk. The one that's still all messed up, that's Herman's. Are you feeling any better, or do you want a bucket beside the bed?"

But there was no reply; a little later still the two doors closed, one right after the other, and then everything was still.

Laura remained with her ear to the door for another half hour, then went to the window and pushed aside the checkered curtains. It was fully light out now, over the garden lay a thin mist; in the distance, beyond the branches of the apple tree, the sky was turning pink and purple. Laura felt her eyes sting. *Don't,* she said to herself, but her lower lip had already begun to tremble.

"Oh, goddamn it!" she said. "God, god, god, goddamn it!"

. . .

"You think that bus is really going to come?" Herman asked. "Or is it the way it always is with public transport, that they think: *Aw, who's going to take a bus on a day like today? You know what, let's just stay in the garage.*"

Laura watched as Herman wandered over to the bus stop, his hands in the pockets of his jeans; then she looked at Stella, who was acting as though she hadn't heard Herman.

They were putting up a good front. At breakfast, too, Laura had watched for signals, for outward signs like blushing or bags under their eyes, or something much clearer than that, scratch marks or hickeys. But there was nothing. They acted normal—everyone was acting normal. Maybe that was it, she'd thought, that they were all doing their very best to act normal.

They were hushing it up. They were keeping it under wraps. It had been tacitly agreed that no one would talk about it. A tacit agreement among all those present, except for Laura. David had not given her even one meaningful or conspiratorial glance when she finally came down to breakfast, the last one to appear—a role usually reserved for him. In fact, he hadn't looked at her at all, he had gone on much longer than necessary with smearing his slice of brown bread, first with butter, then with peanut butter. Laura heard the wood in her chair creak when she sat down—that's how quiet it was— until Michael asked David to pass the butter. The silence and the acting normal could mean only one thing, and that was the conclusion Laura quickly drew: they were sparing her, at least they were trying to spare her, but precisely by sparing her they were confirming exactly what Laura was afraid of.

Or wasn't that it at all? Here on the village square, doubt suddenly struck. Were the others all standing together, had they all moved away from her, or had Laura herself gone and stood a few yards from the biggest tree, the better to see Herman as he walked through the rain to the bus stop? She'd had less than two hours' sleep, her eyes were half shut, and in the pit of her stomach something zoomed, an empty, hungry feeling, even though she'd eaten a bigger breakfast than usual. Could she be imagining the whole thing? Were her senses in a tizzy from lack of sleep, was she seeing things that weren't there? After all, everyone had acted *normal,* at the breakfast table Herman and Stella had exchanged no more glances. Or did the absence of such glances point to the very worst? She didn't know what to think. After breakfast everyone had gone to pack their bags, she had straightened up the house and mopped the floor, even Herman had helped out: he had carried the dishes the others had dried to the living room and spent a lot of time neatly arranging things in the crockery cupboard with the glass doors.

"Laura?" he had called out at one point.

And when she approached, her heart pounding, he held up a coffee cup for her to see; she had tried to look straight at him without lowering her eyes or averting her gaze— without bursting into tears.

"Hmm?" she said.

"The cup I broke while I was drying it? The cup that used to belong to your grandma?"

"Hmm?" she said again, because she hadn't the slightest idea what he was talking about.

"I glued it. Good as new, isn't it?"

Now Laura looked at her friends as they huddled under the tree. At Stella. Did Stella know about the cup? Or had Herman kept it a secret from her?

"What day is it today?" Herman shouted from the bus stop. "Saturday, right?"

Everyone turned to look at him. Everyone but Laura, because she had already been keeping an eye on him for the last five minutes. "On Saturday, the bus only comes once every three hours," Herman shouted. "We've been standing here like idiots for half an hour."

And then it happened. A car came from the direction of Retranchement. A green car, Laura had no idea what make it was, but that didn't matter anyway, because Herman was already holding up his hand. He raised his thumb.

Later she would remember the whole thing like a movie played in slow motion, frame by frame, without any way to run it back.

The green car stopping. The window opening. On the passenger side. Two men in the car. Herman leaning down to look through the window. Herman holding up two fingers for all to see.

"There's only room for two!" he shouted.

Here the film stopped completely, with all of them looking at each other.

"Stella!" Herman shouted. "Stella, don't just stand there. Come on, let's go!"

27

A LITTLE less than a month later, in the last week of September, the junior classes left for their field trips. That whole month Laura had done her best not to let on; not to David, Ron, Michael, and Lodewijk, but especially not to Stella. She did her utmost to remain Stella's "closest friend," hard as it was at times for her to listen to Stella's stories about Herman; how much fun he was, what a great sense of humor he had, which movies and concerts they'd gone to, how their relationship had at first met with disapproval from her parents—who were now separated completely—but how Herman, for example, didn't let himself be intimidated by her father, the psychologist. One time her father had reluctantly agreed to have Herman come along to dinner at the trendy restaurant where he took his daughter every two weeks, to help her get used to his new girlfriend, twenty years younger than he (and a former patient). At one point the conversation turned to choosing a profession, to what Stella and Herman wanted to do after they finished high school. Stella wasn't quite sure, but said that in any case she wanted "at least four children," upon which her father gave her another of his pitying looks.

"And you know what Herman said?" Stella said to Laura—it was around eleven o'clock, Stella had called her friend right after she came back from the restaurant.

"No, what?" Laura was sitting on her bed with her knees pulled up, eyes closed, chewing on her thumbnail, but there wasn't much thumbnail left to chew.

"He said: 'Now that's what I call a clear plan. Large families, I'm all for them.' And then he started talking about his own parents, about how depressing things were at home, how he couldn't stand being the only child anymore, stuck in between all the bickering or, even worse, the long silences. He said: 'When there's a divorce, when the father goes looking for someone younger, for example, four children can turn to each other for support.' And then he looked at my father and at Annemarie, that's her name, Annemarie. I thought I was going to choke. But it was so good of him. Don't you think? To dare to say something like that?"

"Yeah," Laura said. "Ow!" She had bit into the exposed skin under her nail.

"Later on, Herman started talking about psychologists," Stella went on. "About how it wasn't really a profession at all. You don't become a psychologist, he said, you either are one or you're not."

Laura was only half listening as she sucked on her bleeding thumb. Then Stella began telling her about Herman and kissing. Laura had closed her eyes even tighter when her friend told her that Herman was sort of clumsy in everything he did. "He's so thin, too," she said. "You can feel everything. But at the same time, he's so sweet. You know, a while back we'd been messing around in my room for a long time, we went pretty far, my mother had gone out to see a play with one of her girlfriends and they could come home any moment, every once in a while we lay there and stayed quiet to see if we heard the door, and then I ran my hand over his hair in the dark and over his face and suddenly I felt something wet around his eyes. He'd just been lying there crying, without a sound. 'What's wrong?' I asked him, and you know what he said? He said: 'Nothing. I was just lying here thinking about how happy I am.' Don't you think that's sweet? I almost started crying too. Sometimes he acts tough and cracks those nasty jokes, but he's really very sensitive."

What Laura really felt like now was hanging up; she held her hand in front of her mouth so Stella wouldn't hear her groan, but Stella just rattled on. That's the way she always was on the phone: even if you didn't say anything back, not even "yeah" or "no," or even little grunts of confirmation, just so the other person knew you were still listening. Anyone but Stella, for example, would have asked if Laura was still there: *Hey, are you still there? You still listening?* Not Stella. Stella's own voice—her own story—was enough for her.

Meanwhile, the story had meandered on to another evening, yet another evening when Herman and Stella had been alone at her mother's house. How they had watched a movie on the couch, and how they had tried to go further, further than they had before, not just long, wet French kisses and petting, but really far.

"Sure, okay!" Laura suddenly responded to an imaginary voice. "I'll be there in a minute."

"He had his hand on my butt," Stella went on. "And from there he moved his fingers up front. Real sweet, real slow, and I had his . . . I'd been teasing him there a little with my fingers, not quite tickling him, but I could tell by his breathing, we were probably both thinking that it might happen that night, but then suddenly—I'd move my fingertips up a little—suddenly I felt it, this sort of tremor went through his body, and then I felt it on my fingers . . . What did you say?"

"My father," Laura said. "My father wants me to come down for dessert. I have to go now."

"Okay, sleep tight."

That was one of the advantages of Stella never listening. She also never objected to what you said: that eleven-thirty, for example, was awfully late for dessert. *Sleep tight.* She probably hadn't even heard what Laura said.

On the fourth day of the Paris trip, after the requisite visits to the Eiffel Tower, the Louvre, and Versailles, they had dinner at a Vietnamese restaurant in the Quartier Latin and ended up with a little group at the hotel bar. Miss Posthuma hadn't even gone along to the restaurant: after their endless walk through the gardens at Versailles she had said that she was "worn out," that tonight she was going to "hit the hay" early—the same way she had the first three nights too. At the hotel entrance Harm Koolhaas had announced that he was going out for a stroll. When Jan Landzaat asked if he wanted him to come along, the social studies teacher said there was no need for that. "Just a little stroll along the Seine," he said. "A little fresh air." Laura had seen the two teachers wink at each other.

The six of them were sitting and standing around the bar; first there had been eight of them, but Lodewijk and Stella had gone upstairs around eleven. Mr. Landzaat ordered a Pernod, David and Herman were drinking beer, and otherwise there were only the two girls from the parallel junior class, Miriam Steenbergen and Karen van Leeuwen, both with a glass of white wine with ice on the bar in front of them. Laura wasn't sure what to order, not until Jan Landzaat handed her his glass for a taste. Later she could no longer be completely certain what had come first, the glass with the unfamiliar beverage that tasted of a mixture of pears and anise at her lips and then on her tongue, or the thought of the hands of a ten-to-fifteen-years-older man on her body—the mouth with the long teeth against her mouth.

"I'll have the same," she said as she looked into the history teacher's eyes—a long look, longer than normal in any case; she couldn't see herself, of course, but she felt her eyes smolder, and Jan Landzaat did not look away. He looked back, long too, longer than might strictly speaking be appropriate for a teacher to look at one of his students.

"Un Pernod, s'il vous plaît," he told the barman, without taking his eyes off her. For just a moment his hand rested on her forearm, quite quickly, then he pulled it back, but she knew the others must have seen it. Maybe not Miriam and Karen, who were busy talking to each other, but David and Herman for sure; ever since Stella had gone upstairs, Herman had been looking at her more—maybe she was imagining it, but even when she couldn't clearly see him, she felt his gaze wander in her direction from time to time.

She had never thought of Jan Landzaat as a real possibility; he was attractive, the fact that he was married and had two young children formed no moral hindrance for Laura; how he explained or didn't explain things at home was his own business. There had to be a kernel of truth to those rumors about his behavior at the Montessori Lyceum, otherwise they wouldn't have existed, she told herself. The history teacher was a *womanizer,* even if Laura didn't know the English word for grown men who felt attracted mostly to seventeen-year-old girls.

Jan Landzaat presented himself. The opportunity presented itself. That, in the end, was the primary but also the only reason why she took the elastic band out of her ponytail and shook her hair free; she would see how far things went, she thought, as she placed a cigarette between her lips and asked the teacher for a light.

She didn't have to check to see whether the others had noticed. It was quiet at the bar, the conversations had lulled—between Miriam and Karen, but above all the conversation between David and Herman. All eyes were on her, she knew that.

28

THE WEEK after they got back from Paris, David suggested that he and Laura stop for a drink at an outdoor café in Vondelpark. "I need to talk to you about something," he said.

They were on their way home from school; they often cycled back with a larger group as far as the corner of Stadionweg, where they would split up. David and Stella usually biked the last stretch together: Laura lived at the edge of the park, David in the city center, on Looiersgracht.

"What'll you have?" David asked, trying to catch the waitress's eye.

"Do they have Pernod here? Probably not." Laura smiled at him a bit naughtily, but David didn't smile back.

"I wanted to talk to you about that too," he said.

Finally, they both ordered beer; Laura thought David would start in right away about her affair with the history teacher, but he didn't.

"I've been thinking about Zeeland," he said. "Actually, I wanted to ask you something. Ask you first, to hear what you think, and the others after that."

"Well?" In two weeks' time they were planning to go back to the house in Terhofstede, with the same group; this time, though, a few things would be different. Two days after they got back from the field trip to Paris, Lodewijk's mother had died. And this would be the first time that a "couple" would be there: Herman and Stella.

"It's your house," David said. "Your parents' house, but still. Mostly your house. However you look at it, it's up to you to decide who goes along and who doesn't."

Laura didn't say a thing, just looked around to see if their beers were coming.

"So what do you think about Herman and Stella?" David asked. "I mean, it *was* pretty weird, the way it went . . . at least I thought so. I mean, Herman's my friend, but I thought the whole thing was out of line. That's what I told him too."

"What did you say to him?" Laura asked, suddenly concerned. She considered David her best friend, the kind of best friend you'd never get involved with romantically, and therefore all the more reliable. David was just a sweet guy, maybe a little too sweet; he always wanted to do the right thing by Laura, but despite all his good intentions it seemed as though he tried to protect her too much, the way a parent might shield a child from shocking or bad news. That made her feel claustrophobic at times, but she never dared say so.

"I told him he should have waited till we got back to Amsterdam," David said. "With Stella, I mean. I thought it was out of line to do that in your house. In your parents' house."

"But why? What's so out of line about hooking up with my best girlfriend?" Laura tried to make it sound as normal as possible—calm, collected, as though it made no difference to her—but there was no way she could get the underlying sarcasm out of it; David must have heard it too.

"Exactly that: your best girlfriend. I think that's weird, you don't do things like that. That's not being respectful of other people's feelings."

Laura felt a sudden flash of heat at the base of her throat;

she had to do her best now to make sure that heat didn't reach her face. "What feelings? What do you mean?"

"Laura, I'm your best friend. There's no need to try to fool me. I saw it with my own eyes. And I probably wasn't the only one. The way you looked at Herman. How you tried so hard not to let anyone see that you liked him. I watched it happen, the way you completely fell apart when he and Stella—"

"Fell apart?" Laura felt the tears welling up in the corners of her eyes, she covered her face with her hands in an attempt to hide them from David. "What are you talking about?"

Then she actually started crying. David rose from his chair, then reconsidered and slid his chair around the table, a little closer to her.

"I'm sorry," he said. "I didn't want . . . This is exactly what I didn't want. Does Stella know what you think about this? How you feel, I mean? Have you two ever talked about it?"

"Oh, that fucking bitch!" Laura said. It was out before she had even thought about it—but it was precisely what she thought.

"Yeah," was all David said; he raised his arm as though to put it around her shoulders, then let it drop.

"I wish she was dead," Laura said. It was a thought that had never come up in her before, not that explicitly, but she sensed that some other force—some other voice—was expressing her feelings perfectly, without a single thought beforehand. In any case, it came as a relief, as though she had finally stuck a finger down her throat and vomited; the queasiness was over now. She stopped crying, wiped the tears from her eyes, and smiled at David. "I *wished* she was dead, for a while there," she said. "It's better now, actually."

And David smiled back; that was what made him her best

friend, Laura realized again, he didn't say the wrong things, he didn't say, for example, that you couldn't say things like that about your best girlfriend.

"All things considered, it just seems wiser to me if Herman and Stella didn't go along to Terhofstede this time," David said. "I already hinted at that to Herman, but I haven't said anything to Stella. Herman understood, I think. But of course it's up to you."

"What did he understand?" Laura suddenly felt icy inside—her crying jag seemed a thing of the distant past, centuries ago, as though she had never cried in her life.

"That it might be difficult for you. He hadn't meant to hurt you, he said. If it bothered you, he was willing to stay home. That's a possibility too, of course, that Stella goes along but not Herman."

"*Hurt* me?" Laura spoke very quietly, she was completely in control, she told herself. She looked David straight in the eye. David, her "best friend," but then a best friend who believed too fully in his own goodness—in his own good intentions. There was no way she could get angry at him, he would never understand that, but not being able to get angry at him made her even more furious. "What did you say to him, exactly?"

"Laura . . ." David slid his chair back a little, so he could get a better look at her. "Laura, I didn't tell him anything except what was already clear as a bell. Everyone saw it. Herman's not blind either. He understood right away, that's what I thought was so good of him."

So this was the price one paid for having a best friend, Laura realized. You also had to accept it when they ruined everything for you. Out of the goodness of their heart. Out of *pity.* She thought she really might have to vomit at any moment.

"I have absolutely no problem with Herman and Stella coming along," she said. "Absolutely no problem whatsoever."

"Laura . . ."

"Don't 'Laura' me. It's my house, isn't that what you just said? My parents' house? Okay, then Herman and Stella are very welcome there too. End of discussion." She stood up, their beers still hadn't arrived. "I'm going. See you at school tomorrow."

29

THEY WERE sitting on his living room couch. Landzaat had his arm around her shoulders; on a low table at their feet was a bottle of red wine, two glasses, and a dish of peanuts.

"What do you feel like?" he asked. "A movie? Or shall we go get something at that restaurant we went to last time?"

It was the Friday evening before the fall vacation began. Laura and her friends would be leaving for Terhofstede the next day. That morning the history teacher's wife had left with their daughters for a holiday park in the woods; he was going to join them there tomorrow.

"I don't know," Laura said.

It was the first time she'd been to his house, a house that in no way went against her expectations. For, in fact, she'd had no expectations at all. At least none that made a difference now: well-filled bookcases with hefty biographies of Alexander the Great, Napoleon and Adolf Hitler, a stereo installation with tall, black speakers, framed photographs of the Landzaats at a beach somewhere, Jan Landzaat building a sandcastle with a pail and shovel; also a few pictures of older people, their own parents probably, and a photograph of the teacher standing beside his wife on the stairs of some building, he in a suit and bow tie, she in an ankle-length bridal gown, both of them smiling.

"We don't *have* to go anywhere," he said. "We could just stay here."

He hadn't shown her the rest of the house. The bedrooms. She wondered whether she would get to see them, or whether he would try to limit her presence here to the couch. *The bedroom,* she decided; she wasn't going to settle for the couch.

"I don't know," she said again.

The role of indecisive young thing fit her perfectly; let the older, more experienced male take the initiative. She lifted her legs up and tucked them under her, stuck the tip of her thumb in her mouth for a brief moment. "I'm kind of tired," she said.

"You've barely had any wine," the teacher said. "Are you hungry? I could fry some eggs, we can eat them here, then talk a little or watch some TV. Does that sound good?"

She shrugged. His fingers were toying with her hair now, close to her ear. It wasn't unpleasant, but at the same time she suspected that he knew all too well what women and seventeen-year-old girls liked and didn't like—or he'd picked it up from some magazine or book, the erogenous zones and how to tinker with them best. Jan Landzaat was an experienced lover, as she had noted on the two occasions when he had taken her to a hotel along the highway outside Amsterdam. Too experienced, maybe. Studiously experienced. He took his time, he was no slouch. He knew what he was doing, she had nothing specific to complain about, but still, it always felt more like gymnastics than ballet, more like a point-perfect exercise on the balance beam than a dance that drew you in, than movements that could thrill. He was patient, attentive, he waited for her—the first time there had been a few misunderstandings as he looked at her with big, questioning eyes, whether she was there yet, whether he

himself could start in on the final cartwheel before the landing. Laura looked at the history teacher's grimace of effort.
She saw everything: a blue vein pounding on his left temple,
the glow of the nightlight beside the hotel bed reflecting
off the saliva on the long teeth in his half-open mouth, his
somewhat-too-large Adam's apple bobbing up and down as
though he were struggling to swallow something—a chunk
of meat, a herring—that was stuck in his throat. At such
moments, doubt struck. At first she had been curious about
the body of a grown man, but after a few times the teacher's
gymnastic routine seemed mostly ridiculous. She thought
about Stella's stories about Herman—about his clumsiness.
In her sophomore year Laura had had a boyfriend, Erik, who
was now no longer at the Spinoza Lyceum. They were both
very young, of course, and one evening—they were sitting
beside each other on the bed in her room, Laura had turned
off the light and lit two tea warmers—he confessed to her
that he was completely ignorant, that she was the first girl he
had really kissed, and that he was embarrassed by his inexpe-
rience. Laura took his face between her hands and whispered
sweet words in his ear. Comforting words. It didn't make
any difference, she thought he was sweet, he should just relax
and surrender to her completely, then everything would turn
out fine. It was glorious, she thought, Erik's tender, virginal
fumbling; when she closed her eyes she thought of a snowy
landscape, a landscape without footsteps, a gentle rise covered
in fresh snow where no one had walked before, while she led
his hands and fingers to where she wanted them. Other boys
had followed, boys like Erik, who all thought that girls like
Laura—girls who were much too pretty—would be put off
by boys who didn't know the first thing about sex. And,
one by one, she reassured them. *Let me do it. Close your eyes.
Do you like it when I do this? And this? You don't have to swill*

your tongue around like that, it's not homework, look, just the tip, like this, and real softly, come on, take some of this off, this only gets in the way. She helped them take off their sweaters and T-shirts, to loosen their belts—sometimes it made her feel like a mother undressing a little child, but that only made it more exciting.

"I have to go to the toilet," Laura said; she put down her glass of wine beside the plate of peanuts.

"End of the hallway, second door on the left," Mr. Landzaat said.

The toilet turned out to be a full bathroom as well. Before sitting down she inspected her face in the mirror above the sink. This evening she had gone for the no-makeup face, she saw the red blotches on her cheeks, probably from the wine. No personal items were out in the open, she would have to look inside one of the cupboards or drawers to find out which perfumes and creams the history teacher's wife used. In a glass on the sink was one toothbrush—the toothbrushes belonging to Mrs. Landzaat and the girls were doubtlessly in a glass too at the moment, but in the bathroom of a cottage in the woods.

Laura hiked up her black leather skirt, lowered the toilet seat, and sat down. She closed her eyes tightly and suddenly wasn't sure she'd be able to let Mr. Landzaat lead her to the bedroom later on. She stood up, flushed the toilet just for appearances, and looked again at her red, blotchy face in the mirror. She longed intensely for clumsiness, for boys like Erik—like Herman.

A hair had fallen in the sink, she saw as she opened the tap and splashed cold water on her face. A long, black hair, her own. Mrs. Landzaat was a blonde. After a bit of a struggle,

Laura succeeded in sliding the black hair away from the wet bottom of the sink and picking it up between her fingers.

She was about to toss it into the wastebasket under the sink when she stopped and reconsidered. Actually, it wasn't so much an act of reconsideration as a flash of inspiration, maybe even a brilliant one.

Holding the long, black, wet hair between her fingertips, Laura looked around the bathroom. On the inside of the door, two terry cloth kimonos hung on a hook; Mrs. Landzaat had probably figured that the kimono was too bulky for a week's stay in the woods. When Jan Landzaat entertained underage students here at home, nice girls who thought he was a cool teacher, he probably—after some playing around in the shower—let the underage student put on his wife's kimono, only to peel it off her again in the bedroom.

Laura hesitated between the pocket sewn onto the kimono and the collar, then slid the hair under the collar. Sooner or later Mrs. Landzaat would turn up the collar of her kimono and pull out the hair. A pensive look would appear on her face.

"Laura? Are you all right? Everything okay?"

His voice outside the door; how long had she been in here, anyway? She stepped over to the sink and turned on the tap.

"I'm coming," she said. "Be there in a minute."

And then, as she pulled back her hair and looked at her own smile in the mirror, she had another idea—an idea that was perhaps even more brilliant than putting the black hair under the collar.

She hadn't put on any makeup, but she had left her earrings in; little earrings, two gleaming gray pearls her mother had given her a few months back, for completing her sophomore year with such solid grades.

She took off one of the earrings. She leaned down and put it on the floor behind the toilet. Then she stuck a finger down her throat.

"Laura?" Jan Landzaat called from outside the bathroom door. "Laura?"

"I'm not feeling very well," she said when she opened the door at last. "I think I'd better go home."

30

HERMAN CAME up with the plan.

"We walk to the Zwin and back," he proposed on the third day. "And we don't say anything. Not a word. If we want to tell each other something, we do it with sign language. But let's try to keep that to a minimum too."

It was around three in the afternoon, they were having a late lunch of bacon and eggs. Miriam Steenbergen, the newcomer to the club, had just a bowl of muesli with fruit.

"And the one who says the least, wins," she said. "For every word, you get three penalty points."

Herman didn't even bother to look at her. "It's not about points, Miriam. It's not a contest. It's about the experience. What happens to you when you're not allowed to talk? When you walk out of doors and the only thing you hear is the birds? Birds, the wind, and the sound of the waves."

Miriam had only recently become David's girlfriend; a week before the fall vacation started, he had called Laura.

"Who is it exactly?" Laura had asked, because she couldn't connect the name to a face.

"Blond hair, almost to her shoulders," David said. "She's in the parallel class. Friends with Karen."

"Sorry, David," she said. "I really don't know who you're talking about."

"Remember the field trip to Paris? When we were all at the hotel bar. When you and Landzaat . . . they were both there too. Karen and Miriam."

Because Laura still couldn't put a face to the name, and because David couldn't see her anyway, she shook her head and rolled her eyes. "Oh, her," she said. "What about her?"

Then David started in on a long story, a story with lots of details—so many details that Laura knew right away that things were serious between David and this faceless girl. First he'd gone to the one café, then to another, and then back to the first one and was just about to go home—when Miriam suddenly wandered in. He had never really noticed her before, he admitted (which helped to explain why Laura had also been unable to link any physical attributes to the name Miriam), but on that particular evening, four days ago now, her face had suddenly been "beaming," he didn't know how else to put it—and while she was beaming their eyes had met.

Laura knew exactly what he was talking about. Last summer she had seen Stella beam like that, but she didn't tell David.

"You always figure it's a cliché from some romantic movie," David said. "Until it happens to you. The light had a lot to do with it; she came in out of the darkness into the light of the café, then semidarkness when she came over to me, but the light never left her face, like the heat of a fire, the glowing ashes after the fire is already out, I mean."

At this point Laura couldn't suppress a yawn, she covered the mouthpiece with her hand so David wouldn't hear, but that probably wasn't even necessary. He was so caught up in his own story—it had already been going on for at least fifteen minutes, Laura reckoned, and seeing as they hadn't even made it out of the café yet there was no end in sight. Still, she didn't dare to interrupt her friend or tell him to get on with it; David was a kind and quite handsome boy, but for as long as Laura had known him he had never had a girlfriend. Deep in her heart, she knew why; it had to do with the way David shrank from every form of physical contact. A shock went through his body whenever you simply laid your hand on his forearm; at more intimate moments of contact—an arm around his shoulders, a hug, a kiss on the cheek—he would shudder as though you had dropped an ice cube down the front of his shirt. After that happened a few times you stopped touching David, to keep it from happening. David and a girl together, that thought had never occurred to her before, it was something you almost didn't dare consider, almost as unimaginable as what your parents did in bed.

"So I was thinking," David said fifteen minutes later, after the story had ended in Miriam's room. "It's up to you, Laura, it's your house, but I was thinking: it's all so new, I can't just leave her alone now."

Laura didn't help him, she didn't say: *But there's no reason to leave her alone, just bring Miriam along.* For David's sake she was pleased, with his infatuation and his new girlfriend, but on the other hand she didn't feel like it at all, a new face—especially not a face she still couldn't place. "So what I wanted to ask is whether Miriam could come along to Terhofstede," David went on, at the moment when the silence between them had started to grow painful.

"Do you think that's a good idea?" Laura said. "I mean, you haven't known her that long. None of us know her." She hated herself for being so purposefully obtuse, but on the other hand she wanted nothing more than to hear her best friend thrash about.

"Maybe you're right," David said. "Maybe I should just stay here. With Miriam."

"Don't be such a jerk," Laura said, hoping that David

wouldn't hear the shock in her voice. "Of course you're coming along. And if this Miriam is so important to you, then she's coming along too."

Two days later, in the school cafeteria, she saw David and Miriam together for the first time. Miriam was, above all, short, with a round face that could best be described as "open." And—she had to hand it to David—she really did beam. "Hi!" Miriam said to Laura. "David has told me so much about you, I bet we're going to be good friends." And then Miriam leaned over in order to—as Laura realized too late—kiss her on both cheeks.

"Yeah," Laura said as she—there was no way around it now—kissed Miriam back. "About you too."

For a moment she wondered whether all the things David had told his new girlfriend about her also included her affair with Landzaat, the history teacher, but the next instant she realized how ridiculous it was to wonder about that. Everybody knew about it, after all, everybody except the teachers. But that was what teachers were there for, to have no idea of what was really going on at a school.

The affair had lent her a certain status, albeit not always in a positive sense. Sometimes she picked up on the things that were being said behind her back. According to some of the boys, she was a "slut," and some girls called her a "whore," but most students thought it was pretty much "cool" and "fresh" for a girl to turn up her nose at her contemporaries and seduce a grown, experienced man. A married man at that. A blackmailable man. In fact, no one doubted that it would end that way, that the revelation of Laura's relationship with Landzaat would destroy his marriage.

From the start, what irritated Laura most about David and Miriam was that they couldn't keep their hands off each

other. Here, in the middle of the cafeteria, where at least
five hundred students were at that moment sitting or standing to eat their sandwiches, ordering coffee and sweet iced
cakes from Arie, the cafeteria manager, David was plucking
at the back of Miriam's purple sweater, then putting his arm
around her waist and pulling her up against him. Miriam,
in turn, never let go of his sleeve, holding him by the wrist
and caressing the palm of his hand with her fingers. Every
twenty seconds she turned her head to one side and planted
a little kiss on his throat, which was as high up as she could
get without standing on tiptoe.

It annoyed the hell out of Laura, she had no desire to
be around all this plucking and pecking. It reminded her of
a thirsty man coming in from the desert, a castaway who
had spent weeks bobbing around on a raft, or, even more,
of an emaciated stray, a starving dog that wolfs down two
pounds of hamburger, plastic packaging and all, without taking a breath—and vomits it all back up the next minute. She
looked at Miriam and asked herself what was with this little,
beaming girl, whether she had been out in the cold for too
long as well and had a lot of catching up to do, or whether
she was just stringing David along. Not much chance that she
had ever been with a boy who was as wild about her as he
was, Laura decided, and was about to walk away when Herman suddenly joined them.

"Hey," was all he said as he looked from David to Miriam, and he took a step back when Miriam tried to kiss him
on the cheeks too.

"Miriam may be coming with us to Terhofstede," Laura
said, noticing the way Herman's eyebrows shot up for a moment.

"Well," he said. "That's nice . . . for David." His gaze

crossed Laura's—more than a meaningful look, it was above all one of desperation. *Do something!* his eyes begged her. *Come up with something!*

"We still have to discuss the sleeping arrangements," Laura said. "I mean, is it . . . have you talked to your parents about it? Do they know that there will be boys going along?"

"My father's a gynecologist," Miriam said, as though that explained everything. "And my mother has already met David, she thinks he's darling."

Then they started kissing, not just a little bit, but the whole hog, they pulled out all the stops. Through their cheeks Laura could see their tongues at work, and she in turn tossed a desperate glance back at Herman.

"Can I get you something?" Herman said, nodding toward the counter at the back of the cafeteria. "Coffee? I hear there's a special on pink glacé cakes today."

Beside the exit to the bike shed, they found a vacant table.

"Yes, it's certainly nice for David," Herman said. "But that's about all you can say for it."

"Yeah," Laura said. She tugged at the plastic wrapper of her glacé cake, but when it didn't tear right away she laid it unopened on the table.

"Did he drive you nuts too?" Herman asked. "With that story about how he met her?"

Laura burst out laughing. "Yeah! You too?"

"First one café, then the other, then back to the first one . . . I thought I was going out of my mind. But okay, he's my friend. When a friend's talking, you let him finish, even if it's all a load of bullshit."

"But still . . . I'm happy for David, really, but . . ."

"Maybe he should have shopped around a little longer. Let's be frank about this, Laura. We're glad our friend has a girlfriend, but—tell me if I'm out of line—there's something about this Miriam that is incredibly irritating. I could see it on your face right away, just now, when I came up to you guys."

"Yeah, I don't know exactly what it is. Maybe that she tries to act so nice and spontaneous. The way she tries to kiss everyone right away. The way she hangs on David."

"He hangs on her too. We can't blame the poor girl for that."

"No, but right in the middle of the cafeteria? I don't know, it seems so . . . so childish."

She pulled the glacé cake toward her. Herman took hold of the plastic and tugged on it gently. "May I?" he asked.

"Go ahead, I'm really not hungry."

"No, that's not what I meant . . ." He took the plastic packaging between his teeth and tore it open. "Here you go."

"I don't feel like having a girl like that around the whole week in Zeeland. But I can't tell David that, can I? What I don't get is that he can't figure it out for himself."

Herman shrugged. "What do you expect? Love is blind. Young people in love. The most glorious thing there is."

Laura couldn't help laughing, but when she looked at him he looked away and pretended to be absorbed in the packaging of his own cake.

"Yum," he said. "You know, there's no expiration date on these things anywhere. Maybe they're timeless cakes. How does yours taste?"

Laura didn't answer, she waited patiently until he looked at her again.

"I was thinking," Herman said, laying his cake back on the table. "I talked to David about it a bit, and he thought it was a good idea. But then, in the state he's in now I don't know whether he's any good to me. That's why I wanted to approach you about it."

Finally, he looked at her. And Laura looked back.

"What?" she said.

She clasped her hands behind her head, leaned back in her chair, and shook her hair loose. Then she pulled it up into a sort of knot and let it fall again. Meanwhile, she kept looking at Herman—maybe she was imagining it, but it looked as though his face had turned a fraction of a shade darker.

"So I was just thinking," he said quickly, sliding his cake back toward him. "The last time in Zeeland. In fact, we didn't do anything then. I mean, not *really* anything. We made those drawings for Lodewijk's sick mother, of course, but when we were all doing that together it occurred to me: This is fun, isn't it, making something together like this? Voluntarily? Doing it for Lodewijk's mother, after all, was really sort of volunteer work, right?"

Laura was only half paying attention, she wondered whether maybe she should try something else with her hair, but decided to listen anyway.

"But Lodewijk's mother is dead now," she said.

"Exactly. That's what I mean. There's nothing we *have* to do. But that's no reason for us to do *nothing*. Maybe, in fact, it's the only real reason to do *something*." He pushed the cake away again, to the edge of the table, and then halfway over it, until it was just teetering on the edge. "My idea was this: We don't take anything along with us to Zeeland. Nothing that isn't our own. No music, no magazines or newspapers, no books, only our own things. Michael's saxophone, Ron's guitar, Lodewijk's bongo drums if need be, and I'll bring my movie camera. I bought this really simple camera about six months ago. Eight millimeter, made in East Germany. It doesn't even have a battery. You have to wind it up. Anyway, here's the idea: we don't read anything, we don't listen to anything, there's no TV in the house anyway, so that's easy. We don't let ourselves be influenced by the outside world. We go shopping and buy enough for three days. And then we see what happens. What happens inside your head when you're not allowed to do anything. No, wait a minute, I'm putting that wrong: we're allowed to do anything, we're just not allowed to fall back on things from outside. People get bored and pick up a book, but isn't it a lot more interesting to see what happens with you when you *don't* pick up a book? Oh yeah, and Lodewijk has a tape recorder. We'll take that along too. We can record things if we feel like it. Music, conversations, stories. I think it will be great. An experiment. Maybe it will bomb and we won't do anything at all. But even then you can't really say that it failed. Then the conclusion of the experiment is simply that, apparently, we don't do anything."

Herman brought his finger down hard on the edge of the glacé cake, which shot up high and flipped a few times, but before it could fall he plucked it out of the air.

"Oh!" Laura said.

"That's a trick," Herman said with a grin. "You can learn a trick if you practice long enough. But creating something new, you can't learn that, you only find out about it by doing it."

He took the cake between his fingers and squeezed it until it was completely flat inside the packaging. "Sorry," he said, "I don't mean to sound like someone who knows how it all works. Like a teacher." He looked straight at her as he spoke those final words, and now it was a struggle for Laura not to blush. "So what do you think? David thought it was a good idea. Back before he fell in love."

"So what are you going to film?" Laura asked.

"What?"

"What you're going to film. I didn't even know you had a camera. I guess you've already filmed some stuff."

"Oh, lots of things. With David. For instance, I went over to the flower stand—there's a flower stand across the street from my house—and David filmed me from the window. We live on the third floor—and I waited until a couple customers came along and I fell onto the ground in between all those people. It was really great, I'll show it to you sometime. Those people don't see the camera, and I act like I'm in a bad way, I have a seizure, a sort of epileptic fit, and then they help me to my feet and I just walk away. You see the people and the man who runs the flower stand talking to each other, like: 'What was that all about?' Fantastic!"

Laura tried to picture it, Herman having fits in front of a flower stand. She looked at his twinkling eyes and laughing face and she couldn't help herself, she started laughing too.

"Oh Jesus!" she said. "You mean you just went and *did* that?!"

"We did it one time with Miss Posthuma too. During study hall. David went up to her desk, supposedly to ask something. And I sat all the way at the back with the camera. She had no idea at all that she was being filmed. So David acts like he's going to ask her something, and she looks up at him, and then David slowly sinks to the ground and starts flapping his arms and legs around, having a spaz attack. Oh, it's so . . . I keep the camera on David for just a few seconds, then I zoom in on Posthuma's face. Priceless! That lady is so clueless! No, she's not even really clueless, it's something else. It's the face of someone who has never experienced anything in her whole life, and now all of a sudden she has. And we got that on film. For posterity."

"Oh, you guys are terrible!" Laura laughed. "It's pathetic!"

"You're right. It *is* pathetic. But not because of what we did. It was already pathetic, even without us. What time is it anyway?"

"What?"

"Next period we've got that physics exam, right? Did you work on it?"

Laura felt her face grow hot, while her stomach seemed to fall a few yards, like in a Ferris wheel going down. "Is that today? I thought it was after the fall break!"

Herman looked at her, then put down the glacé cake and laid his hand on hers. "Don't sweat it. You can call in sick, right? Then just make it up after the vacation."

"Karstens isn't going to believe that. I rode into the bike shed this morning at the same time he did. He even said good morning."

"You could suddenly get sick. Even deathly ill." He grinned, took his hand off hers, and held up the package with the cake in it. "From eating a glacé cake that was long past its expiration date, for instance?"

Laura tried to laugh, but only half succeeded.

"Oh, I'm such an idiot!" she said. "I wrote down the wrong date in my diary. And it's not the first time." She looked at her watch. "Five more minutes . . . What are you doing, Herman?"

Herman had pulled the plastic wrapper off his cake and was holding it in front of her face. "Take a couple of bites. Then stick your finger down your throat. Throw it all up. Here, on the table. Then I'll help you down to the concierge's office, to report that you're sick. I promise."

Laura stared at him. He smiled at her, but it was no joke, she could tell by the look on his face, he really meant it.

"But . . ." *But I'm too chicken to do that,* she almost said, but that suddenly seemed like a bad idea. "What about you?" she said instead. "Then you'll be too late for the exam too."

"Don't worry about it," Herman said. "I didn't study for it either." He leaned over, picked up his backpack, and put it on the table. "On purpose," he went on. "I wrote down the right date. But then I thought: of all my exams, this may be the best one not to study for."

"Oh?" Laura's expression invited further explanation, or at least tried to, but at that moment she was more concerned about the test and what she was going to do. Karstens, the physics teacher, was a little man; in the bike shed this morning he had remained seated on his bike for as long as possible, he never got off until he thought no one was looking, then he heel-toed it to the classroom, where he hoisted himself up onto his high stool and never came down again. "Leprechaun Karstens" was what the kids called him, but from that stool he exercised a real reign of terror. He laughed openly at the girls for their scant aptitude for the exact sciences, he humiliated them in front of the whole class in order to boost his popularity with the boys. There was no way in hell she could tell Leprechaun Karstens the truth: that she had written the exam down wrong in her diary, and whether she could please make it up at a later date. She could already see his beady little eyes, like those of a squirrel, or more like those of a magpie or crow, an animal that seems to be listening carefully to you but then suddenly pecks you right in the face. *That wasn't very smart of you, young lady . . .* She could already hear him say it, then he would address the whole class. *Miss Laura here has failed to study for her exam. Are there any other candidates who would prefer to move right along to the school of domestic sciences?* She had heard that Mr. Karstens had children. Unthinkable, that a woman could tolerate this sneaky little man beside her in bed without vomiting.

"What is it?" Herman asked. "What are you laughing about?"

"No, I was just thinking: if I think about Leprechaun Karstens long enough, I might not even have to eat that cake."

That made Herman laugh too.

"Sure, why work yourself into a lather for a reject like that?" he said. "That's the conclusion I've come to. I've had it. I can't force myself to do it anymore. I have to get out of here. Having mediocrity poured all over you, hour after hour, it's bad for your mental health. It's a physical thing with me too. I start itching all over, I break out in a sweat, I start stinking. A classroom, it's a sickness, bacteria everywhere, and the source of the infection is up at the front of the class."

In Herman's face Laura saw something she'd never seen before, something grave, the ironic tone he tended to adopt had almost disappeared.

"But you could leave, right?" she said. "Go to another school, I mean?"

"I wouldn't do them the favor. No, they're going to have to *send* me away. They'll have to say it right to my face. 'We hate you, Herman. We'd be glad to get rid of you.' But of course they don't dare to do that, it would mean they've failed as a school."

"But how can you do that, *make* them send you away?"

"You can always do something. *I* can do something. It's a sickness, that's the way you have to look at it. You finish your finals, but by then you're already contaminated; you graduate, and you're terminally ill. There a couple of possibilities. You can blow up the school building, but that wouldn't help; they'd just rebuild it, here at the same spot or somewhere else. You can also combat the source of the infection. Smoke out the whole mess. With whatever it takes.

In a sick body they do it with penicillin, with radiation, or chemicals. First you have to draw up a diagnosis. Maybe it's going to take insecticide or agricultural pesticides, maybe it requires sterner measures. And even then, the question is whether doing that would solve anything. It's like being attacked by an army: you can mow them down by the hundreds, but they keep coming. The teaching colleges churn out thousands of new ones each year. But hey, *I'm* not the one who's going to take those measures; first of all, I'm no doctor or healer, but what's more, I'm not going to risk my own future. Under the present legal system, the healers are the ones who go to prison for years, maybe even for the rest of their lives. I don't want to do them the favor."

He rummaged around in his bag and pulled something out. A movie camera, Laura saw. A little, flat model without a handgrip. Herman began turning a crank on the side of it, and Laura remembered him talking about the windup mechanism.

"There's only one thing I ask of you in return," he said. "I'll help you with the hall monitor later on and everything. And I'll tell Karstens that you went home because you were deathly ill. In exchange, I'm asking you for permission to film you as you vomit all over the table. I promise that I won't do anything with it without asking you first, Laura. You'll be the first one to see how it turns out. Slap a nice sound track under it, you'll be amazed."

She didn't quite know what to say, how to react.

"The cap," she said at last, pointing at the lens of the camera that Herman now had pressed against his left eye. "You forgot to take off the lens cap."

.   .   .

At this hour of the day, just before lunch ended, there were usually crowds of students hurrying to their classes, but now the main hall was uncommonly still. The hall monitor was not in his glass booth. Laura glanced at her watch, then at the big clock above the entrance.

"It's only three minutes before," she said. "Where is—?"

"Look, there," Herman said.

He pointed to the corridor to the right of the stairs, where a group of students and a couple of teachers had gathered.

"Karstens," someone said, when Herman and Laura began edging through toward the physics lab. "Probably fainted," someone else said.

The classroom door was open. In front of the board, which was covered in equations, was the table and the teacher's high stool. Of Leprechaun Karstens himself you could see only his legs sticking out from under the table, his legs and a pair of buffed black shoes; one trouser leg had crept up a little to reveal a brown sock and a stretch of pale, hairless shin. The rest of his body was blocked from sight by two men squatting beside the table. "Hello, hello!" they heard one of the men say, and recognized the voice of Joop, the hall monitor. "Are you awake, sir? Can you hear me? Help is on the way. Hello, sir, are you still there?"

She looked over and, because Herman was nowhere in sight, turned all the way around.

There he was, his back pressed up against the wall on the other side of the corridor, the movie camera held up to his left eye and aimed at the door of the physics lab.

"Well there you have it, Laura," he said when she came over to him. "If you had studied for that exam, it would all have been for naught."

In the distance she heard an ambulance howl.

31

THEY LEFT the house in midafternoon.

"We start as soon as we get past the gate," Herman said. They were standing in the kitchen waiting for Miriam, who was still on the toilet. "After that, not another word. We walk to the Zwin and back. Only when we're back inside are we allowed to talk again."

On the long, straight road from Terhofstede to Retranchement they were all still a little gigglish, but once past the last houses of the village their expressions grew serious. Lodewijk walked alone out in front, followed by Michael and Ron, and at a little distance by Stella, Herman, and Laura. David and Miriam walked a ways behind the rest, their arms around each other's waist.

At first Laura hadn't been sure what to think of the whole idea—a typical boy idea, she thought, perhaps even a typical *Herman* idea—but as she climbed the steps up the dike and down the other side into the Zwin, she had to admit to herself that it worked, that something was happening, at least in her. In the distance you could hear the waves break on the beach, a gull dove with a shriek; and then there was the wind, rustling through the bushes and thistles. It was indeed as though, after holding your hands over your ears for a long time, you could suddenly hear again, really hear, each separate sound. Somewhere back on the other side of the dike a church bell tolled and she counted the strokes—four. After the fourth stroke the silence was overtaken again by the waves, still too far from them to see at this point, and she felt flooded by . . . a feeling of happiness, she thought at first, but that wasn't it; it was located somewhere lower down, more like in the pit of her stomach. She looked around, wondering whether the others felt the same thing, or at least something similar, but at that point there was no one else close by, no one to look at her and see the joyful—no, that wasn't it, it was something else for sure—expression on her face. Lodewijk had just disappeared behind a stretch of dune, Michael and Ron were too far away, and David and Miriam were still at the top of the steps across the dike—kissing, Laura saw, and she looked away quickly. Only Herman and Stella were close enough, but Stella was peering into the distance, her arms crossed, and Herman had pulled out his movie camera and was panning slowly, in a full circle.

The night before, Herman had asked everyone to stay in the top-floor bedrooms for fifteen minutes, until he called them to come down. When they came down, they saw that he had tacked a white sheet to the wall in the living room, and arranged all the available chairs in two rows. "A night at the movies!" he shouted, twisting the knobs of a projector he had set up atop a stepladder. "At home I always play some music in the background, but now you'll just have to imagine that part."

When Ron asked how Herman had smuggled the projector all the way to Terhofstede, Stella said, "He had it in his duffel bag. I wasn't allowed to say anything. It had to be a complete surprise for everyone."

The first movie was the one that showed Herman falling to the ground in front of the flower stand; there was something undeniably comic about it, and they all laughed. Unintentionally comic, to a certain extent, Laura thought: when Herman fell to the pavement in front of the flower vendor and his two customers, then went into a feigned spasm—waving his arms and pedaling in a half circle with his feet against the paving stones—you could see even more clearly how skinny he was; the jeans and short-sleeved T-shirt he wore made his bare arms look like pure skin and bones. As he spun around, the T-shirt crept up and revealed the pale, slightly hairy stomach that Laura had seen the night of David's party. She couldn't help but think of spaghetti, spaghetti that stood rigid and upright in the pan at first, before sinking slowly into the boiling water.

"Look," Herman said. "Check this out."

The flower salesman was watching Herman flounder about from a safe distance, as though unsure how to react to the situation. But the two customers—a middle-aged woman and a girl, a mother and daughter probably—reacted as though he were some poor misfortunate who had taken a nasty fall. The older woman leaned down and touched Herman's shoulder, upon which he jumped to his feet, shook the woman's hand, and then calmly walked away from the flower stand. "Watch this," Herman said. "This is good." The women turned and consulted with the flower vendor, who took a few steps forward and watched as Herman exited, bottom screen left. "Look, David got this just right," he said. "He doesn't follow *me* with the camera, he keeps it on the people who stayed behind. We didn't agree on that beforehand. It's brilliant."

The woman, the girl, and the flower man looked like they were still in a quandary about what they'd just witnessed. The camera had now zoomed in further, you could clearly see the flower vendor's shrug and his arms lifted in the universal gesture for *Don't ask me.* "This is beautiful," Herman said. "You toss a stone into a pond. All we're seeing now are the ripples that the stone caused. In a full-length movie you would have to go on until the water was completely calm again. The woman buys her flowers and pays for them. She goes home with a question in her mind. She can't stop thinking about it. But then I guess the roll was finished, right, David?"

What came next were shaky, unfocused images, shot in an elevator from the looks of it, in which Herman and David shook their fists in close-up, then took turns giving the camera the finger and shouting. "What are you guys saying here?" Lodewijk wanted to know, but no one answered him. "Wait," Herman said. "Watch this." Now David appeared on the screen. He walked casually down the aisle in a classroom, until he got to the teacher's desk. "Posthuma!" Michael said. "Oh, Christ!"

"Wait," Herman said. "Watch this." David leaned down over Miss Posthuma's desk, as though he was going to ask her something, then slid slowly to the floor. First the camera remained briefly on David, who was trying to simulate an epileptic fit by spastically moving his arms and legs, then it zoomed in on Miss Posthuma. "Watch this," Herman said. "Watch, watch, watch . . ." By now Miss Posthuma's face filled the entire screen, she was looking down at David, who was presumably still flopping around on the floor, but then suddenly she looked straight ahead—straight into the camera too. Initially it was hard to tell whether she saw the camera and Herman; she just stared into space a bit, almost in a kind of trance, her slightly watery eyes seemed to look right past the camera, but then her lips started moving, they formed words, a sentence. There was no sound, they couldn't hear what the English teacher was saying, but there was no longer any doubt that she was speaking directly to the camera. To the cameraman. To Herman.

"You never stopped filming!" Michael said, and there was both amazement and admiration in his voice. "What's she saying here, Herman? What did she say to you?"

"Wait!" Herman said. "I want you to look. At that face. Do you see it? Can you see it happening?"

Miss Posthuma's lips were no longer moving, the camera zoomed out very slowly. David, who had apparently stood up in the meantime, crossed the screen on his way back to his desk. Then the camera stopped moving, Herman didn't zoom out any further. Miss Posthuma was still sitting motionless at her desk.

"This is it," Herman said. "This is the moment. A grown woman who has never experienced anything, suddenly experiences something. Only she doesn't realize yet what it is."

"And didn't she say anything else?" Ron asked. "I mean, you kept filming her the whole time. Didn't she send you to Goudeket or something?"

"That's the whole trick," Herman said. "Don't stop too soon. If I had stopped filming after David got up again, it would have been nothing. We would have had nothing. Now we have the image of a woman in all her astonishment at life. Both her own life and the lives of others."

"How old are you two, anyway?" Miriam asked.

"Do you remember that old game?" Herman said, as though Miriam hadn't spoken. "Ringing doorbells, but then not running away? I did that with my friends when I was eight or nine. You ring somebody's doorbell, and when they open it you say: 'Oh, that was stupid of me! I forgot to run away.' It's sort of like that. The same astonishment. The same expressions. The only difference being that we didn't have a camera back then. Afterward I realized that doing that was actually a pity, I mean with Posthuma. I bet her amazement at the mystery of life would have been much greater if we hadn't filmed it. Now it's sort of like a nature film. Animals drinking. A giraffe at the watering hole thinks it hears something, or sees something. That's how Posthuma looks. As though she's seen something moving in the water. But she doesn't realize that it's a crocodile floating there, she still thinks it's a log."

"Did you really use to do that?" Michael laughed. "Ring doorbells and then just stand there?"

"I bet you two think you're really funny, don't you?" Miriam said. "Tormenting the poor woman like that."

"You see it all the time," Herman said. "The giraffe thinks it was mistaken and goes on drinking, and suddenly the crocodile spurts forward and drags it underwater. Sorry, Miriam, I wasn't finished yet. Did you have a question? Was it for the director or for the actor?"

The only thing projected on the sheet now was a bundle of white light, the reel spun wildly, the film came loose and began looping over the projector, then over the floor. Herman stopped the reel with his hand and turned off the projector.

"No, I was only wondering what you two think you're doing," Miriam said. "If you want to act like idiots in front of a flower stand, okay. But Miss Posthuma, she's an awfully easy victim, isn't she?"

David, who was sitting beside his girlfriend on the couch, laid his hand on her forearm, but she pushed it off right away. "Miriam . . . ," David said. "Miriam, maybe you shouldn't take it so seriously."

"David, my dear, I don't take *you* seriously at all," Miriam said. "Don't worry about that. But Miss Posthuma . . . The way she looked . . . so, so . . . helpless. I think that's taking things too far, that's all."

"But that's precisely it," Herman said. "Like you said: helpless. Those animals in the nature films are always helpless too. It's not the strongest animal in the herd, but the *young* gazelle that is pulled underwater by the crocodile or mauled by the lion. So pitiful! But still, we keep watching."

"But it's not a nature film, Herman!" Miriam said. "Miss Posthuma isn't an animal. I think you talk about it too easily, like it's suddenly not a person anymore but some animal in a nature film."

"We're animals too, of course," Ron said. "That's what we are, whether we like it or not."

"Miriam," David said. "It's just a joke, don't take it so personally."

"You can also look at it from a different perspective," Herman said. "Why, in fact, is Miss Posthuma so helpless? She's a teacher. Are all teachers helpless? Not if you ask me. What we're seeing is someone who has lost their way, an old, weak creature that has wandered away from the herd. Like you said: an awfully easy target. Is that also what you say when you watch lions or crocodiles tearing apart that old buffalo? 'Come on, guys, that's a bit too easy, isn't it?' Things have to eat. It's natural selection. Teachers aren't helpless. It's more like a herd, a herd consisting of individuals of an extremely mediocre species, true enough. A school of gray fish: as long as they stick together they're better armed against attacks. Inside a school building they don't have to worry much and can just go on talking through their hats with their boring stories, hour after hour, they don't give a shit that everyone fell asleep a long time ago or has already died of boredom. Outside, in the wild, you can cut one off from the herd. Then, all of a sudden, their blathering doesn't mean a thing. They'd probably shit their pants right away if you drove them into a corner. In real life, all that bullshit about physics equations won't get you anywhere. And that lousy English Miss Posthuma tries to teach us is even worse. *How do you do? My name is Hurman.* Give me a break! What if you were attacked on the street in some slum in Chicago or Los Angeles. What do you say then, Miss Posthuma? *How do you do?* Or do you say something else? Something that fits the situation a little better? *Shut the fuck up, you sick fuck! Go fuck yourself!* Which syllable receives the main stress in the word 'motherfucker'? Hello, Miss Posthuma? Hello? Shit, she fainted. Oh, no, she's dead."

First David started laughing, then Michael did too. Lodewijk glanced at Laura and raised his eyebrows. "How are you doing otherwise, Herman?" he said.

Then everyone had to laugh, Herman almost harder than the rest—everyone, that is, except for Miriam. It took something like thirty seconds before Laura saw it: Miriam was crying.

"Miriam?" she asked. "Miriam, what's wrong?"

She was weeping almost soundlessly, only sniffing now and then and wiping her eyes with the sleeve of her sweater. "Don't you hear it?" she said quietly. "Don't you guys hear what he's saying?"

David put his arm around her shoulders and pulled her up against him. "Miriam . . ."

"And you too!" she shouted, so loudly and so suddenly that it startled everyone else. "Shut your face with that 'Miriam' shit!" She pushed David's arm off her shoulders and stood up—in two attempts, the first time she didn't push hard enough and landed back on the couch. "Fuck! Cunt!" she screamed: two words Laura hadn't expected to hear coming from this round, open face that wanted to kiss you on the cheeks all the time. "Go fuck yourselves, all of you!" She was already at the door, she yanked it open and slammed it so hard behind her that a candle fell from its candlestick on the mantel and landed on the floor; right after that came the sound of hiking boots pounding up the stairs to the attic, where another door slammed with a loud bang.

Laura looked at David; like everyone else, probably, she expected him to get up and run up the stairs after his girlfriend. But David remained seated.

"Well," he said, "I guess that's clear enough."

The one who did get up was Stella.

"Where are you going?" Herman asked—his voice didn't sound threatening, perhaps, but there was something about it that made Stella blink.

"Just up to her," she said. "I don't . . . I don't like this at all."

"Sit down," Herman said.

Stella's jaw didn't quite drop, Laura noticed, but almost. "What did you say?" she asked.

"What I'm saying is that you should sit down for a bit before maybe going up to her. And in fact, I don't think you should go up to her at all."

Laura glanced over at David, but he had his head down and was pretending to pluck at a piece of lint or something on the thigh of his jeans.

"When someone's hysterical, you have to let them calm down first," Herman went on. "During the initial phase, you can't get through to them."

No one said a word for quite a while after that. Laura caught herself staring at something on her lap too.

"Well, shall I go then?" Lodewijk said. "Then it's not so clearly a girl coming to comfort another girl."

They all had to laugh at that, a laugh that broke the tension and brought relief, and they looked at each other again; even Stella, who was still standing at the door, laughed a little.

"I wish you all the success in the world, Lodewijk," Herman said. "But I don't give you much of a chance. No, really, I think it would be better if we waited a bit."

In the silence that followed, Laura pricked up her ears, but didn't hear anything from the attic.

"Maybe I overdid things a little," Herman said. "I completely realize that not everyone thinks those films are funny, but you can talk about that without getting hysterical about it right away, can't you? I mean, did we fight like this last summer? Or at school, the last few months? That's what I'm trying to say. In fact, I don't think we ever argued at all before that cow came along."

Laura glanced quickly at David again. David was no longer staring at real or imaginary bits of lint on his trousers, but at a spot somewhere on the floor; when Laura followed his gaze she saw, close to one of the table legs, the candle that had fallen from the mantelpiece.

"Aw, well," he said, "maybe we should just let her calm down a little."

Without meaning to, Laura looked over at Stella, her best friend, who was still standing with her hand on the doorknob—her former best friend, she corrected herself. After what happened during the summer vacation, the most you could say was that their friendship had normalized. Stella had stopped keeping Laura on the line with lengthy accounts of all-too-intimate details of her relationship with Herman, and Laura in turn had tried to do everything in her power to act *normal*. Laura hoped that one day they could be best friends again, maybe after Stella broke up with Herman, but deep in her heart she didn't believe that anymore. It was like getting a spot on your dress, or on your favorite blouse; you pour salt on it right away, you wash the blouse at two hundred degrees and the spot is gone. But the colors have faded too—you hang it in the closet and never wear it again.

Now, however, Laura and Stella looked at each other almost like they used to, and Stella rolled her eyes, breathed an inaudible sigh, and nodded toward David, who was still slouching on the couch. And Laura nodded back, to show that she agreed with her friend. *What a wimp, not to stand up for his girlfriend. Cow or no cow, any kind of man would have gone after her right away.*

Lodewijk stood up. "Shall we do it then?" he said to Stella. "You can take care of the girl things and I'll represent the 'practical boys' standpoint."

"Maybe someone should go who's a bit more neutral," Michael said. "Ron or me. Or Ron *and* me. I mean, you're Herman's girlfriend, Stella. And you, Lodewijk . . . yeah, how shall I put this . . ."

"Yes?" Lodewijk said, grinning broadly. "Do tell. What was it you were going to say, Michael?"

"I don't have to explain that to you, do I?" said Michael, grinning back. "At least, I hoped I wouldn't have to explain that to you."

"I'll go with Stella," Laura said. She got up. "Better that way. Just girls. Women . . . I almost said 'woman to woman,' but that reminds me too much of my mother."

"And then?" Herman said. "What are you two going to say?"

"You don't even want to know, sweetheart," Stella said. "Just be glad you're not there. Right, Laura?"

.   .   .

Miriam was sitting on the edge of the bed, her head in her hands, her suitcase open at her feet; there were clothes in it that looked as though they had been pitched in there in a hurry. Yes, Miriam was the only one of them who brought a suitcase; that too said something about who she was, Laura knew, even though she wouldn't venture to say exactly what.

Stella and Laura did the things one does in such cases. They sat down on the bed, on either side of Miriam. Stella put an arm around her. Laura said: "I think you shouldn't take it so hard. It was nothing personal. Herman never means it personally. Right?"

At that final *Right?* she leaned forward a little to look at Stella. But Stella had just put her head up against Miriam's and didn't look back.

"I figured, I'm going home," Miriam said through her hands, which were still in front of her face. "I wasn't going to stay here another minute. But then I thought about how late it is. There's probably no bus at this time of night, I figured."

"But that's nonsense, isn't it?" Stella said. "To go away because of something like that. It's nothing personal, it never is with Herman."

It took a full second before Laura realized that Stella hadn't even heard what she, Laura, had just said. Miriam was sitting up now, she'd taken her hands away from her face.

"That's me, Miss Practical," Miriam said. "I want to go away, but the first thing I do is think about the bus schedules. That's what makes me so different from you, that's why you all think I'm a cow."

Laura knew that one of them—Stella or she—should now say something like *Hey, where did you come up with that? We don't think you're a cow at all!* But she knew how contrived it would sound, so she waited for Stella to say it.

"You people don't even see it," Miriam said, before the

silence became too painful. "I'm probably the only one who does. That's why he hates me. And because of him, you all hate me too. No, no, you don't have to say anything, don't bother, I wouldn't believe you if you did. Tomorrow I'll be gone. Then you can all go back to your happy-go-lucky little lives without a practical cow like me around to get in your way."

Miriam hadn't bothered to wipe the tears off her face— maybe she had just forgotten, or maybe she simply didn't care, Laura thought. The wet spots that gleamed under her eyes and on her cheeks did not make her round face any prettier, and that was putting it mildly. Laura was reminded of the little boy who lived upstairs in their building, she babysat for him sometimes to earn a little pocket money. He was about six, a spoiled little six-year-old boy who started crying whenever he didn't get his way. Laura never let him have his way, at least not right away. She would watch him as he started to cry and stamp his feet, for as long as it took to make her wonder how anyone could love an ugly child like him. Only then did she give him the lollipop or the extra spoonful of sugar on his yogurt that he'd been whining for the whole time.

"What makes us happy-go-lucky?" she asked. "And why shouldn't you be that way too?"

Now Miriam finally used the sleeve of her sweater to wipe her face; the wet spots became red smudges. "I don't really know if you want to hear that," she said. "And whether I feel like telling you about it. Besides, Stella's with Herman. No, it's not a good idea."

For the first time since they'd sat down here on the edge of the bed, Stella looked at Laura. "That doesn't matter," she said, rolling her eyes a bit. "Really, it doesn't, Miriam. Even I don't like *everything* about Herman. I think those films are funny, but I know exactly what you mean. That sometimes it seems like they don't take it into account, David and Herman, how nasty the experience can be for someone else."

"Aw, David . . . ," Miriam said: it seemed like she was planning to say more, but she only wiped two fingertips across the spots under her eyes.

"What?" Stella asked. "What were you going to say?"

"I don't know," Miriam said. "I mean, I think David is really sweet, but when I'm here I also see how spineless he is. I don't know if I really wanted to see that. Whether I can go on with him now that I've seen that side of him, I mean. And then I see him in that movie with Miss Posthuma and I think: *That's not the way you are, you only do that to act cool around . . . around . . .* Oh, just listen to me! Who am I to say that's not the way he is! I've only known him for about a week."

And what about us? Laura thought. *Do you think we're spineless too?* She looked at the girl's round, teary face and suddenly she found it unbearable to think that this Miriam, who—it was true, she'd said so herself, hadn't she?—had known them for barely a week, was already equipped with judgments about who was spineless and who wasn't. She braced herself, in her thoughts she stood up from the bed and said something. Something like *Well figure it out for yourself, Miriam. You really are a cow. It was more fun last time, when you weren't with us.* But she didn't get up.

They hadn't heard the footsteps on the stairs, there was only a little knock and the next moment the door opened. Herman was standing there.

"Excuse me," he said. "I hope I'm not intruding, but before things get completely out of control, I want to say something too." He took a step forward. "To you, Miriam." There wasn't much space in the bedroom, Herman's legs were almost touching Miriam's knees, she had to tilt her head all the way back to look at him.

"I want to tell you that I'm sorry," he said. "I'm not going to say that I'm sorry about the movies, because David and I really had fun making them, but maybe I ranted on a bit about Miss Posthuma. I think you're right, Miriam. After all, they're people too, teachers. I went too far. I'm sorry about that."

"Okay," Miriam said.

And then Herman leaned down, he took Miriam's head in his hands and laid his own head on her hair. "So will you come downstairs and make us happy? David's a bit confused too, but I know he'd be very glad if you came down."

Herman had turned his head to one side, his cheek against Miriam's hair, his face turned to Laura, not to Stella.

As he was saying that Miriam should come downstairs and make them happy, he looked at Laura and winked.

32

WHEN HERMAN came over and walked beside her on the beach, Laura couldn't help thinking about that wink. They had left the thistles and the tidal creeks behind; David, Miriam, and Stella had almost reached the waterline. Ron, Michael, and Laura paused to wait for Herman, but he gestured to them to walk on, without taking the camera from his eye. In the distance, in the direction of Knokke, they saw a dot that could only be Lodewijk.

When Ron and Michael walked on to meet the others by the water, Laura slowed without really intending to. Herman still had the camera held up to his left eye, he kept his right eye shut. Above the sound of the surf and wind, Laura could hear a rattling from inside the camera, a toilsome rattle like an old, un-oiled clock.

First Herman filmed the beach—literally the beach, the lens pointed down at the sand. Then he walked past Laura and turned around. Standing with his back to the sea and walking backward, he slowly panned up until he reached her face.

"I'm going to tell you something now," he said. "You don't have to say anything back if you don't want, but then at least I have it for later. On film."

He had spoken very quietly, but Laura still glanced up

past Herman at the others. They were too far away to hear anything above the sound of the waves, she thought. She looked back at the lens, and at Herman's closed right eye.

"You're the only one I've ever wanted, Laura," he said. "Ever. I thought maybe it would go away, but it only gets worse. You don't have to say anything, it's enough if you just keep looking. I see it, I can see it."

He halted, less than ten feet from her. There were two things she could do, Laura realized. She could keep on walking, past Herman and the camera, out of the picture. Out of his picture, out of their picture—forever. Or she could stand still.

She took three more steps, then stopped. She looked straight into the lens. She didn't say anything, she *thought* what she wanted to say.

"With me, it happened right away," Herman said. "At David's party, the first time I met you. Was it like that right away for you too, Laura? At that party?"

She didn't answer, she didn't nod or shake her head. She kept looking straight into the lens.

Yes, she thought, *for me too.*

33

AFTER DINNER that evening, Herman set up the projector on the stepladder again and tacked the sheet in front of the window.

"There's one more little film I'd like to show you," he said. "Something we didn't get to yesterday . . ." He glanced over at Miriam and smiled. "But I promise, no more nasty jokes, Miriam. And definitely not at the expense of others."

They were all sitting or slouching on the couch, in the easy and less-easy chairs around the table. "It's not a very long film," Herman said, to explain why he hadn't set them up in a semicircle this time. "But I'm very curious to hear what all of you think."

First a flickering white light appeared on the sheet, then a title, written in capitals with black Magic Marker on a piece of cardboard: LIFE BEFORE DEATH.

"Michael . . . ," Herman said, and Michael picked up his saxophone, moistened the reed with his tongue, and stuck the mouthpiece between his lips.

Then a dinner table appeared on the sheet, a man and a woman eating across from each other, above the table was an antique hanging lamp. "My parents," Herman said. "That's all I'm going to say. I just want you all to watch."

The man and woman at the table didn't look at each

other, they used their knives and forks to cut the food on the plates in front of them. In the foreground was a third plate. That plate was empty.

At a snail's pace, the camera moved closer. Michael began to play, a simple, rather sad melody line that seemed vaguely familiar to Laura, but she didn't know why—something from a movie, she thought.

The camera angle lowered, the cameraman had taken a seat on the remaining chair, now he zoomed in on the empty plate, then panned up to the man, to Herman's father.

For a moment the man kept chewing, then he raised his napkin to his lips, wiped them and looked to the right, into the camera. There was something in the way he looked, Laura saw, as though he was doing his best to look amused, but his eyes were empty and dull. The corners of his mouth curled up in a failed attempt at a smile. Still looking into the lens, he said something, there was no sound, they couldn't hear anything, but the lips moved as they spoke a short sentence. Panning quickly, the camera moved to the far side of the table and the woman was on screen. Herman's mother. She too looked straight into the lens. She was wearing glasses with black frames that curled up slightly on top, which gave her a catlike look. She too smiled at her son—a dejected smile it was, sad, but it was real. Then you saw a hand holding a wineglass. Herman's mother took a sip, then quickly another, now she was no longer looking into the lens but straight ahead, at the spot across the table where Herman's father was seated. It wasn't really a look, more a sort of gaze, the way you gaze at a fire that is slowly going out. The camera started moving again, apparently the cameraman had stood up and was backing off slowly, until the dinner table with the two parents eating at it once again filled the entire frame.

"I recognize it," Lodewijk said, once Herman had turned

off the projector and Michael had stopped playing. "That music."

"Why's it called *Life Before Death*?" Ron asked.

"You tell me, Lodewijk," Herman said.

"It's what they play at military funerals," Lodewijk went on. "In America. At Arlington! Now I remember, one of those military cemeteries, outside Washington, DC, I think, with all those rows of white crosses. I saw it on TV a while ago, some documentary about Vietnam. A coffin with an American flag draped over it, and then a soldier with a trumpet. Damn, it was a trumpet, not a saxophone! But that was good, Michael. If I'd known you were so good, I would have asked you to play that at my mom's funeral."

They were quiet for a moment, probably all thinking about Lodewijk's mother's funeral a few months back, Laura supposed. It had been at a hilly cemetery somewhere close to the dunes. And because his father wasn't around anymore either, Lodewijk, as the only child, had organized the whole thing himself: from the color of the mourning cards (a purple border instead of the customary black) to the music (two French chansons, his mother's favorite music: *"Les Feuilles Mort"* sung by Yves Montand, and *"Sous le Ciel de Paris"* by Juliette Greco). Lodewijk had followed his mother's wishes to a tee. Just before the summer vacation, a few weeks before she died, a sound had woken him in the middle of the night. He went to see what it was and found his mother in the big recliner in the parlor, in front of the window; by then she could barely move on her own, it was little less than a miracle that she'd been able to get from her hospital bed to the chair. The bed was a real hospital bed, as Lodewijk had explained to his friends, one of those with a motor-driven head and foot end and metal rails along the sides. It had a metal bar with a cord and a handle, so she could pull herself up, and an alarm button that sounded a buzzer you could hear in the parlor of their own house and in the house of the helpful neighbor lady.

On that particular night his mother was sitting at the window in her white peignoir, a notepad on her lap, the curtains open; she hadn't turned on the lamp, she was writing by the faint light that came from outside.

"Oh, Lodewijk," his mother said when she saw her son in the doorway; she had trouble breathing, Lodewijk could see her chest move up and down in the semidarkness. "Oh, my sweet boy."

On the notepad she had jotted down the last instructions for her funeral, and the names of those who were to be invited. It wasn't all that much: the way her name should be noted on the mourning card, that she wanted to be cremated, and that the coffin was to be closed.

"Sometimes they make a little window in the coffin," Lodewijk told his friends. "So you can catch a last glimpse of the person's face. She didn't want that. During those final weeks her face had turned all yellow. And swollen. She didn't want people to see her that way; those last few weeks before she died she stopped receiving visitors too, and she wanted people to remember her real face."

That's the way she'd written it down, it all fit on one page of the notepad. First her name: her first name, her husband's surname, a hyphen, and then her maiden name; beneath that the word *Cremation,* and then below that the two words concerning the little window: *Closed coffin.*

The rest of the little page was filled with the names of those who could come to the funeral. All the way at the bottom she had written *Lodewijk's friends*: he could decide that for himself, who and how many (or how few) of his friends he wanted to invite.

Lodewijk had pulled up a chair and sat beside her. At first they sat there in silence, but then his mother suddenly said that what she really regretted was that she wouldn't get to see Lodewijk's back.

She spoke very softly, Lodewijk had to lean over closer to her lips to make out the words.

"What did you say?" he asked. "What is it about my back?"

It must have taken a minute before his mother answered.

"That I won't get to see you go out the door and into the world," she said at last. "That I won't be around anymore."

They were already past the stage of lying to each other, the stage when his mother still regularly asked Lodewijk whether he thought she looked horrible, and when he replied each time that it really wasn't that bad—because he still assumed that that was what she wanted to hear. One afternoon she'd asked him to fetch a mirror for her, the little mirror in her makeup bag, and Lodewijk had pretended to search long and hard in the bathroom (he had found the makeup bag right away, in a little drawer among the lipsticks and eyebrow pencils his mother had stopped using long ago), then came back to say that he couldn't find it; fortunately, his mother had fallen asleep while he was gone. And when she woke up an hour later she had forgotten about the mirror, or at least she didn't mention it anymore.

No, that phase was far behind them. Which is why Lodewijk didn't say, *What are you talking about? I'm going to graduate next year. You'll be there for that, in any case.* He didn't say anything at all, just laid his hand on hers, clasped her thin wrist with his fingers.

"I'm actually very happy," she said. "I'm pleased you have such nice friends. That makes me happy. That you have your friends to fall back on, later on."

A few months earlier, before the summer vacation, when his mother could still walk, they had gone one Saturday afternoon to buy herring from the fish stand around the corner. She walked one step at a time, and had to stop every few steps to catch her breath. Lodewijk had had plans to go with his friends that afternoon to a rock concert in the Amsterdamse Bos, and he was just putting on his jacket to leave when his mother called him. "I suddenly feel so much like having a herring," she'd said. Lodewijk offered to pop out and buy her one, but then he saw the look in his mother's eyes. When they got to the herring stand she no longer had the strength to stay on her feet; from the back of his stall the fishmonger brought out a plastic chair for her. "It's so nice to be able to do this," she'd said. "To do this with you, while we still can." It was the last time they went to the herring stand together.

"I want to tell you just one last thing, sweetheart," his mother said now. "And I want you to keep it in mind. You are who you are. Always keep being yourself."

Lodewijk waited, expecting her to say more, but the only sound was his mother's labored breathing in the dark. After school tomorrow, he thought, he would bring her a herring. Two herrings, so they could eat them together. After a few minutes he lifted his mother in his arms and carried her back to her bed, she weighed almost nothing these days, no more than a full bag of groceries.

Another thing Lodewijk had arranged for the funeral was that, after the French chansons were over, the coffin was not to be lowered through the floor. But that was the way they always did it, the funeral home people tried to explain to him: after the final piece of music or the last speech, the coffin disappears. It sinks into the ground, down one level, to where the ovens are. But that seemed too dramatic to

Lodewijk. "No, not even dramatic," he said. "Completely kitschy." He was reminded of what his mother had said about him being who he was. Himself. There were no speeches. After the final notes of *"Sous le Ciel de Paris"* they all shuffled slowly past the coffin, then outside. It was a lovely day, everyone was happy to be out in the fresh air again, Laura recalled. The trees around the cemetery were big and old, and birds were singing. Somewhere just outside the cemetery they heard the clang of a railway crossing, and then the hiss of a train passing at high speed. There was food and something to drink in the auditorium, but most of them soon took their glasses or coffee cups back outside. They stood there for a while, talking beneath the trees. Here and there people were laughing again. Beside Lodewijk's group of friends there were a few of his mother's more distant family members, plus her sister and a few cousins, a few colleagues from the office at the music school where she had worked for the last six years after her husband died.

Laura couldn't help but notice the way people glanced furtively at her father. As always, the famous face gave no sign that it noticed the glances; it was only eleven-thirty, and Laura's mother and he were the only ones who had already poured themselves a glass of red wine. She heard her father telling Lodewijk that the music was lovely, then he started in about a woman he'd had as a guest on his show, a university professor who had written a book about coping with bereavement.

The original idea had been that Lodewijk would move in with his mother's sister, who had a house in Arnhem, a city where, he said, "no one should ever want to live." If he moved to Arnhem he would have to start over at a new school, and what was maybe even worse, he would be too far from his friends. Friends who, as the aunt also understood by now, were very important to Lodewijk at this difficult moment in his life, and who could perhaps do more for him than some vague family member he had visited only on four Sunday afternoons a year throughout his youth. For a very short time the aunt had considered moving temporarily to Amsterdam, but—to his great relief—had finally abandoned the idea (which Lodewijk referred to as the "worst-case scenario") as too impractical.

At the very end of the funeral, when almost everyone was getting ready to drive back to Amsterdam, Laura and Lodewijk were standing together when the aunt came to say goodbye. She was a little woman, just like Lodewijk's mother: she had to stand on tiptoe to kiss him on the cheeks.

She had barely turned away when Lodewijk wiped both cheeks with the back of his hand and made an ugly face at Laura.

"Blech," he said quietly, but in Laura's mind still a little too loudly. "At least we've got that out of the way."

Laura burst out laughing. "So what now?" she asked. "What are you going to do now?"

Lodewijk stepped up and put his arms around her. "I'm a poor little orphan now, Laura. Will you take good care of me?" He had laid his head on her shoulder as he hugged her, but then he pulled back and looked at her. He was grinning broadly—looking relieved, mostly, Laura saw.

"You can always come and live with us, you know," she said. "Meals, a room, there's plenty of space."

"Thanks. But first I want to see how it goes on my own. Throw open the windows. The first thing is to get that hospital smell out of the house."

Laura went by Lodewijk's house a few days later, and was struck by how light it was, so much lighter than when his mother was still alive. There were empty pizza boxes on the parlor table, and dozens of garbage bags lined up in the hall.

"What's all that?" she asked.

"My mom's clothes, mostly. And all those sweaters and vests she knitted for me."

Laura looked at him, she wanted to say something, but didn't know quite what.

"I need to do it now," he said. "Later on I might grow sentimental. Get attached to all the wrong things. I want to make a new start. Can you still smell it?"

"What?"

"That hospital odor. It had seeped into everything. Into the curtains, the bedding, even my clothes. But I sponged down the whole house, and I kept all the windows open for three nights."

Laura sniffed, she smelled something, but it wasn't a hospital, more like cleaning products and soap—and a vague, oniony smell, probably from the pizza boxes.

"You still can't get that Herman off your mind, can you?" Lodewijk asked suddenly.

"What?" Laura said. "What are you talking about?" *Don't blush,* she told herself. *Don't blush, not now.*

"Laura, sweetheart, you don't have to play make-believe with me. I saw the way you looked at him at the funeral. How you looked at him *the whole time.* And I can't blame you. He *is* a bit skinny, and he's certainly no Mick Jagger, but I know what I would do if I were you. I know what I would do *myself.* That type. Not really masculine. Wonderful! I can stare at that for hours."

Laura looked into Lodewijk's eyes and saw something she had never seen before: the new Lodewijk, a Lodewijk who would no longer wear knitted sweaters, who would be who he was from now on, the way his mother had made him promise, who had chased away the hospital smell and would be himself.

"Ron asked why you named that movie *Life Before Death,*" Miriam said. "I'm curious about that too."

"I'm glad you mentioned it," Herman replied. He was back at the dinner table now, and at first it seemed as though he was teasing Miriam as he put on a mock earnest expression and closed his eyes for a moment, but when he opened them again he smiled at her. "That you *both* asked. No, but seriously. Life before death. Because that's what it is, because that's what we're seeing. Two adults who have nothing more to say to each other just go on living. They stay together 'for the children's sake,' as they say. But the only child in the house is me. They didn't ask me a thing. That's too bad. I can see their situation from a greater distance. I could provide them with advice."

"But your father's got someone else, doesn't he?" Miriam said. "It could be that he'd rather be with that other woman, but that he doesn't dare to go away. Precisely because he has a child. Because he has you."

Laura saw how Herman's expression suddenly stiffened; it lasted less than a second perhaps, Laura looked around at the others, but she was almost certain that she was the only one who'd seen it.

"If my father were to ask my opinion, I would strongly urge him to buzz off as fast as possible to that cute new girlfriend of his," Herman said. "I would tell him that he's not doing me a favor by sitting at the table with that bored, deadpan face of his. But maybe your parents are nice, Miriam? I don't know. Maybe you do have parents like that. They do exist. I know a couple. Laura, for example, has nice parents."

Laura was startled to hear her name, she didn't dare to look at Herman, but then she did anyway. And Herman looked back. She counted to three, then lowered her eyes. Right away she felt the heat rising to her cheeks; she rubbed her fingers over them in the hope that no one else had seen. The way he had looked at her! She'd never been looked at that way by a boy. She was used to a whole spectrum of other looks: languorous looks, yearning looks, hopelessly infatuated looks—thwarted looks, above all, yes, if there was one thing that all those looks had in common it was the realization that permeated them: that they didn't stand a chance. That she, Laura, was simply a bridge too far for most boys.

Herman's look was different: as a matter of fact, he had never tossed her a losing glance, she realized now for the first time. Never once. From the moment he had spoken to her beside the ransacked table at David's party (*So you're Laura*) up to his declaration of love in the midst of silence, just a few hours ago on the beach.

If we were here alone now, he said during the whole three seconds in which he held her gaze, *we'd know what to do. We've had to wait for months, Laura, we have a lot of catching up to do.*

"Still, when I hear *Life Before Death,* I tend to think of something positive," Miriam said. "Not that you're already dead and just go on living, but that you get everything out of life before you die. You know what I mean?"

Herman looked at her, and this time his expression didn't harden; an amused smile appeared on his face.

"See how easy that was?" he had said to Stella and Laura the night before, after he apologized to Miriam. They were standing at the foot of the attic stairs, Miriam had gone to the bathroom to wash away the worst traces of her crying jag. "She's not very smart," he said. "She's just oversensitive, I think that's sweet."

Later that evening Miriam settled down on the couch with a book of crossword puzzles. Herman raised his eyebrows, then poked Michael and then Lodewijk and Ron too.

"What have we here, Miriam?" he'd asked, when he could apparently contain himself no longer.

Miriam was concentrating so closely on her crossword puzzle that she didn't hear Herman the first time around.

Laura remembered the tense silence that had come over the group then, when Herman called out in a sarcastic tone: "A crossword puzzle!" And then again, but this time with a slightly different stress: "A *cross*word puzzle!"

"Well, what's wrong with that?" Miriam had asked.

"Nothing," Herman had answered. "Nothing at all. One has crossword puzzles, and that's a fact we have to live with. As long as no one feels the need to solve them, there's not much of a problem."

"What kind of self-inflated bullshit is this, Herman? Is this off limits too? Like all the rest? TV, newspapers, the— what do you call it again?—'non-self-made music'? Are we only allowed to read really impressive books? Well, I don't happen to like reading, and there's no TV here. So maybe I can do something for myself, so that I don't get bored? Or would I be better off sitting still and thinking deeply?"

Laura glanced at Herman, then at the others. David was busy again examining something on the thigh of his jeans, Ron and Michael were sitting on either side of Herman, their arms crossed; they were looking at her almost reprovingly, as though she had done something that really could not be tolerated around here. Lodewijk was in the easy chair by the fire, reading, or pretending to. Stella was at the table writing, a letter probably, every two days she wrote a long letter to her mother.

The way Herman looked at Miriam, though, was anything but a rebuke; he seemed, above all, amused.

"Miriam," he said, "you shouldn't take things so personally right away. Yet you brought it up yourself. Listen, as far as I'm concerned, you don't have to do anything. But apparently, when you think you get bored. At least that's what you said. Is that right? Do you feel bored when you think?"

Miriam let the book of puzzles fall to her lap, she took a deep breath and tapped her pen against her front teeth.

"What's wrong with crossword puzzles, Herman? You still haven't successfully explained that to me."

"Nothing, in principle, but I said that already. I only wonder what goes on in the mind of someone who is searching for another word for 'sailboat.' With seven letters. I can't help but think that it's mostly a way to kill time. And time doesn't need killing. Time is our friend. As long as we learn to experience it."

At that point Miriam surprised Laura, and everyone else too probably, by bursting into laughter. "Oh, Herman," she said. "How lovely! Are you going to give us yoga lessons? Or is it meditation? What exercises must we do precisely in order to experience time? Our *friend* time?"

Even more surprising perhaps was Herman's reaction; he stared at Miriam, speechless, for half a second, then started laughing too. "Sorry," he said laughing. "Yeah, now I hear myself too. I hear myself talking. I'm going to try it one more time, if you'll permit me, Miriam. What goes on in your head while you're solving a crossword puzzle?"

Once again, Laura thought she was the only one who had seen it, but this time she was less certain: the half second of total panic in Herman's eyes when Miriam laughed at him.

He had regained his footing with lightning speed though, it's true, within that half second he had found the emergency exit.

"I think about things," Miriam said. "Or maybe I'm fretting about something. Then I start on a crossword puzzle. Ten minutes later I've forgotten what I was thinking about, what I was worrying about. I'm busy solving something. Something *outside myself.* Something that has nothing to do with myself and my own, limited way of thinking. One hour later I've finished the whole puzzle. And I've totally forgotten what I was fretting about. I can recommend it to everyone."

"Okay," Herman said. "That's clear enough. At least it's clear enough to *me.*" There was still a bit of doubt and hesitation in his voice, but his tone was no longer sarcastic—he smiled at Miriam. "I won't keep you from it any longer."

That had been last night. Laura remembered that she hadn't liked it much, this sudden mutual respect between Herman and Miriam. Above all, things mustn't get too cozy between those two. She wondered whether Miriam was really as stupid as Herman had thought—and whether he himself realized now that he had been mistaken.

All in all, Laura would rather have seen it end in a new clash and a crying jag, she'd even considered trying to steer it in that direction—but decided against it, it would have been too obvious.

Now she was glad she'd kept her mouth shut. Miriam had changed from the "dumbest" girl in the group to an ally within the space of a single evening. That could prove handy later on, when Herman told Stella how things stood. She didn't have much to worry about as far as the others went, she figured. Michael and Ron always sought confirmation from Herman before doing or saying anything. David was still solidly Herman's best friend, albeit a friend without a backbone. Lodewijk, in fact, was the only free agent in the group. Lodewijk always spoke his mind right away; there was no doubt about it, he had become stronger since his mother's death.

Laura looked at Stella sitting beside Herman, her arm slung around his shoulders. Right after dinner Herman had announced that he was going to the garden to smoke a cigarette. Laura was just heading into the kitchen with a pile of dirty dishes, and as he passed he brushed her forearm gently.

Laura found him behind the shed.

"I'm going to tell her tonight," he said.

"Tonight, when?" Laura asked.

"Before bed, in any case. It's painful. It's going to be real nasty. But still, it would be weird . . . Anyway, that would just be weird."

Laura leaned into him. He tasted of tobacco smoke, he was indeed very thin beneath his T-shirt, she could feel the bones sticking out under the skin of his hips and then, when her fingertips reached the front of his body and crept up slowly, his ribs. But his tongue was less clumsy than she'd expected, based on Stella's detailed reports.

"Come on, let's go inside." He pushed her away gently, he was panting. "If someone sees us like this . . . if they find us out here . . ." He tugged softly on her hair. "That would not be good," he said.

It was long past midnight. They had gone on chatting for a while about the movie Herman had made of his parents. In the end, Herman agreed with Miriam that *Life Before Death* was perhaps not the best title after all. Then he had talked a bit about the script he and David were working on, for a longer movie this time. A feature film about a high-school revolt. The uprising would begin after a teacher had wrongly sent a girl out of the class, but unrest had of course been brewing within the student body long before that. At first it was to be a purely idealistic uprising, a revolt against injustice, but as the days and weeks passed—the students had occupied the whole school, the teachers were being held hostage in the gym, the building was surrounded by the police and the army—the leaders of the uprising would be faced with increasingly difficult decisions. To press home their demands, they forced a teacher to stand blindfolded at one of the classroom windows.

"All the other windows have been covered with newspapers," Herman said. "So then you've got a number of possibilities. Either the students have no way of going back and really have to hurt the teacher in order to maintain their credibility, or else the blindfolded teacher is the signal for the army to rush the building. The revolt is brutally crushed."

And at that point Stella stood up and stretched.

"I think I'll go upstairs," she said. "Are you coming up too?" she said to Herman.

"I was thinking . . . ," Herman began, but then fell silent.

"What?" Stella said.

"Shall we . . . I don't know . . ." He stood up, he didn't look at Stella. "I actually feel more like taking an evening stroll. Just the two of us."

The Book's the Thing

34

"I JUST wanted to tell you," you begin—but you stop as a truck turns into our street with rumbling motor and screeching brakes, making further conversation impossible. As we wait for the truck to pass—the white walls of its closed bed are decorated with blue letters: the name of a moving company, a cell-phone number and a website—I look at your face.

We're standing on the corner by the garbage containers; I had just dropped a bag into one of them, and when I straightened up, suddenly you were standing there. What started as a fretful look, as though you were trying to recall who I was, now made way for something probably meant to look awkward or shy. It doesn't suit you particularly well, an awkward or shy look, it's as though all the muscles in your face struggle against it—but maybe it's the first time they've ever tried it, and they just don't know exactly how.

Huffing and hissing, the moving van comes to a halt in front of the café across the street; two men in blue jeans and white T-shirts, also printed in blue letters with the name of the moving company, hop out of the cab and pull open the back doors of the truck.

"I wanted to thank you," you say.

I raise my eyebrows and wipe my hands on the back of my jeans. I could ask what you want to thank me for, or I could skip that and show right away that I know what you mean.

"Oh, that was nothing," I say, choosing the latter. *Anyone else would have done the same.* But I don't say that. Besides, it's not true. Anyone else would have done something different. No, that's not true either: anyone else would in any case never have done what I did *for those reasons.*

For the moment there's nothing else left to say, so we both look at the moving van in front of the café, where the two movers have now gone inside.

"No, really," you say. "You wouldn't have had to. My wife is very grateful. And so am I."

The men come back out with a pile of chairs.

"One time you would go in there and they wouldn't have any milk, the next time it would take them half an hour to bring you your beer," I say, "by which time, of course, the head on it had gone completely flat. But that they'd go out of business *this* quickly, I never expected that."

"I've been thinking," you say. "About what you asked me last week. Last Saturday. At the library."

"You said you don't give interviews anymore. Almost no interviews. Or only by rare exception."

"That's right. But I'm prepared to make an exception. For you. What was it again, what did you say it was for?"

"For . . ." I suddenly can't remember what I said at the library. *For a website?* Could be, but I really can't remember. "As part of a series," I say. "A series in which writers—"

"Would next Tuesday be all right for you?" you interrupt.

"Tuesday? Tuesday's fine."

"It's a date. We're going to H. again for a few days, but we'll be back by Monday at the latest. Tuesday's the annual Book Ball at the theater. We don't have to be there till nine. So if you could come by around five . . ."

35

WE'RE IN your study: a plain desk, an expensive office chair and bookcases—your wife just brought us some tea and cookies.

Are you dreading the gala this evening?
"Yes and no. I feel a certain reticence, but that always goes away as soon as I'm past the red carpet. Aren't you going to record this?"

No, that won't be necessary.
"But you're not taking notes either."

No.
"You'll be able to remember everything?"

Probably not. But that doesn't matter. It's about the information as a whole. Didn't you once say: "A writer shouldn't want to remember everything, it's much more important to be able to forget"?
"By that, I mostly meant that you need to be able to separate the useful memories from the useless ones. It's handy if your memory does that for you. But it almost never works that way. We remember things that are no good to us. Phone numbers. I once read somewhere that when we memorize phone numbers we're misusing our memory. Phone numbers can be written down. After that we're allowed to forget

them. And that we should use the space then freed in our memories for more important recollections."

Do you need evenings like this evening?
"What do you mean?"

I mean, are they indispensible? Or could you, for example, just as well stay at home?
"No, not indispensible, certainly not. As I said, they're a part of the whole thing. You see a few friends. You talk to colleagues you never see anywhere but there. Once a year. And if you go, you have less to explain than if you don't."

You mention friends and colleagues. Does that exist, friendship among writers? Or do they mostly remain just colleagues?
"Among writers I have more colleagues than friends, if that's what you mean. A few of those colleagues also happen to be very good friends."

"Happen to be," you say. Does that mean that being colleagues makes it difficult to be friends?
"No, on the contrary. If you ask me, you can be good friends with a colleague whose books you don't particularly enjoy reading. And the other way around too: that a writer you think is good turns out to have an intolerable personality in real life."

Is that a hard-and-fast rule?
"A rule? How am I to see that?"

You should see it in the sense that perhaps it's always that way. That friendships can exist only between writers who find each other's work fairly ho-hum. That you can never be friends with a colleague who is more or less your equal, who writes books that stand comparison to yours. Let alone with a colleague who is better than you.

"Jealousy exists. Envy. Why do I sell much less than colleague R? Why does L always come in right at the top of the best-seller list? I mean, these days it's no longer such a circus for me when it comes to sales figures, but back in the days when I wrote the occasional bestseller, I felt as though I needed to apologize all the time. Sorry, my book is selling well. There are people who want to read my books. I'm so sorry. Next time I'll try to write something no one wants to read."

Among women, among girls, one often sees that a pretty girl chooses a very unremarkable girl as her best friend. Not an ugly girl, no, an unremarkable girl. The unremarkable girl's function is to cast her pretty friend's beauty into even sharper relief. At the disco, it's immediately clear that the pretty girl will get the pretty boy and the unremarkable girl will get the nerd. Is it that way with friendships between writers? That the successful writer, for example, surrounds himself with less successful writers? As "friends"?

"That's a striking comparison you make there. It could very well be. One does, indeed, rarely see two beautiful women who are best friends. That's too much competition."

Take your colleague N, for example.

"What about colleague N?"

At this moment, he's your most direct competitor. In your age category, perhaps your only competitor.

"You're right, he suffers from no lack of attention. Completely deserved, by the way. I should say that right away. *The Garden of Psalms* is also, without a doubt, his best book."

Do you really think so?

"Well, let me put it differently. *People* consider it his best book. The critics. My own taste is different, but he is good in his own way. I see that too."

But you don't wish you'd written it yourself?
"No, no, not at all. I mean, however good it may be, I find the style . . . the subject matter, how shall I put it . . . a bit too *easy*. And that title. Why not call things by their name?"

Would you have had a better idea for the title?
"Not right off the bat. I mean, I'd have to think about it. But *The Garden of Psalms* . . . I don't know, it's as though the title was already there before N used it. That's not good."

N recently changed publishers.
"Really?"

He hasn't done badly by the switch at all.
"But the important thing is the book itself, first and foremost. If the book's no good, all those posters around town won't help."

Do you really believe that? You sound a bit like your own publisher. "The book's the thing," isn't that what he always says? But do you believe that as well?
"Quality will always win out, I'm convinced of that. A good book can get by without posters or an author who speaks so glibly on all kinds of talk shows."

But isn't it also the times that are changing? Isn't "the book's the thing" just another way of saying, "in any case, we're not going to push it"?
"In the days when my books were still being bought and read widely, at least, that wasn't necessary."

You're referring to Payback?
"*Payback* was the first big success, but a few of the other books that followed didn't do badly either. *The Hour of the Dog* . . ."

But these days it's all subsided a bit, right? Liberation Year, *of course, is still "the new M." But do you mind my asking how many print runs it's had till now?*
"There's a new one coming up. But you should also know that the first print run was quite large."

What kind of numbers are we talking about here?
"I'd have to ask for the exact figures. But they're the kind of figures a debuting author could only dream of."

Until recently, you and your colleague N had the same publisher.
"That's correct."

In the interviews about his new book, N wasn't very complimentary about his former publisher.
"We found that rather bad form too. By 'we' I mean the collective authors. That kind of thing is simply not done. It's the kind of 'kick them when they're down' tactic one usually sees only on the soccer pitch."

But was he right?
"About what?"

Was he right to say that his former publisher, and now your publisher alone, has lost all contact with reality?
"He still has a very impressive list. One author who runs off can't change that."

But they're all authors who are closer to the grave than to the cradle, if I may put it that way.
"Age is not a factor here. There are plenty of examples of writers who only really blossom at an advanced age."

Do you count yourself among those? Do you feel that your best work is yet to come?

"I never think that way. I go from book to book. If I knew that I had already written my best work, I could just as well stop right now."

But meanwhile, the sales of N's latest book are astronomical.
"That's true, and I'm happy for him. I sincerely mean that."

Do you ever dream about that, that one of your books might take the bestseller lists by storm?
"The answer to that is the same as my earlier one. As to whether my best work is yet to come. I don't worry about bestseller lists. No self-respecting author should."

Let's talk about Payback. *Your most successful book to date. Do you also consider it your best book?*
"No, definitely not. People ask me that sometimes. But I wrote better books before that, and afterward, too, if you ask me. *Payback* took on a life of its own. Apparently, I struck a chord somewhere. An open nerve."

And which chord was that, in your opinion?
"A writer should never try to analyze his own work too deeply in retrospect. That can be crippling. Overly deep analyses by others can be fatal too. Sartre needed a whole book to interpret Jean Genet's work. After that, Genet never wrote another word. But all right, it was a long time ago, so I'll try to answer you. Even though I believe I've formulated that answer before this, so please don't expect anything earthshaking."

An "open nerve," you said. I've never heard you say that before. Personally, I find that much more evocative than a "chord."
"The particulars were well known. Everyone was shocked by that affair. Two young people—still children, really—do away with a teacher. Or at least make him disappear. No

body was ever found. I remember it so well, the newspapers of course weren't allowed to publish pictures of the culprits. To protect their privacy. But a couple of magazines did anyway. We saw their faces. A school picture. That girl with the long black hair. The boy with his blond curls. Not exactly two killers you would pick out of a lineup later on. Pick out of a lineup *in retrospect*. On the contrary. The girl was absolutely the prettiest girl in the class. But I looked hardest at the boy. He wasn't bad-looking either, maybe even more handsome than most of the other boys in the picture. But then handsome in a way not all girls like. I can't recall exactly what it was. A face that was a little too thin, a slender body. Gawky. What happens with a boy like that when the prettiest girl in the class chooses *him*? I asked myself. I saw a story in it right away. Just a story at first, then later it become a complete book. Did he do it for *her*? That was what I asked myself. That was the question I would try to answer by writing the story."

But that wasn't the nerve.

"No, the nerve was how recognizable it was. Every parent's nightmare. Children who look normal in a school picture may turn out to be killers. And not just the parents' nightmare. Also for their own age group. It's still one of the books read most often by high-school students. Could that boy or girl sitting beside me be a murderer? Does that nice neighbor, who always feeds the cats when we're on vacation, have his wife's chopped-up corpse in the freezer? They were normal children, the ones we saw in the school picture. Perhaps a little more than normal. A pretty girl, a handsome boy. Not losers."

There was also someone else in that picture.

"You've seen it?"

It's on the Internet these days. A number of other pictures too. The little house in the snow. The teacher's car. The nature preserve where he might be buried.

"That's right, that teacher was also in the school picture. I cut it out of that magazine back then and hung it on the wall above my desk. Every day, before I started writing, I looked at that picture for a few minutes. It was taken a couple of months before the murder, that's what made it so trenchant. *There they are,* I thought each morning. *There's the victim, and there are his killers. In one and the same classroom. He still doesn't know a thing. They don't know yet either.* At least, that was my assumption. That the idea came up only much later."

But in your book the idea came up beforehand. And not just after the teacher came by the holiday home.

"It was difficult. I struggled with the motive. Or let me put it another way: I simply couldn't believe that they would have done it *just like that.* And of course, *just like that* wasn't interesting for a book. In dramatic terms. Dramatically speaking, a murder is better if it's planned beforehand."

And do you still see it that way? What I mean is, did you actually believe in a murder that happened just like that, *but decided that a murder like that wasn't dramatic enough for your book?*

"That's an interesting question. I asked myself the same thing while I was writing it, and afterward too. Whether there really was a motive. That teacher had had an affair with the girl. She breaks it off, but he keeps bothering her. He goes to find her at the holiday home where she's staying with her new boyfriend. Motives aplenty, you might say. An adult—an adult in a position of power—imposes himself on a couple of minors. They could have reported him to the police. Maybe that wouldn't have helped much, but the teacher would have been fired at the very least."

But these days, do you believe a bit more in the just like that
theory? In the lack of a motive?

"There are any number of classic situations in which the
balance of power is out of kilter right from the start. In
which the stupid ones sometimes have more power than the
intelligent ones. The few intelligent ones, I should say. An
army, a prison. A sergeant humiliates a recruit who's smarter
than him. Guards torment a prisoner. At a high school, the
balance of power is not so very different. A high-school
teacher is not among the most intelligent of the species, and
that's putting it very mildly. A physics teacher will hardly
be the one to develop a new theory of relativity. Generally speaking, they're sort of stuck in the middle. Lame and
frustrated. You can keep that up for a few years with empty
talk about idealism and the transfer of knowledge to coming generations, but in the long run a frustrated intelligence
like that devours itself from the inside out. Teachers don't
stick around long enough to get old. That has nothing to do
with their ability or inability to maintain order. Day in, day
out, they stand in front of a classroom full of intelligences
just as mediocre as their own. In principle, things can go on
that way for years. But every year there are also a few people in the class who are more intelligent than them. They
can't handle that. Just like a soccer trainer who was once a
mediocre player himself, teachers will try to frustrate an
intelligent student wherever and whenever they can. The
soccer trainer makes his best player sit on the bench. The
teacher can't give low grades to the student who's smarter
than him. That student already gets those. Only mediocre,
hardworking students get good grades. The above-average
intelligence is bored to death in high school. A C-plus is the
best he can do. And so the frustrated teacher thwarts him
in other ways.

"Deep in his heart, what the frustrated teacher hopes for is that the goaded student will explode. You can go on tormenting a prisoner until he finally stabs a guard to death. In the barracks, the recruit who has been provoked will yank the machine gun out of the sergeant's hands and open fire. The employee who has been sacked returns to his former place of work and kills the personnel manager and his secretary before taking his own life. But that still happens only rarely at high schools. Whenever one or more of the students finally settles accounts, it's automatically front-page news. We are shocked by it. We are conditioned to have it shock us. A high school! What's become of the world when high schools are no longer safe? But we see no further than the ends of our noses. What has always surprised me, in fact, is that it doesn't happen much more often.

"For years, a student is made a fool of by a teacher—by an inferior, mediocre intelligence. One day the provoked student comes into the classroom to get even. He restores the natural order of things. Sometimes a student like that will go wild and wreak vengeance on the whole school. On the innocent. Innocent in the objective sense, perhaps, but seen from a broader perspective those are the stooges who are now getting a taste of their own medicine. The obedient students, the eager beavers who have spent all those years trying to cull favor with their teachers. The weaklings who have lowered themselves. During the nightly news shows after a massacre, all the attention focuses on the culprits. People say that they had been acting peculiar for years. They had watched violent films, of course, and played even more violent games on their PlayStations. The 'wrong' books were found in their bookcases and desk drawers. Biographies of Hitler and Mussolini. They also dressed weirdly or extravagantly, of course, and were severely withdrawn because they didn't take part in all kinds of school social activities. But then you can still wonder: Who is more disturbed? The student who wants to be left in peace, or the student who takes part voluntarily in all kinds of idiotic activities meant to develop his or her 'social skills'? In an army, it's always the socially skilled who volunteer first for an over-the-top suicide charge. Those who function well in a group will find it easier to herd the villagers together onto the village square. To torch the houses and then separate the men from the women."

In your book you chose to use the perpetrators' perspective. For the moment, let's leave aside the question of whether they were actually perpetrators in the usual sense of the word. Did you ever consider trying to meet with them? To ask them what happened? Or what might have happened, I suppose I should say.

"Of course I considered that. I would have been interested to find out more. On the other hand, though, I realized right away that it would curtail my freedom. My freedom as a novelist. As it was, the teacher's disappearance was only a pretext. I could fill in the rest myself. What do they call that: 'based loosely on the facts'? I was afraid that, if I actually succeeded in meeting the boy or the girl, I would hear things that would endanger my novel, the way I saw it in my mind's eye."

So you already had it planned out? Before you started?

"No, no, absolutely not. All I'm trying to say is that I didn't want to risk curtailing my freedom by being confronted all too abruptly with the facts. My imagination had to do the work. I've already told you about my premise. The relationship between the two of them. Pretty girl, a somewhat less handsome but still reasonably attractive boy. Who has the power over whom? As far as that goes, that teacher wasn't interesting. He is only the victim. No one deserves to be bumped off for something like that: stalking a female student. But you can never completely shake the feeling that he, at least in part, brought it down on himself. That's what we read back then in the first newspaper reactions, that's what we heard in the conversations, both on TV and in the cafés. A grown man, a teacher who does something like that, can't count on much sympathy. But I wasn't interested in his motives anyway. Grown man falls for young girl, you can be sure he wasn't the first man to have that happen. He is rejected, can't take that and goes crazy. He turns into a bothersome stalker. Our sympathy rarely focuses on men who pant on the telephone, men who follow young girls all the way to their doorstep, who stand guard under their bedroom window at night. From that moment on, in fact, the girl becomes the victim. If she had gone downstairs, walked outside and kicked him hard in the balls, we would all have applauded."

You talk about the novelist's freedom. About his imagination, which could be obstructed by too much knowledge of the facts. But the reader is very much familiar with the facts. Of the most important facts, in any case. One reads your entire book knowing how it will end: with the teacher's disappearance.

"That's true. As a writer you're free to use that, I think. It's about the imagination, how do you as a writer fill in the blank spots: Could it have gone this way or that way? The real facts, the ones everyone knows, I should say, serve only as the perspective within which the narrative takes place. There are plenty of examples of that: you write about a Jewish family in Germany in 1938; everyone knows then that something is going to happen, that the sinister shadow of the future is already looming over the characters. These days a lot of writers—especially American writers—have their story begin on the morning of September 11. Or one week before. One day. Six months. It makes you read that story differently. Throughout the entire book you're waiting, as it were, for the first plane to slam into the North Tower. That's also the way I started on *Payback*. A teacher, a boy, and a girl. A high school. A holiday home in the snow. All the ingredients are laid out on the counter. The only thing left is to prepare the meal itself."

The only difference being that everyone knows roughly when World War II started. The same way everyone knows—now, in hindsight—that neither of those planes flew into the Twin Towers by accident. But in Payback, *you fantasize blithely about exactly what might have happened in that holiday cottage. Using what you call your imagination, you saddle the suspects with a theoretical murder.*

"Something else occurs to me now. Because we were just talking about September 11. There is a fifteen-minute gap, a naive eternity, between the first plane and the second. Witnesses all thought it was a horrible accident. The dime only drops when the second plane hits. 'Oh, my God!' you hear them all shouting. But, as a writer, I'm much more interested in those minutes in between the two planes. In the accident. The belief that there are no evil intentions at play. We all look at it differently now. Now we see the footage of the first plane, and we already know. The accident is gone completely. It was there once, but it has disappeared for good. It's the writer's task to bring back that naive belief in the accident. To let us relive those minutes between the first and second planes. Today we sometimes see the Twin Towers in movies or TV series from before September 11, 2001, and you know right away that this is a fairly old movie, if you couldn't tell already from the clothes and the cars. But those towers in a feature film also remind me of the old archive footage of German cities. A German city in 1938. You see streetcars and crowded cafés, mothers pushing prams, men playing chess in a park, and you know: This will all be laid to waste. Later, all this will be gone completely.

"In the same way, with the same perspective, I often looked at that school photo tacked up above my desk. A normal school photo. There are thousands, hundreds of thousands of photos like that. They're all different, in that there are other people in each of those photos, yet they still all look alike. There are more similarities than differences. A teacher, a man or a woman, is posing with his or her students for the school photographer, the clothing and hairstyles usually tell you roughly when the picture was taken. Everyone is posing, everyone is looking straight into the camera, except perhaps that one student who doesn't want to be there, the eternal troublemaker who would like to leave school as quickly as possible, and often there are also one or two jokers who are sticking out their tongues or holding up their fingers in a V behind the head of a fellow student, but those exceptions too are what make the school photos look alike. Sometimes though, with the passing of time, the photos take on more significance. That boy with the pale face and the greasy hair is now a famous writer; that girl with the round cheeks and pigtails is now an anchorwoman on the eight o'clock news; that handsome boy with the sunglasses pushed up on his forehead rose quickly through the ranks of the underworld and was shot and killed a few years ago in the parking lot of the Hilton Hotel. And then of course you have the class photos charged with portent, photos of classes in which more than half the students will not survive the war. But in those photos, too, the tone is largely set by innocence. The faith in a future. Every morning, before I started writing, that's how I looked at the photo of Class 5A at the Spinoza Lyceum.

"These days there's a program, it's called *Classmates*; it didn't exist back when I started on my book, but I thought about it later on. That you would bring together that whole class and let each of them tell *their* version of that school year. They're all in that picture. Herman and Laura of course, first of all, and the teacher, Mr. Landzaat. Obviously I changed all the names, but Mr. Landzaat is an improbable name for a book anyway, sounds a bit too suspect, too unbelievable. You always start by changing the names, then come the facts, at least insofar as they're available.

"But to come back to that photo: I always looked at the protagonists first, then at the bit players, the other members of that group of friends. David, Lodewijk, Michael, Ron. I looked them in the eye, one by one, and I tried to figure out what they were thinking, what they *knew,* only later of course. The class picture was taken at that empty moment of innocence, the vacant space between the first and second planes, just after the summer vacation. Of course I asked about that, about when those pictures were usually taken: it was shortly after the start of the school year, after that same summer vacation when they went together to the house in Terhofstede, but still before the three protagonists came into alignment. Laura only hooked up with Mr. Landzaat during the junior-class field trip in late September; Herman and Laura became a couple during the fall vacation in October. In December, on Boxing Day, Mr. Landzaat visits Laura and Herman at the house in Terhofstede and disappears. None of that can be seen in the class photo, there are no signs; most of the students look serious, a few are smiling, many of the boys have their hands in their pockets: on the one hand they want to show their indifference to the fact that a class photo is being taken, on the other they want to be sure they look good in the picture. A class photo doesn't show just a single individual, not like a passport photo or vacation snapshots. You can throw away a passport photo and have another one taken, as often as it takes to satisfy you, or perhaps I should say as often as it takes to be *passable*. We can dispose discreetly of vacation snapshots that aren't flattering, or at least not glue them into a photo album. We stuff them into a shoebox that we run across every couple of years. 'Oh, no, not that one! I look so terrible in that!' and we try to yank the picture away from the person with whom we're delving through photos on the couch. Then it disappears again for years. A class photo is a very different thing. We can't allow ourselves to look bad in it, because later, a few weeks later, everyone in the class will see it. Hence all the serious expressions, the stiff poses, the mortal fear of looking stupid, laughable. The photo can't be secreted away somewhere, because the whole class has it. 'Look at that expression on Henry's face, he looks like he had to pee so badly!' 'Oh, Yvonne's teeth! Oh, I feel so sorry for her!' 'Theo, did you wash your hair before you came to school that day? Never do that again!' You take the class photo home with you, you can hide it from your parents, but then parents aren't likely to say that it makes you look like a retard: their love ruins their eyesight. You wish you could destroy the photo, tear it into little bits, or even better, burn it. But you know it's no use. You have twenty-eight classmates, twenty-eight copies of your ugly face are in circulation for all eternity."

You didn't mention Stella.
"What?"

Stella. *You just reeled off the names of their group of friends. But
you didn't mention Stella.*
"I didn't? I didn't realize that."

*She's in that class photo too, right? She wasn't sick that day, was
she?*
"Yes, I know she's in the photo. Standing beside Laura. Two
best friends. The boys are also all standing together, the way
friends do. I have it here in a drawer, but I don't have to look
at it anymore, it's etched in my memory."

And do you sometimes take it out and look at it?
"No, that chapter is closed. That book is finished. As I said:
I could draw it for you, from memory."

You don't mention her in your book.
"Who? You mean Stella? No, that's right. In fact, I don't
name anyone, it's fiction, I purposely kept the minor characters vague."

*But there's a difference between keeping something vague and leaving
it out completely. In your depiction of the friends' club, there's only
one girl, Laura. In* Payback *she's called Miranda.*
"I felt as though I had to choose. And it definitely was not
an easy choice. I had to choose between two storylines. Or
rather: this book needed one storyline, and that was enough.
A second one would only have weakened it. I chose for the
teacher, the boy, and the girl. No other diversions. A tragic
love story. A fatal conclusion. Or at least the suspicion of a
fatal conclusion. That seemed more powerful to me. A difficult decision. I did start on it. I made an attempt, but it didn't
work. Look at it this way: I didn't leave her out on purpose.
Initially, I didn't *want* to leave Stella out at all. On the contrary. There were mornings when I looked at the class photo,

and the one I looked at longest was *her*. I was completely fascinated. She's one of the only ones who doesn't look into the camera, although you have to examine it closely to see that. She's looking straight ahead. No, that's not right either. She's looking at *herself,* it took me weeks to finally see that. Those big eyes, that smile, that sweet face, an *open* face too; it's open, but as an outsider you can't see a thing. At most, you see that the face is *dreaming*. It's sufficient unto itself. It's full of itself.

"You have people, I know a few, certainly among my colleagues, who never actually look *at you,* they probably don't even see you, or at least they see you only in relation to themselves. They ring your bell, you open the door and you see it right away in their faces, in their eyes. They're not happy to see you, let alone do they wonder whether they've come at a convenient moment. No, they're happy they came. They're happy *for you*. They're happy for you that they are now standing there in front of you. That they've taken the time and gone to the trouble to ring your doorbell. *Here I am,* they say with their faces all aglow. *Enjoy*. That's the kind of expression Stella is wearing too, right in the middle of that group with all her classmates. There's no real reason to look into the camera, at the school photographer. No, the school photographer should be pleased to have her in the picture. The way she is. All by herself.

"When I finally figured that out, every morning for weeks I looked almost exclusively at *her*. Not at her classmates, in the same way she didn't look at them. I think she *never* looked at her classmates, at least not the way we, as quote-unquote normal people, look at each other. At most, she gauged the reactions in the faces of others, the way those others reacted *to her*. She was, of course, a very pretty girl, but pretty in a different way from Laura.

"In the photo, Laura is the prettiest girl in the class, the girl all the boys chase, of whom all the boys dream. She's completely aware of that, which is at the same time her handicap. When girls are too pretty, they easily become isolated. Without being able to do anything about that themselves. *Unapproachable,* we think when we see the prettiest girl in the class, *she doesn't even know I exist.* And from that moment on we avoid all contact. In order to keep from being disappointed, or even worse: from being completely humiliated. We're afraid the prettiest girl will look us over from head to toe and then deliver a crushing verdict. A verdict from which we'll never recover, that we will carry with us for the rest of our lives. Sometimes even literally, in the words literally used by the prettiest girl with regard to your person: *You don't actually think*—that's how the devastating rejection almost always starts—*that you stand a ghost of a chance with me, that I even knew you existed before today? I would strongly urge you, as of today, to never—I repeat: never—speak to me again.* And so we do all we can to avoid exchanging looks with the prettiest girl. We're in no hurry to have her point out the category to which we actually belong. Not *her* category, in any case.

"Stella's beauty is of a different kind. Precisely because she is so sufficient unto herself, she is beautiful in the way a landscape can be beautiful: a green, rolling landscape with a few sheep grazing on a hillside, a snowy mountain peak at sunset. That landscape doesn't care whether we enjoy it. It's always been there, tomorrow it will still be there, and the day after tomorrow too, and a hundred years from now. She gives off light, but at the same time she absorbs it, as something that goes without saying. She'll never wonder why, it's just always been that way. She wonders about it as little as the earth's surface wonders why the sun shines on it. Or better yet: the light of the moon."

*The difference being that a landscape can't be rejected. You yourself
say that a landscape doesn't care whether we enjoy it. But a landscape also doesn't care whether we reject it.*

"That's the way I always looked at the class photo too. Every
day. I looked at Stella's face. A boy has declared his love
to her, he is standing a few yards away, among his friends.
She finds that only natural. At that moment, everything is
still fine and dandy. The teacher is sitting at his desk. He is
breathing, even though we can't see that in the photograph.
What we can see in the photograph is that the teacher in
question is taken with himself. He's sitting there cheerfully
amid his students, in a checkered shirt with the two top buttons open, at a time when teachers still tended to wear jackets
and ties. He wants to be one of them, he insists that they call
him by his first name, he's trying to smile with his mouth
closed. Standing beside Stella is Laura, her best friend. But
Stella probably has no idea that her best friend is the one she
should watch out for most. It wouldn't occur to her; girls
like Stella believe unconditionally in the trustworthiness of
their best friends, just as she believes in the trustworthiness
of her boyfriend. Of Herman. It would never come up in
her, in Stella's, mind that her boyfriend is actually attracted
to her best friend, or that in a few weeks' time that friend is
going to hook up with the jovial teacher in order to draw
Herman's attention. What happens in the mind of a girl like
Stella when she realizes one day that not she, but someone
else, is the chosen one? That she has only been used as a
diversionary tactic? She thought it was normal that Herman
would want to start something with her, just as she would
have thought that was normal for any other boy; what boy,
after all, *wouldn't* fall for a girl like her? And then, one day,
quite unexpectedly, out of the proverbial blue, he breaks up

with her. And not only does he break up with her, but he tells her he is trading her in for Laura. For her best friend."

But you didn't do anything with that. In Payback, *Stella isn't mentioned at all. As though she never existed.*

"There was nothing I *could* do with it. I mean, there was nothing I could with it because of the way things went. Because of what happened afterward. I did try. In the first draft, I still had two girls. But it didn't work. I realized that I needed to focus on one thing and one thing alone. The teacher's disappearance. What Stella . . . What she did . . . That would distract readers too much from the essence of my story. It might throw the whole book out of balance. You read books sometimes that give you the impression that the writer was trying to sweeten the pot. That he thought that one central premise wasn't enough. It's quite understandable too. Every writer has that urge, you work on a book for months, often years, you're sick and tired of it, the story is starting to bore you, and to combat that boredom you toss another element into it, a surprising twist, something spectacular. But there's a very real chance that adding that element will destroy the book's balance right away. Maybe the writer is bored, but the reader isn't. Not yet. The writer forgets that the reader doesn't spend months or years with a book. Only a couple of days, or a week at most. He doesn't get enough time to become bored. *Payback* is not some five-hundred-page doorstop, I knew from the start that half that would be enough. Stella would have been a new narrative line. That would have made it a very different book. There was a very real chance that that one new narrative line wouldn't have been enough. That happens often. Two storylines can be confusing, while three or five aren't, then it's simply that kind of a book. But I didn't feel like writing that kind of a book. I felt that the teacher, the boy, and the girl were enough."

But in reality we also make do with any number of storylines, don't we? Why is it that writers are always so afraid of that?

"Because one expects a certain degree of order in a novel; a clearer, more compact reality. Actual reality doesn't worry about that compaction. A writer has to chop into reality. For example: an acquaintance of mine was recently hit by a garbage truck. The ambulance took him to the hospital with a broken leg, and there he was told that his wife had just been admitted to that same hospital: one hour earlier she had fallen off her bike and broken her arm. That's a true story. The kind you would never make up. In the book version, only one of the two remains: either the husband with the broken leg *or* the wife with the broken arm. It's up to the writer to decide which one gets cut out of the book."

In Payback, *of course, you already made that decision by giving your imagination free rein. In your book, the boy and the girl finish the teacher off and hide the body in an ingenious fashion. While in real life there was never any solid evidence to indicate that. The teacher no longer disappears in the literal sense of the word. The reader knows how it went.*

"Yes, I thought that was fascinating. What might have happened? That question, in fact, remains interesting. We still don't know how it went."

But don't you ever have the feeling that you, as a writer, have a certain responsibility with regard to reality? There is no Stella. The teacher is murdered in cold blood. It may all be your own imagination, of course, but little is left to the reader's imagination.

"Maybe I was unconsciously hoping for a reaction, who can say?"

You mean a reaction from the murderers? From the suspects, I should say?

"First of all that, yes. As I've already said: I myself never tried to make contact, to the extent that they would have allowed me to; I didn't want any explanation on their part to get in the way of my imagination. But afterward . . . Once the book was published, I noticed that I started asking myself whether they were going to read it. Whether they would feel like refuting my solution. And whether their refutation might expose them. Maybe even betray them. Please note: morally speaking, it didn't interest me at all. They were right in whatever they did. But still, one remains curious. We're always curious about the fate of someone who disappears from the face of the earth. But I wasn't thinking only about Herman and Laura, I also thought about the others, about what they knew. Within close groups of friends like that, nothing remains a secret for long. You confide in each other. The way I imagined it, Herman and Laura would have wanted to tell someone their story. In fact, I was sure of it. You can't walk around with something like that for years, or even weeks. One day you simply have to try to tell someone. David was very close to both Herman and Laura. So was Lodewijk. My speculation was that one of the others from that group of friends might want to react to the book. That they would approach me, anonymously or not, with their version of things."

And did that happen?

"I don't know . . . I could simply say that I never received a direct reaction from anyone involved, and be finished with it. But on the other hand . . . by now it must have passed the statute of limitations. But you have to promise me that this will remain completely off the record. I wouldn't want to get anyone into trouble, forty years after the fact."

Perhaps you could tell me first whether it changed your view of what happened. Whether the new information made you think differently about precisely what went on in that house in Terhofstede.
"Yes, it did."

And then there is a knock at the door. You say "yes" again, but this time with a question mark behind it. The door opens and your wife comes in. In a little over an hour the two of you have to be at the book ball; you might expect that she has come to ask what you think of her dress, that she has come to ask you to close the zipper on the back of her dress, that she would be at least half or three-quarters of the way dressed for the party, but she is still wearing her jeans and white sneakers—the untucked tails of a white shirt (a man's shirt, I can't help but notice, maybe one of yours?) are hanging loosely over the jeans.

She's holding a thermometer.

"We're almost finished," you say—apparently you haven't noticed the thermometer, or at least you ask no questions about it.

"[. . .] hasn't been feeling well all afternoon," your wife says; she mentions your daughter's name, the name I'm still leaving out; you know her name anyway, and it is indeed no one else's business. "But now she's really running a fever." She takes a few steps toward you and holds out the thermometer, but you are looking only at her. "I don't like the idea of going away while she's sick in bed."

"But Charlotte's coming in a bit, isn't she?"

"I don't know," she says. "I'd rather not leave her alone with Charlotte. I would just feel much more comfortable staying with her myself."

You stare at her. I think I know more or less what is going

on in your mind. Without your wife, without your much-younger wife, you won't be complete at a party like this. As though you were being forced to show up in the nude; no, not in the nude, in just your boxer shorts.

"But . . . ," you start in, but your wife is too fast for you.

"You don't have to go by yourself," she says—and then she looks at me for the first time.

36

THE LAST two times it had been more than she could take. She couldn't stand it anymore. That was why she held the thermometer up to the lightbulb. It was, in fact, a completely ridiculous and unnecessary thing to do. As if M would actually check the thermometer! Still, the black digits made it somehow more *real*: 101 degrees. Thermometer in hand, she knocked on the door of his study.

The last couple of years she had started dreading it a week beforehand. Like a visit to the gynecologist. A hollow feeling between navel and abdomen. It started with wondering what to wear this year. A different dress each year. Bare shoulders. Bare arms. And most important of all, of course: the décolleté. How much to show off. In her experience, it was the women whose shelf life had expired long ago who also sported the deepest décolletés. The same went for women who were too fat, for women who smoked, for the redheads. The women with faces on which two packs of Gauloises and two bottles of red wine a day for twenty years had left their mark. Pits and craters and stretches of dead skin—a face like a polluted river in which the last fish had bobbed to the surface years ago. But with a deep décolleté they could draw attention away from that face. The skin there was none too young either, usually too red or too tanned, but the men's gazes often remained hanging there. First they looked at the bared no-man's-land, and only then at the face.

After that the program began. The male and female authors gathered in the big theater. They looked at each other, said hello with a nod of the head or waved to each other from a distance. What they paid particular attention to was the seating arrangement, to who sat where. A moment of suspense, each year anew. Not for her and her husband. They knew beforehand, of course, where they would be seated. That never changed. Second row from the front, in the middle. But most colleagues had no fixed place. They could end up somewhere else each year. Those who sat all the way at the top, up in the second balcony, didn't even count. The same went for the side balconies. Writer L hadn't put a word on paper for years; these days he sat behind a pillar where no one could see him. G had been at the top of the bestseller list for three months, hence her spot in the front row of the lower balcony. And then of course there were the old hands who never failed to show up. A couple more of them dead each year. The spots they vacated in the middle of the theater were assumed by other aged men and wrinkled women. The policy was to be accommodating toward literary widows. During their first two years of bereavement they were allowed to keep their regular seats. After that they were quietly banished to the second balcony, or simply not invited anymore.

Most publishers organized a dinner for their authors before the ball started. The lucky ones went to a real restaurant, but in recent years the buffet dinner had becoming increasingly popular. Her husband's publisher ("subpar results," "recession," "sector-wide structural malaise") had switched to the buffet last year. She remembered the long line waiting to be served by the college-aged temps, who ladled casserole and mashed potatoes onto their paper plates. The hot plates were silver, but the line of hungry faces reminded her of a soup kitchen. Of breadlines in a region struck by natural disaster.

Before the actual show began, a few speeches were given. No one was anxious to hear them. The speakers were always gray-haired men in suits, who said right at the start that they would "keep it short." For the last decade or so the whole event had been sponsored by the Dutch Railways, and while the representative from that organization was giving his speech she wondered whether she was the only one thinking of delayed departures, frozen switches, and stranded passengers. After the show, which usually featured a hand-me-down nightclub performer or a singer-songwriter whose career was on the rocks, or—even worse, if that was possible—a writer who thought he was funnier than his colleagues, the big loitering began . . . the endless mingling in the catacombs of the theater.

Thermometer in hand, she went to her daughter's room. Catherine had been mopey all day, complaining of a headache and nausea, but there was nothing wrong with her appetite; after finishing two pieces of toasted white bread, she had asked for a third.

"Drink your milk first," Ana told her. "If you're still hungry after that, you can have another one."

That was when the prospect presented itself to her: an evening at home with her "sick" daughter, beneath a blanket on the couch, watching a DVD of some animated film she and Catherine had already seen a hundred times before. Anything was better than the theater corridors, the predictable conversations, the publishers, the journalists, the "nutty" decorations on the walls and ceilings, even in the restrooms. And last, but definitely not least, the writers themselves . . .

Put a hundred writers together in one space for a party and you get something very different—in any case, not a party. With M she usually stuck to one round of the corridors, a nod here, the briefest possible conversation there, a photographer asking them to look into the camera for just a moment, their heads *a little closer together, yes, that's it, now smile, you look so serious, it's a party isn't it?* After that one round they settled down on the stairs to the right of the second-floor men's room. Before long, the others would join them there. M's colleagues, writers whose greatest similarity was that none of them had long to live. The oeuvre would soon be complete, the folio edition of collected works was ready to go, the obituaries had mostly all been written, the lucky ones (or unlucky ones, depending on how you looked at it) already had a biographer who had established a bond of trust with the prospective widow.

N always snapped at his girlfriend. Or ridiculed her to her face. She, too, was much younger than he was, but no more than twenty years or so—not nearly as big a difference as between M and herself. Unlike most writers' wives, N's girlfriend also did something herself, though Ana could never remember exactly what. Something with websites, she thought. Something that required no skills.

And then you had C, who was somewhere in his eighties too by now but tried to wear his seniority as boyishly as possible, like a pair of worn-out sneakers, ripped jeans, and safety pins; he liked to be seen in recalcitrant clothing: no sport coat, let alone a tuxedo; just a T-shirt with V-neck that revealed a landscape of sagging sinews, razor burns, and three or four snow-white chest hairs. Halfway through this landscape, which shifted from red to dark purple on its way down, C's Adam's apple looked as though it were trying to break out through the skin, like an oversized prey—a marmot, a rabbit—that has been gulped down by an overly rapacious python and become stuck in its gullet. Behind the lenses of his spectacles his dilated pupils floated in the whites of eyes that were no longer completely white, trashed as they were by any number of broken capillaries; they reminded her most of some raw dish, something on a half shell, an oyster, something you had to slurp down without looking.

And each and every one of the old writers looked at her, Ana, like children waiting for their favorite dessert at a birthday party. N literally licked his lips, he didn't care that his girlfriend was standing beside him, when they said hello he first kissed her on each cheek, then let the third and final kiss land just a little too close to the corner of her lips, almost as though by accident. But it was no accident. Meanwhile he did something with his fingers, something right above her buttocks, his thick fingertips pressed softly against the spot where the zipper of her dress started, right over her tailbone, then slipped down a fraction of an inch.

"You're looking lovely as always, Ana," he said. Then he stepped back: before letting her go completely, his hand slid to the front, by way of her buttock and hip to her abdomen, before he pulled it back. "We should go for coffee sometime. Just the two of us. Sometime when M is traveling abroad." This latter remark was always accompanied by a big wink, he wanted to be sure she saw it only as a compliment and not a serious come-on, but his eyes traveled downward right away, resting on her lips for a few moments before descending further, to her breasts. "No, really, if I didn't have Liliane, I know what I'd be doing," he said—and this time he didn't wink.

The other old men were less forward, but they all looked. They looked when they thought she didn't see them; C's oyster eyes had a predilection for her buttocks, and she always felt the gaze of D, the travel writer, somewhere around her left ear, as though he wished he could clamp her earlobe in his doggy, wine-stained lips, then use the tip of his tongue to fiddle loose her earring and swallow it. Van E, the artist, had eyes like a mole, or some other animal that spends more time in darkness than in light; he always kept them squeezed in a tight squint behind his glasses and probably thought she couldn't tell where he was looking: at her legs— first her thighs, then lower and lower, by way of her calves to her ankles.

A recent addition to their little club on the stairs was K, who was about thirty years younger than the rest. K was what people called a modest writer. "Modest writers are the worst kind," M had said once, referring to K. "In actual fact, of course, they're not modest at all. They only act modest because, in their hearts, they consider themselves better than the rest. *I can act normal,* the modest writer figures. *I can act normal because my greatness is beyond any shadow of a doubt. I'm like the queen, who can ride a bike like a* normal *person might, because everyone already knows she's the queen.* For readers, too, the modest writer is a delight. *So normal!* they tell each other. *You can talk to him like a* normal *person. He didn't act as though he was one whit better than the rest of us normal people. Not arrogant like M, not aloof and cerebral like N.*"

In interviews, K had more than once expressed a certain disdain for M's work ("a writer from the past, a writer whose work will quickly be forgotten once he's gone"), but whenever they met he always pooh-poohed the critique: "I hope you didn't mind. It wasn't really that bad. I didn't mean anything by it, you know I admire your work as a whole."

K looked at Ana differently than most of M's aging colleagues who gathered on the stairs beside the gents'. Or rather, he didn't look at all. No randy perusal from head to toe, no suggestive kisses on the cheek, not even raised eyebrows or the faintest trace of flirtation. They were closer to each other in age, amid the fogies K could have considered himself the most likely of the lot, but he was the only one in the group who acted as though there was no pretty woman within a few feet of him. Once, when Ana had complimented K on his latest book—a village history smeared out over three generations—she had at some point used the word "special." She remembered the sentence in which she'd done that, word for word: "I'm only halfway through the first section, at the point where that priest drowns. I can't say a lot about it yet, but in any case it's really special." She had lied about where she was in the book, she wasn't anywhere near halfway through the first section, after ten pages she had decided that it wasn't her cup of tea—but the drowned priest was mentioned in the blurb.

"I don't think I'm special at all," K had replied grimly, fixing her with his cold gaze; a neutral gaze above all, as though he wasn't talking to an attractive woman his own age but to a postal clerk or a bailiff. "Just because I happen to be a writer doesn't make me any more special than anyone else."

Ana had said something about his book, not about his person—and at that moment she suddenly understood M's aversion to modest writers.

"What do you want to watch? *Dumbo,* or the real movie about the two dogs and that cat?"

She sat down on the edge of Catherine's bed and showed her daughter the thermometer again. "A hundred and one, Papa thought it was a good idea too, for me to stay with you. How are you feeling now?" she asked, touching Catherine's forehead with her fingertips—it wasn't warm, or at least no warmer than usual.

"Not very well," Catherine whispered. "Can we watch a movie right now?"

Dumbo was one they'd seen together more than a hundred times, but the film about the adventuresome journey by two dogs and a cat across the United States, based on a true story, was one Ana had bought only a couple of weeks earlier. The first time they watched it they had cried together, the second and third times, too, even though they knew by then that it had a happy ending.

"Let's wait a bit, till Papa's gone," she answered. "In half an hour. Papa and that man are going to the party. Do you remember that man? The downstairs neighbor? The one who brought us to the house in H. when the weather was so bad?"

It was more like forty-five minutes in the end, but then at last they were lying together on the couch in the living room. Catherine beneath a blanket, cuddled up against her mother. During the forty-five minutes that had passed, Ana had used an adhesive roller to pick the lint off of M's tuxedo, she'd said something about his hair ("Nonsense, it looks perfect"), and then, for the third or fourth time, urged him to simply tell the truth at the party. *Our daughter is ill, my wife insisted on staying home with her.*

After forty-five minutes she heard the front door close at last, then the doors of the elevator. She went to the kitchen and made popcorn in the microwave, poured a glass of lemonade for Catherine and red wine for herself. For a brief moment, as she was carrying the tray from the kitchen to the living room, she had a slight feeling of regret. No, not really regret, more like a gently gnawing sense of guilt. She could have gone along with M, she knew how important it was to him, how he reveled in having his wife by his side on such occasions. But she already did so much, she told herself, from the very start she had bravely shouldered the role of *the wife of*. Still with pleasure, during the first few years, lately less and less so; she didn't know exactly why that was, perhaps it was the predictability. Like with the cocktail parties at the publishing house. The summer party, the autumn party, the New Year's party, the spring party ("in the garden, if the weather's nice"), there was no end to them. There were peanuts and dishes of olives on a table in one corner of "the French Room"—almost all the self-respecting publishers were housed in a canal-side mansion with marble corridors and gilded wainscoting—while the bottles of beer stood growing tepid. M's colleagues greeted her politely but without interest, they never asked how *she* was doing, how she was getting along at the famous writer's side, they only asked indirectly about *him* ("Is he working on something new?" "How did he react to that article, the one that said he no longer counts as the voice of his generation?" "Was he serious about what he said in that interview about the Nobel Prize?"). The colleagues fell into two categories: those who were more successful than M, and those who received less media attention and therefore had to make do with fewer sales. The colleagues in the first category were usually amiable, although it could also be seen as condescension. "It's such a pity," they said. "That last book of his really deserves a much wider readership. It's puzzling." The second category started in right away about the posters and public-transport campaigns, about the talk shows that were all too pleased to make time for "big names" like M.

"The publishing house has a limited budget, unfortunately," they said. "But that doesn't mean they have to spend it all on the same authors." And then they would go on to wonder aloud whether their work might get the attention it deserved at another house. "Just between the two of us, I sometimes think about going elsewhere."

All they'd really talked about at the last cocktail party was N, who truly *had* left, suddenly, out of the blue, without whining about it for months beforehand. From one day to the next he was gone, his switch made all the papers, and his next book with his new publisher was an instant bestseller. "I should have done this long ago," he repeated in almost every interview dealing with the publication of *The Garden of Psalms*. "I should have traded in that old chicken coop long ago for a house where you're not bumping your head all the time." The authors who had remained behind in the chicken coop never spoke their mind about N's departure. They all agreed, however, that it wasn't "comme il faut," the way it had gone, that one "simply doesn't do that," at least not in that way—just slipping away with no prior notice, and then "fouling one's own nest" with sarcastic comments about your former publisher. Amid all of this, M's publisher moves about the room like a birthday boy at his own party, a birthday boy who can't really enjoy the party himself because he has to divide his attention among all the guests. A bit of chatting here, a horselaugh there, not in too much of a hurry to talk to the critic from the weekend literary supplement, not lingering too long with the bestselling author; no one must get the feeling that he's not considered important enough. M's publisher is a master at the game; when he gets to Ana, he touches her elbow gently.

"Well? How are things at home?" he inquires, but she doesn't answer right away; she knows that by "home" he doesn't mean their actual family life. And sure enough: "Is he working on something new?" he asks after that brief silence.

Ana admires him for how skillfully he maneuvers among

all those sensitive egos, but in the course of the years she has also grown truly fond of him. A sort of secret understanding has developed between them, an understanding based on the mutual, always unspoken knowledge that it is of course all a bunch of nonsense, these writers and their attention issues, the publisher who—like the soccer trainer—always receives the blame when things don't turn out as hoped, but rarely or never a compliment when he succeeds in making a book successful. She shows him, indirectly, that she feels for him, and he shows her that he appreciates that.

"Oh well, you know, something new . . ." She raises her glass of white wine to her lips and takes a sip—the white wine, too, is almost at room temperature; the bottle has probably been on the table beside the peanuts and olives for the last few hours, or else the new trainee forgot to put it in the fridge first. "He never stops working, he's in the study almost all day, you know that, but he never tells me what he's working on."

"It would be too bad if *Liberation Year* were to drop out of sight too soon," the publisher says, looking around to see who he'll talk to next—she doesn't blame him for that, he has to hurry, there are already people gathering their coats at the door. "I have great expectations for the Antwerp Book Fair. Marie Claude Bruinzeel is going to interview him there, in public. That can really get the discussion about the book off to a good start."

Ana knows Marie Claude Bruinzeel's reputation, based on her interviews in the Saturday literary supplement. They're the kind of interviews that leave no stone unturned. Marie Claude Bruinzeel has the tendency to focus on the vermin that hide beneath those stones; the worms, beetles, and pill bugs that can't stand the light of day and go scuttling for safety, and she doesn't put the stone back where she found it, no, she actually holds it up for a while longer. "Do you still dream sometimes about a winning smash, an Olympic gold medal?" she'd asked a diabetic table-tennis star who'd recently had a leg amputated. At first Ana had been shocked, the question seemed impertinent, and tears had actually come to the table-tennis star's eyes, but later she had realized that it wasn't such a strange question after all. *Do you still dream . . .* Well, why not? Why shouldn't people with only one leg still dream? Then, right away, she starts wondering what Marie Claude Bruinzeel will ask M at the book fair. *Do you still dream of writing a bestseller? A book like* Payback? *Do you still dream that you might . . .* She thought about it for a moment; a question about his work or the dream of future successes won't expose any creepy pill bugs. *Do you sometimes dream of being younger? Of living to see your daughter grow up? Even if it's only to her eighteenth birthday?*

"Will you be there too?" the publisher asked. "Will I see you in Antwerp? We could go to that fish restaurant afterward, if you two feel like it."

She shakes her head. *I don't think so,* she feels like saying, *I don't want to leave my daughter alone too often.* But there's a different reason, actually. Antwerp is too close, there are no surprises in store there anymore. In other cities, yes. Rome, Milan, Berlin. Sometimes she went along with M when he traveled abroad. As long as the engagement was still a ways off, he looked forward to it. But as the departure date came closer he grew increasingly nervous.

"I should have canceled," he'd say, "but it's too late now."

"You could always say you're sick," she said.

"That would be boorish. They invited me a year ago. If I canceled now, they'd panic."

"But what if you really *were* sick," she tried, for form's sake. "You couldn't go then either, could you?"

He looked at her as though she'd suggested that animals might be able to talk.

"But I'm *not* really sick," he said—and a few days later they were standing together at the airport check-in. The ladies at the desk recognized him occasionally, if they were older than thirty. They would give him their prettiest smiles—some of them even blushed—and treated them with great respect. "I read your latest book from start to finish, in one night. Have a lovely trip, Mr. M!" The younger girls treated him like the old man that he was. They raised their voices almost to a scream when handing him his boarding pass, and drew a circle around the gate number and boarding time, as though they assumed that he was already hard of hearing. The rudest among them looked at her and then at him and then back again—they made no attempt to disguise their curiosity. *Is this his daughter, or some crumpet forty years younger than he is?*

M wasn't fond of flying. In the duty-free zone he always went to the bar and knocked back a couple of beers before boarding.

"Look at that," he said, pointing at a group of men in long robes and women in veils. "Let's hope they're not on our flight. But maybe they'll blow themselves up here before we leave the ground. How many beers have I had, anyway? Three or four?"

On the plane he always wanted an aisle seat. After flipping through the in-flight magazine from back to front in record time, he would breathe a deep sigh and look at his watch. A book was useless; he couldn't read on a plane, he said.

"I thought hippos were only allowed to travel in the cargo hold," he said a bit too loudly when the stewardess, who was indeed rather portly, stood right beside his seat to demonstrate the use of the oxygen mask and life preserver and accidentally brushed his hair with her elbow.

"How many does this make?" he asked, popping the top off his can of Heineken before tearing the cellophane from the double-decker sandwich with cheese spread. "I can't eat this," he said after sniffing it. He pushed the button on the console above his head. "We seem to be hitting turbulence," he said when the fat stewardess came hurrying toward him down the aisle.

But after the landing—in Milan, in Frankfurt, in Oslo—he usually perked up quickly enough. As soon as he saw his foreign publisher's publicity person in the arrivals hall, holding up a sign with his name on it, he relaxed visibly. From that moment on he played his part—the role of Dutch writer with a certain reputation abroad—with verve. In the taxi he asked all the usual things. *How many people live in the city? That opera house, was it rebuilt brick by brick after the war? Do you have problems with immigrants here too?*

The usual itinerary followed. Interviews in the lobby of his hotel, and that evening a dinner at a restaurant with staff members from the publishing house and a few local bigwigs. During those dinners he answered his hosts' questions. Ten years ago, foreigners had never asked so many questions about the Netherlands. They never got further than the standard clichés. Drug abuse, euthanasia, and same-sex marriage. But then the politically tinted murders took place, and these days they asked about only one thing: the rise of right-wing extremism.

When they did, he would apply the knife to his veal escalope or Norwegian sea bream, take a sip of wine, and smile affably.

"First of all, I need to correct you," he said. "In the

Netherlands, it's not about right-wing extremism *pur sang*. That's what makes it so difficult to dismiss right off the cuff. The Dutch extremists, for example, are great advocates of gay rights. And our brand of extremism is not at all anti-Semitic, not like in most other European countries. The very opposite, in fact: the right-wing extremists in our country are among the most outspoken supporters of the state of Israel. And when it comes to social equality and care for the aged, you could almost call that particular party a socialist one."

But the Netherlands had been the most tolerant country in the world for decades, hadn't it? What happened to that tolerance all of a sudden? his hosts wanted to know.

Putting down his knife and fork, he used the tip of his napkin to wipe an imaginary bit of escalope or bream from the corner of his lips.

"Perhaps we should start by redefining the term 'tolerance,'" he said. "After all, what does it mean to be *tolerant*? That you *tolerate* other people? People of a different color, different religious beliefs, people with earrings and tattoos, as well as women who wear headscarves, people with a different sexual orientation. But there is really nothing to tolerate. By using the word 'tolerance,' you're simply placing yourself on a higher plane than those you tolerate. Tolerance is only possible when one fosters a deep-rooted sense of superiority. That's one thing we Dutch have never lacked, and it's been that way for centuries. We have long considered ourselves better than the rest of the world. But now the rest of the world is suddenly thronging to our borders and taking over our houses and neighborhoods. Suddenly, tolerance isn't enough. The newcomers laugh at us for our tolerance and see it primarily as a sign of weakness. Which in the long run, of course, it is."

Then dessert arrived. The people from the publishing

house ordered coffee with liqueur, but he said he was tired and wanted to get back to the hotel.

During those interviews, Ana would wander through the more exclusive shopping streets. Sometimes she would buy a purse, other times a shawl. In the afternoon there was a buffet lunch at the Dutch embassy.

"It used to be easy to represent the Netherlands abroad," the ambassador sighed. "But these days we're always on the defensive. It's often hard to make it clear that right-wing extremism in Holland is different from in other countries. Just look at their attitude toward gay rights and Israel."

There were times when she enjoyed those trips abroad, with just the two of them, but the worst were the festivals or book fairs with a whole delegation of Dutch writers. When just the two of them were abroad they would snuggle up together in their hotel bed, order a bottle of wine from room service, and watch reruns of some old Western series, dubbed in the local language. At such moments they were almost happy—or at least she felt so.

But when an entire division of Dutch writers would descend on a foreign city, such moments were rare. The Dutch could never exercise moderation. They always made a contest of seeing who could stay up latest. They would sit at the hotel bar until the wee hours of the night. Some of those writers shouldn't have been drinking at all, the whites of their eyes were already the color of old newsprint, but they always took "one more for the road." At breakfast the next morning they bragged about how late they had gone to bed. They winked conspiratorially at other colleagues who had gone on into the wee hours too. With that wink they shut out the others, the pussies and weaklings who had considered their own well-being or who simply preferred not to go to bed too late.

"No," she says to M's publisher. "I don't think I'll be going along to Antwerp. I think I'll stay with my daughter."

"But . . ." Someone taps the publisher on the shoulder, a female author whose coat is already draped over her shoulders, it was so much fun but she really has to leave now, they give each other three little pecks on the cheeks. Ana knows what the publisher's objection would have been. The holiday house. The house outside H. is barely fifteen miles outside Antwerp, a half hour's drive, no more than that. They've done that before. One time, after a festival where M had read, the publisher and his wife had actually slept over. Now that he's finished saying goodbye to the female author, his glance ricochets around the French Room, which is a good deal emptier now, and then he looks at her again.

It's possible that he's forgotten what they were talking about. She's had time to think about what she'll say if he pushes on. *It's too close.* He'll understand that, she's sure.

But he doesn't press the point. He lays a hand on her forearm, squeezes it gently for a moment.

"I understand," he says.

Some movies only get better once you know how they're going to end. The two dogs and the cat escape from their new, temporary home and start on their quest for the old one. On their journey straight across North America they navigate somehow—by the stars? The magnetic pole?—the movie doesn't explain that, in any case it's something only animals can do, an ability humans lost long ago. During the fight with the bear, Catherine had crept up even closer to Ana, the bowl of popcorn was almost empty, Catherine hadn't even touched her glass of lemonade. Ana herself definitely felt like another glass of wine, but she didn't want to get up now and go to the kitchen, she was afraid of interrupting something.

She had vowed not to think about the book ball—about M being on his own at that party, first wandering the corridors, then at his regular spot beside the men's room—in order to lose herself completely in the film, but she only succeeded partway. When the cat came out of the bushes as the first of the trio and ran across the lawn toward its owners, she tore open the packet of tissues she had waiting and handed one to Catherine.

"Oh, Mama," her daughter said when the youngest of the two dogs followed from the bushes. "Do you think that old dog made it too? Or is he dead?"

Catherine had started crying quietly, she pressed the tissue to her eyes. Ana was crying too, perhaps even harder than the first three times she'd watched this.

"I'm not sure, sweetheart," she said. "I really hope so. But I really couldn't say."

37

THE LONG line of guests at the entrance forms the first hurdle. There are klieg lights and TV trucks with satellite dishes on the roofs, photographers and cameramen lined up behind the crush barriers on both sides of the red carpet. The trick, M knows, is to exude a certain nonchalance, to feign patience as naturally as possible, with an expression just a tad ironic and complacent. *This is the forty-fifth, what, fiftieth time I've been here? Try telling me something I don't know.* M has mastered the trick like no other; after all, he really *has* lost count, he's never missed a year. On his own at first, or with another new conquest on his arm each time, later with his first wife, and an eternity by now with Ana. There are other—younger, less famous—colleagues who clearly have a harder time with that, with exuding such calm indifference. They stand there with their coats half unbuttoned, their party clothes showing a little, the dress they bought specially for this occasion, the coat they picked up from the cleaner's only a few hours ago; any way you look at it, it's clothing that has been *thought about.* That red coat, isn't it just a little *too* red? Isn't that sequined dress a little too flashy? The rare guest attempts to defy etiquette: a T-shirt bearing the logo of a soccer team, white Nike high-tops with black laces, a weird cap or a crazy hat (nutty glasses don't cut it here, nutty glasses are the uniform of the elite)—M himself abandoned that defiance years ago, he would like to erect a monument to the inventor of the tuxedo. The tuxedo, of course, is a uniform too, but then a uniform that—unlike the canary-yellow spectacle frames—makes us all equal, in the same way the military or school uniform does. When a man in a tuxedo stands among other men in tuxedos, you no longer look at the clothing but at the face, at the head sticking out above that white collar, black tails, and tie. All in black and white; it's brilliant, everything else takes on new color above an outfit like that, including gray hair—even one's facial complexion, be it ever so pale, will never be as white as the shirt.

His features are striking, M knows. The strikingness of those features is something age has never been able to corrode. Of course he mustn't pose on a beach in his swimming trunks anymore, and it's better if they don't come by early in the morning to find him in his striped pajamas at the breakfast table, but in the pronouncedly masculine uniform that the tuxedo is he looks like one of those old Hollywood actors on his way to the Oscars or the Grammys. To the—what do they call that again—Lifetime Achievement Award. A prize for one's entire life. It's no fantasy or wishful thinking; he's seen himself in the news footage, in the pictures in the paper the next day. He's no slouch, he leads a healthy life, he's a moderate drinker, he even has to be careful not to lead *too* healthy a life, he noted, after seeing last year's footage. Something about his face (not his teeth, he definitely must not smile, as long as he keeps his lips sealed there's no reason for concern), his cheeks were sunken, too deeply sunken, no longer charming, as though they'd been vacuum-sealed from the inside out. Perhaps he wasn't the only one who could see the foreshadowing in his face, the foreshadowing of that day when he would live on only in his work (or *not* live on, he had seen how quickly that went with most of his late colleagues). A skull. A death's-head. He had started eating more, he had asked Ana to prepare prime rib and pasta dishes with bacon and cream, a slice of cream cake for dessert or a Magnum Almond from the freezer—within a few weeks the prescient death's-head cheeks had fairly disappeared.

A few yards ahead of him in line is N, who knows like no other how to do that, stand in line. His hands are in his pockets, he already has his long mohair coat draped over one arm. He stands there the way you'd stand in line in a bakery shop. One sliced whole-wheat and two bread rolls, please. At first M sees only the back of his head, but then N steps over closer to the crush barrier and brings his lips closer to the TV reporter's mike; behind the reporter, the blinding light of a camera flips on. The light shines straight through N's hair: like a low-hanging sun above a dry and barren landscape, it underscores the depth of the almost-eighty-year-old creases and lines in his profile, but at the same time gives him something kingly—something *imperious,* M corrects himself right away.

Close to the entrance, a new torment begins. The party has a different theme each year. Sometimes it's straightforward—the animal kingdom, youth, the autobiographical in literature—but there are also years when they have obviously been desperate to come up with something, anything. M recalls one year when it was about birds and nests, no one knew whether it was supposed to be about the nesting instinct, about eggs, or about something much more horrible than that.

At the theater entrance, at the end of the red carpet, awaits the evening's major television moment: the reporter from *News Hour* who asks any author who counts, however slightly, to say something about the theme of this year's Dutch Book

Week. The tone of the question is usually slightly ironic (*If you could be reincarnated as an animal, which one would that be?*), but the reply, of course, is the important thing. The snappiest answers are the ones that are finally aired, mumbling and stuttering doesn't stand much of a chance, not unless it's the mumbling and stuttering of a big literary name: a famous writer who starts to sweat and stutter or can only come up with platitudes has a certain news value too. Whatever the case, it's always an unequal battle: the reporter from *News Hour* has had almost a year to dream up his cutesy question, but the writer has to say something eloquent on the spot, right there under the bright klieg lights. A one-liner or two, in quick succession, that's the best. "Since when are people no longer animals? But even if they aren't: coming back doesn't really appeal to me, one time around seems like more than enough."

This year's theme is "Resistance—Then and Now." When he saw the announcement in the paper almost a year ago, M had groaned. There was no escaping it, there was no way he'd make it into the theater unnoticed, the war was his trademark. Even if he succeeded in slipping in behind a colleague, they would drag him back in front of the camera by the sleeve of his tuxedo. *Are there things you still resist? If you had to go into hiding, with which colleague would you like to do that? And with which colleague absolutely not? Do you see similarities between the rise of right-wing extremism back then and the way it is today?* A question about the truth concerning the resistance was impossible. That was still too touchy. The resistance in the Netherlands had been negligible. Nowhere else in Europe was so little resistance offered. Any German soldier told that he was to be stationed in Holland breathed a sigh of relief. Thank God not the Ukraine, Greece, or Yugoslavia, where the partisans showed no mercy to recruits taken prisoner. In the Netherlands you had the beaches, the tulips, and the pretty girls. Everywhere you went you were treated amiably. At a village party you could ask the girls to dance without getting a knife in your back. Without a homemade fragmentation bomb going off under a haystack. In Russia the girls got you drunk, then cut off your balls in the shed. The rare Dutch act of resistance seemed to disappoint and distress the Germans more than it made them truly angry. They reacted as though they had been betrayed by a sweetheart. They picked up a few chance passersby from the street on a Sunday afternoon, lined them up along a ditch, and executed them. Not too many, not whole villages like in France, Poland, and Czechoslovakia. *Why did you people have to go and do that now?* it seemed the Germans were asking. *We were having such a good time!*

Now M is almost to the entrance. He turns his head to locate his downstairs neighbor, who has lingered further back in line. *Come on,* M gestures, *come on, it's time to go in.*

"Mr. M . . ."

The reporter from *News Hour* holds the mike up in front of his face. The lamp on the cameraman's shoulder pops on.

Here comes the question.

And there—smoothly, in one go, he needs barely a second to think about it—comes the answer.

38

It's HALF an hour after the show has ended; they are standing and sitting on, or leaning against, the stairs beside the
men's room. N is there, and C, W, and L—they're not quite
all present: a few minutes earlier, S had taken the arm of a
young PR manager from his publishing house and, with a
wink at the others, headed downstairs to the dance floor.
Van der D has gone to fetch drinks, in accordance with the
time-honored, roundabout procedure in which one must
first stand in line to buy tokens and then move to the next
line for the drinks themselves.

Tokens! Chits! If M were to sum up the Dutch national
character in one word, it would be "chits." He's been all over
the world, he feels he has every right to sum up the character of his own country in one word. In France, Spain, and
Italy the chit has yet to be invented. In Germany they give
you twenty at one shot; that's also a way to undermine one's
confidence in the value of the chit. In Holland you never get
more than two. No matter where, at the library, a literary
café, a book festival—everywhere you go you're handed an
envelope containing the program printed on a sheet of white
paper, and two chits. Once those chits are finished, you have
no further right of appeal.

He had attended the Academy Awards ceremony once,

years ago, when the movie version of *By a Slender Thread,* his best-known book about the war, received an Oscar nomination for Best Foreign Film. After the ceremony, waiters had made the rounds with silver trays filled with glasses of champagne, Jack Daniel's, and white and red wine. The fancy tables with their linen cloths were loaded with platters of lobster and oysters on ice. Not a chit in sight, not like at the film festival in Holland where he had to "get in line just like everyone else," as one of the bar employees snarled at him after the premiere of *Payback.*

He talks briefly with C, N, L, and W about the show, which N calls "a travesty" and C "a disgrace." He puts in his own two cents by commenting that he would rather spend his time in the waiting room at the dental hygienist than at these horrible shows before the party itself is allowed to begin.

"You mean at the dentist's?" N asks.

"The dental hygienist," M says. "No need to make it worse than it is."

"It goes with the territory," C says.

"I'm thinking about skipping the whole show next year," N says.

They glance at each other, they know that's not going to happen: they remember all too well that N (or S, or Van der D, or C) said exactly the same thing last year.

A tall man in a tuxedo joins them. M recognizes him as N's new publisher. First he embraces N, then shakes hands with the others.

"Excuse me, I really have to take this," he says, still holding M's hand and looking at the display on his cell phone. M hadn't heard the phone ring. "Where are you? Where *exactly?* Okay, I'll be right there."

He winks at M and puts the phone back in his pocket.

"How's it coming along?" he asks.

"What?"

"*Liberation Year.* How many copies? Second run? Third run?"

M is aware of the reputation of N's new publisher. The rumors about the huge advances. They say he uses those advances to brazenly steal authors away from his colleagues, something that's officially not done among publishers.

"Reasonably well," M says. "I'm not dissatisfied."

The tall publisher looks at him impertinently, mockingly.

"'Not dissatisfied.' That sounds a bit grim," he says; he coughs and grins almost simultaneously. "I haven't seen it in the Top 60 yet."

M shrugs. "Well, you know," he says as calmly as he can—but his face suddenly feels flushed—"I don't really pay much attention to that. Not anymore," he adds. "Not at my age."

"The books in that Top 60 are all garbage anyway," C says.

"So your colleague writes garbage," the publisher says, with a little nod toward N. "That's news to me."

"Oh, but I didn't know . . . ," C says. "That book's been out for a year already! Is it still on the list?"

"One year to the day, next week," the publisher says. "We're going to raise a toast to that at the house. You men are all invited. And, if you'd like to talk sometime," he says, turning to M again. "A cup of coffee, or a beer at the end of the afternoon."

M says nothing, he glances at his empty champagne glass.

"No strings attached, of course," the publisher goes on. "But I really think it's a terrible pity. A book like *Liberation Year* deserves a much wider audience. Ask your colleague here, if you like. Ask N. He'll tell you that I'm not nearly the bastard they think I am. The bastard they *say* I am. In any case, I haven't heard N saying things like 'not dissatisfied,' not since he's been with me."

"We've talked about it before," N says, turning to M. "It's opened whole new worlds for me. Like after a cataract operation. Suddenly, you can see again."

N actually underwent a cataract operation a few years ago, so he knows what he's talking about. But that they had talked about this before was simply not true. M may have become a bit forgetful in the last few years, but he would definitely have remembered something like that.

"That reminds me, suddenly . . . ," the publisher says. "Did you have a special reason for that, M? For what you said about the Dutch resistance?"

M has no idea what he's talking about; he looks at the publisher questioningly.

"Wait, I've got it right here," the man says, and pulls out his cell phone again. "On *News Hour,* at the entrance, wait, I've almost got it . . ."

M realizes only too late that within the hour, through the miracle of technology, they will all see and hear their replies to the reporter; he only actually believes it, however, when he sees himself on the display of the cell phone the publisher is holding up for him.

"There . . . here it comes," the publisher says.

C, L, N, and W all crowd around the phone. Van der D also comes up and joins them at that moment, carrying a little tray with glasses of red wine.

"Here we go, you were thirsty and I gave you a drink . . . ," he says.

"Ssh!" L says. "Man, now I missed it!"

"Wait, here it comes again," the publisher says.

He does something with his fingertips on the display, and

there it is again, tiny but razor-sharp, the image of M leaning over to the reporter's microphone.

This time he doesn't look at the screen himself, he looks at his colleagues' faces.

His words are clearly audible.

A silence descends, insofar as one can speak of silence amid the hubbub around the stairs. C's jaw has literally dropped. Remarkably enough, it doesn't make him look older, but younger. *More boyish,* M corrects himself; *at our age you've seen everything, but rarely something that truly amazes you*—what he sees on C's face, though, is not amazement but dismay.

N is the first to break the silence.

"Well, well," is all he says.

"Yes," the publisher says. "That's what I thought, too, the first time around: Am I hearing this right?"

"What were you getting at?" C asks. "What were you trying to say, for Christ's sake?"

M looks into the eyes of his slightly older colleague. Is he crying? It's hard to say. As a matter of fact, C always looks like he's crying. M shrugs. What he would really like is to see the film one more time—he'd like to be able to think, *It's not that terrible, is it?* Would like to say that. To his colleagues. *There's nothing wrong with that, is there? It's not that terrible?*

He tries to do just that, but nothing comes out. He moistens his lips with the tip of his tongue.

"But that's already passed the statute of limitations, hasn't it?" Van der D says. "I mean, they won't be breaking down your door tomorrow, will they?"

It was meant as a joke, but no one laughs.

"I don't know what got into you," N says. "To make it worse, the timing is miserable. Especially after that magazine interview. Maybe you should have kept your mouth shut for once."

What interview? M wants to ask, but the next moment he realizes that it can be only one interview. That's strange, isn't it? Marie Claude Bruinzeel had promised to send him the text beforehand, but he never received it.

There's also something else. He doesn't like N's tone at all. That's not how colleagues talk to each other. And especially not with other colleagues around.

"We live in a free country," he said. "We were once *liberated,* if I remember correctly. So that we could once again say whatever we like."

"Well, if it had been up to your father that liberation never would have taken place," N says. "Then all of us here"—he points around him at the colleagues, at the publisher—"would be in a concentration camp. And that's only if we were lucky. Probably we would all have been taken out into the woods, shot, and dumped into a mass grave long ago."

M stares at him. Where is this coming from, all of a sudden? N is an arrogant, completely self-important shithead, everyone knows that, but he can't remember him ever using this tone with him before. With everyone standing around. The fact that M hasn't read the magazine interview himself now puts him at a great disadvantage. He looks at the others. C lowers his eyes, W averts his gaze, L shrugs, Van der D acts as though there's something floating in his wine, something that requires all his attention. The only one who isn't avoiding his gaze is the publisher—the look in his eyes is no longer triumphant, it's downright defiant, eyes in search of a row.

"Could I ask you to leave my father out of this?" M says at last. "My father made his own decisions at the time, but he's no longer around to defend them now."

"The point is that perhaps you should be a bit more conscious of what you're saying," N says. "You in particular, M.

In your books you've always made clever use of your past and your background. That also gives you a certain amount of responsibility. When someone like you says things like this about the Dutch resistance, it's different than it would be coming from some half-baked idiot. Especially in combination with all the dirty laundry that was aired in that interview. No, I find it absolutely tasteless."

But the theme is resistance, isn't it? M wants to say back to him. *The theme of the party? If you make resistance the theme of a party, you can't go complaining afterward when someone makes a few critical remarks about it?*

"That we're all allowed to say anything we like doesn't mean that we *have* to say everything, does it?" C says. "I don't get it, M. Especially not coming from you, with your background."

Oh my God, here we go again! M thinks. *Freedom of expression . . . and then especially the* limits to *that freedom.*

"I agree with you completely, C," M says in a conciliatory tone; at least he *hopes* it sounds conciliatory, because inside he's already boiling like—a pan of water: you can turn down the gas, but the water won't cool, not for a while. "Except there are some things that *have* to be said, because otherwise no one will say them these days. I'm not out to offend anyone; the two things are confused far too often: exercising one's freedom of expression and demanding the right to offend whomever we please."

"But there are cultures, religions, I don't have to name names, that are offended awfully quickly," Van der D says. "So are we supposed to censor ourselves and keep our mouths shut just because someone might feel insulted?"

"The point is to not apply a double standard," M says. "If I stand in front of colleague N's door every day and scream that his girlfriend is a whore, have I any right to complain when, on the third day, that girlfriend or N himself comes down and punches me in the face? Or do N and his girlfriend have every right to do that? They can, in any case, count on our sympathy. Or should we keep it simple and say that N and his girlfriend belong to a backward, medieval culture and that they are offended far too readily? That they have no right at all to defend that backward culture against insults?"

Besides his rage, M also feels light; he feels himself drifting away slowly, being lifted into the air: in the same way that they, as by some fortunate circumstance, were also drifting a bit further away from his remarks about the Dutch resistance.

"Each and every day," he goes on, because no one else is saying anything. "'Liliane is a whore! Liliane is a whore!' I assert my right to express myself freely. Maybe I'm wrong, N," he says, addressing his colleague directly now. "Maybe she's not a whore at all. But I'm allowed to say so. After all, we live in a free country."

"You're a pitiful figure," N says. He adopts a sad expression as he says it, which makes the countless wrinkles and folds in his cheeks and around his eyes seem to deepen even further—the landscape of gorges and deep valleys above which the sun is now going down. "In fact, I've known that for a long time, but today I know for certain."

"And *The Garden of Psalms* is a tired shit-cake of a book," M says—the water has stopped boiling, the gas has been turned off, the pan placed in the freezer: he feels calm. This calm, this *icy* calm, is something he hasn't felt for ages. "But I don't think I have to tell you that. I think you know that yourself already."

"And that from the writer who keeps churning out books about the war, year in and year out? We all fell asleep long ago, M. I think you're the only one who hasn't realized that yet. Why don't you write about something else for a change? About your mother, for example. In that interview you spend three pages whining about your dear mother, but in all those flog-a-dead-horse war books of yours we never read a word about her."

39

I'm washing my hands in the men's room when the tumult begins. First there are only a few excited voices. Then the screaming grows louder, the voices become distinct, with distinguishable words and sentences. "Cut it out!" "Stop . . . knock it off . . . knock it off . . . You hear me? Knock it off, right now!" "Grab him! . . . Grab him, goddamn it!"

There is a loud thud against the door of the men's room, as though someone has fallen or been pushed forcefully against it.

"Pervert!" a voice screams. "Dirty piece of shit!"

A dull boom, the wood cracks: *That was someone's head,* I think right away, *the back of someone's head hitting the door—* being hit *against the door.*

"I'll kill you, you pig! I'll rip your fucking lungs out!"

The show in the big theater was over more than an hour ago. I won't dwell too long on the show itself. You look at your watch a few times. You sigh deeply. When the woman comes on stage on her bicycle, you start to shift in your seat and groan. Everyone saw it. We all saw that the bike had wooden wheels, that the woman was wearing clogs and had a yellow Star of David sewn to her worn coat. You could feel it run through the audience. Everyone held their breath.

Then the woman started talking. With a weird accent, the
way drama school actors think normal people in Amsterdam
talk. "Chrise Amighty," the weird voice said. "Here I bike
all this friggin' way out to the farm on wooden wheels to get
some spuds, and the Krauts confiscate my tater peeler!" The
audience laughed. It was a laugh of relief. We were watching
a *sketch*. We were *allowed* to laugh, no one was going to recite
any poetry in honor of the resistance, thank God for that.
But after that first wave of relief, the laughter dwindled. Vicarious embarrassment settled over us like a cloud of gas. An
odorless but deadly gas. "Tulip bulbs? *Tulip* bulbs?" the actress shrieked. "Go tell that one to the floralist!" No effective
antidote has yet been found for vicarious shame. It's something physical. It hurts in a place you can't get to. You could
leave, try to sneak out of the theater as quietly as possible, but
you don't budge. Vicarious shame is contagious. Not only
does it infect the people around you, in the end it also makes
its way back to the source of the embarrassment. It was only
a matter of time before the cloud of gas drifted up onto the
stage. The actress began speaking faster and louder. She was
probably in desperate search of a point where she could cut
the monologue in half. Away! Away from this stage, into the
wings, the soothing fit of weeping in the dressing room—
anything was better than going on acting cute in front of an
audience that apparently didn't think it was cute at all.

Then it was over at last and we shuffled out of the theater.
You looked left and right, shook someone's hand, someone
else tapped you on the shoulder. You introduced me: the
mayor, the cabinet minister, a colleague: "Ana stayed home
with our daughter, she's ill, this is my neighbor." The mayor,
the cabinet minister, and the colleague all shook my hand
just to be polite, their eyes lingered on my face for less than

a second, then they turned away, sometimes quite literally, with their whole body. And so we finally reached the stairs beside the men's room.

I won't try to claim now, in hindsight, that there was tension in the air from the very beginning. But maybe you thought so? I don't know, something in your colleagues' faces, their glances, the way they looked at each other more than at you. I could be wrong, though, I don't actually know how writers look at each other—maybe they always look that way.

In the men's room, I am not alone. There are about five of us at the sinks. Famous faces, less-famous faces, an awfully famous face is just coming out of one of the cubicles.

When the shouting starts, we all look at each other. No one wants to be the first to go out. Excited voices are still coming from outside the door, but a little further away now, the ruckus seems to be moving—a thunderstorm passing, the number of seconds between flash and rumble is increasing, soon it will all be over.

Finally, I'm the first one to the door, the first one to open it and step out.

At the foot of the stairs, two old men are on the ground. Or rather: one old man is lying on his back on the dark red carpet, the back of his head pressed at an uncomfortable-looking angle against the bottom step, the other old man is sitting on top of him; he raises his fist and punches the man on the ground in the face. The carpet is sprinkled with glass.

A semicircle has formed around the two combatants: men in tuxedos, men in sport coats, men in jeans. At a safe distance. No one does anything. No one intervenes. There are women in the semicircle too: women in evening gowns, women with nutty hats and even nuttier dresses—but the women are standing a little back, behind the men.

"You pig!"

I suppress my first urge to go rushing over, to grab your fist, which is now poised in the air for the next punch, to say that enough is enough. I put my hands in my pockets and find a place among the lookers-on.

I do what the others do.

I do nothing.

40

IT FEELS good, he hadn't known it could feel so good. He plants his knuckles hard against N's upper lip, he's already done enough damage to the nose; there had been too much ambient noise to actually hear it crack, but he'd felt it. Perhaps he should have done this long ago, maybe not only to N (to N, too, of course, in any case to N!), but also to all the others who had foiled him all his life. All those failures and near-failures who begrudged him his success. Sometimes the talking has to stop and one must act. During the war, collaborators were shot and killed in their own doorways. Talking is something you do in peacetime. *Yes, you should have done this long ago,* he knows now, raising his fist in the air once more.

In his long life as a writer he has done a lot of talking, but even more often he has been silent. Dozens, maybe even hundreds of insults and left-handed compliments, below-the-belt taunts, unfounded accusations: he has swallowed it all. Usually he kept his mouth shut, turned and looked the other way, got up from the table. But sometimes he was awfully close. *One more word,* he told the other person in his thoughts. *One more word and I'll shut that mouth of yours once and for all. One more insult in the guise of an ironic comment and that face will shut down for good.* But it had always been as though the other person realized in the nick of time that he was toying with his own well-being—perhaps with his life. Something in M's eyes must have warned him, a minimal change in M's breathing had told the other person that they were about to cross a line: two cars racing at each other down a narrow road, which one will swerve first and run off the road? Almost never, M realized to his regret, had the other person turned their back on him, they must have realized just in time that they were dealing with a dog. A dangerous dog with its teeth bared, a dog in a barnyard where they had no business being. Always maintain eye contact with a dog, walk backward slowly, never turn your back on it. No, they were smarter than that: they quickly changed the subject in order to save their own skin.

The eye. The eye is a soft target par excellence; his fist doesn't land quite right, his wedding ring nicks the brow, blood wells up between the hairs and runs into the swollen eye. *Like a boxer,* it occurs to M in a flash. Muhammad Ali. Joe Frazier. But when an eyebrow keeps bleeding, they have to stop the fight. That would be a pity, he's not finished yet.

At first, just after he had grabbed N by the lapels and slammed the back of his head against the men's room door, colleagues, publishers, booksellers had tried to separate them. Hands on his shoulders, on his upper arms, at his wrists. But that's over now. He knows how it works: *Too dangerous.* They probably saw the look in his eyes, the grimness with which he went to work. The others are now only spectators. Onlookers.

Then M feels it between his legs, in his groin. N's knee has come up and hit him there, intentionally or not, precisely at the spot you have to hit when you're trying to get away from an opponent who's on top of you. He gasps for breath, there's no pain yet, just deep nausea, he has to be careful not to puke all over N's face, he thinks, and the next moment the head lifts itself from the step: he wonders how that can be, how the hell that's possible, he had assumed that he'd had him pinned completely, both knees on N's upper arms, his right hand squeezing N's throat. Now something really is coming up through his gullet, he opens his mouth wide to let it out, it's only air, warm air, it reminds him of the air in an underground subway station, the air that an onrushing train pushes out ahead through the tunnel. It tastes sour, he notes then, the pain rising at the same moment, the pain spreads out from his balls all over his lower body, the tears well up in his eyes—and at that moment, at that very moment, N's forehead slams hard into the bridge of his nose.

I literally saw stars . . . That's how people often describe the sensation after a hard blow or fall. But it's not like that: it's more like flashes of light, a reel of film flapping loose from the projector, sunlight reflected off a windowpane rattled by the wind, like lightning from a violent storm right above your head. And immediately after that comes the blackout. There is nothing that comes after, or at least there is no chronology. Between N's forehead hitting his nose and the moment when M himself is lying on his back on the soft carpet of the theater, there's something missing—for good, as it turns out.

He opens his eyes and sees N standing there—at his feet, his colleague is rubbing the bloodied knuckles of one hand with the fingers of the other.

"Goddamn," N says to no one in particular. "Goddamn it . . ."

And then there are already hands and arms helping M to a sitting position. A hand holding out a glass of water. Another hand wiping something from his face with a paper napkin.

Someone has squatted down beside him, it takes a

moment for him to focus, to slide the two images of a face on top of each other, to form one face. The lips move, but he hears nothing, only a hissing sound. The flashes of light have come back.

"What?" he says—he can barely hear his own voice either, as though he's swimming underwater.

The face moves up, leans toward him until the mouth is close to his ear.

"I'll take you home," M makes out.

The Teacher at the Blackboard

41

JAN LANDZAAT, history teacher at the Spinoza Lyceum, pulls on his socks and shoes. It is the day after Christmas, the radio forecasts are calling for heavy snowfall.

He sits on the edge of his bed, his hair still wet from the shower. He thinks about Laura. Then he tries not to think about her. It works, for five seconds. He sighs, brushes back his wet hair with his fingers. He hasn't shaved since the start of the Christmas vacation, four days ago—and maybe not before that either, he can't remember. But this morning everything is different. A new start, at least that's how it felt as he drew the razor across his soapy cheeks and, with each swipe, saw a bit of his old face reappear.

Of his *new* face, he corrects himself right away. Last night, as he'd wolfed down his lonely, reheated Christmas dinner, he was still a loser. Someone for whom you could feel only pity. Self-pity—he was home alone after all, there was no one else around to feel anything for him. The magic moment, the turn-around, the insight, took place as he was unscrewing the top from the whiskey bottle. The discovery, in fact, that the bottle was only one-third full: not enough to drink himself into a senseless coma, in any case, not the way he had on the first three nights of the Christmas vacation. A buzzing coma, with no past or future, a test pattern with the volume turned off.

"Here's what I'll do," he said out loud. "Tomorrow I'm going to drive past the house in Zeeland, but I'll be a different person."

The sound of his own voice in the otherwise silent room startled him. He hadn't spoken since five that afternoon, it felt as though something first had to be dislodged at the back of his throat: dried spit and mucus, with a warm nicotine taste from the two packs of cigarettes he had smoked each day for the last couple of months—since the fall vacation.

He had taken the tray with his half-eaten Christmas dinner—a piece of turkey breast in a sauce of walnuts and dark chocolate—from his lap, put it on the couch, and stood up.

"I'll drive to Paris," he said, starting to pace the room. "I have friends there. I won't be staying in Zeeland long, I have to move on. 'It wasn't that far out of my way,' I'll say. But after that I won't bother her anymore. That's how I'll say it, too: 'not bother you anymore.' That way, I'm openly admitting that I did bother her in the past."

It wasn't a little ways out of his way, but a big ways, no plausible little detour in any case, but he counted on a boy and girl of seventeen accepting that lie. He had thought about himself at seventeen: how he and a friend had hitch-hiked to Rome with no idea of the best route to take, by way of Austria or Switzerland or France; all that mattered was that, about four days later, they actually ended up in Rome.

The friends in Paris, that was something different. They definitely had to be believable, they had to at least *sound* believable, and so he had come up with two real names for them: Jean-Paul and Brigitte. A couple. A childless couple, he decided quickly enough—if he had to juggle even more names in his mind, he might slip up. To help him remember Jean-Paul and Brigitte he had devised last names for them as well: Jean-Paul Belmondo and Brigitte Bardot.

Maybe he wouldn't have to mention the names at all, but because he knew them, they existed. "Back in college," he now replied to the question that had not been posed, pacing back and forth across the room. "For my master's thesis about Napoleon. I spent a year at the Sorbonne. We were all in line for the same movie, Jean-Paul asked me for a light. After the movie, *Zazie dans le Métro*"—or did that one come out only much later?—"we went for a beer on Boulevard Saint-Michel. That's how we got to be friends, and we've stayed in contact all these years."

He felt like a cigarette, cigarettes helped him to think clearly, but his new face, the face of that other person he would be from now on, had stopped smoking—quit completely. He had reached the kitchen by now, where he used his paper napkin to wipe the remains of the turkey into the pedal bin. Then he unscrewed the top from the bottle of whiskey and held it above the sink. "No," he said then, screwing the cap back on. "I'm not an alcoholic. A non-alcoholic doesn't have to protect himself from himself. I can control myself. A bottle with a third still in it speaks of more self-control than an empty one."

But what about the smoking? He looked at the clock on the wall above the kitchen door. A quarter past nine. He needed to think, to think about tomorrow. "At midnight on Christmas Day I quit smoking," he said. "Forever," he added after a brief pause.

Lighting up a cigarette, he went back to pacing. There wasn't a lot of room in his new house: a living room with a sofa bed and a kitchen with a little balcony. Two hundred square feet, the landlord had said. A hundred and eighty, not counting the balcony. "But tomorrow I can take my pick of a hundred college students lined up to have it for this price," he said, looking Landzaat over from head to toe with almost shameless sarcasm, as though he had long figured out exactly how things stood with this unshaven grown man, "so I'd advise you to decide today."

He hadn't shown his children these two hundred (a hundred and eighty) square feet, not yet. He would pick them up at the house, or else his wife brought them to a spot they'd arranged beforehand on the phone—like at the entrance to Artis Zoo this afternoon—and later she would come and pick them up again. This afternoon she hadn't even stepped out of the car, she simply stayed in the driver's seat with the engine running, she hadn't even rolled down the window when he'd walked around to talk to her about what time she would pick them up. She had merely held her hand up to the glass, with all five fingers spread. *Five o'clock,* he saw her mime with her lips; she waved to their daughters, but didn't look at him again.

That's what I'll do. Still pacing, he had arrived at the glass door in the kitchen, the door to the balcony. He saw his own reflection in the pane, not crystal clear, but just right. A grown man in jeans and a sweater. Unshaven—at the moment, still, but tomorrow not anymore.

He looked at his reflection in the kitchen door. "That's how we'll do it," he said. "From now on, I'm above it all."

The first thing he did on the morning of that day after Christmas was spend half an hour in the shower. He washed his hair three times. Then he lathered his face with shaving cream. His lonely Christmas dinner of the night before already seemed an eternity away, like something from a former lifetime. When he took the turkey breast out of the oven, he had been unable to hold back the tears. Tears of self-pity. He had seen himself as the lonely man he was, from a distance,

as in a movie: a man prepares a gourmet meal for his sweetheart: he lights the candles and pours himself a little glass of
wine beforehand, but the sweetheart doesn't show and the
audience starts reaching for their hankies—they know she
has someone else.

For just a moment, a fraction of a second, as he conjured
the first stretch of smoothly shaven skin from beneath the
white lather, he felt his eyes start smarting again, but he pulled
himself together. He thought about Laura. He thought about
her as someone without whom life had a purpose as well.
Stand above it, he told himself. That's how you have to show
up there. *I just came to say hello and goodbye. I'm on my way to
Paris. But we can still be friends, can't we?* No, that was no good,
that sounded too much like begging, as though she would be
doing him a favor by consenting to be just friends. Ask no
questions, he said to himself. Avoid the interrogative completely. *They're expecting me in Paris this evening. We can still be
friends.* Now, without wanting to, without being able to stop
himself, he thought of Herman—and at the same moment
the razor slipped sideways across his cheek. It drew blood
right away. Not much, just the way that goes with shaving
cuts: as soon as the blood gets a whiff of the outside air, it
keeps on flowing. "Fuck!" he said—more at the thought of
Herman than the blood. What did she see in that skinny kid
anyway? You could hardly call that a man, could you? He
picked up a towel, carefully wiped away some of the foam,
and dabbed at the cut.

Ever since Herman had started going with Laura, he behaved differently in the classroom. He leaned far back in his
chair with a pen between his lips, his long legs sticking out
from under his desk. But even more than his shiftless posture,
it was the look in his eye. *I'm with her now, and you're not,* that
look said. He should really say something about it, sprawling

like that in a classroom wasn't done, but he held himself in
check. He knew the skinny boy's reputation; he could imagine how he would react. *Does it bother you?* The bleeding had
stopped faster than he'd expected, with great care he shaved
around the thin red stripe on his cheek. *The reason I sit like
this is because what you say doesn't interest me at all.* He had to
be careful not to cut himself again. Breathe calmly. What
was it Herman had asked him last time? Something about
Napoleon . . . no, now he knew: about Napoleon's *maîtresse.*
That high-handed tone! The insinuating look on his face as
he pronounced the word "maîtresse." He had tried to ignore
the question, but wasn't able. He had let himself go. *And why
should* you *suddenly be so interested in* that? he'd asked—the
whole class must have seen it, must have heard the tremor
in his voice. And then he had looked at Laura, Laura who—
ever since the fall vacation—had sat beside Herman at the
back of the class. He had looked at her with a helpless gaze, in
his mind he counted to ten, by *five* he was still no less afraid
that he would burst into tears right there on the spot. First
Laura had lowered her eyes, but when he reached *seven* she
looked at him. For half a moment, *eight* . . . she had smiled at
him, and then, *nine* . . . she shrugged. It was like a beam of
sunlight at the close of a rainy day, the hope of a tiny bit of
warmth that might dry your soaked clothes. With that smile
and that shrug Laura had, if only for the space of a second and
a half, distanced herself from her new boyfriend.

After school he cornered her in the bike shed. "I have to
talk to you!" he panted, and she glanced around a few times
before answering him. "What about? We've said all we have
to say." At that moment, from the little tunnel linking the
bike shed to the school basement, came the sound of laughter; a few senior boys were walking to their bikes, lighting
their cigarettes and roll-ups as they went. "I saw you," he said

quickly. "This afternoon in class, I saw how you smiled at me and shrugged." He paused for a moment and took a deep breath before asking the next question, the question that had kept him awake night after night, tossing and turning in his bed, for the last few weeks. "Are you happy with him, Laura? Are you really happy? That's all I need to hear."

Laura raised the pedal on her bike with the tip of her right shoe—so she could hop on and ride off immediately, he realized. "I smiled at you and shrugged this afternoon because I felt sorry for you, Jan. I thought you were pitiful. I don't want the whole class to see you like that, I can't stand it. I mean, look at yourself, the way you look. How you . . . how you smell. You shouldn't want to do that to yourself."

Then she took off on her bike. When she had to pass the smoking seniors, she hopped off, but she didn't look back.

It was Laura's words that handed him the key to his current metamorphosis. He would no longer elicit her pity, he would look fresh and well rested, he wouldn't smell anymore, at least not of alcohol and dried sweat. He was finished shaving, he sprinkled himself with aftershave, not only his cheeks, chin, and neck, but also his chest and belly, armpits and arms. Later on, at the house in Zeeland, when she opened the door for him, he would smell like a fresh start.

A towel around his waist, he made coffee and fried three eggs with ham and melted cheese. *I mustn't ask that anymore,* he thought, *whether she's happy with him. I just have to be there*—he didn't know how to formulate it any more clearly than that, but somehow it covered the feel of what he wanted to make happen. *Be there.* A certain nonchalance. That's the feeling he would elicit: that he was cured of her. A healthy, clean-shaven, fresh-smelling man who was sufficient unto himself. A grown man. A man who was old enough and stood above it all. Whose knees didn't start knocking at the sight of a schoolgirl who had dumped him, traded him in for someone her own age. Only in that way could he be a viable alternative for her. The self-assured, grown man who came by only because it happened to be on his way, simply to deliver to her the message that he had moved on. That he wanted to tie up the loose ends, together with her. He wasn't going to call her anymore. He wasn't going to stand in front of her bike in the shed to keep her from getting past. He would not—and this was the episode of which he felt most ashamed, he stopped chewing on his omelet and began groaning at the recollection—follow her home and hang around under a streetlight until deep into the night. Yes, he would round it off, close the book, turn a new page and then he would drive on to see his friends in Paris.

Meanwhile, however, the seed of doubt would be sown. Laura would see them beside each other at the table. She would realize again why, not so long ago, she had been attracted to him. Beside the skinny boy he would come out looking good. Anyone would come out looking good next to Herman. How could it be? How could it be, for Christ's sake? He looked almost like a girl! Around one wrist Herman wore a knotted leather strip, around the other a thin, woven lanyard of beads. And then those rings on his fingers, the flaxen hair on his cheeks. And his teeth! His teeth were too weird to be true. To call them irregular would be putting it mildly. Those front teeth that curved inward and the open spaces between his canines and the molars behind made him look more like a mouse than anything else. A mouse that had been smacked in the teeth by a much bigger mouse. How could a girl be drawn to that? They were teeth that let the wind through, a girl's tongue would have a hard time not getting lost in there. Granted, when it came to seduction, his own teeth weren't exactly his ace in the hole. But he had practiced it in front of the mirror, how to smile without his lip pulling back to show his gums and expose the full length of his uppers. Whenever he couldn't help laughing, a reflex he'd developed made him hold his hand in front of his mouth. Don't forget to brush your teeth well, later on, he noted to himself. Nothing was as deadly as a chunk of bacon or white bread in the gap between teeth that were too long anyway.

He laid the plate with the knife and fork on it in the sink and turned on the cold water. The frying pan was still on the stove. He looked at his watch, he wanted to leave on time, he didn't want to run the risk of getting caught in the blizzard. On the other hand, it would be strange for someone who was going to Paris for a couple of days to leave dirty dishes lying around. He'd do them later on. Before he went out the door. First he had to brush his teeth.

He smiled at himself in the mirror above the sink. His hair was almost dry now, he pulled it back and looked. The bags under his eyes, that was a problem, they hadn't just gone away after one night of not drinking. He sprinkled a little aftershave on a cotton swab and pressed it against the grayish-blue hollows under his eyes. Then he opened the door to the balcony. Atop the railing was a thin layer of fresh snow that had fallen during the night. He swept it together with his fingertips and rubbed his face with it, his eyelids and the bags. As though I went for a long walk this morning, he told himself when he saw the result in the bathroom mirror. The bags were still heavy, but the contrast between them and the rest of his face was already less striking.

He sought out a pair of jeans, his favorite plaid lumberjack shirt and his ankle-high hiking boots. Holding a pair of thick woolen socks and the hiking boots, he went back into the living room and sat down on the edge of the sofa bed.

He thought about Laura, then he tried not to think about her. "I can't stay long," he said out loud. "I need to be in Paris by dark."

Suddenly he couldn't help thinking of his little daughters. About yesterday at the zoo. The chickens and the geese and the pig at the children's farm there, the parrots on their perches, the monkeys, the lions, and the crocodiles. All the way at the back of the zoo they had found the polar-bear habitat. Two polar bears were asleep amid the artificial rocks. Carrots and heads of lettuce floated in the water—it had snowed yesterday too, the pointed tips and ridges of the artificial rocks were covered in a thin layer of white. His first thought had been that the polar bears, in any case, would not suffer from the cold, that the difference in temperature must be less pronounced for them than for the monkeys, lions, and parrots. But they were a long way from home. And this habitat, with the dirty water in its cramped swimming hole, was above all claustrophobic. An exercise yard, no more than that. It reminded him of the room he had rented, and at the moment when those two images—his lonely room and the polar-bear habitat—were transposed, the self-pity came roaring up: like gall from a tainted meal it rose from his stomach, through his gullet to the back of his throat.

"What's wrong, Daddy?" his eldest daughter asked. She took his hand. His younger daughter tossed the bears the last slice of stale brown bread they'd brought with them, but it ended up in the water amid the lettuce and the carrots.

"Nothing, sweetheart," he said.

He didn't dare to look at her, he didn't want to cry when his daughters were around. The hangover from the night before (six cans of beer, two-thirds of a bottle of whiskey), which had till then remained sleeping in its basket like a big hairy dog, now stretched itself slowly, walked up to him and licked his hand.

"You said, 'What a shitty rotten mess!,' Daddy."

"Did I say that?"

His daughter didn't respond.

"I feel sorry for the polar bears," he said. "That they're so far from home. That they have so much room to move around at home, but here they have to live on a little rocky shelf."

"Are we going home now, Daddy?" His younger daughter shook the last of the crumbs from the plastic sandwich bag into the polar-bear habitat.

"How about if we go and get french fries first?" he said.

In the cafeteria, where he ordered three portions of fries with mayonnaise, two colas and two bottles of Heineken, he felt how the cold had crept into his clothing. He stood up, took off his coat first and then his sweater. He had already finished the first bottle of beer. He tried to warm up by swinging his arms back and forth. Much too late, he noticed the worried looks on his daughters' faces, as though they no longer dared to look straight at him.

That evening his wife called.

"What did you do?" she said before he could speak.

"What?" He had just slid the turkey into the oven and was flipping through the TV guide in search of a suitable program to accompany his dinner.

"They're all upset. Because you . . . I hope it's not true, because they said you were *crying,* Jan! What were you thinking of, Jan?"

He couldn't remember doing that, but he had a suspicion that it was probably true.

"It was cold. I had tears in my eyes because of the cold, I told them that too."

"Please, Jan! I only wish you had the guts to admit it. That you could be honest with me. But no, of course not," she added after a brief silence.

"Okay, okay . . . I felt badly. The polar bears . . . you should have seen those polar bears. It just got to be too much for me."

He heard his ex-wife sigh—and the next moment he felt surprise at how easily he had admitted that word into his thoughts: "ex-wife." She wasn't his ex-wife, not yet, they were living apart for a while only after his ex-wife (wife!) had found an earring behind the toilet. *I have no idea,* he'd said. *Are you sure it's not one of yours?* He was no good with earrings; he wouldn't swear that he could recognize a pair of his own wife's earrings if he saw another woman wearing them on the street.

"Don't go thinking that I'll start feeling sorry for you when you act like this," she said to him now on the phone. "Or that you'll get to see your daughters any more often. In fact, you'll achieve just the opposite."

A gentle snow starts to fall as he lays his bag on the backseat. In plain sight. That way they can see with their own eyes that he won't be staying, that he's only making a brief layover on his way to Paris.

"Don't come on too strong," he says out loud and starts the engine, which turns over only after a few tries. "You've just come by to say hello. You plant something, a little seed in her mind. Then you leave."

He twists around in his seat and unzips the bag. The whiskey bottle is on top. He glances around furtively, but at this hour, on Boxing Day, the streets are empty. He unscrews the top and takes a big slug.

"You've got the drinking under control, so you can take a little now and then," he says. "You won't show up drunk, but you will be loose and easy."

After the second slug he feels the heat crawling beneath his clothes, he looks at his face in the rearview mirror; he's looking good, his cheeks are rosy, an open and warm look in his eyes. He screws the top back on the bottle, jams it down between the emergency brake and the seat, and drives slowly down the street and around the corner.

42

WE'RE SITTING in your living room: an Italian designer sofa, a glass coffee table, a chaise longue from the 1960s. Your little daughter is already in bed. Your wife has brought out beer, wine, and nuts.

After I first tried to install the projector on a stool balanced on a pile of books (photo books, art books, books of above-average girth and size), your wife came up with the idea of using the little stepladder. I went with her to get it, from a closet beside the front door, a cupboard containing the electricity and gas meters and a few shelves for cleaning products and other household items.

"Are you sure the timing is okay?" I asked without looking at her—by then I was halfway into the cupboard; I moved aside a vacuum cleaner, a bicycle pump, and a red bucket with a mop in it, so I could lift out the stepladder. "I mean, he doesn't seem completely himself at the moment."

"He still complains about being nauseous and seeing flashes of light," she replied. "And sometimes he goes completely under. It's not that he falls asleep. No: he goes under. I called the family doctor today and he says those are normal symptoms of a serious concussion. He should just take it easy for a week, the doctor said. And keep waking him up, in any case, when he goes under like that. No TV, no newspapers, no reading for a week."

No eight-millimeter movies, I almost said—but your wife said it for me.

"You're right, at first I didn't think it was such a good idea," she said. "Maybe these aren't the ideal circumstances. Are there a lot of them?"

"Two or three. I can also come back some other time."

But your wife shook her head.

"He's so excited," she said. "There's no talking him out of it now."

You didn't want to go to the emergency room. We picked up our coats from the checkroom, but it was only when we got outside, on the square in front of the theater, that I realized you were in much worse shape than I'd thought.

My wife. Ana. Ana is still inside.

I assured you that there were only the two of us. That your wife had stayed at home, with your sick daughter. You stopped for a moment and said you felt nauseous. By that time your left eye was swollen shut. We had washed away the blood as best we could in the men's room, but there were still spatters on your white shirt, just below the bow tie.

People—colleagues, publishers, others who had been invited to the party or not invited at all—looked at us as we made our way to the exit, once, then a second time, *yes, that's M, it's really him, what could have happened to him, do you think he fell down the stairs?*

That was when you started talking about flashes of light. *A storm. There's a thunderstorm coming up.* I already suspected that you had a concussion, and tried again to get you to go to the emergency room. I said we could take a cab, that it would be better if someone looked at it—but you didn't want to hear.

I got in a few good licks, didn't I? You saw it. I wasn't finished with him yet. I should have finished it a long time ago.

You grinned and slammed your right fist against the palm of your left hand. I had to promise not to start whining about the emergency room again. You wanted to walk home, but after only a few steps you stopped again.

What's that noise?

You tilted your head to one side and pressed two fingers against your right ear, as though it was blocked—as though there was water in it. I said nothing, only looked at you.

For a moment there I thought I heard a plane, but now it's gone.

At the taxi stand I held open the back door of the cab for you to climb in. By then you had forgotten that you were planning to walk home, and you climbed in without protest.

You had, I said, indeed got in a few good licks. I thought the message was clear enough, but you acted as though you had no idea what I was talking about.

Yeah, yeah. We're going home.

I meant to ask you about the reason for the fight, but it wasn't the right moment for that. Home first. Your wife would be shocked by the sight of your battered face and bloodied shirt, but maybe she was the one who could convince you to at least see a doctor.

You were slouching down in the seat, your head against the window. I thought you had fallen asleep, but it was something else, your body rocked apathetically to the taxi's movements, when we went through a curve the back of your head floated free of the door and then bonked against it, without waking you.

I grabbed your arm, I had to shake you hard a few times before you opened your eyes.

Ana! Where are we? We have to go back! Ana's still in there!

Once I had reassured you, you started in again about the thunderstorm and the flashes of light. I was just about to lean up to the driver to say that he should take us to the emergency room anyway, when I saw that the taxi was already turning into our street.

This is it, I said, *here, here it is, third doorway on the right.*

You tried to ring the bell, but I stopped you just in time. *It's late,* I said, *we don't want to wake anyone and startle them*—I took the key out of my pocket and opened the front door.

In the elevator you leaned back against the panel with buttons and shut your eyes. Your left eye was, as noted, already swollen shut, so in fact you closed only your right eye. I had to get you to move aside a little so I could hit the button for the fourth floor.

I think I have to throw up.

Less than a second passed between this announcement and the actual vomiting. I tried to sidestep it, but there wasn't much room in the elevator. I didn't dare to look down, I suspected that it had spattered up against my shoes and trouser leg too, and I tried as best I could to breathe only through my mouth.

One thing I always wondered was how that teacher, that Landzaat, how he found out that you two were spending Christmas vacation at that cottage.

You wiped your lips with the back of your hand and looked at me with one bloodshot, watery eye.

I just kept breathing. *Keep breathing calmly,* I told myself. Meanwhile I looked into that bloodshot eye.

You had said "you" almost in passing. As passingly as you

had spoken earlier of the thunderstorm. Of your wife, who you said had remained behind at the party.

I wondered, in short, which part of your brain had addressed me at that moment. The part that no longer knew exactly where you were and with whom, or another part, the one you sometimes hear about with older people: they no longer know where they put their reading glasses a minute before, but the way their mother kissed them good night seventy years earlier is still etched in their memory.

I in turn could have asked you all kinds of things then, but I was afraid that if I did, that part of your brain now meandering through the distant past would shut down on me—and never open again.

That's why I said, without looking away from your one good eye, that I had sometimes wondered about that too. I said it without looking away from your eye. I said I'd always meant to ask Laura about that, but that I kept forgetting to.

The elevator came to a stop at the fourth floor. I pushed the door open as quickly as I could.

Is it possible? I asked myself that at times. *Is it possible that Laura consciously lured that history teacher to the little house? For my book, for* Payback, *it wasn't absolutely crucial. But afterward I thought about it a lot. What about you, Herman, what do you think?*

You searched for something in your pants pockets, then breathed a deep sigh. This time I was too late. Before I could stop you, you had rung the bell beside the door.

In a moment your wife will open the door, I thought. This was probably my last chance.

I said that I had new material for you.

I know you do. From behind the door came the sound of approaching footsteps, then of a dead bolt being slid aside, a lock being turned. *I have new material for you too, Herman. New*

*material that I'm sure will interest you. It's time to lay our cards on
the table. It's rather late now, but why don't you come by tomorrow
night. Sometime after dinner, for example. Would that suit?*

I start with the movie of the flower stand. There is no sound,
let alone music, only the projector's rattle.

"That's right across the street from here," you say.

"Yes," I say. "The flower stand used to be right over there,
across the street. They only moved to our side of the street
later on. And where the café is now there used to be a snack
bar, you can't see it very well in this shot, but it was there.
A cornet of fries with mayonnaise cost twenty-five guilder
cents, a slightly bigger one was thirty-five."

I walk onscreen. A lanky boy, hair down to his shoulders,
a T-shirt that's too small for him, jeans, ankle-high (green,
but the color you have to imagine for yourself) rubber boots
with the tops folded down.

Christ, I was so skinny then! I think; I glance aside, at you
and your wife. Your wife is on the couch, you have settled
down comfortably in the chaise longue. Playing across your
lips is something that can only be an amused smile.

"Watch this," I say.

I/the lanky boy collapse in front of the flower stand, I use
my boots for traction on the paving stones and spin around
in a half circle, moving my left arm spastically the whole
time. At first the florist and his two customers, a middle-
aged woman and a girl, look on in bewilderment, but without intervening. Then the boy gets up, shakes the woman's
hand, and walks off camera, bottom left.

I hear you laugh. I glance over again, but you don't look
back at me, your gaze remains fixed on the wall, on the
flickering image. By then David and I are in an elevator, this

elevator, the elevator here in our building, making faces in close-up into the camera.

"Fantastic!" you say. "I knew this existed, but of course I've never actually seen it."

Now Miss Posthuma, our English teacher, appears. She is sitting at her desk in front of the chalkboard as David walks toward her. She looks up at him, it looks like he's going to ask her something, but then he falls to the floor. David does more or less the same thing I did at the flower stand: spastic movements, fits, knocking his head repeatedly against the leg of the desk. Now we pan up slowly and see our teacher's face, dumb with amazement. Even more than with the florist and his two customers, there is total bafflement here. The camera zooms in, David is spinning on the floor in a much smaller space, barely eighteen inches from her feet under the desk.

"Watch," I say.

The camera zooms in further on Miss Posthuma's face. Now she is no longer looking at David and his gyrations, but straight into the lens—at me.

She doesn't look angry, more like sad, her lips move.

"What is she saying here?" you ask. "Do you remember?"

"No," I say. "Something like: What do I think I'm doing. What it is I think I'm up to. Something like that."

I remember it all too well, it has always stuck with me, even long after my visit later that year to her deathly silent apartment out by the bridge, to run through my reading list with her—and long after her death too.

She said something about me, something about which I asked myself in stunned surprise, right there and then, whether it was true. Whether this seemingly sexless woman had perhaps seen something for which I had neither the proper distance nor degree of insight. Later, at her apartment,

I wondered whether she would come back to that, it was probably the main reason why I had turned down her offer to drink "something besides tea" with her.

"This got you into a lot of trouble later, didn't it, Herman?" you ask.

"Yes," I say.

"I remember," you say. You pick up the glass of red wine from beside your chair and raise it to your lips—but don't sip at it yet. "They thought these films were pretty crazy. I mean: that flower stand and the things you two do in the elevator here. In hindsight. That's the crux of the matter. In hindsight, it takes on a different meaning. Especially this, with the teacher. No respect. That was the conclusion, wasn't it? Someone with no respect for a teacher won't find it very difficult to snuff another teacher. "

"Yes," I say. My throat feels dry, I raise my bottle of beer to my lips, but it's empty.

"And that film script, I think that was the last straw. About taking hostages at your own school. That you all get together and blow up the place. A 'normal student' wouldn't do that either, would he? But that's bullshit, of course. In hindsight, all you can say is that you were far ahead of your time."

"Would you like another beer, Herman?" your wife asks.

I nod. "Love one."

"All that jabbering after the fact," you go on as your wife heads to the kitchen. "It's like with a troubled childhood. Someone mows down fifty people at a high school or a shopping mall. During the investigation, their troubled childhood is always unearthed: divorced parents, an abusive father, an alcoholic mother who moonlighted as a prostitute, the 'severely withdrawn' killer who 'always kept to himself and often acted erratically.' But for the sake of convenience they forget the tens of thousands, perhaps hundreds of thousands of withdrawn loners who had a childhood at least as troubled as the killer's but who never hurt a soul, let alone assaulted or murdered anyone."

"But in *Payback,* you made that same connection."

"Only because it was better for the book. Omens. Signs of things to come. Besides the film of the teacher and that screenplay, the main thing was probably that physics teacher. That you went on filming while he was lying dead in his classroom. Anyone who would do that is probably also indifferent toward life, toward the lives of other teachers, that was the way people reasoned back then. At first I went along with that line of reasoning. Once again: for the sake of the book. A book in which a couple of boys make funny movies at a flower stand, fool around with a teacher, and film another teacher who has died on the spot, but who commit no murder later on; who, on the contrary, go on to college, start a family, and end up as head accountant at an insurance company—that's not interesting to read about. They blend seamlessly into the gray masses of those who perhaps do wild or crazy things when they're young, but who grow tame as adults. A writer can't do anything with that. By the way, did you bring that one, the one with the physics teacher?"

Your wife has taken a seat on the couch again; I raise my second bottle of beer to my lips. There is Laura. She is sitting at a table in the cafeteria of the Spinoza Lyceum, forty years ago, she sticks her finger down her throat, she gags, but after that nothing happens. She grimaces, then smiles at the camera and shakes her head.

"What a lovely girl," your wife says. "What is she doing?"

"I suggested to her that she barf up a pink glacé cake, so she could say she was too ill to take the physics exam," I say.

"She gave it everything she had, but in the end she couldn't do it."

Meanwhile, Mr. Karstens's gleaming black shoes and lower legs can be seen, but the screen is then quickly filled by the table, the rest of the body too is blocked from sight by the men—the hall monitor and two teachers—who are squatting beside him.

Then Laura is back, she is standing beside the door of the physics lab and looking around, then she waves to the camera and starts pushing her way through the crowd of students who have gathered outside the classroom. She looks into the camera, no, this time she looks just past the camera: at me. She says something, wags her finger, almost scoldingly: *Don't!* But then we see her laugh. She laughs and shakes her head.

"People should really have looked at it the other way around," you say. "Or no, not the other way around. Differently. What I mean is: Imagine you're walking down the street and suddenly you hear something that isn't quite normal, a plane flying much too low, or in any event something unusual, an unusual sound, a sound that stands out from the normal street noises around you. You look up and you actually do see a plane. A passenger plane. It's flying right above the rooftops. *This isn't right,* that's your first thought, *something's wrong here, that plane is much too low.* You happen to have a movie camera with you. A video camera. You point the camera up in the air, and less than ten seconds later you see that plane slam into the side of a skyscraper. A tower. A building more than a hundred stories tall. You *film* the plane as it bores its way into the tower. An explosion, a ball of fire, wreckage flying everywhere. Six months later you are charged with a murder.

The police search your house and find the film with the passenger plane drilling its way into the tower. Are the detectives allowed to assume that you have always had little respect for human life, because you filmed the deaths of hundreds, perhaps thousands of people? Simply because you happened to be there, on the spot?"

During the film of my parents eating at the table we are mostly silent. Me too, I don't comment, I realize that it is too bare without music, without Michael's saxophone. Maybe I shouldn't have showed it, it occurs to me once it's almost over.

"Why did you call it *Life Before Death,* Herman?" your wife asks once I've stopped the projector and am threading the next reel.

"Well, that was the thing in those days," I say. "Pompous titles. It allowed you to make something out of almost nothing. After all, it's only my parents. I had plans for a sequel, but when my father moved in definitively with his new girlfriend a few months later, I didn't feel like it anymore."

In the next movie we are back in Terhofstede. You see us walking, on the road to Retranchement, at the bend in the road to be precise: I had run out in front in order to see them all coming around the curve.

"Lodewijk," you say. "And the one with the curly hair is Michael. Ron. David, that girl beside him, I always forget about her, his girlfriend, what was her name again?"

"Miriam," I say.

"Laura," you say as Laura comes by, walking arm in arm with Stella—but you don't mention Stella's name.

Then we're in the Zwin. I film a thistle, and then the white surf in the distance, David and Miriam who have remained behind on the dike and are kissing.

We see Laura from the back, her long black hair, the prints her boots leave behind in the sand.

I catch up with her and pass her, I film her from the front. Laura has stopped—she's looking straight into the camera, she brushes the hair out of her face. She looks. She keeps looking.

I mount the final reel on the projector. A white landscape, a snowstorm, a blue sign with the name of a place on it— RETRANCHEMENT, CITY OF SLUIS—covered in a ridge of snow, but there's also snow stuck to the front of it; a red stripe runs diagonally across the sign.

Laura. Laura carrying a plastic shopping bag, a white woolen cap on her head; the camera zooms in—there is snow on her eyebrows, on her lashes—until the screen is filled with her face and goes from out-of-focus to black.

"They never found this movie," I say. "I had just brought it to the shop to have it developed when they came and took all the others."

Footprints in the snow, the camera pans up slowly, we see the start of a bridge, the railing of a bridge, ice below—the frozen water of what must be a river or canal.

On the far side of the bridge we see Landzaat, the history teacher. He waves, no, he gestures really: *Come on, let's go, hurry up.* He turns around, takes a few steps, then looks back and stops.

It looks like someone has called his name, that that is why he's stopped. He has turned left after the bridge, now he points straight ahead and raises both arms.

For a moment he stands there like that, he's a fair distance away, but from his gestures, his body language, you can tell that he is saying something, maybe asking something—little white clouds are coming out of his mouth.

He starts to walk back, comes up onto the bridge a ways, then stops again. He says (or asks) something. He points.

Then he shrugs, turns and walks back to the end of the bridge, heads right.

43

FOR THE first half hour of their trudge through the snow, Jan Landzaat and Herman barely speak. Sometimes they walk beside each other, and then, when the path grows narrower and the snow deeper, in single file.

Landzaat hadn't slept a wink all night; he had tossed and turned, quietly, not making a sound, but the bed creaked at the slightest movement. With wide open eyes he had stared at the wooden planks on the attic ceiling, the checkered curtain at the window he had left open, the beams and planks illuminated by a streetlamp outside—he was sure that in that light he could also see the clouds of his own breath.

He had pondered, a feverish (there was no other word for it) pondering, his head glowed with all the thoughts tumbling over and scraping past each other. He had to pee, but he remained in bed until it started hurting, only then did he go downstairs.

Step by step, inside his churning, spinning head, the contours of a plan had begun to take shape. A plan which, somewhere around first light, he had christened "Plan B"— he laughed, without making a sound, at the name: Plan B. It sounded like something from an adventure novel, an action film in which the commandos take the island from the rocky north coast rather than crossing the mined beach in the south.

He had in fact already carried out the first part of his plan, without knowing at that point how it had to go. Last night, when the decision had finally been made that he would spend the night here, he had fetched his traveling bag from the car; his traveling bag and the bottle of whiskey, with less than a quarter still left in it.

There was no premeditation. Acting on impulse, he had slid in behind the wheel and screwed the top off the whiskey bottle. Tilting his head back to let the burning liquid flow down his throat as smoothly as possible, he caught sight of the little light built into the car ceiling, just behind the two front seats. In front, beside the rearview mirror, was another little bulb. A light put there to allow one, for example, to read a map at night.

The ceiling light was there for the passengers in the backseat. Sometimes his daughters asked him to turn it on when they were driving home at night, so they could read a magazine or a comic book.

Two or three times in the last year they had forgotten to turn off that light after they got home. The next morning the battery had been dead and he'd had to mess around with jumper cables or call the automobile association.

He took another slug, turned on the light, screwed the top back on the bottle, put it in his bag, and climbed out.

That was the first phase of Plan B. Whatever happened, the car wouldn't start the next morning. He hadn't seen a phone in the house. They could always call the automobile association from a house in the village, but he would immediately point out that the road service probably couldn't get through in weather like this. He would suggest that they go for help at a garage.

He guessed that they wouldn't send him out alone in the snow, that after some hesitation Herman would go along to show him the way—but Laura wouldn't, Laura would stay at home.

He had guessed correctly.

They arrive at a narrow bridge across a frozen canal; at that point Jan Landzaat is walking out in front. Without thinking about it, he crosses the bridge and turns left on the other side. On Christmas Eve, alone in his pitiful studio apartment, when his initial plan (a plan he could now, in hindsight, refer to as Plan A) began to take shape, he had searched around a little for a road map, but all his maps were at the house, as he in fact already knew.

At that point he had thought about the glove compartment of his car: there were always a few road maps in there, maps from the last summer vacation, perhaps even a map of France, but certainly one of the Netherlands.

He made a mental note to stop at a gas station along the way and buy a map of France, if there wasn't one in the car already. That would make his "friends in Paris" even more believable.

The next morning he ascertained that, indeed, the glove compartment contained only a map of Holland. He knew more or less how to get to Zeeland Flanders, he had been that way before, to Knokke, where his daughters had driven up and down the boulevard in pedal cars while he and his wife sat at an outdoor café and shared a plate of shrimp croquettes while knocking back a bottle of white wine.

Retranchement was still on the Dutch map, but Terhofstede wasn't. He didn't think it would be too difficult to find, though. The best thing would be to drive to Flushing and take the Breskens ferry. Retranchement was only about ten miles from Breskens.

Where is that exactly, Retranchement? I've never heard of it. They had been lying close together in their hotel bed, the bed in a hotel along the main road to Utrecht, Laura had leaned across him to take a pack of cigarettes from the nightstand. Their affair had been going on for only two weeks: the first time they did it fast, like in a movie, clothes left behind at the door, underwear and shoes in a hasty trail from door to bed, and then, after a cigarette or two, again, slowly, attentively, waiting for each other. *It had been so long since I'd been there,* she'd said of her parents' house in Zeeland. *When I was little I thought it was a great adventure, but later on I started getting bored, with only my parents and my little brother.* He asked her precisely where that was in Zeeland, just to ask something, not because it really interested him, it was only that, when he heard the funny, un-Dutch name Retranchement, he had thought she was pulling his leg.

It's not actually in Retranchement itself, it's in a little village close by, Terhofstede. Last summer we went there with a group of friends. Then it was fun again.

On that last evening at his place, the evening when she had lost her earring in the bathroom, she'd told him that she was going there again with the same friends that fall.

One evening, a few days before the Christmas vacation, he had called her. "Don't hang up right away!" he said quickly. "I have something important to tell you." He heard her sigh at the other end; he tried not to think about the last ten times he'd called her and only breathed into the phone.

"Please, Jan," she said. "Please. Just stop this."

"You're right," he said quickly. "I'm stopping. That's what I'm calling about. To tell you that I've stopped."

He was drunk, he did his best to keep talking in the hope

that she wouldn't notice, but he felt his words slipping away, struggling to keep their balance—while yet other words kept sticking together.

"Jan, I'm hanging up now. I don't want to talk to you."

"Wait! Wait a minute! Let me finish, I'm almost finished. Then you can hang up."

He was half expecting to hear the dial tone, but she didn't hang up; she didn't say anything, but she didn't hang up either.

I miss you, Laura. I can't live without you. Without you, I'm not going to go on living either. Before the year is over, I'm going to put an end to it.

Covering the horn with one hand, he reached for the whiskey bottle and raised it to his lips.

"I want to meet you one last time," he said after the third gulp. "No, it's not what you think," he added promptly when he heard her sigh again. "I don't want anything from you, I promise. You decide where. In a café or something, wherever you like. Tomorrow. Or the day after."

"I can't, not tomorrow. And the day after tomorrow I won't be here anymore. I'm going away."

He felt an air bubble, somewhere just below his midriff, a bubble that needed to get out now. He covered the horn again and tried to burp, but the only thing that came up was whiskey, whiskey and something else. *Where are you going?* No, he mustn't ask that.

"My parents are going to New York," she said.

"Are you going to New York! That's great! So you're leaving the day after tomorrow? Well, maybe we can—" *Maybe we can meet up tonight, then?* But that was not a good idea, he had no idea what time it was—he'd known what time it was when he called, but meanwhile he'd lost track completely.

"I'm not going along," she said. "My little brother is."

And that was the moment when he'd known—despite his drunken, pounding head, he realized that he should ask no further. Her parents were going to New York. With her brother. She had the whole place to herself, there was no reason to go away, but still she was going away, she'd just said so.

With him! He closed his eyes tightly. For three whole seconds he thought about Herman's unmanly body, his stringy, unwashed hair, the little, beaded bracelet around his wrist, his stinking rubber boots, his malformed teeth. *Fucking shit, how can she do that?*

"I've got an idea," he said. "I'm going to leave it completely up to you. You don't want to meet up now. You *can't* meet up now. So let's just agree that you call *me*. Whenever the time's right for you. Maybe you think right now that we shouldn't meet up at all, but that's not true, Laura. But you decide when. I won't call you again."

At the gas station where he stopped between Goes and Flushing they didn't have a French map, but they did have a detailed map of Zeeland province. That morning in the attic, by first light, he examined it. The closest town of any size was Sluis. Terhofstede was on the map too, and he did his best to memorize the route—both there and back again.

That was why, when they reached the bridge over the canal, he had almost automatically turned left. That's what he thought he remembered seeing on the map. No, not "thought he remembered," he remembered with one-hundred-percent certainty that this was the way to Sluis. That was also why he hadn't turned around when Herman called him. For the last fifteen minutes Herman had been lagging a bit, meanwhile they had left behind the last houses of Terhofstede and now only passed the occasional farm, a bit further back from the road. They saw no one at all, only once a growling watchdog that ventured a few steps from its yard but quickly turned back.

"We have to turn right here!" he hears Herman call out for the second time, and this time he does turn around.

Herman is still standing on the other side, at the start of the bridge, he's holding something up to his eye, a telescope, Landzaat thinks at first, but then he sees it is a camera. A movie camera.

A movie camera! Herman is filming him—maybe he has been filming him for a while, while he was lagging behind. His first impulse is to yank the camera out of Herman's hands and toss it in the canal. Into the frozen canal. He pictures the way the camera might bounce once and then break into pieces. No, not that. Not a good idea. Silently, he counts to ten.

"Are you sure?" he shouts. "I thought Sluis was in that direction."

He points. He points toward Sluis, toward the spot beyond the trees and a few more whitened fields and dikes lined with pollard willows, to where he is sure Sluis must be.

"No, here, to the right," Herman shouts back—Herman is still standing on the other side of the bridge; in the silence that follows Jan Landzaat hears a new sound that he can't quite place at first, a quiet rattle. *The camera! He's just gone on filming! He's filming what it is I'm going to do.* "I've done this before, the fastest way is to the right."

Slowly, he turns and starts walking back to the bridge. As slowly as possible, to win time, to give himself time to think. He can't imagine that Herman could be wrong about this. To the right, along the canal, is the opposite direction; it will only take them further and further away from Sluis.

And closer to the sea, to the bird sanctuary. The Zwin, that's what it was called—he'd seen it on the map that morning.

His Plan B was every bit as simple as it was elegant, if you asked him. He hadn't even spent the whole night thinking about it: the initial outline had been there in less than a second, half a second at most, in a clear flash. He lay staring at the plank ceiling in the light of the streetlamp, but the idea was so clear and blinding that the yellowish light on the planks and beams seemed for that half second to turn a fraction of a shade darker.

In a little while, his car would refuse to start. He would go walking with Herman and Laura, or only with Herman, or completely on his own, to Sluis—he figured he and Herman, just the two of them, was the most likely scenario.

Somewhere along the way he would have to shake Herman, he didn't know how, but it shouldn't be too hard. If need be he could just take off running, yes, that wasn't such a bad idea. "He just took off running," Herman would report later, it would sound completely unbelievable, so implausible that Herman would only incriminate himself.

Once he had given Herman the slip he would have to find a suitable place. A remote place, a hollow in the dunes close to the bird sanctuary, behind a bush or amid the reeds along a frozen ditch, a place where they wouldn't find him too quickly, at least not before the next day, when the search began.

At that remote place he would use a big stone or a heavy branch (a stone would be best, but he wasn't sure whether there would be any of those along the road or in the fields around here) to hurt himself so badly that he would lose consciousness. Practically speaking, he didn't know whether it was possible to knock yourself out with a big stone (or a heavy branch). In any case, it would have to produce a lot of blood. He figured that he could let the big stone come down a few times on his nose, mouth, and eyes before he passed out. It would have to look like he'd been battered by someone who hated him. And even if he didn't succeed in knocking himself unconscious with a final blow to the temple, that would be no real disaster. The most important thing was not to be found right away, at the earliest in the course of the next day—by which time, at this temperature, conscious or no, he would have frozen to death.

There were a few technical catches: he could leave no fingerprints on the stone (or heavy branch), but he would be wearing mittens anyway, so that was no problem. And then there was the snow, or the footprints in the snow, rather. Only his own footprints would be found, nothing belonging to a possible murderer. In selecting the remote spot, therefore, he would also have to make sure it wasn't all too far from a road or path. A road or path with plenty of footprints from walkers and other passersby. From the path to the spot where the corpse (his corpse!) would be found, he would walk back and forth a few times to wipe out all the tracks. As though the murderer had tried to cover the tracks, he thought with a grin, lying in his cold bed in the attic.

Conclusions would be drawn swiftly enough. Everything would be brought out in the open, but what did that matter? He wouldn't be around to see it.

A teacher visits two students at a house in Zeeland Flanders. He and the girl had once had a brief affair. The next morning his car refuses to start. The boy offers to lead him to a garage in Sluis. But they never get there. The boy returns home alone. His statements seem confused (to say nothing of suspicious). *He just took off running.* The next day (two days, three days, a week later), the teacher's body is found in a ditch or a hollow in the dunes. His head has been battered with a large stone (heavy branch). An autopsy will determine whether he was beaten to death or whether it was the cold that killed him.

The accounts given by the two students sound less than believable. At first, both of them are held for questioning. But after only a few days the detectives assigned to the case will begin to doubt whether the girl is guilty. Because Laura herself, in the best of all possible scenarios, will have started doubting whether Herman has really told her everything. He came back to the house alone that day. The teacher had supposedly taken off on his own. Would Laura, in spite of everything, continue to believe in Herman's innocence? It didn't really matter much anymore. Her life, too, would be largely ruined. It wouldn't be long before people began questioning her version of events as well.

That girl, do you think maybe she put that boy up to murdering the teacher?

After that the suspicions would never be completely dispelled, she would be associated with the murder for the rest of her life—as an accomplice. *We'll never really know the whole truth.* That was enough, nothing else was needed.

It was already almost light in the attic; a gray, cloudy day, he noted after pressing his face against the icy window. The plan made sense, down to the slightest detail, even those details he himself could never have anticipated beforehand.

The teacher, Laura and Herman would claim, had said he'd only made a slight detour before driving on that day, or the next morning, to see friends in Paris. But it wasn't a slight detour at all, you couldn't call it that, not with the best will in the world. Wasn't it strange that someone going to Paris would have no guidebook or map of that city in his car? Or at least a map of France?

Imagine that there was a thorough police investigation and that, besides the evidence already rapidly piling up, they discovered that the car's battery was dead. Run down, because a battery doesn't just go dead. When the battery was charged, the roof light would go on. Aha, so that was it! The car wasn't locked. It would have been easy as pie for one of the students to sneak out during the night and turn on the reading lamp, so that the teacher couldn't leave the next morning.

At that moment he had heard them talking downstairs, very quietly, almost in a whisper, but in this house every sound went straight through the thin wooden walls and floors. What could they be talking about? He had to go downstairs quickly now, he would surprise them by making breakfast. He would pretend to be cheerful. Most people on the verge of suicide were cheerful for the last few days, that's what those closest to them always said afterward. The future suicide smiled a bit more than usual, he played games with the children, he told jokes—and the next day they found him hanging from a beam.

He shivered as he picked up his cold clothes from the chair at the foot of the bed. And as he put on his socks and shoes, he suddenly thought about his two daughters. His little daughters would grow up without a father. What's more, for the rest of their lives they would be the daughters of a murdered father, a father whose life had been taken by brute force. He thought about his wife. In a certain sense, she would be getting her just deserts, she would never recover. She would feel guilty, about what he wasn't quite sure, but he believed it was true: his wife would think she could have prevented his death if she'd been a little more accommodating. If she hadn't threatened him with seeing his daughters less often, perhaps not at all anymore. With a little more compassion, she could have cured him of his obsession with a seventeen-year-old student. She would be consumed with regret at her own stubbornness. She would age quickly. Later, she would have a lot to explain to her growing daughters. *But why did Daddy go away, Mom? Was it really so bad, what he did? Shouldn't you have helped him instead?*

And it was there and at that moment, as he pulled on his clammy socks and slid his feet into his ice-cold shoes, that he'd had his second brilliant flash of inspiration.

A modified Plan B.

Yes, he thought. That's how I'll do it. Much better. Better for everyone: not least of all for myself, but in any case better for my girls.

44

Landzaat and I would walk out to the Zwin. At that moment I didn't know what I was planning to do out there, but whatever happened we were not going to Sluis, not to a garage.

In a certain sense it was all very illogical, I was quite aware of that. The sooner we found a garage, after all, the sooner Landzaat's car could be fixed, and the sooner he could go away too, away, out of our lives.

But that morning I wasn't running on logic anymore. The history teacher had arrived uninvited. He had forced his way into our lives, which had been timeless up till then— ever since he'd arrived, everything was taking too long. He didn't go away, he remained hanging around like a musty, lingering smell.

We might find an open garage in Sluis. A mechanic might come back with us to look at the car, or else they'd send a tow truck to pick it up, a tow truck of the kind that could actually make it through the snow. There was a chance that the repair would take a few days, that they would have to order parts. Would Landzaat volunteer to move to a hotel in Sluis while they waited? Would he go back to Amsterdam?

But even so, what then? Imagine the car could be started today, that they could push him out of the snow—that

Jan Landzaat would *finally! finally!* be able to travel on to his friends in Paris. Would we really be rid of him? Would Laura be rid of him? Or would it start all over again after the Christmas vacation?

The teacher may have lost the battle, but he had not lost the war. Landzaat himself had said that once during history class. It was some kind of famous quote, I didn't remember who said it. Jan Landzaat already realized that he had nothing to gain here in Terhofstede, I was convinced of that: he had given up for the moment, he would cut his losses and, if the engine started, he would really leave.

But what about a week from now? A month? Would he give up completely, would he put Laura out of his mind for good, or would he simply start all over again? With other means. With a new tactic.

No, I had to do something to make sure it was over for good. Something that would remove him from our lives forever.

That was why I sent him the wrong way after he crossed the bridge. That was why I filmed him too: as evidence, although at that moment, I didn't know what of.

After the bridge the path widened into a road, a dirt road, or maybe a real one covered in asphalt: the thick layer of snow made it impossible to tell. It didn't really matter, of course, but because the road was so broad we could—at least theoretically—walk beside each other, which was absolutely the last thing I wanted. By then my body literally balked at getting close to the history teacher, and so I slowed down every once in a while, to at least stay a few feet behind him. But then Landzaat would slow down too, forcing me to choose between dawdling even more or coming up alongside him. Maybe he was suspicious, or maybe he was simply on his guard after seeing the movie camera—maybe he wanted to keep me from filming him candidly again.

Up to that point there had been no conversation, not even the start of a conversation. I had resolved not to start talking; first of all because I didn't feel like it, and secondly—

"Have you made movies before with that thing?" Landzaat asked; at that moment he was walking two feet out in front of me, but he slowed so that we could walk beside each other. "I mean, you must make movies. No, what I really mean is: What kind of things do you film?"

I didn't answer right away; I realized that I preferred the silence that had reigned till then. It had not been an uneasy silence—maybe for him, but not for me.

Not answering him at all was out of the question. The teacher would probably only shrug and say something like *If you don't want to talk, fine by me. No skin off my nose.*

It would grant him a kind of moral superiority, and we couldn't have that.

"All kinds of things," I said.

"Really? All kinds of things? Or mostly teachers?"

I had put the camera back in my coat pocket, inside the pocket I weighed it in my hand: it was pretty heavy, but not heavy enough to use for anything but making movies.

"You've developed quite a reputation in the teachers' lounge," Landzaat said. "You and David. With the things you two do. Playing tricks all over the place. Acting like an idiot in class and then filming the teacher's reaction."

I said nothing, it felt best to say nothing, to see first where he was trying to go with this.

"Don't misunderstand me, I'm not condemning it right off the bat," he said. "I was young once too. Playing jokes on teachers, I did that in high school too. But in the teachers' lounge I noticed that one or two of them were really upset about it."

After the fall vacation I had edited all the films back-to-back. By then, the teacher mortality rate had reached its high-water mark—in hindsight you could even say that it had already passed that point by the start of the Christmas vacation. First Mr. Van Ruth, the math teacher—unfortunately, I didn't have him on film. Then Miss Posthuma, found dead in her apartment less than a week later, and in late November Harm Koolhaas's fatal trip to Miami, which ended in a (botched) holdup. We hadn't done anything with him either, he simply wasn't the right type for it—"too vulnerable by nature" was David's comment, and that said enough already. I did of course have footage of Mr. Karstens, but only of his lifeless body lying in his own classroom, half hidden beneath the desk in front of the chalkboard.

I had mounted all the films back-to-back and given the whole thing the working title *Life Before Death II*. It was perfect, that title: teachers also didn't realize that their lives were empty and senseless, that those lives had ended on the day they decided to make teaching their profession. It was like a nature film of a herd grazing on the savanna, or better yet, of a school of fish in the ocean. Oblivious to almost everything except the water in which it moves, the life of a fish starts somewhere, at a random moment, and ends somewhere else, at perhaps an even more random moment. That end is often both swift and brutal. Another, bigger fish or a bird or a seal waiting patiently beside a hole in the polar ice takes the fish in its jaws, beak, or teeth, bites it in two, and swallows it down.

I had tried to furnish it with English-language narration—nature films are almost always dubbed in English. *Miss Posthuma is seeing something she has never seen before. Mr. Karstens will never teach again.* I thought about the narration I could later dub beneath the footage I'd made of the history teacher. *Mr. Landzaat has followed his instincts; he has followed his dick to the end of the world. Now he is lost in the snow, wondering, "How did I get here?"*

What was it Landzaat had just said? *I was young once too.* The horror of it, what emptiness, when you could make that kind of pronouncement about yourself. It reminded me of my father. My father, who had tried to act so casual when I came home drunk one night from an outing with my friends, long past the time we'd agreed on. Paternally casual. My mother's eyes were red and teary. *I was so worried! I thought you'd been in an accident!* The gesture with which my father silenced her . . . *I used to drink a bit too much too sometimes. That happens when you're young.* After that I had to throw up, I didn't even have the strength to get up off the living room couch, let alone make it to the bathroom: everything came out all at once, a bucket being tossed, a toilet flushing—it spattered all over the wall-to-wall carpet, but at least the room stopped spinning.

They didn't get angry. My mother came and sat beside me and put her arm around me, my father stood beside the TV with his hands in his pockets and winked at me. I felt my mother's fingers in my hair, she had started crying quietly as she spoke reassuring words. Normal parents would have let me clean up my own barf, but they had stopped being normal parents long ago. *I'm going to my room. I need to lie down.* And I stood up, I left them behind with their sense of guilt. Less than a minute later I could hear them fighting, I couldn't understand what they were saying, but I could sort of guess.

I could make *Life Before Death II* end with Jan Landzaat. With Landzaat on the bridge back there, or with a couple of new shots later, out in the Zwin. His face at the moment he realized we had gone in the wrong direction, that we had to walk the whole way back, but that it was probably already too late to reach a garage in Sluis before it closed. *I don't know,* I would say. *I guess I must have been mistaken . . .*

Would he fly into a rage? Or would he remain a teacher under all circumstances? Someone who knows nothing himself, but has been hired to aid and abet others in their ignorance. A grown man barely in his thirties who says of himself that he "was young once too." *As a teacher, he must repress his natural urges. But so far he hasn't behaved like a proper teacher. Now . . . he is paying the price for his carelessness . . .*

Yes, I would have to look him straight in the eye, cold as ice, later, when I told him we would no longer make it to Sluis before dark. I would film him, keep on filming him, in his dismay, his despair, perhaps in his rage. But not yet, for the time being I needed to reassure him—we were on our way to Sluis, to a garage, if everything worked out he could drive on to Paris tomorrow morning.

"Come on," I said. "Really upset about it . . . I don't believe that. They're grown-up people, right? Who was actually so upset about it?" I asked for form's sake, because of course I already knew; this was meant more to keep our "normal" conversation going. *Mr. Karstens didn't seem particularly upset,* I thought—but I didn't say that.

"What are you laughing about?" Landzaat asked.

"No, I was just thinking about Karstens," I said; and it was at that moment, that one careless moment when I spoke before thinking, when I said exactly what I had meant not to say from the beginning, that I made up my mind—that I suddenly knew what I was going to do. "At least he didn't seem too upset when I filmed him. On the contrary."

I could tell right away from the second and a half in

which Jan Landzaat didn't reply. The time he took to think it over was what gave him away. I felt a wave of triumph rise up from my collar: it was going to be much easier than I'd thought.

"Do you think that's funny?" he asked. "At least that's how it sounds: as though you think it's really funny. And what do you mean by 'when I filmed him'? What did you guys do, for Christ's sake?"

Bingo! I thought. *Gotcha.* You hold a piece of sausage above a dog's head, two feet above its head. You can't let your concentration flag for even a moment, otherwise the dog will take a piece of your finger when it jumps at the sausage.

"Karstens wasn't actually a friend of mine," he went on after a brief pause, during which he took off his black mittens, rubbed his hands together and stuck them in his pockets. "Just a different kind of teacher than I am. But I don't think that's any way to talk about someone."

"What do you mean by 'a different kind of teacher,' Landzaat? Do you mean a teacher who doesn't try right away to stuff his dick into one of his students? Who just does what he was hired to do? I can't imagine Mr. Karstens climbing down off his stool to force himself on one of the girls in the class. Getting down on his knees and begging them to play with his wiener."

This was fantastic. It *felt* fantastic. It was like being able to throw open the window at last after a long, stuffy day, to let in the fresh air—no, it was more than just fresh air—to let a fresh *wind* blow through. But even more than an open window, it felt like something that was sort of forbidden, but still necessary: busting a pane of glass in order to yank on the emergency brake.

The teacher had stopped in his tracks, he turned halfway

around to face me, but I walked on; a few yards further I stopped too and turned around.

"The big mistake teachers like you make is in thinking that they're different," I said. "Above all, that they're nicer. That's what you think too, that you are above all else a nice teacher. Not strict like Van Ruth and Karstens. Not deathly boring like Posthuma. But we don't care fuck-all about nice teachers. Give us the real thing. Real, instead of artificial. You're pure fake, Landzaat, everyone can see that. Everyone except for you."

He looked at me, his eyes weren't angry, more like dull: crestfallen. He took a few steps in my direction, but I quickly walked backward, pulling the movie camera out of my pocket and taking the cap off the lens.

I needed to crank it up a little and then turn my back on him. I needed to give him the chance to do something to me, something irreversible, in any case something that left marks; I needed him to lose his self-control and fly off the handle. I was doing this for Laura, I told myself, I was not a born fighter, in a head-on fight with the history teacher I was bound to take a beating. I would have to get him to the point where he knocked out a couple of my teeth or blackened both my eyes. A battered and bloody face, a split lip with two front teeth broken off, that would be the best thing. The footage would speak for itself. Jan Landzaat would be drummed out of the Spinoza Lyceum and slapped with a restraining order at the very least, if he didn't go to jail for six months or so. I thought about his wife, his two young daughters; I imagined them talking to their daddy through a little window in the booth in the prison visiting room. With one of those closed-circuit telephones, like in American movies: the daughters would press their hands against the window, and their father would do the same on the other side. Tears would be shed. His wife might forgive him to a certain extent, but she would never let him share her bed again.

"I bet saying all that makes you think you're pretty tough," he said, approaching now with somewhat bigger steps—I pressed the viewfinder against my eye and took equally big steps backward. "But I know exactly what kind of petty little man you are, Herman. It's a wonder you could ever get a girl like Laura, that you could get any girl at all with that skinny body and those pitiful teeth of yours."

I stopped, another possibility was to let him get closer and then unexpectedly hit him in the face with the camera, against his upper lip or the bridge of his nose—but I had to stay calm, I told myself. I mustn't ruin everything now by losing my self-control; I was so close.

"Don't go thinking that a girl like Laura will stick with you for very long," Landzaat said. "Maybe girls think that's fun for a while, a little boy they can lord it over, who they can make do whatever they want, but they go looking for a real man soon enough."

The history teacher had stopped less than two feet from me; I looked at his face through the viewfinder, but I didn't start filming. *Not yet, wait just a bit,* I said to myself.

If I got in the first blow, I might have a chance. I could break his nose with the camera, he would grab his nose with both hands while the blood sprayed in all directions, and in that unguarded moment, while his defenses were down, I could kick him in the balls. After that it would be up to me to decide how far to go. Where I would stop. But it would be a mistake, I realized, it would be a victory for Jan Landzaat. A teacher assaulted by a student. Whatever the exact cause, precisely why he was here in Terhofstede would fade into the background. From a culprit, an underage-girl-stalking teacher, he would become a victim. The turncoat is blindfolded and hoisted onto a rail amid a raging crowd. What happens to him after that we still find a bit pitiful, we forget the why behind it, the reason—we forget that this is a collaborator. No, I warded off the thought of getting in the first punch as quickly as it came up. I had to keep my wits about me, I warned myself again—not hand over the reins now, not while I was so close to my objective.

I pushed the button on the camera. I knew what I was going to say, how I would push him over the edge. And I would have it all on film: his face contorted with rage, with a bit of luck also the first swing, and then the consequences.

"You know what it is, Landzaat?" I started in, but at that moment I heard my camera make an all-too-familiar sound. *Fuck!* I thought, but I thought it with such force that it escaped audibly from my lips too. The film roll! The film was finished and unraveling inside the camera. There couldn't have been a worse moment! I hadn't been paying fucking attention, I shouldn't have used the camera back there on the bridge. It had two ORWO-brand reels, manufactured in East Germany; Double-8 was what it was called, two times 8mm, you could film for two and a half minutes, after that you had to open the camera and turn the reel around, preferably in a dark place, for another two and a half minutes of moviemaking. There was no way I could do that here, outside. I had to decide fast. Whether to go ahead now and live with the fact that it wasn't on film, or wait and try later to get him riled up all over again. I knew exactly what I was going to say, the question was whether I'd be able to dish it out later with the same impact. It was something about Landzaat's wife and daughters, something Laura had told me once. I would start with that, and if that wasn't enough to get him to take a swing at me, I would take it a step further. After all, he'd asked for it. I would tell him something Laura had told me about him one evening, a few days after she'd broken off the relationship. I'd always tried to avoid hearing too many details about the affair, whenever Laura started in about it I tried to change the subject as fast as possible: I found it too disgusting to listen to. This was a couple of days after she broke it off. She was sitting on her bed at home, crying; her parents were in the living room watching TV, we had been kissing a bit, and then she told me. It was something physical, something about Landzaat's body that she could never stand, something she'd kept trying to get over during the couple of weeks it had lasted, but never succeeded. *You know from the start that you'll never stick it out too long with someone with . . . with something like that,* Laura had said. *It's like someone with a shrill voice,* she said, *or a weird odor. At first there are other things that make up for it, but in the end you know that you'd never want to grow old alongside that shrill voice or weird odor.*

Then she went on to tell me precisely what it was about Jan Landzaat that had inspired her aversion from the start. She had to repeat it a couple of times, because at first I didn't understand what she was talking about, and after that I didn't believe her. But then she'd started crying and swore that it was really true—and I took her in my arms and pressed her against me, I whispered in her ear that I believed her.

If I were to confront Jan Landzaat with this bodily detail, here and now in the snow, it would be as though I were rubbing his face in his own vomit and forcing him to eat it—but this was worse than vomit.

He'd thought he could insult me with his comments about my appearance and my lack of masculinity, but that didn't get to me. I knew who I was. I knew above all where my strengths lay. I knew enough not to fly in the face of my own nature by trying to play the irresistible macho man; everyone, especially the girls, would see through that right away. Sure, I was too skinny. Physically, I wasn't strong, I didn't have a seductive set of teeth. At the age of ten I had worn braces for a while, at first my teeth had sort of protruded, but after wearing the braces they were pushed too far back; on my way to school once, in a fit of rashness, I had taken the retainer out of my mouth and tossed it under a parked car.

But I was different—or rather, I *had* something different. At thirteen I had my first real girlfriend. She was going with a much older boy at the time. A handsome guy. The athletic type. Biceps, long hairy legs that looked good in shorts. But also yawningly boring, as I noted while a group of us were standing around talking, after the school's annual track and field day. The girl was part of that group too. The boy had his arm around her waist, but I could tell from the way she started looking around whenever he started talking, about the weather, about his baseball team winning the finals, about how hungry he was. And how tired. I could almost *see* the girl sigh. I looked at her, I kept looking at her, for as long as it took for her to look away. *I wouldn't bore you,* my eyes told her. *Never.* Then I said something that made her laugh. She laughed, the handsome boy didn't, he only raised his eyebrows and looked around pensively, as though he suddenly smelled something strange. *It's your eyes,* the girl told me the next afternoon when we were lying on the bed in her room. *The way you looked at me yesterday. And now you're doing it again!* During the fall vacation, Laura had said something along the same lines. *When I look into your eyes for too long, I get all wobbly. You don't hide anything. You can see exactly what you're thinking. Who you are.* Not all the girls felt that way, of course, they didn't all melt when I looked at them. I knew my own limitations. But if those other girls felt like dying of boredom beside some fashion model, that was up to them.

"What is it?" Jan Landzaat asked.

I had stopped in my tracks. I looked around. About ten yards from the path, at the bottom of the embankment sloping down to the canal, there were some bushes, a thicket, no more than that—but exactly right for what I had in mind.

I would turn the film around. I *had* to turn the film around. I needed to get it on film, how the teacher flew off the handle. Without pictures, there was nothing.

With my back to him I would try to turn the reel around under my coat, without letting too much light in. I didn't know what time it was or exactly when we'd left the house, but it seemed like it was already getting dark.

"I have to piss," I said.

45

AT THE moment you lost consciousness I was in mid-sentence, right in the middle of my account of how I came home later that evening, my embrace with Laura in the snow beneath the light of the streetlamp.

Here's how it went: First your daughter came into the living room, in her pajamas. Blinking her eyes in the bright light. "I can't sleep." You didn't look at her, you looked at your wife right away. "Come on, come with me, we'll go back to bed." Your wife told me she would be right back, that I didn't have to wait for her to finish my story.

Where's . . . where is he? Laura asked, and she stopped kissing me for a moment as she squinted into the darkness, peering up the darkened road I'd just come down.

I . . . I lost him, I said.

It had been a while since you'd last mumbled "yes" or "oh," or even nodded your head. Behind the lenses of your glasses your eyes were still open, like normal, the lid of the swollen left eye had even crept up a little since yesterday and was already revealing a fraction of an inch of eyeball. I was in the midst of that last sentence when I realized you weren't moving *at all* anymore. Total motionlessness. Rigidity. It was not like being asleep. This was a clock. A clock that's been running normally and then you suddenly realize that the hands stopped moving a few minutes ago. There's something you've missed: a train, an appointment. Time has slipped away, time has literally stood still. You, in any case, arrive too late. I spoke your name. I asked whether everything was all right, but in fact I already knew. You weren't going to answer me. I also knew what I had to do. I would have to get up, put a hand on your shoulder, and shake you—or, at the very least, shout for your wife.

But I did none of that. I fell silent. I kept my mouth shut. I looked at you in a way I had never looked before. The way you rarely look at people. Maybe at those closest to you, the woman asleep beside you in bed, your child napping in the crib.

So this is it, I thought. *This is what the world looks like once you, Mr. M, are no longer around.*

The back of your head was leaning against the headrest; at that moment, for those few minutes (or was it more, fifteen minutes, perhaps?), you existed only in your work. In the work you'd left behind; nothing more would be added, the readers would have to make do with this.

"Well, she's back asleep." I hadn't heard your wife come in. "Would you like another beer, Herman?"

I raised a finger to my lips and nodded at your motionless form in the chaise longue.

"Aw," your wife said, tiptoeing a few steps in your direction. "He's been so tired. Since yesterday. I wonder whether we shouldn't have called the doctor again."

Then she was beside you, leaning over you.

"But . . ." During the brief silence that followed—without

a doubt the longest brief silence in my life—during that one moment when she still had her back to me, I took the opportunity to put on my most surprised expression. "His eyes! His eyes! His eyes are still open!"

She started shaking you, first by the arm, then by both shoulders. She called your name a few times—a little too loudly if you asked me: I was just about to say that she should be careful not to wake your daughter, when she turned around to face me.

I don't know if she could tell right away. Maybe I'd adopted the surprised expression a few beats too early, so that now there was only a glimmer of it left, a vague recollection at most of my feigned surprise.

Yes, in hindsight—now—I think she did see it, the color of her eyes shifted slightly, one shade darker, like spilled wine, a wine stain, still glistening at first, that sinks into the carpet the next moment.

I was expecting her to start screaming at me, to blame me for something. *Why are you just sitting there? Do something!*

But she didn't scream. She only shook her head. Then she picked up her cell phone from the coffee table and called an ambulance.

Before the ambulance arrived we tried to bring you around. Your wife opened the top buttons of your shirt and slapped your cheeks softly a few times, but there was no reaction. You were still breathing, you were just somewhere else, at a spot where maybe you could still hear us, but from which there was no return. Perhaps you felt your wife's hand against your cheeks, but then as though they were hands from another world, a parallel world where you'd been not so very long ago, watching forty-year-old black-and-white movies.

And then there was the moment when your daughter was suddenly standing in the living room again; I saw her before your wife did, she was staring wide-eyed at her mother as she shook you by your reluctantly earthbound shoulders.

For the second time that evening, I did nothing. I looked. First at your daughter, then at your wife, and then at you. There was nothing left for me to do. I could stay and watch, but I could also go away, it wouldn't make any difference.

"Mama."

At last your wife turned around.

"Catherine!"

She held her arms out wide, grabbed her, held her tightly to her chest, cuddled her. "It's nothing, there's nothing wrong. Daddy's sleeping. Daddy's just sleeping."

Then your daughter wriggled her way out of her mother's embrace, took a step to one side, and placed her little hand on your forehead.

"Daddy's sleeping," she said.

46

DADDY'S SLEEPING—BUT those are words he no longer hears.

He's still there: he thinks—his mind thinks its final thoughts—but the sounds have now been banished. He is a writer. He can describe his final moments, the transition from life to death, no longer on paper, but still in words—in a final sentence.

He knows the accounts of people who have "come back from the dead." Those accounts usually speak of a "very clear, *blinding* light at the end of a tunnel," of a "lighted gateway," of a "sense of peace." Death is not at all terrible, these revenants say, merely a joy-drenched transition from life to a new phase.

But those who came back from the dead had never been truly dead, that's the one factor that binds them all, he knows now. In the last few years he has often—increasingly often—thought about his parents. His parents who supposedly were waiting for him on the far side of that "light" and that "gateway." With open arms. Like on the playground. Yes, he would go running to them like a child after a long day at school, his father would lift him high into the air, his mother would cover him in kisses.

Life was about that long: a boring day at school, the endless hours spent mostly staring out the window.

The greatest advantage, he knows now too, is the disappearance of fear. You don't have to be afraid of anything once you're dead. He has, in essence, always been afraid, he at least possesses enough self-knowledge to realize that—he is not the adventuresome type, as they say. There are two kinds of writers. The first kind has to go everywhere himself, he has to experience it all himself in order to write about it. This first category of writer goes big-game hunting in Africa, shark fishing in the Gulf of Mexico, he races out in front of the bulls in Pamplona and dives for cover during a mortar attack in a hot, distant country rife with diarrhea and nasty, stinging insects—a country he would never have visited if there hadn't been a war on. He needs to *experience* things, if he doesn't experience anything, the writing engine will not turn over.

The second category of writer mostly stays at home. When he actually changes his address, he does so at most once or twice in his life. He nurtures constancy. The familiar. At a restaurant he will always order the same dish. And it's almost always the same restaurant. When he goes on vacation, it's always to the same country. To the same hotel.

It was like with a story. Like with a book. What is it we look for in a book? That someone goes through a process of maturation—that he achieves insight? But imagine if that process and that insight simply aren't there? Wouldn't that, in fact, be much more like life itself? People who actually go through a process of maturation are as rare as hen's teeth. To say nothing of those who gain insight. No, in the real world we remain the same. We go to the theater and see a movie and decide to change our lives, but the next day we've forgotten all about that. We resolve to be kinder, to listen more carefully. We keep that up for the better part of a morning.

After that we go back to snarling as usual—snarling is that one old, worn-out housecoat that fits us best.

He wonders how it will go with him, with himself—with his own story. He's seen it happen to dead colleagues. Suddenly their books are back on the bestseller list. Not for long, a couple of weeks at most, but still . . . He tries to put himself in the shoes of those who buy a book by a recently deceased author. A book they apparently didn't own yet. Maybe they had never even heard of the writer in question, maybe it was only the newspaper obituary or the article about the writer's funeral that gave them the idea. "Hyenas" is what colleague N called that category of readers, that category unto itself, in an interview once. "Vultures." But that wasn't true. Such readers had at most heard the hyenas howl in the distance, they had seen the vultures circling and realized there was something there for the taking.

He had only tried to imagine what must have happened. Back then. Forty years ago. He had never written detective novels or thrillers, but he had always enjoyed reading them. Those books brought back something of that old joy in reading, the old, carefree, avid reading: in the same way he'd devoured the books he had stolen from the shop when he was sixteen, without worrying too much about genre. In those days, all books were equally exciting, in the old-fashioned sense that you wanted to find out how they ended.

But somewhere around his eighteenth birthday—a point that coincided more or less with his earliest urges to write—he had been driven out, once and for all, from the paradise of carefree reading. From that moment on a distinction was imposed between literature and the rest: the other books. From then on literature was either good or bad. Bad literature he read with a gnashing of teeth, growling and fidgeting in his easy chair, furious in fact at such pretentiously formulated impotence. But with the good literature too, something of the original pleasure was ruined once and for all. Whenever a book was truly good—very, very good, perhaps even a work of genius, a masterpiece—he kept asking himself how the writer had done it. He would pause after each paragraph, sometimes after each sentence, and then read that paragraph and that sentence over and over before going on. Sometimes he turned the sentence into pabulum by reading it over and over so often that it finally kept as little of its original flair as a meal cooked to death and then warmed up again and again.

There was also another difference between literature and all the other books. It was, in fact, the same food from two different restaurants. On the right you had the restaurant with the Michelin stars, on the left the Burger King or McDonald's. The point was that you didn't always feel like nibbling at sophisticated tidbits, didn't always feel like spearing a minuscule piece of goose liver from an otherwise as-good-as-empty plate. Sometimes you felt more like a hamburger with bacon and melted cheese and a soft, soggy bun that left the grease dripping down your chin—but that was always accompanied by a sense of guilt. A sense of guilt so overpowering that M, whenever he visited a Burger King, kept looking around skittishly to make sure he saw no one he knew. Caught red-handed! Like running into someone outside the door of a whorehouse. After reading a thriller or a detective novel, he had almost the same feeling: a great emptiness. Was that all there was? A few hours after eating that Triple Whopper with bacon and cheese he was hungry again too, as though both stomach and brain had completely repressed the memory of that guilty meal. A detective novel was a furtive visit to a whorehouse, a real book was a conquest each and every time, the woman at the hotel bar in that foreign city, the conversation that consists more of glances than of words—and then the elevator upstairs.

Along with Ana, he sometimes cast a furtive eye at detective series on TV. "The vet did it," he would shout after ten minutes. "Wait and see, that nice veterinarian who's helping them search for the body right now."

"Ssh!" Ana would say. "Don't do that, otherwise it's no fun anymore."

But he was always right. It took a great deal of effort to suppress a triumphant grin whenever "the nice vet" was taken into custody at last.

It was in that same way, forty years ago, that he had looked out over the fields around Terhofstede, had walked back and forth to Retranchement and then followed the canal to Sluis. He had found a room in a simple boarding-house in Retranchement, and left on foot for the Zwin after breakfast the next day. There, atop the sea dike, he looked out over the thistle and haulm-covered flats of the inlet—it looked like it was low tide. He put himself in the position of his characters. Of Herman. Of Laura. But above all, of the history teacher. Of Jan Landzaat.

Imagine, he thought for the first time there, at that same spot, that the teacher had simply disappeared of his own free will. That he hadn't been killed by Herman and Laura and then buried in some secret, or at least unfindable, location. He had thought about the detective series, about the most improbable yet still just barely credible scenario—about the nice veterinarian.

He had tried to imagine this same landscape when it was covered with ice and snow. The sun that was already going down by four-thirty on that day after Boxing Day, the day when Jan Landzaat and Herman left on foot together for Sluis to find a garage for his disabled vehicle. Imagine that the history teacher had been planning all along to get rid of Herman somewhere along the way; perhaps not in the literal sense of getting rid of him, not by harming him, but much simpler than that: by disappearing, by giving him the slip when he wasn't paying attention. That he had waited patiently for such a moment to arrive, and that when Herman withdrew into the bushes along the dike to take a piss—as Herman himself had stated, as he had never stopped stating—Landzaat had seized the opportunity and slipped away quietly.

As a writer, this version of events was inconvenient for M. Inconvenient for the book he had already decided to write, even though he was still unsure which way the plot would go; it would be better if the whole hike to Sluis had been invented by Herman (and by Laura), and if the history teacher was long buried and in the ground two days after Christmas. Unfortunately, though, there was that witness, the to-this-day-unidentified witness who the papers said had seen Herman and the teacher close to the canal, albeit not in the direction of Sluis but out toward the Zwin.

After that, of course, anything could have happened; no new witnesses turned up. Herman could have murdered Jan Landzaat and then buried him at some spot in or close to the Zwin. Then he could have returned to Terhofstede and told Laura that he had "lost" the teacher.

But back then, forty years ago, as M stood on the sea dike, that version of events had suddenly seemed highly improbable. Herman would have had to do it with his bare hands; in a struggle with the healthy, full-grown Jan Landzaat he would definitely have come out on the losing end. He would have had to take him by surprise, from behind, using a stone, or some weapon he'd brought from the house—a hammer, a hatchet, something he could easily hide under his coat—to knock him out. But the more M thought about it, the less likely that seemed. It seemed more premeditated than Herman or Laura was capable of. And even though the witness had stated that he'd seen Herman and Landzaat heading toward the Zwin, that didn't mean Herman had intentionally lured him out there in order to kill him: after all, Herman could have gotten mixed up too—he may have known the surroundings better than the teacher, but maybe he'd had a hard time getting his bearings in that white landscape.

M had walked from Terhofstede to the canal. There was a bridge there, but no signpost; on the far side of the canal the road split, one side going north toward the Zwin, the other to the south, toward Sluis. From the split in the road you still could not see Sluis, not even on a clear summer's day: nothing, no steeple or buildings, those came only later, after the canal bent off gently and the old fortified town popped up from behind the trees. Jan Landzaat and Herman, in any event, had never reached Sluis.

Atop the sea dike M had closed his eyes and sniffed at the wind. In the distance, on the horizon, he saw sticking up into the air the cranes of what was probably a harbor. Which way would he himself have gone? he'd asked himself that afternoon.

In the police interviews with Laura and Herman, in what had leaked out about those interviews, the "friends in Paris" came up a number of times. But no one else, not Landzaat's wife, not his colleagues or former classmates, had ever heard of such Parisian friends. Still, the history teacher had been "on his way to Paris"; at least that's what he himself claimed—once again, according to Laura and Herman.

M imagined a figure: a lone figure in a pure white landscape, this same landscape in winter, the harbor cranes in the distance.

Had Jan Landzaat gone to Paris? Had he taken the train? And had he then gone into hiding with his real or imaginary friends?

And if so, why? M wondered. In order to disappear? Had he had his fill of life as a teacher? Of his life in general, his family life? Had he hoped to pin the blame for a murder that had never been committed on two innocent students?

And there M's imagination balked, or rather: that was as far as he was willing to think about it. For his book, for the book he was already planning to write, he wanted to focus solely on Herman and Laura. On two students who had bumped off an overly obtrusive teacher. Bumped him off justifiably—this last aside applied only for the discerning listener, for those who could read between the lines. An all-too-intelligent teacher who outfoxed everyone, that was no good to him. It would make the story hard to swallow, to say the very least.

Still, he needed to know for sure. He couldn't have reality suddenly coming along to spoil the broth. Which was why, during an interview on the Sunday afternoon cultural program, when the host asked whether he was working on "something new," he had said that he was considering writing a book about the affair. A few months had already passed. Herman and Laura had been released on bail, due to a lack of solid evidence. They were even allowed to return to school, to make up for the time they'd missed while awaiting the results of the investigation.

"You mean a sort of *In Cold Blood*?" After posing the question, the host closed his eyes and pursed his lips; he wanted everyone, including M, but above all the viewers at home, to know that he was no slouch, that he had perhaps actually even read Truman Capote's book.

"No, not so much that," M had replied. "Capote wrote

that when the facts of the crime were already widely known. Two men rob a remote farmhouse in Kansas because they think they'll find money there. The final take is quite disappointing. While they're about it they murder, yes, in cold blood, an entire family. What I'm thinking about is something different. I want to let my imagination do the work. After all, we still don't know exactly what happened during those days around Christmas, which proved so fatal to the history teacher. The investigation has reached an impasse. I'm going to look into the affair. In fact, I've been doing so already for a while. I don't pretend that I'll be able to solve the mystery, I'm thinking more along the lines of a reconstruction, up to the point where we no longer have any idea. Making use of the imagination. Fantasy. Maybe we've all overlooked something."

The next day most of the Dutch daily papers had run the news, some of them even on the front page. M TO WRITE BOOK ABOUT CASE OF MISSING TEACHER, was the headline in *Het Vrije Volk*. A WRITER AND HIS IMAGINATION: NEW IMPETUS FOR SOLUTION OF UNSOLVED MURDER? announced both *De Telegraaf* and *De Courant/Nieuws van de Dag*.

M waited. Meanwhile, he went on writing his book. The writing went quickly; soon he had finished his first rough draft. He and his publisher decided on a publication date in the fall.

About three weeks after the interview, he found a blue airmail envelope in his letterbox. A French stamp, a Paris postmark.

Dear Mr. M, was the salutation of the letter, written on light blue airmail paper.

47

JAN LANDZAAT, history teacher at the Spinoza Lyceum, pulls on his socks and shoes. The shoes are the same ones he was wearing the day after Boxing Day, when he walked by way of the Zwin to Zeebrugge and spent the last of his cash on a train ticket to Paris.

For the first few weeks he had thought about Laura almost every day. No, not *almost* every day: every day, every hour, every minute. Laura's eyes, Laura's mouth, Laura pulling her black hair back into a ponytail and then shaking it loose again. Laura saying *You shouldn't want to do that to yourself,* that time in the bike shed when he had laid both hands on her handlebars to keep her from riding off. At that last memory he groaned quietly and shook his head. *I won't bother you anymore,* he said silently, but sometimes, without realizing it, he said it out loud too.

The final variation on his Plan B meant that he was no longer dead. The morning after Boxing Day, sitting on the edge of the bed, he had worked out the new version down to the minutest details, then thought it through again, checking for blank spots and loose ends, and then approved it as being exceptionally believable—all within the space of five minutes.

He would disappear. Somewhere on the road to Sluis

he would shake off Herman, just like in the initial version of Plan B. But now he would no longer withdraw to a remote spot in the dunes and hurt himself badly with a stone (or piece of wood). He would not have to freeze to death. He would no longer be found and buried—it was this final image, above all, the image of his coffin in the auditorium at a cemetery, a coffin on which his daughters would place flowers and drawings (*Isn't Daddy coming back at all anymore? No, not anymore*), that had made him change his mind.

He would only disappear. First Herman would come back to Laura with his dubious story, then both of them would have to explain that story—which would grow more dubious with each passing day—to the police. *Took off? What do you mean, took off? And left his car behind? And all his baggage? Do you really believe that yourselves? Or is there something you two aren't telling us . . .*

Precisely how he would deal with the practical side of it, that was something he could think about later. It didn't seem like it would be too tough, there were so many people who disappeared. He had almost no cash left, he couldn't go to a hotel, he couldn't call anyone: no, he literally had to disappear from the face of the earth. A few months, half a year, a year . . . He would see how it went. Herman and Laura would be indicted, even though there was no evidence, no body, but still, everything pointed clearly in their direction. From a distance he would follow the course of the investigation, he would have to go somewhere where he could buy Dutch newspapers, no further than Belgium or France—and suddenly he thought of Paris.

For those closest to him (for his daughters—his wife could go fuck herself!), he would only be missing. Everything would seem to indicate that he had been murdered, true, but as long as no body was found the hope—however slim—of a happy ending would remain alive. The proverbial glimmer.

After those six months (or that year) he would come back. He would report in somewhere. Amnesia. He would feign amnesia. Not for too long, he probably wouldn't be able to keep up the act for more than a few days. When he was reunited with his daughters (with his wife, who would tearfully forgive him for everything), his memory would return by fits and starts. *Daddy! Daddy!* He would raise his eyebrows, frown. *Yes, it's coming back to me . . . something is coming back . . .*

A week later his memory would have returned almost completely. By then he would remember how he and Herman had hiked to Sluis. Then nothing else, not for a long time, until he finally woke up in the snow, half frozen to death, he didn't know what had happened, hit while his back was turned and left behind for dead, perhaps? He really couldn't remember. Then, for a long time again, nothing. He had walked, yes. Walked and walked. Then another huge gap in time, a vague memory of a bridge over the Seine. What do you think, Doctor? What could have happened to me?

48

DADDY'S SLEEPING—HE feels the little hand on his forehead, the hand of his young daughter, for whom he will be a memory from this evening on. A memory still reasonably clear at first, but which will fade quite quickly. After that comes the gradual forgetting, the life carried forward in a photo album: *Look, this is Daddy holding you on his lap.*

They had drunk a cup of coffee together outside a brasserie on the corner of Boulevard Saint-Michel and Saint Germain-des-Prés. The waiter had asked M solicitously whether everything was all right, whether he wasn't being bothered by the unshaven man in his torn, filthy winter coat who stank of stale wine. And M had held out his hand reassuringly above the tabletop, *everything's fine, everything's all right, we'll be leaving in a moment.*

From the very start, from the morning when he had opened the airmail letter, there was something M had been unable to stomach. His book was more or less finished: he had always relied on his intuition, he knew when a book was really finished. The teacher showing up out of nowhere, the teacher with (feigned!) amnesia, it was all just a bit too much, a narrative line that was no longer needed. But so as not to scare Jan Landzaat away too quickly, M had pretended to be interested in this new angle.

"When I saw Herman standing at the bridge with his movie camera, I thought for a moment that I was going to have to cancel my whole plan," Landzaat said. "After all, I couldn't just run away anymore, he'd be sure to film me then. But in the end it turned out to be easier than I'd thought."

"What makes you think, by the way, that I'll actually keep this to myself?" M asked. "Why shouldn't I go back to Amsterdam tomorrow and go to the police right away?"

"Because you're a writer," the teacher said. "You can't let something like this go. You want to keep it all to yourself."

As darkness fell they had walked down to the Seine. Jan Landzaat had showed him the bridge under which he had slept for the last few months. But M was only half listening. It was, above all perhaps, the *news value* that he couldn't stomach. The spectacularity. His book didn't need that at all. The focus would shift far too much to the teacher. He was looking for something else—maybe a more timeless book. A normal story in which two students rid themselves of a teacher. Simply because it's possible. Because the possibility presents itself—the recovery of the natural balance.

It happened without forethought. They had walked down the steps to the quay and were standing under the bridge. In the meantime, M had been thinking about what he was going to do. First he would tell the teacher that he needed to think about it. Then he would never contact him again. He would leave the book precisely the way it was. Jan Landzaat could show up suddenly if he felt like it, but not in M's book.

"I need to get back to my hotel," M said. "I'll think about it."

"But not too long," the teacher said. His eyes gleamed wetly in that face with its filthy, sticky beard. "I miss my daughters. I really miss them."

Maybe there was something else, M thought at that

moment. Maybe it was actually something else he couldn't stomach. He'd always disliked people who came to him with ideas for his books. *I thought about you right away. It's really something for a novel. But, okay, I'm no writer. So if you want to use it, it's yours.*

It was completely dark by then, they were standing beside each other at the edge of the quay, looking out over the river at the dancing lights of the bridge reflected in the black water. M glanced around, but the waterfront was deserted. He took a step back, putting Landzaat between him and the edge.

The history teacher must have thought at first that M was reaching out to shake his hand goodbye. But the hand came up and rested against Jan Landzaat's chest.

Spreading his fingers, so he could apply more force, he shoved him hard. The teacher waved his arms wildly, shouted once, then fell backward.

Back in Amsterdam, M waited a month. Closing his eyes, he could see Jan Landzaat's head appear above water once or twice, but with that winter coat and those hiking shoes it was a lost battle; the current was strong, the head was already smaller the second time, and much further away too. In M's memory the man shouted something again and raised his arm.

People on the bridge, or further down along the waterfront, might have seen the drowning man, maybe even tried to help him. Maybe the teacher had actually succeeded in struggling to shore further downstream, under his own power.

But after a month, when M had heard nothing, he called his publisher to say that the book was finished.

"Have you got a title already?" his publisher asked.

"Payback," was M's reply.

.   .   .

Now he can't feel the hand anymore either. He is already gone. There is no light, no tunnel, no gateway. *Good thing too,* is his final thought. Imagine if there were. He thinks about the excuses and the pretexts he would have had to come up with, how he had used his parents in his books, had *misused* them—as they could rightly claim if they had actually been able to read those books "up there," where they had ostensibly been all this time. He had missed his mother more than he had missed his father, it was better to be honest about that. But the thought of spending the rest of his life, no, the rest of his death, of spending all eternity—whatever one was supposed to imagine by that—in her company had always seemed unbearable to him. Better the missing than the presence, he knew that was the way it was, but he doubted whether he could ever explain that to her.

And now? How would it go now, now that things had finally reached that point?

The first thing they would probably notice was his battered face, the black eye, the swollen nose, the bruises.

"What happened?" His mother would squat down in front of him, throw her arms around him, brush the blue-and-yellow spots carefully with her fingertips. "Have you been fighting?"

I fought for you, Mama.

But instead he would avert his eyes; just like seventy years—an eternity—ago, he would come up with a lie.

"I fell down," he would say, and just like back then, he would add details to make the lie stick. "Today, on the way home on my bike. My front wheel got stuck in the tram rails, I fell over the handlebars, hit my head on the street."

The real liberation, as he knows now, as he has in fact

known all along, is that his parents aren't around anymore. That they have been gone so long. That was his own liberation year: the year they passed away.

And so his relief is great when he sees that there is no gateway, no light—no playground he has to cross to his father and mother waiting at the fence.

There is nothing.

About the Author

HERMAN KOCH is the author of eight novels and three collections of short stories. *The Dinner,* his sixth novel, has been translated into forty languages and was an international bestseller. He currently lives in Amsterdam.